Chloe's Story

Ice and Fire

D.S. Harders and Diana Terrill Clark

i

Ice and Fire

ISBN 10 0692980156
ISBN 13 978-0692980156

Front Cover by Evan Short
Cover models: Diana Hughes and Scott Harders
Mask by Nokturnel Eclipse
Long sword by Sabersmith
Editing by Anne-Marie Pritchett

Acknowledgements & Dedications

The authors would like to thank Diana Hughes, Jerry Sanders, Daria Eden, and all the beta readers who helped with this book. You are all wonderful.

D.S. Harders dedicates this story to Mom and Dad. Thanks for making me, guys.

Diana Terrill Clark dedicates this story to Betty Jaeglar who inspired her and gave her the love of books that made any other vocation impossible.

About the Authors

Born and raised in Arizona, Mr. Harders spends most of his time surviving in the southwest region of Arizona. When not avoiding plants and animals that want to put holes in you, he spends his time writing and working on local films.

Diana Terrill Clark has written her whole life and has found it impossible not to make up stories about everyone and everything to the occasional dismay of those closest to her. She loves dark chocolate, coffee, and Jameson's, not necessarily in that order.

Ice

Chapter One

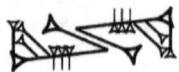

Death. Demise. Entropy. It has many names, but no matter what you want to call it, it's the ending of life and one of the few things all living beings share.

Humanity has written countless volumes on the subject; from the scientific to the philosophical to the spiritual. In most cases they all say the same thing. While our physical processes stop sooner or later, most agree that there is something more we can't account for, that thing that is often called a soul. Even physics tells us that energy does not simply cease to be. It may change states, but it does not just end.

One thing is certain, and I've learned this first hand—you can't fully comprehend death until it happens to you. I'm not talking about any physical pain that might be involved. I'm talking about what can only be described as the emotional impact.

It's more than just your life passing before you, which you get like a TV show detailing your every action. It's every choice you made, how it played out, and if it was for better or worse. It's like your very own St. Peter judging you and deciding your fate. Given some of my choices through life, I sometimes wonder if I deserve to go to Heaven.

Speaking of, there's no way to properly describe Elysium, partly because memories of it are hard to keep a hold of. Somehow it's a place that is timeless. Ageless. While there's no word invented that can truly describe it, home is what comes best to mind.

Perhaps the reason why is because the souls of those loved ones who have passed on are also there. They smile at you, happy the see you and the feeling of family is beyond intense. It is this seductive blanket that smothers you with its love and makes you want to stay.

Yet I couldn't stay. Some force I couldn't identify ripped me away from that idyllic place. Before I knew it, I was sailing through clouds and then falling back to Earth at a rate that would leave one dead when you hit the ground. Good thing I already was.

Mental note, resurrection is no fun. Think of that pins and needles feeling you get when blood flows back into a limb that fell asleep and magnify that over your entire body. Every inch of your skin on fire, every breath and movement ripples and flares with tingly, excruciating pain.

Then just like that, I'm back on Earth, blood coursing through the veins of my once-dead body. I am not happy. I am tortured. I am Jack's raging bile duct. The loss of my wife and daughter is a now-fresh wound, callously torn open.

As I catch my breath and the pain subsides, my eyes fly open as I gasp. The first thing I see is a ceiling, dingy brown and sporting a few bullet holes. Then the scenery changes.

Don't ask me how I know that it's her, but Goddess looks down at me and smiles warmly. Just like that, I realize what has happened and why I was once again ripped from my family.

Anger. Bitterness. It's hard to describe the emotions that surge through me. Scrambling to my feet, I ignore the stench of death that hangs in the room. Stumbling away from the destruction that lays scattered about, I escape out the shattered door and into the parking lot.

Sunlight bathes my skin with its warmth and a slight breeze kisses my face. Inhaling deeply, I struggle to control my raging emotions, a feat that seems Herculean in nature.

Coming to a stop at the edge of the parking lot for the Ute Mountain Travel Center, I gaze at the high desert terrain that stretches out to the west. Taking in a deep breath, I close my eyes and realize that's a big mistake. The faces of the ones I love—my wife, daughter and Chloe—are right there when I do, haunting me. A void grows in my chest, making it difficult to breathe.

I'm struggling to hang on to the vague and fading memories of my family welcoming me with bright smiles and open arms. They were at peace, happy. They had moved on from mortality; they were content. I felt oddly comfortable with that, ready to stay and forget everything about my mortal life. Even though I had just been ripped from Chloe, I was at peace.

Of course my thoughts are on more than just my dead wife and daughter. My heart has been ensnared by someone else as well—Chloe. I can only assume she survived. I spotted nothing but dead raiders inside, and Truck is gone. Besides, if the bandits had won, they would have taken my weapons and they never would have left all the guns that are littering the floor. No, she lived. I know she did. And it looks like she took all of those bastards out. *That's my Angel.*

I want nothing more than to follow her to the bunker I sent her to, so that we can fall into each other's arms. I don't care how much I hate myself for falling in love with another woman. In my heart, I feel my wife has forgiven me—the same woman who so briefly greeted me during my recent death and abruptly-recalled afterlife. She was joyful to

3

see me, and I felt no recriminations from her, only love and a calm peace.

Yet a part of me still feels like I've cheated on her. How do you reconcile being in love with two women without feeling like you're cheating? I just don't know.

Suddenly, *She* walks up, shattering my introspection. Dressed in a pristine white toga, most would consider her the definition of perfect beauty. Blonde hair, cropped short, gives the impression of spun gold in the sunlight. Eyes that look like gold flecked lapis lazuli. Leather sandals adorn her feet and the dress stops short enough that her muscular calves are visible. Finally, a silver belt studded with lapis holds a sword with a copper hilt. Oddly, her looks don't move me in the slightest. To me, the perfect beauty is Chloe.

"Hello, my knight. Are you ready to talk?"

"What's to talk about?"

"Don't be like that," she warns darkly. "Not with me."

I probably shouldn't be flippant to a deity, but I'm bitter in more ways than one. I was ripped from both of my loves and brought back at the edge of Colorado, all alone. Yeah, I think I have a right to my current mood. The two lions not far from us don't scare me either. What are they going to do? Kill me?

"Why?" I ask while looking at her sideways. "What will you do? Revoke my breathing privileges—again?"

Goddess narrows her eyes at me. "That could easily be arranged, and to make me do so would make me extremely angry with you."

"Why am I here?" I sigh painfully, seeking to change the subject.

"I need your rage, my knight. There are good people in Las Vegas who are under siege by bandits and need saving."

"Then let me go get Chloe," I state matter-of-factly. "There's no better team than she and I. You know that."

"No." Her answer is quick and emphatic. "While you have a job to do, she has her own. You will go to Las Vegas and help those good people. If, in your estimation, evacuating them to Colorado is the answer, then do so. But I expect you to make that decision objectively."

"And how do you expect me to do all that? My truck is gone and she took all my weapons with her." I look down at my blood-soaked vest. "Well, almost all my weapons."

While my short sword and Kimber race gun are gone, oddly my Steyr and Webley are still on me. It looks like all the dead bandits still have their gear as well. Of course, I imagine my lady was filled with too much grief to think of salvaging anything.

4

My Goddess answers my thoughts. "The many weapons of the dead raiders will give you something of an arsenal. Their vehicles are behind the hotel building. You will consolidate what you need to travel."

"That sounds great, but Chloe even took my sword."

I point to the empty leather frog on my belt. I don't know why I am pushing like this. Maybe I'm cranky after being raised from the dead? Perhaps that's why I'm in a childish mood. It's possible that is one of the side effects of resurrection. But hey, I'm just a tad bitter, so sue me.

Goddess rolls her eyes, yet smiles. "That can be remedied."

Holding out a hand, a sword and scabbard appears out of thin air. It is a similar design to my old blade, but it is a long sword rather than a gladius. Made of bright steel, the grip is wrapped in white leather and copper wire. I take it from her hands and draw it to reveal a fine looking blade. I sheathe it and slip it into the frog before looking at her.

"Thank you. Why are you even talking to me?"

This is the question that has been eating at me since my resurrection. It's hard to put words to the incredible shock of waking from the dead to see your patron deity looking down at you with a smile. Mind-fuck comes to mind.

"Because I need you," she states simply. "My followers were few and far between. But when everything collapsed, you started sending me evil souls by the wagon-load. The simplest explanation is to say that I was in semi-retirement, and you—" My goddess laughs throatily, "—you changed that."

"I changed that?"

"Yes. Well, not just you. Chloe was a brilliant recruit. She is mine now as well. And you probably don't realize it, but the two of you stabilized the L.A. area."

I'm shaking my head. "Why do you even care? You let the Collapse happen."

Goddess gives me a censorious glare. "No, my warrior, mortals let the Collapse happen. They turned their backs on God, not that God cares if one is atheist or devout. More importantly, they turned their backs on reason. So God just—let them do things on their own."

Whoa! While it's a slap in the face, I can't argue it either. Too much stupidity and zealotry added to good doses of arrogance and complacency brought everything we knew crashing down. I saw the writing on the wall too late and couldn't escape L.A. before gangs took over and murdered damn near everyone.

"I warned God that not paying attention would ultimately lead to ruin," she continues with a sigh. "You had Christians who couldn't follow the teachings of Christ. Radical Islam went totally off the rails. More and more humans were dependent on faceless, uncaring

5

governments instead of being self-reliant. Greed at both ends was rampant. Debt was out of control. And don't even get me started on the multitudes who had to feel important by claiming to be a victim of everything they could find. It all collapsed under its own weight and that's why people died by the billions! The world turned into a fucking mess! Pardon my Akkadian."

She grins at her joke before continuing. "Your work, in part, reactivated me. I was able to show God that good followers can make a difference."

"So I got you a promotion?"

Goddess laughs at that. "In a way. You've helped me prove that my teachings of 'love and war' are now far more useful than 'turn the other cheek.' Besides, I broke the rules in bringing you back, and that means I need to make sure you get pointed in the right direction."

"Rules? What rules?" *Gods have rules?*

I can tell she's not thrilled with this question. "We are not supposed to directly intervene. Hopefully, the other side hasn't detected my actions. Otherwise, they can take an opportunity of direct intervention as well. The world has enough evil in it already."

I hang my head. This conversation is giving me a headache. Frankly, this whole situation is giving me a headache. I'm a broken man, separated from the woman I love after I thought I would never love again. All I want is to be by her side, killing bandits with her and keeping her safe.

"I know you miss her." Goddess touches my shoulder and it tingles. "But I can tell you that she made it to the bunker just fine. She is safe and well."

"Thank you," I reply with a sigh.

Suddenly, a memory floods into my mind. It's of me visiting Chloe the night after I died—the conversation as I consoled her, that one last kiss, and then me writing a hidden message on the driver's side window that could only be seen by breathing on it. That message let her know I love her. I drag my mind back to the stark reality I've been thrust into.

What choice do I have?

"Fine. Where am I going again?"

"Nellis Air Force Base."

"Yes Goddess."

"Travel as quickly as you can," she warns. "There is something in the wind. The world is teetering on the edge of a knife. If evil wins, it will be thrust into a thousand years of darkness."

I roll my eyes. "No pressure."

"None at all," she quips at me with a grin that makes me uneasy.

That said, she simply walks towards the desert, not giving me a chance to bow respectfully. The two lions quickly move ahead of her like soldiers on point, looking for hostiles. After a time, they fade from view like a heat mirage and then are gone.

All I can do is shake my head. The world has gone to hell, and the Gods are walking the earth? If that is not the definition of being totally screwed, I don't know what is. Turning around, I walk back into the travel center to start gathering weapons and gear. Fortunately, Chloe left me a couple of my favorite pistols, so I draw my Steyr GB, just in case.

She took all my suppressed weapons. Shit!

Chapter Two

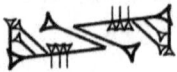

Stripping useful gear would be stomach-churning work to some people. Everyone's gotta be at least a day or two dead, so the smell of decaying corpses mingles with blood and human waste in an enclosed room. Yes, there are some maggots at this point, and yes, they have an extra-special scent all their own. While I've gotten used to these various and interesting odors over the years, the oppressive stench makes me gag a few times.

I'm able to salvage a couple decent tactical vests and various MOLLE pouches, holsters and other gear. I also grab a map of Utah and Colorado, just in case. A couple guys had various lengths of paracord I salvaged and added to the pile before dragging it all outside. How I am going to get all the blood off?

My thoughts are answered as an early winter squall comes out of nowhere and dumps a torrent of freezing rain right on my head. I look up to the sky, giving a glare of minor disapproval before using the opportunity to wash everything off, and that includes myself. When I'm done, the rain magically stops and the sun slowly comes out again as the clouds move west. Shaking off the water, I start going over the haul.

Just about everything the bandits have is civilian-quality. Only one gun is military make, a Chinese-made AK-47. Must have come from drug dealers down south. No other way I can see how a full auto version could have ended up in their hands. Nice thing is that they've got two semi-auto versions as well, so that means a decent number of magazines, a drum and a good amount of ammunition.

There's one other item that catches my interest—a Mosin Nagant in an Archangel stock and five magazines. The raiders put a four by nine power scope on it, and I can still use the iron sights. Evidently, this guy was their sniper. I thank Goddess for small favors. No, I really do. That rain shower was well-timed, too.

On top of that, I've got a number of AR-15s of varying style, a number of semi-auto rifles, a few bolt and lever-action long guns, a couple shotguns and a whole mess of handguns of which only a few share even the same caliber. The Desert Eagle in .44 is another nice find and that goes into my drop leg holster after some adjustments. Just about all the pistols have no extra magazines though, so I'm going to be doing a lot of New York reloading.

Then, there's the issue of stealth. The only way I'm going to have any suppressors is via the proper oil filters. It is important for staying undetected, but also for saving one's hearing. I'll have to start scavenging vehicles and see what I can come up with. Speaking of vehicles, I drag the useful weapons and gear across the parking lot and behind the hotel.

A combination of six cars and trucks sit in the lot. There, I find some food, water and a few more weapons and ammunition. Shit, these boys were definitely loaded for bear. Before I died in the travel center, I recognized one of the now ex-raiders. He was one of the three assholes at the feedlot that had shot me and was going to take Chloe alive.

Fuck me! They came all the way here from Phoenix? Why?

I shake my head, not fathoming the thought processes of idiots. Well, they're dead now. Guess that's all that matters. Even better, Chloe did damn well avenging my death. Before stripping everyone, I tried to get an understanding of what happened after I died. As I looked at the corpses, I could identify all the ones she gunned down. The last guy was the one who shot me, and she gutted him with my sword. I smile proudly.

That's my girl!

I find myself shaking my head in disbelief. I'm proud because she avenged my death, yet here I am, alive and in the flesh. The world has done more than just go to shit, it's gone totally fucking weird. I'm expecting to see Agents Scully and Mulder at any moment.

Shit! I hope when I see her again, she doesn't shoot me in the head, thinking I'm a zombie. I chuckle to myself at the thought.

It takes time, but I consolidate everything into a two door Toyota Hilux with a diesel engine. Piling damn near everything into the truck bed, I drain all the fuel out of the other cars and trucks. The gang wasn't entirely stupid and had all diesel vehicles. The bonus is that I should have more than enough fuel to get to Las Vegas.

With that thought, I sink into despair and collapse into the driver's seat. I don't want to go to Vegas! I want to go to the bunker. Thoughts of Chloe invade my mind, making it difficult to focus on anything else. Why am I being punished? What did I possibly do to deserve this kind of treatment? I feel alone, and I know how to remedy it, but I agreed to the Goddess' terms. For the first time in a long time, I break down and cry.

Yes, even real men have their limits. You work hard and survive the best you can. You internalize and bottle up the shit. You use it to fuel you, to push harder and do better. Yet, all it takes is one thing to push us over the edge and break us down. When my wife was gang raped and murdered along with my daughter right before my eyes, you might say that dramatically changed me.

Now I'm faced with another breaking point. The second love of my life is within reach, likely wallowing in the same kind of grief I am going through. All I have to do is aim this truck in the right direction and save us both from that pain—but at what cost?

My forehead is resting against the steering wheel when my SEAL instructor's voice shouts in my head. *Pain is acceptable. Falling is acceptable. Crawling is acceptable. Crying is acceptable. Quitting. Is not. Acceptable!*

Pulling in a deep breath, I get myself together. I find that cage deep inside me and unlock the latch to let the Beast out. I can practically hear the roar in my ears as I let my animal side back out to play.

I'm going to do this job, save those people, and then get back to Chloe. And once she's in my arms, I'm never going to let her go. Goddess help anyone who dares stop me, because I'll fucking kill them!

I look to the sky. *You owe me huge!*

Starting the truck up, I drive around the backside of the casino parking lot and then onto State Highway 491. Driving through the outskirts of Cortez, I see nothing but abandoned farms with fields full of weeds. With no water being pumped into the area, all the people had no choice but to abandon the place and move on.

The town of Cortez isn't any better. As I approach the 491 and 160 interchange, I see no signs of human occupation. Weeds and grass poke through breaks in the asphalt as nature shows its dominance. Almost every building looks like it was hurriedly abandoned. I see no obvious signs of fighting or looting.

I slow down and stop as I arrive at the interchange. If I make a right turn, I could have Chloe in my arms within just a few hours. All I have to do is turn this wheel and I'd be heading in the direction I want, the direction I should be heading in.

At that moment, the tattoo on my chest flares up in pain and I grit my teeth. As soon as I turn the wheel back towards the left, it stops abruptly. Of course, She's watching me. Her name is tattooed over my chest. How big a fool do I have to be to think that I can outwit a god? Taking a deep breath, I bury my pain deep inside and replace it with anger.

Do the job, get it done, get to Chloe. This becomes my mantra. My raison d'être.

Stomping on the gas, the wheels squeal as I peel rubber. I fly down the 491 and quickly leave the dead town of Cortez in my rear view mirror.

With every mile I put between Chloe and me, the Beast gets stronger and stronger.

Chapter Three

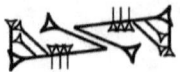

I have a lead foot as I scream down the highway on every straightaway. In retrospect, I shouldn't drive so fast, but emotions are clouding my judgment. In less than two hours, I zip through small desert towns, all of which look abandoned.

In Moab, I stop long enough to use a machine shop that I happen to spot while driving through. Actually, I spotted the solar panels and decided to check the building to see if it had anything of value. The bonus is that now I have an oil filter suppressor on the Mosin.

I'm surprised that no one is living in Moab. The Colorado River flows right along the edge of the town, so fresh water wouldn't have been an issue. Although looking at the arid landscape, it's highly possible that it would have been difficult getting any crops to grow.

When I finally hook up onto I-70, heading west, I notice smoke rising in the northwest. Every time I glance that direction, my tattoo tingles. I'm beginning to get the feeling I've been issued a moral compass, and I'm not really thrilled with that idea.

Approaching the Green River turn off, I slow down and start paying close attention while making sure the AK is within reach. Main Street runs through a stretch of desert for at least a half mile before it looks like it actually enters a town that reminds me of Blythe. With the exception of the fact that I hear distant gun shots.

I gesture to the sky, *How is this my problem? It could be a shooting competition! A county fair?* The tingle in my tattoo makes me curse.

Taking the exit, I pull off on the first dirt road and drive at a crawl so I don't kick up a lot of dust. It doesn't take long to find a secluded spot to hide the truck. Getting out, I quickly load up. I've modified my tactical vest to carry six AK mags, my Steyr GB and my Webley in back. The Desert Eagle sits in my drop leg.

Fuck, that's going to be loud!

From the truck bed, I pull the Mosin out and make sure it's fully loaded. Slinging the AK across my back, I close and lock the truck and then jog off towards the town.

I realize with a pang that I don't have backup anymore with Chloe not by my side. But I figure if I'm supposed to be off doing good deeds, my backup will have to be the one who sent me on this mission. *Right?*

In all actuality, Green River might be smaller than Blythe, but it's the same concept. Farm land hugs a flowing river as it meanders its way south. The town and farms are predominantly north of the interstate. As I move through the desert, train tracks unwind to the north of me, and the bridge for the tracks is about a klick or so away.

Moving past a derelict water tower and some run-down buildings, I glass the area, looking for any hostiles. Someone is guarding the railway bridge, looking about lazily with a rifle slung over his shoulder. The man is wearing your typical bandit style clothing and armor. Funny how the bad guys are wearing a uniform of sorts. I have hours of daylight left, and these people could be in trouble, so I've got no choice but to make a daytime assault.

Making my way closer, I sneak into what was probably a farming field that's now choked with weeds and dead plants. Dropping into a low crawl, I move up to the edge of the field and take aim at the sentry. Silently, I pray the makeshift suppressor works and pull the trigger.

The Mosin-Nagant is a good old, tried and true rifle that has a lineage stretching all the way back to the 1890s. Firing a one hundred and eighty grain bullet at roughly twenty-five hundred feet per second, it's like a freight train. A rifle much like this one is what I normally would hunt deer or black bear with. Today, it's raiders that are on the menu.

The report is decently suppressed and a large cloud of blood appears. The man is thrown into the steel girder of the train bridge and then slumps onto the tracks. Then I wait, listening for someone yelling an alarm or to see anyone run up. It doesn't happen, and I move carefully to his position.

This man is close to death, blood tricking out of his mouth as he tries to talk. He wheezes with every breath. My bullet ripped through both lungs, so he's slowly drowning as he looks up at me with fearful eyes. Normally, I'd let a piece of shit like this suffer, but a little voice in my head that sounds like Chloe pleads otherwise. Setting the rifle down, I draw my knife.

"You don't want my face to be the last thing you see," I whisper to him.

With a slight nod, he rolls his head with great effort and looks at the river. It's a good view really. Flowing waters with lots of green and wildflowers on the banks. Putting one hand on his forehead, I ram my blade into his medulla. Death is instantaneous and he goes limp as a slow, ragged exhale escapes his lips.

13

There's still the occasional shot going off in the town, but I don't see anyone else near my position. Sticking close to the framework of the bridge, I glass along the town and scout out what's going on. All I spot is a couple men on rooftops, along what I think is the main drag. They look like they are supposed to be on guard duty, but are instead paying attention to something happening on the street. My good fortune, their stupidity.

Moving slowly across the bridge, I slip down into a section that looks like it used to be a park. Green, overgrown grass is swallowing walking paths and benches. Between the overgrowth and the trees, I've got plenty of cover to stay hidden as I inch closer.

I can hear shouting and laughing now, but can't make out any distinct words. Of the two that I saw posted up on roofs, one is now looking south, away from the current commotion on the main street. I take aim, verify the other isn't looking and shoot.

My placement is perfect and the force of the bullet snaps his head back. He crumples and then falls off the ledge, hitting the ground. I immediately shift aim for lookout number two while listening for any calls for alarm.

The next volunteer turns and starts walking away from Main Street. He's about to the edge when he glances over to where his partner should be and starts looking around. That's when my bullet rips through his left eye and he drops. Breathing a sigh of relief, I move further up and get a look at the commotion that distracted the guards.

Yep, I was right, assholes.

Main Street is having something of a celebration, but only the raiders are having any fun. The townsfolk appear terrified as a number of armed bandits have tied a man up on a pole and the one raider that is probably the leader is playing target practice.

I take a count of how many bad guys are left. Lucky number thirteen. I've got one on watch about thirty to forty meters down the street to my right, propped up against the wall and lazily standing guard. Another inattentive guard stands maybe sixty meters and on the same side of the street. Quickly I take out both of the men without anyone being the wiser.

And then there were eleven.

After that, I decide it's time to turn the tables and fuck with these guys' heads. Lining up my aim on one of the bandits looming over the townsfolk, I wait until their leader fires another shot at his victim.

"You think some sheriff is comin' to save ya?" The gang leader yells at the people.

The leader places a glass on the head of a young man in his twenties, with short black hair. His white face is pale, immobile in wide eyed

14

horror. Evidently the gang boss considers himself a trick shooter as he rapidly draws and shoots, the glass shattering and dumping fluid on the young man's head. At the same instant, I pull the trigger.

And then there were ten.

Everyone is in shock as my target staggers forward, looking at the blood on his hand and then pitches forward, face first into the street. Every pair of eyes turns and looks at the leader, who is looking at his gun.

"Damnit, Jimmy," one of the bandits yells. "Watch where yer shootin'!"

"I hit the glass!"

"Well evidently you killed Kenny with a ricochet."

"Yeah," one of the other men yells out. "You bastard!"

The bandits gather around the leader, having a heated discussion about how their compatriot just died and it gives me all kinds of time to line up the perfect shot. The townsfolk have faded back, and I think they are expecting a fight to break out. Well, it is, just not the kind they're thinking of. When three of those idiots step into line, I grin and pull the trigger.

Chapter Four

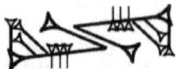

My bullet rips through all three heads of the bandits who were foolish enough to get in a line. They collapse onto the street with a spray of blood. The rest of the gang looks at the corpses and then down the street in the direction they figure the shot came from. All of them have a deer in the headlights look and that allows me to count one more coup on my tally before they break for cover.

And then there were six.

"Who's out there?"

Sounds like the leader yelling. His voice is stupid-angry. This day is not playing out for him the way it was supposed to. I don't answer, and instead wait to see what their next play is going to be. The townsfolk have scattered and are in hiding, which suits me. Fewer people to get in the line of fire. Odds are far in my favor now. I can take six amateurs with my eyes closed. Doesn't mean I'm going to be stupid about it.

The leader finally makes his move, walking out onto the street with a teenage girl as his hostage. His lackeys take up position behind him, arrayed like bowling pins just asking for someone to roll a strike. Only the leader has his gun out, the rest look ready for the shootout at the OK Corral. What they don't know is that I'm Wyatt Earp in this scenario.

"Alright, whoever you are," the leader yells. "You come out right now, or I'm gonna put a bullet in this little lady."

Placing the Mosin in the grass, I grab the AK and walk out, aiming at the leader the entire time. If he so much as twitches wrong, I'm going to blow him straight to Mars and then start in on his minions.

"Well whadda we got here?" Jimmy grins like he's got the upper hand. "You think you some kinda law dog?"

One of the men on his right laughs. "Look at that mask, Jimmy. He thinks he's the Lone Ranger."

Everyone laughs. Hell, even I can't help but smile at the comment. Back in L.A. and Blythe, people only called me Beast. Not once had the concept of the Lone Ranger ever been mentioned before, probably because it's white and not black. Still, I kinda like it.

"You some kind of coward, Jimmy?" My voice is a taunting growl.

"What?" In mere seconds his face is turning red.

"Well, you seem to be hiding behind a woman's skirt. Doesn't seem like the action of an ace gunslinger to me."

I read him right. His face reddens even more, and in a huff, he pushes the girl away. With a cry, she stumbles before bolting into hiding. Jimmy shows me his Colt 1911 with his finger off the trigger. Very slowly he slips it into his hip holster. Waving for his men to back away, he then holds his hands up once more, fingers twitching, waiting for me.

Oh, the thought of burning them all down right this instant is racing through my head. The John Wayne in me keeps saying otherwise though. It's the perfect opportunity for a quick draw shootout. An opportunity for me to see if I'm still as good as I was. The sane, logical part of my mind gives a yelp as I force it back down. I am *so* going to do this.

Yeah, this whole raised-from-the-dead thing is fucking with my head.

Bending down, I place the rifle on the broken asphalt road and then stand up while unsnapping the peace bond on the Desert Eagle. Slowly we both walk forward until we are the rough distance we should be for a fast draw. His men keep apace, but still hang back. All of them look highly confident of the outcome.

"You sure you wanna do this?" Jimmy grins. "Clearly you're a good shot. Could use a guy like you. Appears we got a few openings."

"Sorry, Jimmy. There's a new sheriff in town. You can walk away from this."

"Ain't gonna happen," he states with a confident shake of his head.

"Then draw and face the consequences."

Jimmy and I stare each other down, waiting for who is going to draw first. Tension rises as I gaze at him impassively. I don't give him any emotion to work off of and I'm sure that makes him frustrated and angry. When he goes for his gun, I clear nylon faster than he clears leather. My Eagle roars like a demon from hell.

Let's face facts, any bullet can kill you. A twenty-two long rifle will end you if it hits a critical spot, but otherwise doesn't do much damage. Many fear the forty-five because it's a big, slow moving bullet that mangles you like pit bull. Then there's the forty-four. It doesn't just mangle you, it picks you up when it does and tosses you like a rag doll. That's exactly what happens to Jimmy, but I'm not really paying close attention.

Some of his men are shocked but I'm already laying into them, and two more drop before guns start drawing. Two shoot in pure fear before they even aim, and then I've gunned them down. The last actually gets sights on me and shoots before I put a flat-nosed slug in his gut. I stagger backwards, gritting my teeth at the pain of being hammered in the chest. My luck holds just like my trauma plate does.

And then there was one.

I holster the Eagle and draw my Steyr while ignoring the ringing in my ears. Nine millimeter is easier to come by, and thanks to this little shoot out, I've only got about two mags worth of forty-four rounds left. *So worth it.* Slowly I approach the bandits and start checking.

Well, now I know coming back from the dead hasn't affected my aim.

All but my gut shot volunteer are dead. Jimmy took the bullet with his name on it right in the chest. Pretty sure death was instantaneous for him. In fact, all the others have chest wounds, so they are no longer a threat to anyone. As such, I walk over to Mr. Gut Shot to have a little talk.

The fear in his eyes is easy to spot while trying to scramble away from me in a futile effort. While his gun is too far to reach, I kick it further away anyway. Then I kneel down and glance at his wound before looking into his eyes.

"You're gut shot, kid. These days that's a slow death."

"Fuck you!"

I shake my head. "You're not my type. I prefer brunettes."

While he wants to retort, instead he groans in pain, clutching at his wound.

"Are there any more of you? I counted thirteen, but I want to hear it from you."

His eyes flash in consternation, which tells me what I wanted to know. I got all of them. I bet they even had a stupid gang name like the Evil Thirteen or some other nonsense. Most of these idiots are all the same.

He shakes his head, determined to keep me guessing. I am certainly not going to treat his wound. Chloe's voice is in my head though, telling me to show mercy. In this case, mercy has nothing to do with it. There's no way for me to treat this kind of wound, especially when Chloe has my trauma bag.

"Best I can do is end your suffering."

Swallowing hard, he nods as he closes his eyes briefly. "Please," he whispers harshly.

"Don't look at me, kid. You don't want my face to be the last thing you see."

Rolling his head to one side, he looks down the street, still clutching at the wound the is profusely bleeding. Taking careful aim, I put a bullet into his skull.

And then there were none.

Staying there a few minutes more, I look at the raider I just showed mercy to, and wonder why. Is it because of Chloe? Has her influence made me a better man, a softer man? As I look back at all the dead bandits, I scoff at the thought that I've become softer.

Townsfolk are finally coming out of hiding now and they are shell-shocked, terrified. A timid man in ragged clothes approaches, and at first I think he's afraid to even talk to me. Can't say as I blame him. Masked man walks into town and kills thirteen men in less than an hour, most might think that person is not someone to trifle with.

"T- thank you, stranger."

I stand up and nod. "You're welcome."

Paying close attention, I notice he's wringing his hands. "I'm, uh, afraid you've made things worse for us though."

"How is that?"

"The main gang, they, uh..." Clearly he's not comfortable having this conversation.

"Spit it out," I state calmly. "I'm not going to harm you."

He gives me a nod and looks a little calmer. "They are a few miles down the road in Thompson. There are a lot of them, practically an army. When their friends don't come back in a few days, they'll come here and punish us. I'm sure of it."

Fuck!

Quick thinking kicks in and a plan lays out in my head. "Do you have working vehicles?"

"Yes sir," he replies back with a nod. "We've got a few trucks for bringing in the harvest. We make our own diesel, though the gang normally keeps it controlled so that we don't have enough to get away."

"How many of you are there?"

"Thirty six, sir."

"Then this is what you do. You grab everything you need to survive; all their guns and ammo, warm clothes, food and water. Just what you need to survive."

Quickly I pull out my map of Colorado, open it up, and mark out the route for him. I always carry a red and a black indelible marker in my trauma pouch. Comes in handy if you have to mark the time on someone's forehead after applying a tourniquet.

"You follow this route all the way to Gunnison. You hear?"

He nods frantically. "Yes sir."

"You drive until you run out of gas, and then you start walking. Hell, tow anything that's available as well. All the desert towns looked deserted when I moved through, so you should be safe all the way to Cortez. From there, you need to be cautious. Winter is coming, so keep an eye on the sky. Hole up in a deserted town until spring thaw if you have to."

"Can we hold out that long?"

"Make sure you take enough supplies, take all you've got if you can and ration accordingly. If you have enough fuel, you should make Montrose at the very least. If it's deserted, you'll have more than enough roofs to keep you warm and there's plenty to hunt in that area."

"All- all right," he replies with a nod.

"Now this is the important part," I state while holding up a finger. "North of Gunnison, you are looking for a dark haired woman. You ask for the Angel of Death and you tell her I sent you."

Oh yeah, the mention of her name went over well.

It's not difficult to notice the poor man swallow hard and start to look nervous again. I'm betting they are all civilians, none with any combat experience at all. While I want to feel bad about throwing them into the unknown, I don't have much choice because my tattoo has started tingling, so all I can do is pray to Goddess that they make it safely.

"I apologize," I state calmly. "What's your name?"

"D- Dan, sir. Dan Brandt."

"Nice to meet you, Dan." Taking his hand, I shake it vigorously while smiling politely. "Now don't worry about the name, she's a good woman, the best! She will treat you right. Especially if you remember what I'm going to tell you next."

He nods, a little less shaken. "All right."

"You give her this gun," I reluctantly hand over the Webley I'd given her the first night we met. "You tell her I gave it to you. She won't understand, but tell her that I will get a message to her somehow, explaining things when I get to Las Vegas, got that?"

As he agrees and takes the pistol. I can feel my tattoo is now burning. I'm not sure if it's because I've overstayed my welcome or if I'm saying too much. One thing is certain, I need to finish this up quick.

"I'm counting on you, Dan. Don't let me down. You carry a message far more important than you can possibly know."

"Yes sir."

"Good," I nod. "Now I have to go. Get your people to safety, and be quick. Leave today if you can. Within an hour or two if possible, but be as well supplied as possible."

Before he can even reply, I'm already walking away. I stop at the corpse of one of Jimmy's compatriots who carried a Ruger Blackhawk. Stooping down, I pick it up and check for any extra ammo. Nine extra rounds. I then look at Dan.

"I'm keeping this since you have mine, okay Dan?"

All he can do is nod as I turn and head back. Rapidly I'm picking up my weapons and making for the truck. The tattoo is becoming more insistent and before long I'm jogging to get back so I can get on the road.

As I get to the truck, I glare at the sky. *You ever think about using a carrot instead of a stick?*

Chapter Five

Taking I-70 to I-15 takes me a little under two hours and in that time I don't see anyone. Is this luck or intervention? I don't know and I don't care. I pass more abandoned towns, unable to survive without electricity to pipe in water. When I stop outside of Sulphurdale to fill up the tank, I take stock of how much diesel I've got. Even with the slight detour I'm guessing it should be enough to get me to Las Vegas.

Don't imagine I'm standing there at the pumps, elevator music playing and sunglasses on my face as I watch the numbers spinning and telling me how much fuel I'm buying as I easily pour the fuel into my tank. There's no electricity, remember?

While I still have a few Jerry cans, I check the station anyway. Anything left is going to be in a tank buried under the concrete and you have to figure out how to get it out of the ground. The raiders happened to have a hand pump that, though it is nerve rackingly slow, works well enough to pump into a Jerry can. It's not a lot, but it's something. The job is painstaking, smelly and annoying. But it is better than walking, that's for damn sure.

Looking at the horizon, it's getting late. Turning off of the freeway, I head west on a dirt road a short jaunt and find a secluded spot to camp for the night. While I don't want to stop, I need to eat and get some sleep.

My food choices are slim. There's a bag of pork jerky that actually isn't bad, but I take only a couple pieces, saving the rest as a good source to snack on as I drive. Ultimately I decide on a can of chili, a can of pears and some water to wash it all down.

All my camping gear is in Colorado with my love, who thinks I'm dead. *Fucking hell!* There's really no point in setting a fire. Instead, I just make sure everything is tied down tight and then lock up the truck and try to sleep in the cab.

Yeah, sleep. Like that's going to happen.

Using one of the extra vests as a pillow, I wedge myself into the bench seat. As I lie there, soft moonlight drifts in through the passenger side window as scattered clouds move across the night sky.

I toss and turn. Chloe's face haunts me as soon as I close my eyes. This growing void in my chest feels like I'm bleeding out. What did I do to deserve such torture? Didn't I send Her enough souls? Didn't I prove my love by dying for Chloe? Haven't I suffered enough?

As I roll over, the bruise from the gunshot I took flares up. Clearly I've not suffered enough. With a sigh, I close my eyes and pretend to sleep regardless of the images that haunt me. Somehow, it eventually become honest slumber.

I slowly waken to the sound of someone crying. Through the fog, I swear it sounds like Chloe and that makes me sit up. That's when I find I'm lying in my bed at the bunker and she's sitting at the edge, head in her hands.

Ripping the sheets off, I immediately throw my arms around her and she gasps. My lady stares at me with tear stained cheeks that break my heart even more than it already is. Twisting around, she buries her head into my chest. Gently I gather her into my arms, crooning softly while I run a hand through her soft hair.

"Hey, my angel," I murmur tenderly. "Please don't cry."

"I'm sorry," she chokes out between sobs. "I just miss you so much!"

Pain of a sort no man ever wishes to experience lances through my chest. "I know, I know. I'm sorry, baby. Really I am. I just couldn't let him shoot you."

"I know," she replies, looking up at me with wet, brown eyes. "I wish you were here. It kills me to be here alone, and I don't know if I can do it by myself."

Trying to ignore an agony I can't push away like the physical kind, I hold her tightly. I would gladly die a thousand times if it would save her from going through this kind of anguish. Yet there's nothing I can do, and I despise myself for it.

Tipping her chin up, I kiss her softly. It doesn't take long before it evolves into a burning, passionate embrace. I can taste the desperation and sorrow on her lips as her hands fist into my hair, trying to hold me to her. In return, I tighten my hold, crushing her to me as she moans into my mouth.

23

Tearing my lips from hers, I kiss along the edge of her jaw, all the way to her ear. Her sweet moans fill the air as I suck on her ear lobe, her hands traveling down my back. I can feel her grip tighten against my skin.

"I need you," she whispers with the same agonizing pain if feel.

"I know," I whisper back. "I need you too."

"Please love me?"

"Always, my lady."

Laying her down softly on the sheets, I gladly worship my raven haired goddess. The cries and moans that greet my ears are like a choir of angels. Slowly I lay kisses across her entire body as she writhes beneath me. I can practically taste her anticipation as I make my way to that magical spot.

There are no words that can describe just how much I have come to love this woman. It's not just her beauty, or the sex, or anything physical. It's everything about her, who she is as a human being. This amazing lady who had been a slave for who knows how long, bounced back from the shit she had been through, but didn't want to run and hide. Instead, like a sponge, she soaked up everything I taught her to become one hell of a fighter. In all honesty, she probably was always a fighter. I fell in love with this amazing angel. Couldn't stop myself, really, when I didn't want to ever love again. She deserves my veneration with every breath I have left.

Unleashing my tongue at the apex of her thighs, I send her into a frenzy as she pulls my head closer to her. Many men think that their sexual power is between their legs, but I disagree. I've always felt there's nothing more powerful than having my head between a woman's legs and sending her straight to Heaven.

That's exactly what happens. Her thighs quiver as it approaches, so I hold her hips down. Wrapping my lips around her clit, I suck lightly before fluttering the tip of my tongue right on the spot. Just like that, she screams as her body goes rigid, back bowing off the bed as she damn near pulls my head off my shoulders.

Goddess, I love watching her come.

I wait until her sanity returns, caressing her body lightly as her breathing slowly settles and calms. When she looks at me, her pupils are dilated as she smiles brightly at me. I'd do anything for that smile.

"Wow," she whispers.

"Wow," I whisper back.

Slipping fully onto the bed, I lie down on my back and then pull her onto me. Once more we are all hands, lips and tongues as her breasts press against my chest. My fingers glide up and down her back, across her ass as we both moan into each other's mouths.

Without a word, she straddles my hips and slides me into her. As she gasps, I shudder and growl, grasping her hips as I flex my own. Chloe cries out, head thrown back as I bury myself deeply into her.

Fuck!

A whimper escapes my lady, trying to move her hips, so I loosen my hold to let her take control. Slowly she moves, setting a rhythm and angle that is most pleasing, and the world is centered on her and me. As our dance continues, I sit up and she lets out a surprised gasp as I'm buried even deeper into her. The passionate look in her eyes puts even more fire into my blood.

"I love you, Chloe," I tell her with the deepest of conviction, while gazing into her beautiful, brown eyes. "Don't ever forget that."

Tears flow, and I can't tell if they are from joy or sorrow, but I refuse to let sadness take hold of her. Flexing and rotating my hips, she cries out as her arms and legs wrap around me. Slipping off the bed, still buried deep inside of her, I lift her up and then press her against the nearest wall.

I proceed to ravage her, letting the animal side of me out to play. A growl escapes my throat as I settle into vigorous rhythm. She clings to me, powerless to stop the pleasure and accepting it all. As the beast takes hold, I lose all sense of self as I surrender my rational side. It's just her and I, lost in a sea of passion, the air filled with her sweet, sweet cries as I pound her against the wall.

Chloe tightens around me, exploding into an ear-shattering orgasm, with her lips not far from my ear. With a roar, I give two powerful thrusts and then find my own release inside of her as she continues to cry out.

Then I wake up.

Chapter Six

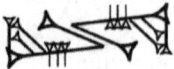

Waking with a gasp, I quickly realize I'm in the truck and it is freezing! Talk about a cold shower. Early morning sunlight streams through the window, assaulting my eyes. They don't hurt near as bad as the ache in my heart. Shivering involuntarily, I groan, then sit up and turn the truck over. Quickly I get back onto the road and turn the heater on, which of course does not kick in as quickly as I'd like.

Memories of my dream haunt me, my pulse still racing as the scent of Chloe lingers strongly in my nostrils. I've not had a dream that vivid since the one she and I shared in Blythe. This must have been the carrot I was asking about yesterday.

As I pull onto I-15, I pour on the gas, hoping that the faster I drive, the quicker I can escape painful memories. Doesn't work, of course. Chloe remains stubbornly on my mind as I race down the interstate with no fear for my life. Why should I fear? The woman I love still thinks I'm dead. If I died here on the freeway, she'd never know any differently. Well, except for Dan. Sending Dan with the Webley would mess with her, especially if there is no follow-up. Shit. I hadn't thought of that.

A painful sigh escapes my lips and I slow down a bit, setting the speed to fifty-five. I figure I'll be in Las Vegas in roughly three hours at this rate. Although I recall I'm heading for Nellis, so I grab the map and double check my routes as I pay attention to the road. Actually, my route is perfect. I-15 passes right along the air force base.

Even better, there's a state route 604 that I can hop on long before hitting the city's outskirts. Given the fact the base is supposedly under siege, sneaking in and getting a lay of the land would be preferable.

Turning my attention back to the road, I scan the desert terrain of what used to be Utah as the miles fly by. To the southeast, dark clouds cover the horizon. My gut tells me a powerful storm is on its way. I might make it to Vegas before it hits—barely. Just looking at it, somehow I just know this is not going to be a good storm.

Pressing my foot down, I speed up, hoping that I continue to encounter nothing but abandoned towns. Every so often, I pass wrecked or abandoned vehicles as I zoom down the interstate in an attempt to outrace the dark monster that is closing in. At no point do I see any human beings.

The miles fly by and I only stop long enough to put the last can of fuel into the truck. Then I'm moving again, as fast as my steed will carry me. I'm paying as close attention to the gauges as I drive. I have no clue as to the condition this vehicle is in, so pushing it too hard could make for a very long and cold walk.

Seconds turn into minutes, which turn slowly into hours. Each tick of the clock feels like an eternity as Chloe weighs on my mind. No matter what I do, I can't stop thinking about her, worrying about her. Of course that dream didn't help. One thing is certain, I have to find a way to get her a message. She has to understand what happened and that I am alive. It occurs to me that she could find someone else if I'm gone too long. I am dead, after all. This thought does not help my mood.

I'm wallowing in so much self-pity that before I know it, the sight of the bones of Las Vegas shows up on the horizon. I slow way down and start paying close attention to the dark clouds looming overhead and a frightful wind kicks up. To the south, a huge dust storm is rolling in, slowly swallowing the city.

That huge cloud of dust strikes just as I'm about to turn onto the 604. I slow down even more, barely able to see the road ahead. In a way I should be thankful, for this storm will handily conceal my movements as I close in on the Air Force base. Again, too helpful to be a coincidence.

Civil unrest was ratcheting up throughout the late twenty-teens and early twenty-twenties. Cops were being shot left and right, neighborhoods burnt to the ground and partisan politics simply fueled the flames in wild abandon. Throughout that time, I wondered just how much the progressives—who were following the communist playbook—thought they were going to transform the United States into a socialist utopia. They forgot that civil wars are rarely civil. In their rush for an ideological paradise, and determined to push their agenda forward regardless of the consequences, they found themselves just as dead as everyone they thought they were so superior to.

Most military bases transformed over the course of that time, large concrete walls sectioning off the military from the civilians—similar to the bases overseas in hostile territory. Nellis was no different. A large wall runs parallel to the 604 before cutting east towards the mountains, near the old motor speedway.

As I get within sight, a sleet-like rain begins to pelt down, cutting down on the dust, and turning it to mud on my windshield. The wall is a monstrosity, with pillars that hold circular guard stations, probably with heavy duty, bullet resistant glass. The gate looks like a steel slab tall

27

enough to allow semi-trucks to drive through. It all reminds me of a high security penitentiary.

Pulling off the 604 onto a small dirt road, I drive towards the mountains to the east. The road is rough and getting wet as I rumble along. When I find a likely looking patch of scrub and mesquite trees, I park it and get out.

Fuck it's cold!

Pulling out my binoculars, I see a number of "technicals" parked away from the wall, and a crowd of people milling about. They've got that bandit look about them as they hide behind their vehicles, trying to shoot at the tower guards. Even the vehicles have the look, with various highway and street signs tacked to them for extra armor.

The raiders are armed with the typical assortment of weapons, and they are severely outgunned. The guards on the wall are decked out with military-issue AR's and machine guns. Cover is the only thing keeping the idiot bandits alive.

Ignoring the bone chilling wind, I pull out the Mosin, sling the AK and start aiming. A hard wind is blowing, but it's almost directly into my face. Right now I'm parked easily two thousand meters from the wall. Kicking into a jog, yet staying low, I close the distance while everyone is focused on each other.

Freezing rain bites at my cheeks as I move forward, getting lower and lower to the muddy ground. I'm able to slip into a ravine choked with plant life. I only start to slip once, but quickly regain my balance. My boots squelch as I cross to the other side and lay down on the upper slope to take aim once more.

Most of these idiots don't even look like they can shoot straight. I do see one guy that's a definitely problem though. He's using an Enfield with a scope, and he wounds one of the gate guards before ducking back down to work the bolt. I aim, waiting for him to pop back up. When he does, I pull the trigger.

While I may have been a medic, I've had quite a bit of trigger time with a number of different weapons. I learned from every team mate, soaking in all the knowledge they had to offer. Just because you are a medic in the SEALS, does not mean you go unarmed. Like the rest of the team, you have to be able to move like they do. Shoot like they do. That includes using weapons outside of U.S. issue.

When I aim for the bandit sniper, I go for center-mass. Between the rain and wind, a head shot would be difficult and I can't afford to waste ammunition. I'm rewarded by watching him slam into the vehicle and drop, his body sliding down and revealing a blood stain. A few close to him look back, trying to spot me.

As I start aiming for my next target, one of them gets clipped by the guards. I drop crosshairs onto the other and shoot. My placement is a little off and the bullet rips through his shoulder, but he falls with a yell. Now they all know they're caught in a crossfire.

There are nine left, four of whom put their backs to the vehicles and start shooting wildly in my direction. Slipping down the bank of the ravine, I move roughly a dozen meters to the right and peek up again. They are shooting way to the left, although a couple shots hit a tree not far from me. Taking aim, I shoot and then shoot again. One man drops and another is wounded. Another three get plugged by the guards.

That's enough fighting as far as the survivors are concerned. Those who are still alive or wounded, pile into a vehicle and then race away as fast as they can. The guards fire a few shots, but like me, let them leave. Ammo is a premium luxury.

One of the guards pulls out with a bullhorn. "Identify yourself."

Climbing out of the ravine, I hold the Mosin up with both hands and walk towards the wall. I'm trying to control my shivering as guards aim at me. Fortunately, they don't shoot me like the target I am as I get close enough to start talking.

Chapter Seven

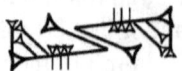

Oh for Goddess' sake!

The kid who addresses me can't be more than twenty. Others tend to their wounded. In fact, if I'm not mistaken, it looks like all of them are young. At least it can be said they are decent shots.

"Who are you? What do you want?"

"I'm here to help," I call back. "Can I come in before I freeze to death?"

"We don't need any help! Especially from on old man."

The beast growls in my mind, but I hold him back. Clearly, I'm being tested and I am not well pleased. At this point, I've been subjected to more than enough heartbreak, disappointment and frustration already. As I start to turn to walk away, my tattoo flares up with pain and I grit my teeth.

"Yeah, kid," I yell back. "I can see you guys are doing a real good job at being trapped in a cage!"

"Fuck you, old man!"

A woman walks up and he comes to attention. I can't make out what she says, but given the look on his face, I imagine he's being dressed down. She must be an officer, or at least someone of higher rank. When she's done, he departs, tail between his legs and the woman now looks down at me.

"My apologies," she yells down. "What do you want?"

"To come in would be nice," I yell back, my teeth practically chattering.

There's a pause, like she's thinking. "I'm coming down. Keep your hands up."

"Yes ma'am."

Keeping my rifle held above my head, I wait in the freezing cold while a fine mist of rain begins falling. The gate opens just enough for one person to walk out. The woman strides toward me, rifle at the ready and two Airmen with her. Not a single damn one of them can be over twenty-five.

Seriously, Goddess? This is what I'm reduced to? A babysitter?

When the woman gets closer, she relaxes slightly. "Thanks for your help, but we didn't need it."

I'm sure I give her an, "are you kidding me" glare. Sporting lieutenant bars, wisps of red hair poke out from under her helmet. Blue eyes size me up and I see fear there. In all honesty, I'm surprised she hasn't shot me. I can tell she's out of her depth and unsure what to do.

Yep, typical second lieutenant.

"You've got wounded that need help, to begin with," I state, trying to control my anger. "And I'm tired of freezing my ass off! So how about you let me in already? That way I can treat your wounded and get warm, lieutenant!"

She looks a little rattled. "You'll have to surrender your weapons."

"Lieutenant, you can have all the weapons I have except my Steyr. No one touches that one."

A look of focused deliberation passes through her eyes and she finally nods. "All right."

Releasing her rifle, she takes the Mosin. Then I carefully hand over the AK and other pistols. Backing away so I can enter, I walk in and look at the two soldiers that are with her while fishing out my car keys.

"You two! My truck is a few klicks that way. Can't miss it, it's got a lot of weapons in the bed. Double time it out there and bring it in."

"You don't give orders here," one of the young men exclaims.

I can't help the growl that rumbles through my throat and his eyes go wide. "I have to treat your people, Airman. Get a move on!"

Looking at his lieutenant, she nods and they dash out the gate. I shake my head and start walking. Quickly the officer falls into step alongside me while yelling for a couple more guards to keep watch on the entrance until the other two return.

"You certainly know how to make friends," she states dryly.

"You've got wounded," I growl back. "There's no time for second guessing and dicking around."

That actually gets a laugh from her. "You've got to be ex-military."

"Navy. Chief petty officer before I mustered out and joined L.A. SWAT."

"Shit," she exclaims. "We've been needing someone like you."

"I know. Get me to your wounded, lieutenant. Then we need to have a serious talk."

Entering one of the towers, we run up the stairs two at a time until we finally reach the top. One of the guards is trying to take care of three wounded. I immediately go to work and assess the patients. Fuck! One of them has a serious chest wound, the lung is filling up with fluid.

"Lieutenant, do you still have your ID card?"

She looks at me like I'm crazy. "Uh, yeah."

"Give it to me." I practically yell while looking at the stricken kid on the floor.

"Hang on, kid."

A face with brown hair and brown eyes looks up at me with the same look I've seen far too many times. That fearful stare, that unsaid statement saying, "I don't want to die." I've gotten tired of seeing young men die while looking at me exactly the same way he is now.

Using the identification card, I place it over the bullet hole to seal the wound. All it's going to do is prolong his agony if we don't have a proper surgical room to treat him, but it's a start.

The other two are more minor and already bandaged so I look to the lieutenant. "We need to get this one to surgery. Please tell me you have a doctor?"

"We do," she says, looking grateful for my assistance. "And your truck just came in."

"Then let's get him into the back and to the hospital!"

Fortunately she chooses not to argue and puts the life of her man before the thought of being given orders by a retired veteran easily twice her age. With some help, we get the young man down the stairs and into the truck. When they hand me the keys, I toss them to the lieutenant.

"You know where we are going, ma'am."

With a nod, she jumps into the driver's side and adjusts the seat forward while I take shotgun. Another soldier hops in the back and keeps my patient covered with a poncho. Quickly we head into the heart of the Air Force base as the storm worsens. Rain has turned to sleet as we drive past the landing strip and finally pull into a hospital.

Hopping out, I rush to my patient as the lieutenant runs in. Fuck, he's not looking good. Breathing is more labored by the second. Doors at the emergency room entrance open and people run out with a stretcher.

I look at the airman that has joined us. "Lift on three. One, two, three!"

Lifting the boy out of the truck bed, we put him on the gurney as it slides next to the truck. Then we are in a rush, wheeling him through as a doctor runs up, stethoscope in hand. As she listens for breath sounds, I'm rattling off my findings.

"Shot to the chest. He's got open pneumothorax. Pulse is weak and thready."

Looking up, first in shock, then gratitude, she acknowledges me with a nod. "Right, we got it from here."

The lieutenant and I stop just short of running into the surgery hallway and I catch my breath. Closing my eyes, I give a silent prayer in hopes that a young man who barely has had a chance to live, gets the opportunity.

"And now I should take you to see the Major," the lieutenant states, snapping me out of my grim thoughts.

"All right." I give her a nod. "You should probably drive. I still don't know where we're going."

Chuckling, she leads me back to the truck. Dashing through terrible weather, we hop in and try to warm up. We're back on the road, driving through a storm that is howling like the animal that lives inside my mind.

Chapter Eight

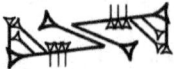

I get a lot of double-takes as I stride through the halls of the Nellis Air Force base air traffic control building. Granted, there aren't as many people as there might once have been. There are at least a dozen Airmen in uniform carrying on as if this is still an active military base.

At the top of the tower, I find it staffed by four people, one of whom is in officer's blues and peering through a hefty pair of binoculars. Outside, the storm is raging so fiercely that one would think it impossible to see even twenty feet. During the climb to the top of the tower, the sleet has turned to white.

"Major Drummond, sir," the lieutenant sates while coming to attention. "I have a visitor to see you."

The major turns to reveal a man that's as tall as I am, graying hair and gray eyes. Against his dark skin, his eyes are striking. He carries a hard edge. A muscular frame tells me he probably still works out. I'm certain he's seen combat at some point in his life as he looks me up and down.

"Lieutenant Hayes," he asks in a southern accent. "Why is this man armed?"

"Because he intervened in a battle with the raiders by killing a half dozen of them and may have saved Airman Burnett's life by giving trauma aid. As such, I felt he should keep his sidearm, sir. He surrendered the rest of his weapons."

I give a perfect salute, which surprises him. "Major, I'm here to help."

Holding the salute until he returns it, he finally speaks to me. "Who are you, son? Name and rank."

"Chief petty officer, U.S. Navy SEALS. Retired. These days I only go by my call-sign, Beast."

All activity stops and they stare at me for a moment before going back to what they were doing. The Major rubs his chin and smiles, slightly. I'm sure he's already imagining ways he can employ someone with my combat experience.

"Follow me, son. Lieutenant, you as well."

We both step into line and following him down the stairs and onto the ground floor. Entering a well appointed office, he bids us to be seated while he opens a liquor cabinet with glass doors. Pulling out a couple glasses, he begins pouring.

"What brings you to Nellis, son?"

"You wouldn't believe me if I told you, sir. Let's just say that I knew you needed help."

The Major hands me a glass with amber liquid in it. "So how do I know you aren't a clever plant by the enemy?"

"How do I know you didn't just poison this drink?"

That said, I take a drink and let a rather smooth whiskey slide down my throat. Already I feel a little warmer. *Oh yeah, that's really good.* With a smile, he sits down at the edge of the desk and regards me with curiosity.

"You are correct. We need help. We've been under siege for nearly three months. We have nowhere to go, and they want in. So far we've kept the bastards at bay, but we don't have an unlimited supply of ammo and they know it."

I nod and take another swallow. "You have any cargo planes that still fly? Fuel?"

"Sure do. Where would we go?"

"Crested Butte, Colorado."

The major looks at me like I'm crazy. I think Lieutenant Hayes does as well. "What the hell is in Crested Butte?"

"Like roughly half a dozen spots in Colorado, it has fertile land, running water all year round and a highly defensible position."

"How do you know this?"

I smile brightly. "That's where my bunker is."

"You're a prepper!" He says that with some disdain.

"Yes sir."

"Well then, why aren't you there?"

"Getting out of L.A. was a nightmare. Heard about your plight from some travelers and figured there'd be safety in numbers. Having some military personnel with experience would be useful in standing watch, setting up defenses and what not."

"You trying to build an army, Chief?"

"No, sir," I state with a firm shake of my head. "Trying to build a safe community."

"Well, you certainly know how to sell it," he states, sitting back a little. "May be problems in getting there. Does this place have an airstrip?"

"It does, but I'm no expert pilot. It's an airfield, but not a major airport. I don't know if it's long enough. We'd need to send a scout to make sure."

"So you can warn your people?" He's sporting a wry smile.

"So we can make sure we can land safely and get everyone sheltered." I shake my head. "Sir, we've both got no reason to trust each other. But if I was working for those piece-of-shit raiders outside, do you think I'd be talking you into flying away? Not to mention pointing out we should be taking the best gear we can with us."

"You do have a point, son." The major chuckles. "You got a plan?"

"The beginnings of one," I state with a grin. "Once the storm lets up, you have a scout plane that can fly that distance?"

This requires some thinking before he gives me a nod. "We've got a Bronco. Even without external tanks, she can probably make it that far. Can't be more than roughly six hundred miles, since that's about the distance to Denver."

"Right. So we send a pilot in the Bronco to verify if the cargo plane can land safely. If so, we load everyone up and get the hell out of here. Do you have ordnance we can use to blow up anything useful that we can't take?"

"You want to destroy this place?"

"We can't leave material in the hands of the enemy," I state somberly. "Any aircraft or weapons we aren't taking we destroy on our way out."

The major actually sits back and laughs. "That proves it! You are most definitely a SEAL."

"Thank you, sir." I can't help the chuckle that comes out of me.

"Well, until this operation starts, you are under my command. Are we clear?"

Quickly I give him a salute. "Very clear, sir."

"Excellent," he states with a grim nod. "Only good thing about this storm is that I'm sure it'll trip up the enemy. Bad side is that it's going to be hell on our solar. Fortunately we also have some wind generators that are probably working overtime."

The Major looks at Hayes. "Lieutenant. Go issue an order for everyone to go to one-quarter lighting until further notice. Then wait for our new guest in the lobby."

Standing up, she delivers a crisp salute. "Yes sir."

We both watch as she walks out, closing the door behind her. Near silence descends over the room, only the howling of the raging storm outside to be heard. Major Drummond clearly has something else to say and I wait for the other shoe to drop.

"I got to admit, you're like the answer to my prayers, Chief."

"How do you mean?"

36

"We've still got enough food to last us a couple of years at least, but water could shape up to be a problem. While the rain and snow will help, and we have a very good filtration system, we will have a water issue at some point."

Giving a somber nod, I ask the most important question. "How many people do you have to evacuate?"

"A hundred and twelve," he states with worry. "Twenty-two of those are middle school kids who were here when massive riots rocked the area and I had to give the order to lock down the base. Then we have some families on top of that."

"Shit!"

"That's right," he states with a frown. "Those poor kids have lost the most of any of us thanks to the Collapse."

"Can we fit everyone on one plane?"

The Major shakes his head before holding up a finger as he rides through a coughing fit. It doesn't sound like a good kind of cough either. I hope he's all right. I just got here, for Goddess' sake.

"We'd need two minimum," he states after a deep breath. "That isn't the problem. The real problem is pilots. I only have one."

I sigh heavily. "Any other good news?"

"Yeah," he replies with a chuckle. "I have a good sized ground crew, so we can get the aircraft up and running in record time. Even mechanics to make sure they are in top notch service."

"Well, I have some flying experience and understand the basics, but landing could be dicey because while I have air time, I have no landing experience."

"We can get you up to speed on the aircraft. We have a flight simulator." Stopping, he starts to look like he doesn't want to say what's going to come out of his mouth. "For right now though, I want you to take command of our security forces. You are the most combat trained person I have now. Most of these people are just kids with no place to go when everything fell apart."

"You sure Hayes is going to be good with that?"

"She has no choice," Drummond states with a frown. "It's an order. Besides, when a lot of our people deserted, she stayed because she felt it was her duty."

"And that's going to make her okay with this?"

"It means she's loyal, and if I say you're in, you're in."

"That is a good soldier to have."

Stepping up, he holds out his hand to shake, so I stand up and do so. "Go ahead and meet up with the lieutenant. She'll get you up to speed."

"Thank you, sir." I deliver a crisp salute and he returns it.

"Dismissed."

37

Exiting of his office, I head down the halls in search of the lieutenant to tell her what could be bad news. All the while my mind is racing, trying to figure out a way to get a message to Chloe.

Chapter Nine

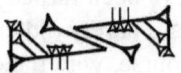

A winter storm the likes of which none have seen in living memory lasts for more than five months. Snow, rain, sleet, and more snow is the constant pattern and continues practically unabated for almost half a year. I think we have a whole two days of sun between storms before getting hammered again. I'm worried. Not only about Chloe, but also over the townsfolk I sent her way. I hope the weather isn't as awful for them.

I couldn't help but wonder if somehow the Collapse caused this to happen, or if nukes happened somewhere and this was the result. Hell, Yellowstone could have blown up and nobody would even know until, well, until the nuclear winter started.

While the cold sucked, it had the added benefit of keeping the bandits at bay for the most part. We had an occasional sniper attempt, but it was too cold so they didn't stick around long. Unless I was nearby, of course, and in that case they were rewarded with a dead sniper. The raiders were simply not equipped for such a winter either, and more than once we saw them running away from a burning house that they'd caught on fire, probably while trying to keep warm.

This whole situation has kept me busy. At first, Lieutenant Hayes was annoyed at being demoted and answering to an enlisted man. But like all good lieutenants, it didn't take long for her to realize it was a good idea, and one that made her job easier. She was wet behind the ears and still had much to learn, even given the hard lessons dealt since the Collapse. In some ways, she reminded me of Chloe—eager to learn and soaking up everything like a sponge.

One nice thing about Nellis was its armory. The Army had set up a depot on the base so they could rapidly ship supplies to any hotspot in the Pacific Rim. This meant large numbers of weapons, ammunition, body armor and other field equipment. It was with this discovery that I was able to replace most of my trauma bag. My tactical vest also has new SAPI plates. Good thing too. The old ones looked like they should have failed already.

The security team consisted of forty-three people, of which less than a quarter had any real security experience. My previous thought at the gate was prophetically correct—I've been turned into a damn babysitter. More than half of these kids are barely old enough to drink, the others aren't even twenty-five. Of course, with the end of the world, some rules might be relaxed. As far as I'm concerned, if a man is old enough to die for his country, he's old enough to have a beer at the end of his shift.

Whipping them into shape was a challenge. These are people who were able to get through politically-correct boot camp. A boot camp that wasn't tough and didn't put them under pressure to make sure they could hack it. By letting them skip out of stressful situations, they were done a disservice which puts both their lives and the lives of civilians at risk. Well, Beast doesn't give any breaks. So I did my best to rectify the mistakes of those who instructed them before me.

Some of them cried. Some of them broke down. But in the end they all banded together and toughened up. By the end of the first month, I was seeing a lot of progress and no lip. According to Lieutenant Hayes, they didn't talk back much because I had saved Airman Burnett's life. Guess I earned some instant respect by doing that.

As for Ms. Hayes, she acted as a buffer between them and myself, which was a good idea. When I scared the living daylights out of them, she found ways to calm them down. When I pushed them hard, she kept encouraging them. I was the bad cop and she became the good cop.

There was one exception in the group—Sergeant Seth Rawlins. A devil dog stationed at Camp Pendleton, he'd been in Vegas doing what many single soldiers do on leave, having fun. When the shit hit the fan, he hightailed it to the base.

The Major didn't see fit to promote him at the time. If I didn't know any better, I'd think there was a bit of an Air Force bias when it came to having a grunt Marine. He wasn't stupid though. Seth had been tasked with not only getting the personnel their initial, squad level training, but also was assigned to run the night crew while Hayes ran days.

To say the he and I got along instantly would be an understatement. Marines love their corpsman, and when he found out I used to be a SEAL as well, he thanked God for sending him some competent help.

My biggest problem was that by month two, everyone was used to me—and my animal side wanted to flee for the hills. It was far too much civilization and not enough killing. At that, I handpicked three soldiers for a two week operation and we made clandestine forays over the wall. I had no choice but to teach them stealth while throwing them to the wolves. Fortunately, I'd toughened them up enough that by now they were picking it up fast.

I'm now on my third foray into the "wilderness" and I've got Ms. Hayes on my six. Joining us is Mr. Burton and Mr. Jackson. I've fashioned makeshift suppressors from the proper oil filters. Having access to a machine shop helped in that regard and now our rifles add to our stealth.

The first few expeditions we didn't find any bandits before needing to turn back. While I've been training these kids to weather the elements, I'm not going as far as to try and kill them like a SEAL instructor would. It is viciously cold, and we don't have exceptional cold-weather gear.

Tonight has been different. We have been able to successfully move up on a group of raiders and they are completely unaware. It was easy to find them, bitching and moaning about how cold it is as they try to stay warm around a barrel fire. Few of them have any weapons within easy reach.

Using hand signals, I start telling each soldier—well, airman, whatever—who to target. Everyone goes on my shot. At that, I start aiming at the one man who is sitting on a couch under the carport who has an AR variant in hand and laughing at his fellows.

The action of my rifle makes more noise than the shot as my target's head explodes against the back wall. All but one man barely has time to even register surprise before they too are gunned down. In an effort to keep from dying, the last man throws his arms up in abject terror as he watches me melt out of the darkness like his worst nightmare come to life.

Pointing at him, I then point at the floor as I growl, low and menacing. Dropping to his knees in compliance, he even clasps his hands on his head as if he knows the drill. I motion for my team to quickly police the dead. As they do so, I zip tie my volunteer's hands. Then I place a cloth in his mouth to muzzle him.

We say nothing, and to the credit of my team, they make very little noise as they gather up useful weapons and equipment. Ms. Hayes gives me a nod that they are ready. Motioning to the bandit with a growl, I get him to his feet and we start moving back to the base as fast and quiet as possible.

"Make a single noise," I whisper to my new friend, "And I'll kill you very badly."

The man nods frantically, but says nothing as I push him forward. The team molds around us and we pick our way through the darkness, heading back for base. The walls loom not far away, so it doesn't take long.

As we get closer, I lean to Ms. Hayes. "Sprint ahead and get the gate open. We'll cover you."

Giving me a nod, she takes off running as the wall ahead, spotlights shining down onto the snow covered street. In order to avoid being detected, we've been using the sewers, something the raiders have not even considered. Of course the Army Corps of Engineers did, and set up steel barricades with locked doors in which the lock was on our side. Fortunately, the Major had the key.

Normally we'd come back the same way, but not via the same entrance. I always made sure to have a sentry on duty for the entrance we were using for that foray. Since I was escorting a bandit, I didn't want to give my secrets away. Not that I plan on letting him live, but it is best to always assume someone is watching.

Kneeling down in the dark, we stay hidden as Ms. Hayes gets the attention of our fellow soldiers. Soon the gate cracks open and we book it. My new friend hesitates, at least until I growl once more. At that he starts moving in the direction I want him to. We slip through the narrow opening before it closes.

Safe inside the confines of the base, the two boys on my team turn and point their rifles directly at my interrogation volunteer. Oh, I can tell they really want to gun this bastard down and be done with it.

"Why is this piece of shit still breathing—sir?"

Jackson adds the "sir" when I start growling at them. The rifles drop and I become less serious, but still keep a good grip on the raider. As Ms. Hayes walks up, I can see the same confusion in her eyes.

"This man may be able to answer some questions for me," I state in an ominous tone. "Now, I need to perform an interrogation."

The man lets out a slight whimper as the lieutenant responds. "What do you need?"

"A secure room, chair, table, and a plastic drop cloth if you got one. Sooner or later, people lose control and end up pissing and shitting on themselves." When I smile wickedly, Mr. Burton turns green and Jackson's dark skin pales.

"Follow me, sir." Lieutenant Hayes heads toward HQ and I point my bandit in the same direction.

"Oh, come on, man," the raider laments. "I'll tell you anything. What do you want to know?"

I stop and look at him, serious as death itself. "Oh trust me, you'll tell me everything by the time I'm done. Now move."

Chapter Ten

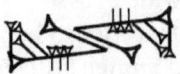

My prisoner is tied to a U.S. issue, steel office chair with dark green vinyl upholstery. After checking his restraints, I exit the room that has been converted into a brig and lock the door. I leave him alone in silence to think about what is going to happen. Imagining what can be done to you is one of the most effective methods of torture.

Everyone immediately speculates about water boarding, trained rats, thumb screws and rubber hoses when it comes to torture. In reality, those are not effective methods. The CIA wrote a nifty little handbook back in the nineteen sixties called the KUBARK Manual. It brings up a very, very important point—physical pain sucks as an interrogation method.

A person in extreme pain will say literally anything to get the interrogator to stop, and often what they confess is not the truth. More importantly, it may not be the whole truth. Once a person is under enough duress, they may babble, yet miss giving you key information in their rush to make the pain stop. After that, they're too terrified the pain will start again to even think straight, let alone give you good intel.

Psychological torture is an entirely different issue. Getting inside their head and letting them think about what can happen is much more effective. Fear of extreme physical pain is far more potent than actually delivering it. Of course, the bad guys haven't read the KUBARK Manual, so they do use torture on their victims, often just for the fun of it. And since they know what awful, painful things they or their friends have come up with, they begin to sweat real fast.

Lieutenant Hayes is waiting in the hallway, wearing a frown when I walk out. Burton and Jackson are not far away either. I think the two young men are happy that the bandit is about to have a very bad day. Instead of saying anything to them, I take Ms. Hayes aside before writing down a list in my notepad.

"I want you to get me the following things, and you need to be quiet about it. Understood?"

With a nod, she takes the paper I hand her and her brow furrows when she reads it. "All this?"

"All of it. Make sure it's in a box so no one can see the contents. Also get me a bucket of sand, make sure the lid is on so no one sees."

"Yes, sir," she states with wide eyes.

Forcing down the chuckle that tries to bubble up, I watch her walk away and then look to the two airmen still standing there. When I point to them, they both swallow hard and look frightened of me.

"You two stand guard until I come back. No one else in or out, understood?"

"Yes sir," they reply in unison.

In all actuality, I hope they talk outside the door, wondering what I'm going to do to my volunteer. It's not a thick door, so the raider would probably hear them. But even if they don't, he's going to be nervous as a cat by the time I return.

Walking away, I go to my room to drop off my weapons and tactical gear. It's still night time, so the hallways are at one-quarter lighting. Major Dummond has continued to keep the order going until we're sure the storms have past.

Once I'm in my room, I groan slightly as I take my tactical gear off and drop it onto the floor before stripping out of my fatigues. To say that I feel old is an understatement. I survived the collapse of the civilized world. I watched my family be murdered. I've even done the impossible and died, then come back to life. All that has left me feeling ancient as I close in on fifty. The only thing that makes me feel young again is Chloe.

I should not have had that thought. Memories of her hit me like a thunderbolt and unbearable loneliness creeps into my chest. Goddess I wish she was here. To have her in my arms. Taking her out to kill bandits. Making her cry out with that lovely singing voice of hers. No matter how hard I try, she's always on my mind. I can't even escape her in my sleep.

Shaking my head free of its errant thoughts, I finish getting dressed. Slipping a holster onto my belt, I place my Steyr in it before grabbing my sword and trauma bag. Heading back out the door, I walk towards an interrogation that I am greatly looking forward to.

Lieutenant Hayes and Airmen Burton and Jackson are waiting for me when I return. She has a cardboard box and I smile, hoping that she has found everything I have requested. One thing is certain, I don't think any of them are thrilled at the wolfish grin on my face.

"Did you find everything?" I make my voice expectant, excited.

"Yes sir," she states in a terrified whisper. "But… we don't torture people."

I can't help but give her a hard stare. "You may have noticed, Lieutenant. We're not operating under the same rule system we used to."

For the first time since meeting me, she actually quails under my gaze. In the past two months, she's gotten to know me better than anyone else on the base. She's seen me operate, seen me kill men with cold, unerring precision. More than once, she's seen my animal side come out to play and bathe in raider blood.

"Yes sir," she replies while swallowing hard.

"Follow me, lieutenant."

Unlocking the door, we walk into the room where my volunteer awaits. The man looks at both of us with terror written plainly in his eyes. I wonder how many of his victims looked at him just the same way before he killed or raped them. I'm sure he now wants to plead for the same mercy others asked from him.

"Set those things on the table, lieutenant."

"Yes sir." Her voice is very soft.

As she does so, I toss my trauma pack next to the table. "I forgot something important," I say with a snap of my fingers. "Follow me."

I open the door and let he walk out, then shoot the man a playful wink before closing it. Taking Ms. Hayes a short distance down the hall and away from prying ears, I decide it's time to explain just what we are going to do.

"I'm sure by now you are wondering why I asked for all those odd items."

"That's obvious," she states with disdain. "You're going to torture him."

I chuckle. "Already have been."

"What?"

"Physical pain is a poor choice for torture. It doesn't work. But the thought of it, oh, that's a different story." I point to the room. "He's in there right now. His mind conjuring up all manner of gruesome thoughts as he wonders what I'm about to do to him. He's doing the interrogation for me."

"Why the blowtorch then? And I'm really afraid to ask what the popsicle is for."

"You'll find out," I reply with a grin. "But trust me, I'm not going to put a mark on him. Your job is simple. Stand there and watch, don't laugh, but look distraught. Okay?"

"Why?"

"You're the good cop. In case he doesn't talk, you rush in after I leave and convince him to talk."

There's a light bulb moment in her eyes and her lips part in shock. "You're a devious, bastard!"

"I had friends in the C.I.A."

Ms. Hayes shakes her head. "I still don't know that I approve."

45

"You don't have to," I state darkly. "This is my job, not yours."

"Yes sir."

Motioning for her to follow, we walk back into the room. Once more the raider focuses on me with wide eyes full of fear. I can imagine the thoughts that have been running through his mind as he tortures himself for me. Opening my medic bag, I pull out a pair of trauma shears and walk over to him.

"Well, Mr. Bandit," I state calmly while cutting his shirt off. "You and I are going to have a long talk."

"I'll tell you anything you want to know," he cries out.

"Yes you will," I reply with a wicked smile that makes him pale. "Problem is, I have to make sure. For all I know, you could be lying to me."

"Awww man." The bandit swoons, and at first I'm certain he's going to pass out or piss himself. "I just hooked up with them to keep from starving. Besides, they aren't the kind of group you can say no to. I've got no loyalty to them."

"Sorry. You backed the wrong horse. Like I said, I have to be sure." My tone is matter-of-fact. Professional.

Pulling another chair over, I screw a hook into the ceiling as he starts whimpering and lamenting. I then put another hook into the closest wall. Every so often I catch sight of Ms. Hayes and she looks very uncomfortable, even though she knows I'm not going to cause him any real physical harm. Looking distraught, just as I asked.

Tying the rope to the wall hook, I then throw the line over the ceiling hook, loop it through his restraints and tie it off. Then I undo the rope tying him to the chair.

Pulling the line, the bandit is lifted out of the chair and into a standing position, hanging just high enough to keep from touching the ground. The man grunts and groans as he hangs suspended in midair.

"Tie the slack off," I call out to the lieutenant.

To her credit, she follows the order and quickly ties to rope off. I then let the bandit go, his toes are barely an inch off the ground. Walking over to the table, I pull it up behind him and start pulling out the rest of the items on the list. Placing a recorder on the table, I hit record.

"What do you want to know!?" He's practically crying at this point.

"What's your name?"

"Sam."

"Nice to meet you Sam," I reply with a chipper tone. "I'm Beast."

Lighting up the blowtorch, his eyes widen. "Wha- what's the torch for?"

"Going to ask you some important questions," I reply as I bring the flame to a nice blue color. "You know, what's interesting about this method is, it won't hurt at first. It's too hot. The flame sears the nerve endings closed, killing them off. Then your body goes into shock, and all you'll feel is cold. Isn't that crazy? Some say you'll smell your burning flesh before you feel it."

I saw this in a movie once, and it's brilliant. Sitting on the table is a tray with a piece of pork on it. I point the torch at the meat, which starts to sizzle immediately. Then I poke his back with the popsicle and he screams, trying to twist away as he thinks he's being burned.

"What do you want to know?" He screams wildly.

"How many of your friends are there? What's the total number of raiders?"

"I- I don't know," he stammers. "Two, maybe three thousand?"

Thousands? Fuck me!

"Who's the leader?"

"Father Roberts," he yells quickly. Answers are coming freely now. "He rescued the prisoners left behind at the High Desert State Prison. Turned them into an army. They all believe he was sent by God himself. They'll do anything he tells them."

"Well, then I've got a message for Father Roberts."

"What?"

I lay the blowtorch down and let it cook the pork chop while I jab the man repeatedly with the popsicle. Screams fill the air, all of it being recorded by the tape recorder on the table. After I've gotten a good amount, I draw my Steyr and pull the trigger.

Chapter Eleven

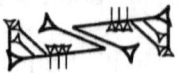

I leave the room with Lieutenant Hayes to find both airmen on guard looking quite pale. A small pool of vomit is on the floor in front of Burton and his face is filled with shame. These poor kids just don't understand the world of shit they've been dropped into. I've been trying to toughen them up, but they still have a long way to go.

"You two are no longer needed," I state plainly to the two airmen. "Go get some rack time. However, Burton, you need to clean up your mess."

"Yes sir."

Both of them look at me like I'm the devil himself, or rather, avoid looking at me altogether. I'm sure at some point, Ms. Hayes will tell them what really happened. For right now, though, fear of The Beast is firmly cemented in their minds. More importantly, I continue to set the standard that my will is implacable when it comes to dealing with raiders and protecting these people.

When they walk away, we wait until they are out of sight before Ms. Hayes and I quickly move into the room. We carry out a body wrapped in the plastic drop cloth and lug it to the parking lot, commandeering the nearest HUMVEE. We speed away from the building toward the rear-most section of the base where the bandits don't go.

The reason they don't go there is thanks to a few Army Volcano mine launching systems the Major put to good use. The systems were mounted on Blackhawks and can lay a dense, thousand square meter minefield in twenty seconds. So the Major laid down a number of minefields in the hills east of the base. After a couple of casualties, the bandits quit trying to make their way around the east side.

The weather has calmed for the moment and is barely drizzling, turning the old snow soft and mushy on top of the thick layers of ice. When we get to the back gate, the guards on duty open it and we keep going. It takes some time, but we finally get to a likely spot near Lake Mead.

Parking the vehicle, I get out. Ms. Hayes follows. Dropping the back hatch, I help Sam out. The poor man is a little worse for wear, but happy to be alive. His legs are trembling as he scrambles to his feet.

"Let me hear you say we have an understanding," I state menacingly, grabbing his attention.

"Ye-yes sir, I won't be back this way. I'm done with that life, I swear."

Reaching my hand out, Lieutenant Hayes places a backpack into my grasp. I shove it into Sam's chest and he wraps his arms around it like it's a life preserver. While I continue, Ms. Hayes is dragging an inflatable raft out.

"You've got enough food for a week if you stretch it out. Only two canteens, but they are both full. One extra set of clothes in your size. Survival kit, knife and a flashlight."

"All right," he replies, but there is a question in his eyes. *Why is he setting me free?*

To be honest, I don't know myself. Ever since I came back, I feel a little different. Sure, the animal side of me is still there, waiting to be unleashed when needed. But at the same time, I've got a sense of mercy I didn't have before, of peace. In some ways, I blame Chloe. Her voice is often in my head, guiding me. It's gotten to the point where I don't argue.

"You will also find an AR-Seven rifle in that pack. It's currently unloaded and it's just a twenty-two, but you can hunt small game with it. I've given you fifty rounds. Don't try to load it until we've been gone for at least an hour." All he can do is nod emphatically as I continue.

"You take this raft, head straight to Lake Mead, and you row to the far side and then keep heading east. You go back to your friends and they'll likely kill you for talking. Best thing you can do is count on yourself."

"Yes sir."

"Now get out of here," I growl menacingly. "Before I come to my senses."

Sam holds tightly to the folded up raft and backpack and runs as fast as he can, often stumbling and damn near falling. I watch the comedy routine for a moment before shaking my head and getting back into the HUMVEE with the lieutenant. It's not until we are through the back gate, she finally speaks.

"Why did you let him go?"

"Because I'm getting soft?" I chuckle. "To be honest, I don't know myself. Gut instinct, maybe. Sam wasn't a hardened raider. He was simply a man caught up in the madness and trying to stay alive. On the wrong side, of course."

"That's it," she exclaims in shock. "Gut instinct?"

49

"Ms. Hayes, that's often all you've got to work on. For the record, my gut has gotten me through some of the worst hell holes in the world."

She frowns, not thrilled with the answer. "Noted, sir."

"Would you quit calling me sir?"

"According to the Major, you are my superior."

I growl at her response involuntarily, and she flinches slightly. "I'm still not an officer. I work for a living."

At that remark, she laughs. It's a common joke in pretty much every branch. Any time a higher enlisted gets called "sir" by the fresh out of boot recruits, the response is always the same. Don't call me, sir! I work for a living.

"What are you going to do with that recording?"

Now it's my turn to start laughing. "Play it over the base's PA system so that the bandits can hear it."

Ms. Hayes eyes go so wide that I swear they are going to pop out of her skull. "What?"

"I'm sending a message. Don't know how well it will work, but if it puts some fear into them, then they won't fight as well."

"Seems like a long shot."

"This is combat, lieutenant. Everything you do is a long shot. And even cheating is fair play. It's always acceptable to try to stack the deck in your favor."

"I'll try to remember that," she states with a grin, "sir."

As we get close to the headquarters building, we both start laughing. While the levity is appreciated, it's also time to start thinking about my next move. I get the feeling this preacher isn't going to give us a break.

Chapter Twelve

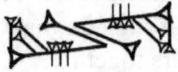

After a successful foray of taking the fight to the bandits, the people of Nellis want to celebrate. Major Drummond, understanding how important morale is, agreed to a little excess and signed off on it.

With the exception of guards and medical staff that are on duty, everyone has shown up to party in one of the empty hangars. I've planned a small celebration for the off-duty staff later. It's an amazing collection of people. All races and religions from all corners of the U.S. mingle under one roof, laughing and celebrating. Not a single one of them care about who is different from anyone else. It makes me actually smile.

Identity politics is part of what tore society down. Claims of racism that typically weren't true, all in an attempt to quash the narrative of an opposing view point. Issues with reverse racism, which is still racism. There were even black students at Berkeley before everything fell apart that were successful at segregating whites and blacks. That's how screwed up and insane things had gotten. Too many people who couldn't simply live their own lives and leave each other alone. Bringing attention to our differences instead of trying to come together. They forgot, I guess, that we all belong to one race: the Human race.

I sit at a table, enjoying what little is left of my meal while the celebration swirls around me. People pat me on the back and give thanks. Even though I organized this, I'm really not in a mood to be here. One incursion does not win this unwinnable war. Besides, there are too many people, too much movement, far too much loud noise. The beast in me is not amused and it all irritates me.

That's the problem with becoming a animal, eschewing your humanity and living in that dark part of the woods all men have inside them. Raiders like to think they live in the same wilderness as myself, but they have not truly embraced their animal side. They dance just enough with the devil to get by and still hold on to some semblance of humanity. Once you follow my path, you are only comfortable with your own pack. For me, that pack consists of only one other person, Chloe.

Fuck! Why did I have to start thinking about her?

Yeah, because there are times I don't think about her? I'd give anything to have her in my arms right now, holding her close, listening to her purr as I run my fingers through her hair. I'd even settle for her laugh as we take out a band of raiders together.

Picking up the beer I've been slowly working on, I step outside the slightly open hangar doors and look up at the night sky. The clouds have mostly cleared up, but I have to wonder for how long. I get a nice view of the stars as my mind is consumed with thoughts of my love. What is she doing right now? What is the weather like at the bunker? Is she still safe? Is she okay? It kills me that I don't know the answers to these questions.

Goddess, please tell me Dan got through with my message?

Across the field of black, dotted with wisps of clouds that are barely illuminated in the moon light, a shooting star with white and green colors streaks across the sky. Is that a coincidence or an answer?

Is that a yes, goddess?

Another shooting star streaks across, and my heart damn near jumps out of my chest. Hopefully that means Chloe knows I'm alive. Impossible to be sure, but she can't miss the significance of that message. It's not like there are that many Webley's floating around, even before the Collapse.

I feel a change in the air as someone steps up beside me. Lieutenant Hayes gazes up at me and smiles. She's changed into civilian clothes, red hair down and in a short pony tail. If I didn't know any better, I'd say she's also put on some makeup. With a beer of her own in hand, she slides up next to me and looks up at the same sky.

"Beautiful night," she states softly. "Nice of the weather to join us in the celebration."

"Don't expect it to last. I think it's just a pause in the storm."

Shaking her head, she takes another drink. "The weather has been rather odd."

"Maybe not," I reply darkly. "I heard rumor that right before the Collapse, the entire Middle East went up in nuclear fire. Probably tossed enough shit up into the air to give us a small taste of nuclear winter."

"Do you think all this snow is radioactive?"

I shake my head. "It's been almost two years. At this point, probably not enough to affect you. Maybe raise your chance of cancer by a percentage point or two."

Ms. Hayes steps up closer. "You certainly do know an awful lot about an awful lot of—things."

"Had to in order to be a SEAL."

"Why?" Her voice sounds a little sultry, but it doesn't really register at first.

"When you are on mission, you are a small team of four to eight men. Each man has to be a force multiplier on his own. For every one of us, there was easily ten to twenty of the enemy. That meant knowing your job, knowing everyone else's job and knowing everything about your terrain, weather, etc."

"That must mean you are really smart, too?"

I realize almost too late that Ms. Hayes is about to kiss me and I stop her. An involuntary growl rumbles through my throat, my animal side warning her she's choosing a bad path. I've killed for my precious Chloe, and the lieutenant does not want to end up on that list. Frankly, I don't want to put her there, so I calmly and gently push her away.

The look of disappointment and rejection is plain on her face. Inwardly I sigh, but go back to looking up at the stars as an awkward silence begins to fall over us. At first she tries to pretend like nothing happened before finally speaking.

"What's her name?"

"Chloe."

"Where is she?"

"Colorado," I reply painfully. "She's at the bunker out there. Hopefully safe and warm."

Ms. Hayes nods. "So that's why you want to take us there?"
"Partly," I nod back, "but also because it's got running water all year round, fertile land, and is well defensible. While winters will be cold, it will still be a good place to live. There's a handful of places in Colorado that are just like it, so as population expands, there are good areas to expand into."

"Wow, you've really thought about this."

I give a snort of a laugh. "Oh yeah, I just didn't pay close enough attention to the signs. I should have gotten my family out sooner. Now they're dead because of my stupidity. At least I saved Chloe and got her out of that mess."

"Saved her?"

"Yeah. She was a slave to a gang of men. Freed her, taught her to kill raiders, and then once my truck was fixed, we left L.A. for good. I think we both needed to get away from that cursed city. Too many ghosts nipping at our heels."

"Fuck! Was it that bad?"

"You have no idea. Worse than here, in a way. There were pockets of them everywhere. Here, they are all organized under one banner. In L.A. there were a thousand different gangs and warlords, all shooting at each other and everyone else in between."

53

"Shit."

"Yes, indeed."

Uncomfortable silence follows before she finally speaks again. "Are we okay, sir?"

"Are you still alive?"

Ms. Hayes looks confused, but nods. "Yes, sir."

"Then we're okay."

I wink and then shoot her a grin. She starts laughing. Clinking our beer bottles together, we both take a drink and look back at the stars while the party continues on inside. All the while, my mind can think of nothing but how to get these people to safety before the Huns outside find a way through the wall.

Chapter Thirteen

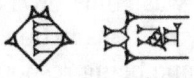

What a horrible winter!

Living in the bunker has made it easy to survive the snow-pocalypse that ravaged the land. I had no idea Colorado got this much snow, but Liz says this is an exceptional year. Liz and I have made forays to both Gunnison and Crested Butte. We found no more raiders, but we did find a few survivors with little to no resources trying to live through the terrible cold. I brought them into the fold, and our numbers increased from two to fifteen. I did not share with them the secret areas of the bunker though. Trust is earned, not given.

We towed some mobile homes into the area, more than we needed because I listened to my gut, the way my Beast taught me to. We found a small bulldozer to start building fortifications. By January, we had a trench and earthen wall that blocked off a natural choke point between two mountains. The only thing not entirely blocked off is the river, which is guarded.

In early January, I was treated to a rather odd event. A small group of people showed up out of the blue. How they survived on foot for so long was beyond me, especially since they were barely armed. According to the man leading them, an old woman in their party had a vision of this place. Said it was protected by the Angel of Death. That gave me quite a chill, believe you me.

There were seven in total. I let them in, trusting my gut again, and initially treated them the same as the others. Nena Kumar was clearly gifted, though. The woman has to be in her sixties or seventies, but is still sharp and perceptive. Short, gray hair adorns her head. Dark brown skin with few wrinkles, remarkable for her age, and her voice is musical and lovely. After she and Liz helped me give birth to Leah, she volunteered to help me watch over my daughter, and she was a godsend.

Now, spring is finally beginning to arrive, thank the powers that be. We had already planned where to plant our first year of crops and started getting the seeds ready. We'd fashioned a mini greenhouse to get some things started early to transplant when the time was right. Everyone looked to me as the leader, and that meant I was supposed to oversee, not work. But I do as I please, so I pitched in wherever people were working, to at least get a feel for what was going on. I did not intend to sit up on high and wave a hand for my minions to do as I said. There is no enjoyment in leading others and being responsible for them if one does not know and love them.

With no bandits in the immediate vicinity, and a vicious winter preventing most people from traveling, we had been living in a peaceful, winter wonderland. The problem was that I had no assholes to kill! I already feel I might be losing my touch. The Angel of Death is just itching to come out and play, but I try to keep that side of me masked so I don't scare anyone.

Liz has stayed by my side through it all as my second in command and my first friend. We were sisters in arms and occasional lovers. I had saved her and she kept me sane, got me through my loneliness and pregnancy. I don't know I could have done any of that had I not found her. I still have not told her I love her, but I imagine she knows why. I keep hoping love will come in time. She is loveable. It's my problem, not hers. I simply know what true love is, and I can't pretend.

Now, teams are planting our first run of seeds and some of the seedlings. I am in one of the small trailers near the wall, playing with my bright eyed Leah. I thought the blue of her eyes would darken as she got older, but they remain the same blue as her father's. She is so beautiful and never fails to make me smile. Even at two in the morning when she needs her diaper changed or to be fed.

This morning I smile at her as I dress her. She gurgles and coos happily, the blue of her father's eyes sending a pang of love and loss into my heart.

"Chloe," Liz yells, "Got movement heading towards the wall!"

I hand Leah gently to Nena and grab my rifle before bounding out of the cabin and towards the defensive wall. In a surge of adrenaline, I run up the earthen ramp so fast, I put cheetahs to shame. Yes, I might be a little excited for some action.

Stopping next to Liz, I pull my Tavor up and look through the scope. Sure enough, there are about two dozen people, lightly armed. They don't look like raiders. Bundled up children are being pulled along in carts, so I revise my estimate to about thirty five souls.

"Families," I state, a little shocked. "Don't shoot unless they shoot first."

All the guards along the wall give an affirmative hand signal, keeping their weapons at the ready as the cluster of people get to within earshot. We will have to parley and find out why they're here.

"That's far enough," I yell out. "What do you want?"

A man in the lead hands off his rifle to a woman near him and walks up with his hands up. Everyone I see is dressed in layer after layer of tattered clothing, blankets and even towels. I don't think there's a single one of them that's properly equipped for cold weather and I can only imagine that they are miserable.

"I'm looking for someone called the Angel of Death," he yells back. "I was told to ask for her."

My paranoia kicks up a notch and Liz leans in and whispers. "This is a trap."

"Maybe," I tell her, "but I want to hear what he has to say."

She grudgingly nods. I can see she is not happy with my decision. My curiosity far outweighs my survival instinct. My reputation is primarily solid in California, so how does this guy know my nickname? Do they have another Nena?

"You can come closer," I point right at him. "Only you!"

The woman behind him says something and he turns, holding his hands out at her. I think she's worried and he's trying to placate her. Turning back, he walks towards the wall with his hands up. Once he is roughly six feet away, I motion for him to stop and he does so.

"Where did you hear that name?"

"A man told it to me," he states truthfully, and my heart skips a beat. "We had to leave our homes. We're being plagued by bandits. Then this man comes along and kills the ones in our town. We were afraid of retribution from the rest of the gang, so he tells us, head north of Gunnison and ask for the Angel of Death. He tells us, 'So long as you work hard, she will give you a home and protect you as well as I did.'"

My mouth goes dry as the hairs on the back of my neck stand up. "What did this man look like? Did he give you a name?"

"No ma'am," he replies with a shake of his head. "Wore a white mask on his face like he was the Lone Ranger himself. Fought like a damn demon. Never seen anyone like that. We figure he musta been military before. Then he tells us to come here and leaves. Seemed to be in an awful hurry."

"Wh-where was he heading?" My voice has too much emotion in it.

"Direction of Las Vegas, ma'am."

I look at Liz. "Let them in, get them sorted per usual procedure. Bring that man to me so I can talk to him."

"All right," she replies, but doesn't look thrilled. I stare at her, and she has a hint of fear in her eyes. I don't like it.

Heading back down the ramp, I'm totally lost in thought, heart pounding, false hope rising in my chest. I try to beat it back down. My Beast can't be alive. A bullet ripped a hole his neck and he bled out as I watched. I held his corpse for hours in that awful place. That's not

57

something anyone could survive. Surely if he had, he would have come here, wouldn't he? Nothing is making sense as I walk into the trailer where Nena is.

"Are you quite all right, Angel?"

I smile at Nena. She always calls me Angel. Even after telling her my name is Chloe, she refuses to call me by anything but that nickname. After the first month, I just gave up trying to correct her.

"Got some people coming in," I say as I take Leah from her.

Nena closes her eyes. "Farmers from Green River. Saved by an animal who walks in human form."

My heart stops. "What did you say?"

"Their leader is almost here. He will tell you." She sighs, opens her eyes again, and smiles reassuringly. "Don't be afraid, Angel. Soon all will be well."

As if on cue, Liz walks in with the man I was talking to and she has a cloth bundle in hand. Respectfully, he takes off his hat and holds it to his chest. He appears terribly malnourished and his layers of ragged clothing look like he's been through a war. It makes me worry about the children that are with them.

"Thank you for taking us in, ma'am." I notice that he's shaking slightly.

"Of course, you're welcome here. In fact—"

I call to a couple of people who are curiously watching the newcomers outside and instruct them to get everyone fed as soon as possible. Grabbing some bread and butter from the trailer kitchen, I sit back down with Dan, urging him to eat something before I debrief him further. Once he's gotten some food, his eyes well up for a moment, and then he bows his head to me. I can hardly stand the sight, so I begin questioning him again.

"Sir, can you tell me more about this man? The one that sent you to me?"

It's easy to tell that my treatment has moved him. I'm almost afraid he's going to break down right here on the spot. He swallows and pulls himself together before he speaks, but still has tears in his eyes.

"Like I said, ma'am. Fought like a demon. I watched with my own eyes as he stood before six of them raiders, including Jimmy who was their fastest. Gunned 'em all down like he wasn't breakin' a sweat. He killed all the others without us ever knowing he was there."

My heart is beginning to race. "You said he wore a white mask?"

"Yes ma'am," he replies with a nod. "Just the upper part like he was the Lone Ranger."

"Then what did he do?"

"That's when he gave me a message for you."

58

"Message!? What message?"

Swallowing hard, he answers timidly. "After killing Jimmy and all them guys, he took me aside and gave us directions. Told us to leave right away with all the food and supplies we could gather. And he had a message just for you. He said, 'she won't understand, but tell her that I will get another message to her somehow, better explaining things, when I get to Las Vegas.' For now, he said he wanted me to give you a pistol."

Liz steps forward with the bundle she's taken from him. My mouth goes dry as I watch her unfold an almost clean square of cloth to reveal the Webley revolver that Beast gave me the day he saved me from the Crazy Eight.

Tears threaten to fall as I pick up the weapon with a shaky hand. I think, no, this can't be right, but there is a nick in the grip where there was one in that Webley. I can't quite accept it, but it must be true.

Oh, Beast! How?

"Why was he going to Vegas?" I look at the messenger who just delivered the most impossible of messages.

"Didn't say," the man states nervously. "Seemed to be in an awful hurry, though."

So close and yet so far away. None of this makes any sense. I know he was dead. There was no pulse, no breathing. I stayed with him a long time, I know he was dead. My beautiful Beast had died in my arms, breathing his final breath into me as we shared one last kiss. Yet I can't refute the pistol in my hands. I never told anyone just what kind of weapon it was, so it was something only he and I could know.

The poor man looks like he's going to shake apart from being so nervous. "I apologize. What's your name?"

"Dan, ma'am."

"Thank you for bringing me this message, Dan. You've done well. Do you and your people have any skills?"

"Yes ma'am. We were farmers in Green River. We managed to save some seed to offer something in exchange, s- so you'd let us in."

Nena is right once again.

"That's excellent," I exclaim with a bright smile. "We are just getting ready to plant, so we could use your help. Very few of us have any real experience."

Dan looks excited. "Yes, ma'am!"

"Liz?" I look at my lieutenant who still does not look happy. "Can you take Dan over to Mike so they can start figuring out how best to employ these people?"

"Sure," she replies softly, but with a bitter undertone. "Come on, Dan."

I thump heavily into my chair and sit there numbly, Leah in one hand and revolver in the other. I'm shocked and lost, my heart torn open and bleeding as memories of Beast rush through me. The flood gates have opened and all the pain and tears flood out of me. If he's alive, why isn't he here? When I begin crying, Leah cries with me. Nena quickly steps over to console us.

Chapter Fourteen

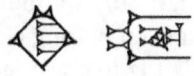

I spend the next few weeks in a haze. Spring has truly arrived, and as the snow melts, my heart heals somewhat. The message Dan brought has caused hope to swell in my chest, yet I cannot allow myself to hope. I know the impossibility of his tale, yet I keep the Webley with me constantly. Hell, I practically sleep with it under my pillow.

Everyone sees the haunted look in my eyes as I try to get through day after day. Liz definitely sees it, and I now see fear and worry in her as I become increasingly distant, Beast consuming my thoughts. She pulls back emotionally as I become more distracted, and I know I am hurting her, but I am suffering too, and can't share it with anyone.

Sitting on the corner of the bed in the bunker's master bedroom, I feed Leah and eye the revolver not a foot from me. My daughter has remained oddly calm throughout my melancholy state. My lovely Leah only cries when she needs to be fed or changed, otherwise she is content to be with me and watch me with her pretty blue eyes. His pretty blue eyes.

Liz walks in, snapping me out of my sadness. "Boss, what's wrong?"

"I- I think I've made a terrible mistake," I tell her, my voice threatening to crack. "Somehow, Beast is alive."

"He can't be alive! You told me yourself, he took a bullet in the throat. He bled out. There's no coming back from that."

I pick up the pistol that has not left my side. "Then explain this?"

"A revolver? It's just a pistol."

"It's not just a pistol, Liz," I say with a shake of my head. "This is the very pistol he gave me the night he freed me from the Crazy Eight. I never told anyone, not even you, just what model of pistol it was. Only Beast and I share that knowledge. And look. There's a mark here in the grip I made when I knocked a tooth out of some raider. This is the same gun."

As this conversation progresses, Liz is looking less and less happy by the moment. She's getting a wild expression I don't like. I know she cares for me, even loves me, but if Beast is alive—that changes everything. He is my love, hell, my life. We had a few short months

61

together as lovers before I lost him. I may be surviving, as he asked me to, but I haven't been truly alive, not the way we were together. I've done my best to push forward, if only for the sake of our daughter. But I have to confess to myself that even putting a brave face on it, I've been lost without him. Now, there's Liz to consider, and I'm guiltily glad I have never been able to tell her I love her, much as I care.

"What are you going to do?" There's a painful, defeated sigh in her voice.

That's the big question and it's one I've thought long and hard on. One of the biggest problems I have is that everyone in our enclave looks to me as their leader and savior all in one. That's a problem because I really don't have all the answers. All I know how to do is kill raiders, and I do that very well. The rest of it? Guess work and delegation. I do my best, but I am not as confident as the people seem to think I am.

"I'm taking Truck and heading to the travel center," I finally answer.

"What!?" Liz is not thrilled. "You can't! We don't know who or what might be out there."

Leah is nodding off in my arms, so I take my daughter and place her gently into the crib. My beautiful girl nestles in and goes right to sleep. Smiling at her, I look at Liz and put a finger to my lips before picking up the Webley and sneaking out of the room. Once we are in the living room, I continue.

"I have to know. I can't go on without some idea of what's going on. Did I leave him there, alive and in pain?" Tears spring to my eyes at the very idea. "No! Damn it, I know he was gone. Did I ever tell you I stayed there almost a full day after he died? He didn't breathe, not once. I was covered in his blood. He was gone. Dead, I know it. But..." I stare at the Webley. "I know it's impossible, but I have to go."

"Then I'm going with you."

I shake my head and take her by the shoulders. Folding her into my arms, I hold her. Desperately she clutches at me just like I did with Beast in the last good dream I had of him. Liz and I are going to have to sit down and have a serious talk soon. Now is not the time though. She's going through enough right now and so am I. Finally I pull back and look her in the eyes.

"We both can't go. You need to stay here and oversee our construction plans. I'll take Mike. He can drive while I watch over Leah and..."

"And?"

"And hopefully get some answers."

"If his body is still there?"

"Then I'll bring him home and give him a proper burial. It's something I should have done to begin with. Doing that will bring a close to that chapter of my life."

Liz nods, and I know she's happy with that idea. What I worry about is the impossible. What if he truly is alive? That's a situation I know will put a strain on all of us. I know where my heart belongs, and while Liz doesn't want to admit it, she knows too.

Fuck! What a mess.

"Alright," she finally agrees softly.

I beam her my brightest smile. "No matter what, Liz, I will always care about you. You know that. I couldn't have made it this far without you."

When she smiles at me, I know she's back on my side. Giving her a warm embrace, I scratch her back softly. I do not want to hurt this woman, because in all honesty, I do care for her. While I may have freed her, she has helped get me through some rough times, got me through some bad dreams.

"I'll keep an eye on things while you're gone."

"Good," I reply with a nod. "I shouldn't be gone more than a day or two, three on the outside, depending on the roads."

"Just be safe."

"I will," I state reassuringly. "Trust me, the Angel of Death is itching to come out and play, so God have mercy on anyone who dares to attack us."

That comment makes her laugh. She knows firsthand just how deadly I can be. She has spread some of those stories across the enclave. Part of me wonders if she did it to help herself feel more important, being close to the dangerous and deadly Angel of Death. She seems to relish the way everyone treats me with a combination of awe and fear. I know she has enjoyed our relationship and benefitted from it. She clings to me as her rescuer, but also, as someone important. Dan's arrival and his news may have changed everything.

"I'll let you get ready," she tells me softly, almost like a goodbye. Her voice is thick with unshed tears. "I'll inform Mike and see you outside."

Such sadness tears at my heart, but what can I do? What is left of my battered heart belongs to a dead man. Or is he dead? As if the world isn't screwed up enough, now we possibly have people coming back from the dead?

Damnit, God! It's bad enough You have to play with my heart! Why do You have to ruin Liz's as well? I try to imagine a place for her in the Enclave that is not at my side. I can, of course, but can she?

Quickly checking on Leah, she's still sound asleep. I grab my cold weather gear and sling my rifle before heading into the armory. Just to be on the safe side, I'm taking the dual P-90 rig and the M249. I also pack a couple smoke grenades and two of Beast's special concussion grenades. Finally I strap on his short sword and I'm ready.

Of course, taking an infant means additional supplies. I grab an extra blanket, clothes and diapers for her to last at least a week. I also make sure Mike and I will have enough food and water for two weeks. While I don't plan to be gone near that long, I want to be safe. I didn't get this far by being stupid and relying on dumb luck. As Beast once told me, wishful thinking is not a survival trait.

Picking up my baby girl, I take her top side and let Nena watch her so that I can load up Truck. I'm not sure who is more amazing, Leah or my nanny. While my darling daughter only cries when she absolutely has to, Nena is the one other person she doesn't get fussy with. Liz, who's been there from the beginning, gets the screaming-fit treatment. So I mostly rely on Nena.

When I exit the bunker with my supplies and head to Truck, Mike is already there and Liz is not far off. He has been third in charge, and one of our few that has real weapons experience.

Mike Wayne is an Iraq veteran. Pulled three tours before losing some good friends and deciding not to reenlist. He came home to Crested Butte, settled down with his family, and tried to put the war behind him. I know how well that didn't work. He and his wife were separated before the Collapse, and only came back together to help each other survive. With the coming of the Enclave, she stays in Crested Butte with their daughters, and he has moved into a trailer here.

The man certainly still looks the part. Black hair is kept short, although these days he does sport a beard and mustache. It contrasts really well against his blue eyes and is helpful in keeping the winter wind at bay, so he says. He's still in pretty good shape, too.

Since he's got experience, I kitted him out with one of the better AR-15s and totally tricked it out with the best gear. It certainly beat his Ruger Mini-14 and he gladly accepted it.

"How goes it, boss?" Mike speaks in his low, baritone.

"Road trip."

He laughs, but Liz does not see anything funny in it.

"So I hear. Do I get to drive your beast?"

My heart stops for a second until my rational mind kicks in and I realize he means Truck. Liz looks like she's just eaten something sour. Just the mention of his name affects us both in vastly different ways. I don't think Mike notices either of our reactions, he's still doing a spot check on the AR, a professional move I approve of.

"Since I need to take care of Leah, you certainly do."

He gives a fist pump and I laugh. After unlocking Truck, I toss him the keys and start loading up. Both Liz and Mike help and it doesn't take long before the job is done. Her lips press into a thin line as she looks over how much food and water I've packed away.

"That's a bit much, don't you think?"

"I'm playing it safe," I reply reassuringly. "On the off chance there's another snow storm, at least I've got us covered while we ride it through. Don't have enough fuel to go much farther than Cortez and back anyway."

"Good point. Just be safe, okay?"

I pull Liz into a warm embrace and then kiss her forehead. Once more she holds me desperately to her. It feels like sadness is coming from her in waves, threatening to swamp us both. Such emotion almost changes my mind, but I squeeze her again until she lets up and I take a step back.

"I will," I promise.

"You'd better."

Nena has come out with Leah cradled in her arms. Taking my daughter, I smile at the lovely old woman before clambering into Truck and buckling her into her car seat. Mike starts him up and we drive out of the compound. Next stop, Cortez.

Chapter Fifteen

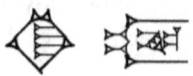

It takes longer than I would like getting to Cortez. While I think spring is officially here, some of the roads are not in agreement. Snow still lies on the ground all over, sometimes in tall drifts that spill onto the road. Ice is also a constant danger and I'm thankful that Mike is used to driving in conditions like this. Going off the road or over the side of a mountain is not exactly the way in which I want to leave this world.

It's also been almost three years since the Collapse. There are no regular road crews anymore. A road gets washed out? It stays that way. Ice builds up over the winter? Too bad. Best wait until it thaws.

Truck is my faithful steed, though. Through it all, he doesn't complain in the slightest. Through snow, over ice, up and down mountains, he's a faithful and reliable trooper. The armored plating makes him heavier, more stable, and easier to drive through tough conditions.

Of course it helps that I have kept up maintenance on him. Working on Truck has been one of the ways I keep from thinking about Beast, though I often end up reliving our battles over the maintenance of Truck, and occasionally shedding a few tears into the depths of the engine when nobody is watching. So shoot me, I'm sentimental.

Oh Beast. Are you alive?

I can't help but have hope, and I wish I didn't. The closer we get to Cortez, the more I dread I'm approaching a waterfall. When I see his dead and decomposing body, it will be like falling over the edge and my hope will be dashed on the jagged rocks at the bottom.

It takes us half a day to finally hook up onto the 491 and start picking our way through to Cortez. We need to be careful and on our game in case raiders have moved in. So far it looks as deserted as when I drove through so many months ago.

"So I showed Dan the list of seeds we have in our bank," Mike states while driving cautiously. "He thinks we can grow all of it."

"Oh?" This is very good news.

"He told me that if we can get enough good glass panes, we could make sunken greenhouses. Dig down roughly four to six feet, we then build a greenhouse over it. Then we can plant a much wider variety of crops while keeping the temperature more stable."

I nod. "Ah, good idea. That would be helpful."

"Very," Mike replies. "He even thinks we can grow those Jatropha seeds."

"That would be terrific! In a few years we could be making our own efficient organic diesel, among other things."

"Agreed. I think we've got more than enough stored fuel for the dozer that we can dig at least a dozen such greenhouses. Glass and building materials is our only problem."

"What about the hotels?"

Mike shoots me a quick glance. "How do you mean?"

"Just about all of the windows there are still intact, right?"

"Hey, that's a good idea, boss. We pull the drywall out, dismantle the walls, encasement and all. If we scour all the hardware stores, I'm sure we can find enough caulking. I highly doubt people looted that when looking for supplies. It doesn't taste very good."

"Good point." I laugh, and Leah giggles with me. Then I have a thought. "What about the coffee beans?"

"I knew you'd ask about that. He says if we can keep the greenhouse warm and tropical, it could be a possibility."

"Now, that is really good news!"

We get out of Cortez without being shot at and head down the freeway, closing in on the travel center and casino to the south. My anxiety grows the closer we get. I find that as it does, Leah starts to fidget more in her car seat. Once again I have to wonder. Does my daughter share some kind of special bond with me? Can she read my emotions somehow?

Taking a deep breath, I try to calm down, if only for her sake. I don't want to agitate my baby girl. In addition, I'm trying to work myself up for the inevitable disappointment that is surely looming. Dan's message, the Webley that is now at the small of my back, but it all has to be a coincidence, right? People don't come back from the dead. Do they?

Mike slows down as the casino comes into sight. I start getting ready. Slipping on the P-90 rig, I pull up the Tavor and start glassing the hotel and its grounds. Through the scope, I don't see even so much as a hint of anyone around. It looks as utterly deserted as the last time I was here—and that doesn't make me feel any better. I ask Mike to circle the building. We find a graveyard of cars where I imagine the raiders parked to get the jump on us, but there is still no movement.

"Park across the freeway," I order while pointing a hauntingly familiar spot.

"You got it."

Pulling Truck onto the side of the highway, I turn and look at Leah and she smiles at me. I can't help but smile back and my precious little girl—our precious little girl. When I gaze into her eyes, I see his eyes looking back at me.

"Mommy will be right back," I tell her while caressing her cheek with one finger. "You be a good girl and guard Truck, alright?"

Leah gives a squeal and I slip out, closing the door. When Mike tosses me the keys, I engage the alarm and Truck gives me a chirp. *Keep her safe, Truck.* We move across the highway with the military precision that I'm used to.

Mike is amazing! Since he was prior infantry, he's one of the few people that meshed immediately with my skill set. The skill-set that Beast taught me. Knowing the hand signals, how to move and how to keep quiet are all important to keep from getting shot.

We encounter no one as we move up to the entrance of the travel center. The stench of death and decay is obvious, though old, and makes my eyes water. Worse, my anxiety has climbed through the roof as I approach. I don't know if I can handle seeing his body. If I can handle what I know is the inevitable death of my hope.

Mike and I sweep in, weapons at the ready, and we find a lot of bodies, but already the picture is different. All the weapons have been taken, and even some of the gear in many cases. My breathing is getting harsher as I move past racks of ruined, bullet ridden clothes and towards the cashier's area. My hands shake and lips tremble, fighting to keep moving forward as my heart is near to breaking a second time.

When I get to the spot where his body should be, my heart stops instead. It isn't there. None of his gear is there. The only sign that he was there is the dried pool of blood from when he bled out and expired in my arms. I can even see the spots were my knees made impressions in the blood stain. The rug I put over him is at least a good ten feet away. I feel faint.

What the... How?

"He's not here." My voice is a horrified whisper.

"What?" Mike sounds as shocked as I feel.

I point at the exact location. "This is the spot. I dragged him right to here, but he was just too heavy to get any further."

"That doesn't make any sense," Mike replies with a shake of his head. "If it was animals, why didn't they take the closer bodies first?"

"Agreed," I state as I frown.

Struggling to find answers, any answers, I start looking around. There's really no useful equipment. Anything left behind is far too bullet ridden to be used. There are no weapons at all, and no ammunition. Then I find something else that chills my blood.

The gang leader, the one I think was responsible for killing Beast. The man that I gutted with Beast's own sword. That is the only other body that I believe is missing. With that realization, a foreboding feeling creeps into my gut.

"Mike," I whisper with dread. "We need to head back. Right now."

"Yeah, okay." His voice sounds strange.

I glance at him, and he's got a sheen of sweat on his brow. Now that I notice it, I realize I'm sweating too. I feel…haunted. *We are so out of here.*

Quickly we leave the store and I make for Truck as fast as I can. This terrible feeling will not leave until we get back to Truck and disarm the alarm. When I climb in, I breathe a sigh of relief when I see my daughter still in her seat.

I smile at her and she smiles back. "Hello, baby girl."

Mike climbs into the driver's seat and I toss him the keys. "We need to get back as fast as we can."

"Sure thing, boss."

Pulling back onto the road, Mike quickly gets Truck up to speed and we are flying down the highway. As the miles go by, this awful feeling in my stomach just won't go away. At the same time, the tenuous hope I had builds a little brighter as the impossible appears to be possible. Through the joy and fear and intermittent dread, I wonder what I will tell Liz.

Chapter Sixteen

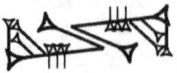

In the next three months, I've continued to lead teams out into the many residential areas outside Nellis. While scavenging was part of the mission, the critical part is ridding the world of raiders and putting fear in the hearts of those who manage to get away. My teams have become expert, and the enemy never see us coming, they just start dying. We put down enough advance groups that they start posting further back.

We had planned well, and in February, we started putting our plan into action. While there was far too much ice and snow still on the runways, the ground crews started prepping the best of the planes in protective hangars. I also started learning how to fly a C-130. Simulators are nice and all, but they're not like real flight time by any means. By the time we were into March, I felt ready, though still worried about making a good landing. Just to be on the safe side, none of the kids and essential supplies would be in my plane.

During this time, I've also taught my team how to set explosives. With the help of some of the ground crew, we've placed 250 and 500 kilo bombs in all the critical areas. When we leave, any arms and equipment we can't take with us will go up like the Fourth of July.

Major Drummond is certainly pleased with our progress. Big problem now is that spring could be here any day now—though who can tell after the winter we've had? That means raider attacks will start up sooner or later. That was okay, I had plans for them as well.

Spotters in the air traffic control tower reported large numbers amassing for an oncoming attack. I was pretty sure they were waiting for a dry day. While we haven't had any blizzards for a while, we still had daily snow or rain, and it was fucking cold! Ice slicked the roads and sidewalks constantly. We had more injuries from slips and falls than from combat, because, let's face it, Las Vegas is not known as a location that would need snow plows and salt for roads. Of course the base was not prepared for this. The thaw, progressed however, and we all waited for the inevitable.

The first morning we didn't have ice, I scrambled the ground crews and we wheeled the OV-10D Bronco out for her scouting flight. While she has enough fuel to easily fly to Colorado and back, they put on an additional external centerline tank as well. The twenty millimeter cannon was her only armament, and they half loaded it to save on weight.

Captain Peter "Slip" McBride is our only qualified pilot. I'd had long training sessions with him learning the C-130 controls. Over time we got to talking and he understood the part of the reason I was sending him was to get Chloe a message. The man knew what I was going through. He lost his fiancée in the Collapse and would have done anything to save her. Unfortunately, she died in the Israeli conflict, unable to escape while there on a humanitarian mission. Yeah, we understand each other.

Pete's an Army pilot, which is ironic, as he is the only qualified pilot on an Air Force base. He and I have traded a lot of good-natured ribbing that is typical between members of the armed forces. There's always been rivalry between the various branches, usually only in jest.

As I walk with Peter to the plane, I hand him the note, slipped in a sandwich bag to keep it protected from the rain. It is just a folded piece of paper with her name on it, so it's not like he can't read it. I don't want it to seem like I'm hiding anything.

"You sure you don't want it in a sealed envelope?" Pete jests. "That way I can't be tempted to read it?"

I laugh. "Nah, it's alright. Just get it to my lady."

"I promise," Pete responds with a smile.

We go through the pre-flight check and once done, I help him climb into the pilot's seat. In all honesty, this is one of my favorite planes. Two seat, twin engine prop job that was used for either reconnaissance or ground attack. I really want to be in that other seat, but the Major has ordered otherwise. He needs me here and I think he's worried that if I leave, I won't be back to help him get his people out. He may be right.

"Fair winds, Army," I tell Pete with a grin.

"Roger that, Navy."

With a laugh, I swing down the canopy and lock it. I get out of the way as the engines start up. As the plane starts for takeoff, I jog to the air traffic control tower. When I get to the top of the tower, Pete's already taxied to the end of the runway and is ready to go.

"This is Victor Victor Six Niner Seven, ready for takeoff."

"Roger that," the Major replies through the radio headset. "You have clearance for takeoff."

We all watch as the plane moves forward, rapidly gains speed, and lifts off. The aircraft quickly sails over the wall. A couple airmen give a triumphant yell as the plane takes to the air and climbs. That's when things get interesting.

"Taking small arms fire," Pete yells. "Taking small ar...."

Suddenly there's static and my heart drops, thinking the worst. Major Drummond picks up a pair of binoculars and looks out the window. I can see the plane and it's still climbing and pulling away.

"We've got us some snakes in the weeds," the major states. "But Captain McBride is still flying and I don't see any smoke. Perhaps they hit his radio."

"Let's hope he makes it," I reply with a frown. "If you'll excuse me. I have some raiders to shoot at."

"Good hunting, son."

Running down the stairs, I'm on the radio and yelling angrily. "Hayes! Where are you?"

"Heading for the north gate, sir."

"Good! I'll meet you there."

Hopping into the nearest HUMVEE, I start it up and punch it. People jump out of my way as I scream down the road parallel to the landing strip, heading for the north wall. As I approach, gunfire is audible. I screech to a halt, park it, and bail out.

Slinging the AK, I grab my Mosin and duck into the tower, taking the stairs two at a time all the way to the top. The few guards on duty are sticking to cover and taking single shots at the enemy which is easily a thousand meters out. No M-4 is going to make that range. Barrel is too short and five-five-six is an inferior round for that long a distance. This is why I always prefer thirty caliber. It hits hard and sends the message, get the fuck off my lawn!

Hayes is already there and knows the score. She's yelling at them to cease fire and conserve ammo. This is the problem with kids. They tend to be glory hounds and forget everything in a mad dash to collect a scalp. You can't count coup when you run out of ammo and get dead because of it.

As I walk to the glass door that gives access to the top of the wall, I grab the captured scoped Enfield that sits in a nearby rifle rack. Pushing out the door, I walk up to the lieutenant and hand her the rifle. It's time for a teaching evolution.

"What this?" She asks while slinging her M-4 behind her.
"Good ole Enfield MK IV," I reply with a smile. "It's what the Brits used in World War One and Two. Their version of an assault rifle, back in the day."

"You served in both of those conflicts, didn't you, sir?" Jackson is already laughing and the other airmen within earshot snigger at the old joke.

"Only in WW Two," I shoot back with a grin. "I was still in diapers when the First World War started."

72

They all laugh, which is good. In the days before the Collapse, the PC crowd was completely destroying the military. No off-color jokes, no sexist jokes, no humor of any kind. Of course, the people making these rules had never seen a day of fucking combat in their lives! They didn't understand that humor of any kind is one of the things that helps keep you and the squad sane. Their rules created a bunch of dysfunctional kids who couldn't handle any amount pressure. Fortunately, I've drilled it out of those that stayed behind when everyone else fled.

The lieutenant is looking at the heavy rifle like I just asked a Millennial to drive a stick. "And what do I do with it?"

"You shoot the enemy with it," I growl. "It's got ten times the range your M-4 does, and Gods help any bandit that gets hit by the big bullet that comes out of it."

I start setting the iron sights for a thousand meters. I'm at least ten meters up, which is going to change my bullet drop, but I'm not an expert enough sniper to do that math in my head. So instead, I'm going to rely on Kentucky windage.

"You can't hit them that far out," Ms. Hayes exclaims.

Ignoring her, I take aim and calm my breathing. The raiders evidently think the same as her, because they are standing out there, flipping us off and laughing at the airmen who couldn't even get close to the target.

When I pull the trigger, the Mosin makes a subdued report thanks to the oil can at the end of the barrel. It takes under two seconds for the bullet to travel the distance, and I'm rewarded by the sight of one of the enemy men falling back with a slight spin. I briefly look to the heavens. That was more than luck.

"What the fuck!?" Jackson mutters in shock.

"You were saying, lieutenant?" As I ask, I cycle the bolt for a fresh round and fire again.

Legends are made, not born, and I've always wondered just how much of them were based on pure, dumb luck. Today is such a day. My second shot claims another volunteer as the idiots stand there in the same shock as my team. My placement is beautiful and I can barely see the man's head snap back before falling. I cycle the bolt again, but now the bandits are running.

Taking careful aim, I attempt to lead the point man as they run for the nearest building for cover. Sending the bullet downrange, the rifle gives me a satisfying kick as I let the recoil roll off me. It's a miss, but that's okay. They aren't taunting my team any longer, and Pete is long gone. I grin at Ms. Hayes while I sling my weapon and head back to my room for some well deserved rest.

Chapter Seventeen

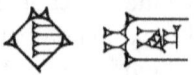

It takes us a little more than two hours to get back to Gunnison. We are on our way up the 135, and I'm trying not to think about the implications of Beast's absent corpse, when I begin to relax. The sight of our defensive wall is up ahead. That's when I see a sight that I never thought I would see again. An airplane flies overhead, heading in the direction of Crested Butte.

"Is that what I think is?" Mike asks, awed.

"It sure is," I reply back in shock.

Liz is on the wall, and as we get close they are already opening the gate. All work has stopped, and everyone is watching the aircraft which is disappearing into the distance. I think it's turning around though.

"Pick up Liz and then gun it," I damn near yell, excited for some strange reason.

"I think he's going to land at the airport."

Mike comes to a screeching halt just inside the wall and I climb halfway out the window. "Get your skinny, blonde ass in here!"

Liz grins, jumps off the wall and clambers in behind Mike and Truck takes off like a rocket. Mike puts the pedal to the metal and we fly down the road as fast as my trusty steed will carry us.

"I'm glad to see you're all right," Liz states over the growling of the engine.

I smile back at her, then pay attention to the road. When her hand grabs my shoulder, I clutch it in response. Not that my life hasn't been a fucking mess since the Collapse, but I get the feeling it's about to become even more so now. Whatever is flying in, I have a feeling it is not going to be fair to Liz.

"So, where's the body? In the back?"

Mike and I glance at each other with the same expression. Liz develops a worried expression as she sinks back in her seat, shaking her head in vehement denial. I just don't know what to say. The impossible appears to be possible.

"We'll talk about it when we get back. I'll tell you everything."

Liz does not look happy, and I'm worried about her. But we're getting close to the airport, so I push that away and try to stay focused because Mike was right. The pilot circled around one more time and the plane is coming in for a landing, looking a little unsteady. In fact, before his wheels touchdown, I'm almost afraid he's going to wreck. Then all three wheels hit the concrete runway, and the plane starts slowing dramatically. I breathe a sigh of relief.

When we arrive, the aircraft is parked at the end of the runway and the propellers are spinning down. Mike brings us to a stop, and I jump out and book it towards the cockpit. The poor craft has a couple bullet holes in her as I come around and find one man in the cockpit.

Shit! He doesn't look good.

Fumbling for the canopy release, I get it unlocked and swing it open. I smell blood. A man in an Air Force jumpsuit looks at me with dull eyes and smiles. The name tag on his suit says 'McBride' in bold black letters.

"You look," he speaks softly and with a smile and takes a labored breath. "Just like… the lady… I'm looking for."

"What?"

"Are you, Chloe? The Angel of Death, Chloe?"

My heart leaps into my throat as yet another stranger uses my nickname. The fragile hope I've been reluctantly carrying blossoms even larger. All I can do is nod numbly and he smiles. With a shaking hand, he hands over a blood splattered plastic bag with a folded sheet of paper in it.

"Promise kept," he states with a chuckle. "Now if you wouldn't mind, I could use some help. Took a bullet in the leg."

"MIKE!"

My voice is a shriek and Mike runs up to help. Thanks to the Army, he's got more medical training than I have, and he is much stronger than I am. Together, we drag the pilot out of the cockpit and Mike goes to work. Hopefully we can get this man stabilized before getting him to the closest thing we have to a doctor. I've got questions that I hope he has answers to.

As Mike and Liz work on the wounded pilot, I slowly back away. Gazing down at the plastic bag with a shaking hand, my lower lip trembles as I slowly open the bag. Pulling out a folded piece of paper that has my name on it, I can feel my heart hammering away in my chest. The anxiety is back as I slowly open it and read:

My Beautiful Chloe;
 I hope this message finds you well. I know you have no reason to believe me, but hopefully Dan from Green River arrived and gave you my Webley as planned.

Yes, I'm alive. Currently I'm at Nellis Air Force Base in Las Vegas. I can't say how I'm alive, but it was important that I come here, not that I wanted to. There are good people here who need saving. I sent Pete to see if the airfield was long enough for landing larger aircraft and to give you this message.

Once Pete returns, I will be coming back to be with you within a day or two at most. I'll explain everything then, some of which even I still don't believe.

I love you, my precious Chloe. I hope you've done good things, my lady.

Beast

Tears of joy fall in what feels like torrents as I drop to my knees. With this note, I know for certain that he's alive. In some impossible way, he's alive. He told me he hoped I've done good things, and that is another thing I've never shared with anyone. The message on Truck's window is long gone at this point, but this proves it.

Somehow, impossibly, my Beast is alive! That knowledge sends my heart practically leaping from my chest. I sit down, put my head on my knees and sob in relief and longing.

I'm so absorbed in my emotions that I don't hear Liz rush up until she puts her arms around me. No doubt she's worried about my sudden, apparent breakdown. I hold onto her tightly as I pull myself together.

"We gotta move him," Mike yells to us.

Sniffling, I give Liz a quick nod that I'm okay and scramble to my feet. With some effort the three of us manage to pick the pilot up and get him into the back of Truck. While Mike stays in the back, I quickly get into the driver's seat and we take off for Crested Butte and the closest thing we have to a real hospital.

"Are you alright," Liz still looks very concerned.

"Yes," I say through happy tears. "He's alive. I don't know how, but he's alive."

In my happiness, I realize too late that I should have kept quiet and broken the news to her more gently. A look of horror flashes through Liz's eyes, followed by shock and grief as her mouth goes slack. In a way, I can't say that I blame her. For months she's been competing with a ghost. Now the impossible happens and that ghost has come back to life.

Fuck! There are better ways I could have handled this.

"How?"

I shake my head. "I don't know, but this message clinches it."

76

Taking the letter from my hand, she reads it. I think she reads it at least a dozen times when we pull up at the clinic and pile out. Then there's no time for words as we get our patient into the building.

"Doc," I yell as loud as I'm able.

Our doctor is James Calvo, a longtime resident of the town. He's lived here longer than I've been alive, a fact he has shared with me on many occasions. The only problem is that his specialty is not humans, but horses. But when all you have is a veterinarian, it's all you have, and you're happy you have someone with any medical knowledge at all. To be honest, he's also caught up quickly and can easily take care of minor wounds, has a surgical suite and at least knowledge of how to do surgery.

"What in the Sam Hill is all the commotion about?" Having survived the apocalypse, I think he's a little miffed that he's one of the few skilled people left to put things back together.

James is balding with gray hair, wrinkles from working in the sun his whole life, and wire rimmed glasses. He opens the door as we rush in, and I note he's wearing his trademarked blood-stained apron. People have taken to calling him, "The Butcher." I would be more diplomatic, but I think he enjoys the nickname.

"We've got a wounded pilot, doc. I need you to save him. He has important information."

"Pilot?" He looks at his new patient. "So I did hear a plane."

"Yes," Mike grumbles. "So if you could work at a speed faster than slow, that would be great. He's got a leg wound and has lost a lot of blood."

"Just 'cause you can shoot straight, Mike," Doc Calvo states sternly while doing a quick assessment. "That don't mean you can talk to me like that. Bring him into surgery and then wash up, Mike. Who's got O-negative blood?"

Mike looks at the two of us and we shake our heads. He rolls his eyes and volunteers to donate if necessary. As Doc disappears into the back to wash up. Liz and I help get the pilot settled before being shooed out. As we leave, my mind is nothing but a cloud of questions. My life has turned upside down in short order.

Leah is in her car seat, sitting on the counter and watching me with her bright eyes. I play with her briefly, but I can damn near hear Liz's thoughts. There is a conversation I'm not looking forward to looming on the horizon.

Chapter Eighteen

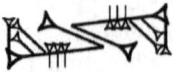

Damn raiders are not making things easy, but then, I'm not making things easy for them either. They quickly learn that the Mosin-Nagant reaches out to a thousand meters. A bunch of those idiots had set up a little over a klick out and were waiting to shoot at any plane that took off, in an attempt to down it. I quickly teach them that I can shoot that far.

Two of them were either wounded or dead when I started dropping rounds on their heads. At that point they scattered like cockroaches, disappearing back into the city as I fired a couple more rounds to make sure they kept going.

After that, we didn't see much of the assholes, but we knew they were there. The many residential districts had numerous columns of smoke coming from them, probably for a combination of heat and cooking. What I couldn't figure out is what they were waiting for?

I wasn't going to let them take the base easily, that was for sure. Taking a page out of the castle siege tactics, I had the security team start setting up bins with large rocks, bricks and other heavy objects useful for dropping on people's heads. We also set up small vats along the walkways, full of oil and just waiting to have the fire lit under them.

While I got security ready for what I felt was going to be a knock-down, drag out fight, the Major was getting the two birds that were chosen, loaded and ready to fly. Hopefully Pete wouldn't be more than a day or so. After that, we'll get out of here as quickly as possible.

Pete will fly our first transport, carrying the children, civilians and bulk of the critical supplies. I will follow right behind with the rest of the people, small arms munitions, and an armored HUMVEE. Even though it's only about five or six hundred miles, both planes will have drop tanks with extra fuel and we will JATO out so that we can take off with max weight.

At that thought I check my watch for the date and frown. I would have thought that Pete would be back by now. Shaking my head, I make my way to check in with the major and see if they've heard anything over the radio.

With our position on the base being tenable at best, I carry both the AK and the Mosin at all times. More than once I've needed to be Johnny-on-the-Spot as a sniper. There have been a few attempts to infiltrate the base, as opposed to performing an all-out attack. We ended up with two wounded and a death from the attempts. The raiders came out far worse, losing eleven.

I find the Major in his office, though I hear his cough long before I see him. He's had that persistent cough since I've been here. I wonder if he's got tuberculosis, but he always tells me that the doctor is treating him and that he's not contagious.

"Chief," he calls out with a smile. "What can I do for you?"

"I was wondering if you've heard anything from Pete."

"Nothing yet. I do hope he made it. Hate the transports flying into this blind. Since you are here, close the door and sit down."

"Yes sir."

Closing the door, I take a seat and wait for him to continue. There's a feeling in my gut that tells me I'm not going to like whatever it is he is about to tell me. Officers tend to give you bad news when they want the door closed.

"Son, first things first. I'm dying."

"What?"

Another coughing fit prevents him from replying right away. It's a dry cough, and that symptom is rarely good. One of the other things I had worried about is that he might have pneumonia, an often misdiagnosed killer. After a deep breath, he continues.

"I've got lung cancer."

Shit!

"And we don't exactly have the drugs to treat it," I state with a frown.

"Exactly," he replies. "As such, I'm not evacuating."

"Sir, you..."

"No," he interrupts, looking determined. "I'm not going to die, like that in front of my people. It's a crappy death and you know it."

"I- can't argue that."

"I'd rather you didn't," he states with all seriousness. "Given that I won't be going, when it comes time for you to leave, I'm giving you a battlefield promotion."

"What?"

"I'll be promoting you to the Navy equivalent of Major, son."

I can't help but close my eyes and grit my teeth. This, right here? This is that last thing I want. Never in my life did I want to be an officer. And now that I can barely stand being around people, it makes even less sense.

Is he trying to get everyone killed? By me?

79

"Sorry, son," he replies with a chuckle. "The people need someone who is capable of leading them. To be honest, you are a victim of your own success."

Groaning at his assessment, I shake my head. *Fuck me.*

"We will have a ceremony and I will promote you to Lieutenant Commander," he continues. "Can't be a Major. You're Navy after all."

I chuckle. "Yes sir."

"You really think Colorado will be a good place to settle down?"

"Yes sir. Many of the places in the area of Crested Butte are rather defensible. There's running water all year round. Fertile ground for growing crops. Fishing. Hunting. While the winters may be cold, it will still be survivable."

The Major smiles. "You really thought this out."

"There are similar places in other states as well," I reply with a grin. "Colorado has half a dozen such locations alone and was the closest to where I was living. Unfortunately everything fell apart so fast, I couldn't get out of L.A."

"Was pretty much the same everywhere. Criminal elements and mobs surged more quickly than we could have imagined, looting and rioting. Turned into a mess in short order. Whole globe went that way almost at the exact same time. Like something in the human subconscious just snapped."

I snort in disgust. "Certainly seemed that way."

"Hell," the Major exclaims. "Even China went off the deep end."

"Sir?"

"Evidently certain portions of the military leadership had created failsafe plans in case of mass civilian insurrection."

This is news.

"Oh?"

"Yeah," he gives a nod. "Best we could figure, they had chemical warfare deployment systems in every major city. Problem was that no one warned the leadership or military before hitting the switch. Everyone died and now China is a dead zone. Haven't heard a single radio transmission from it."

"Dear Gods!"

"Yep, fucking mess. Middle East is irradiated. Russia is as dark as China. No clue on India. Some military has survived in Australia. Perth according to what we've heard. Japan is a bit of a mess, with Tokyo looking like Godzilla tromped through it. All of South America went up in flames, taking the Central America's and Mexico right along with it. Canada may be the only bright spot."

"Really?"

He nods. "Yep. We get a good amount of radio traffic from them. Mostly civilian. Even talked with them. They had riots, but not as bad. Those that survived are rebuilding, although winter was especially rough for them."

"At least the human race isn't done for."

"Not by a long shot, son, not yet. Especially with people like us around to see them safe."

I smile grimly. "Amen, sir."

The poor man has another coughing fit and it sounds like a bad one at that. The medic in me is kicking in, wanting to help the patient in some way. He waves me off as I start to get out of the chair to help him.

"You've got better things to do than tend to a dying man. You go take care of our people, Chief."

"Yes sir," I reply softly.

Giving him a crisp salute, he returns it a little informally. He's looking more and more tired every day. I curse the way some things turn out in life as I perform an about face and leave the office.

Chapter Nineteen

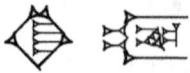

Walking into the hospital, such as it is, I find Doc Calvo sitting at the desk of the front lobby. He's relaxing while he watches a movie on a combination TV/DVD player. Some action film from the sounds of it, and the dulcet tones of automatic fire make me want to sit down and watch it with him, but I have a job to do.

"Hi doc," I state with a smile. "I hear your patient is awake?"

"Yeah. Room two, but don't take too long. He's lost a lot of blood and needs rest."

Inwardly I chuckle. He is his usual, grumpy self. I take out a bag of fresh greens and hand it to him as payment. He glances at the bag and gives me a dirty look, like I just insulted his mother or something. I can't help but laugh.

"Hey, you don't want to get scurvy! And if you just can't stomach it, feed it to your horses."

Giving him a nod, I make my way into the back. I wonder if Doc is like this because of the Collapse, or if he has always been like this. There's not a lot we know about him, and he certainly is not the talking type. He definitely has the grumpy old man act down pat.

In room two, the pilot is resting in a bed. Mr. McBride looks very pale, an IV line plugged into his arm. A similar TV has been set up on a rolling tray and Top Gun is playing. His head rolls over and he smiles slightly, giving me a salute.

"Morning ma'am."

Grabbing a chair, I sit down. "Morning. How are you feeling?"

"Alive," he croaks. "Doc says I landed just in time. Thanks for saving me."

"You're quite welcome." I hold up the message. "What can you tell me about the man who gave you this note?"

To be honest, I still carry what I feel is a false hope. I watched my beautiful Beast die in my arms. All evidence to the contrary, I simply can't believe it's him. People don't come back from wounds like that, especially since the Collapse. Even with the pistol, the missing body and this note, I don't know what to believe.

"You mean Navy?" He chuckles. "Mean son-of-bitch wearing a white mask. Kills raiders like other people take a walk in the park."

The world swims for a moment. Impossible! Inside, my rational mind wars with my emotions. Feelings threaten to swamp me, but it is my rational mind that ultimately wins the war. I narrow my eyes.

"Quit lying to me," I snap. "Who told you to say that?"

The poor man recoils slightly. "Ma'am, I'm not lying. He thought you might not believe it though, so he told me to say this. He left you a message, written in light and breath on the driver's side window of Truck. Only you could know it."

I feel faint and it takes all my strength to keep the swelling emotions from crushing me. Suddenly it's hard to breathe. There's no way anyone could know this. The only other person aware of this detail is Liz. I find it damn hard to believe she'd say anything about it to anyone, let alone a stranger.

"Why did you come here?" My voice is nearly a whisper as I struggle to breathe.

"Aside from delivering that message to you, it was to see how long the runway is."

"What? Why?"

"We've got a lot of people who need to be evacuated," he tells me seriously. "Ma'am, there are kids and families. We have two C-130s loaded and waiting to take off after I deliver my report. Of course, now I'm laid up in this bed. If my radio wasn't shot to shit, I would take a chance with that, but now I guess we're screwed."

Sitting back in the chair, my mind is racing. All these messages and portents are slowly eroding my disbelief. The impossible becoming possible as I try not to cry over this highly emotional issue.

Why did he go to Vegas instead of coming to me in Colorado? Why would he leave me to my own devices for so long, letting me believe he was dead? And why would he let me have our daughter alone, when I needed him the most? Though, I remember neither of us knew at the time he died that I was pregnant.

The pilot, Pete, he says his name is, has been given specific instructions to come here. To check the runway in preparation for bringing two C-130s full of people and supplies to this, specific valley. That does not sound like the actions of some random bandit fucking with me. All this is seriously happening.

"But why leave Nellis? It sounds like a good enough place as any to settle in."

"No, the raiders, there's an army of thousands of them in Vegas. Our people are outnumbered by more than ten to one. We thought we were going to have to slug it out, but your fella shows up and comes up with this plan to evacuate to here. They're going to have to hold out now, though, until I heal up enough to fly back and report."

Great. Now I'm going to lose him to raiders. Again. *God damn it!* Then an epiphany hits me.

"I had gotten my pilot's license shortly before everything fell apart. Can you teach me the differences of your plane to the Cessna 172 Skyhawk I trained in so I can finish your mission?"

He stares at me for a moment, then grins as he replies, "Uh, yeah. Yes, ma'am."

"Good," I reply with a nod. "I'll get you something to write with so that you can deliver any notes they need."

"Thank you, ma'am."

"Thank you, Pete." I stand up. "I have to get things arranged, make sure my lieutenants are well prepared. I'll see you tomorrow morning."

"Yes ma'am." Once more he gives me a salute.

Delivering a smile, I walk out. My mind is so lost in thought, all I can do is give Doc a weak wave as I leave. His grumble in reply reminds me of Beast. Like my man, pleasantries are not really his thing. Besides, I've got a mission to plan and my Beast to rescue.

Just twenty-four hours later, I am as ready as I can be. The Bronco is not all that different from other light planes I've flown. It's a thirty-foot turbo-prop, and the controls are industry standard. Certainly no major differences that I need to worry about.

Pete has made me a diagram of the control panel and written out a pre-flight checklist. We've sat with our heads together since before dawn, and I've only taken breaks to feed my daughter and review the information he's given me.

I am so grateful Nena is with me. She told me weeks ago that I needed to start pumping milk and build up a supply in case of an emergency. I shrugged and agreed with her at the time, and now I see why. My daughter will be fine without me for at least a couple of days. I am taking the breast pump with me because I've learned I can't go too long without feeding her before the pain kicks in. Who knew being a mother could be so difficult and messy?

Liz has alternately cried and fought with me. She's demanded to come with me, and then demanded that I stay. She has a caged-animal look I am so sorry to see, but what can I do? I care about her, she knows it, but she stormed out of the bunker last night and nobody's seen her since. I am worried about her, but she can't stop me from doing this and she knows it. I've shed some tears, too, don't get me wrong. I don't want to hurt her, that's the last thing I ever wanted. But now it is too late to hunt her down, I have to go.

I go over the flight plan with Pete again. He's given me the headings I should take, and it feels odd to not file the flight plan ahead of time, but there is no agency to file it with anymore anyway. I shake Pete's hand and his face is bright through the fever he's developed, but he seems confident since I seem to know what I'm talking about.

In all honesty, I never thought I'd fly again, not with the world so fucked up as it is. But now it's actually a valuable skill, and my excitement has moved to Leah. She's smiling and happy this morning, as if she knows what I'm up to.

"You will be well, I have seen it," Nena's soft voice is a welcome interruption, "And this girl will know a real family."

I smile at her brightly, trying not to be scared that all of this is some hoax or elaborate trap. God that would destroy me after all this hope that has been built up. Nena's reassurance means a lot.

"Thank you, Nena." I kiss Leah's nose, and she burbles happily. "Please, if you can, try to find Liz. I am really worried about her."

"Liz. She holds her future in her own hands, and now she must decide. All our wishing won't make her choose rightly or wrongly, it all depends on the strength of her own heart."

Nena's words puzzle me, but I give a nod anyway. The flight line is chilly and I know I need to leave, but I'm having a hard time saying goodbye to my daughter. She smiles at me, her bright blue eyes so like her father's. I hold her tightly for a moment and close my eyes, inhaling her sweet scent. Then I hand her to Nena and climb into the cockpit.

I've not taken much with me. Cockpits don't have a lot of space, so I only have my Beretta 93, the FN FNX and a combat knife for protection. Not to mention as many magazines for both pistols that I can pack without feeling uncomfortable in the seat. I put one of the AR-15's in the back seat, just in case. I would take the Tavor, but Mike is giving it a full breakdown cleaning and inspection.

I'm wearing a flight suit I scavenged at the airport, and Pete has assured me there is plenty of fuel to get me where I'm going. He's also warned that I need to watch for bandits on approach to Nellis, as they've been harassing the airstrip. All of his information swims in my head and I recheck the preflight list one more time. The bullets that took out the radio and injured Pete haven't done much else to the craft, but we've plugged up the holes anyway, just in case it matters.

Starting up the engines, I taxi to the end of the runway and then escape into the sky. A momentary feeling of joy surges through me as I lift up into the air before reality kicks back in.

I will learn for myself if my Beast is alive, or if this has been some mad trick to lure the Angel of Death to the biggest army of raiders I've ever heard of. I narrow my eyes and realize I will kill them all if it means I am with my Beast again.

Chapter Twenty

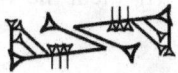

I'm walking the wall with Lieutenant Hayes, performing something of an inspection. Every time one of the soldiers salutes me, I want to rip their throat out. I try not to growl. Too loudly anyway. Stuffing the beast back in the cage, I do my best to be civil. While the night forays have helped, the civilization of Nellis has been irritating me greatly.

"What do you think about the defenses, so far?"

"As good as we can make them," I state with a frown. "We've only got so many people to work with."

"Do you really think they will make an assault soon?"

"Yep. I just wish Pete would get his ass back here. Can't imagine what could be taking him so long!"

"Maybe he had to repair damage from being shot at."

I nod. "Highly possible."

To be honest, I don't like the answer. We need his intel, otherwise we will be flying blind and potentially crashing. I guess if all else fails we could try landing on one of the stretches of road. I just don't know if that will be any better. Besides, if he doesn't come back, we are down our only qualified pilot and no one else has any experience. And that means we're stuck here until we are forced to leave and I am not fond of being forced into anything.

According to weather satellites, we've only got a couple more days at best before the near constant rain is gone. Once we've got obvious clear skies, I'm betting that's when the attack will come.

My head snaps up as the familiar drone of a multi-engine prop plane greets my ears and I have never been so happy to hear it. I whip out my binoculars, searching the skies and after a couple minutes, spot the Bronco. *Yes!*

Pete is circling overhead. I can only assume he's trying to make sure the base is still friendly territory. After a couple circles, he heads north before looping around to come in for a landing. Never have I been so happy to see that Army bastard!

Something about his approach seems off to me. It's not quite as tight and level as I would expect from such a seasoned veteran. At least he's making a good approach and will clear the wall. Or at least he would until the shooting starts.

Fucking raiders!

They've got to be at least fifteen hundred meters out, because they've learned I can shoot a thousand. Lying on the ground and shooting up, they are using an old Vietnamese tactic. Throw enough lead into the air and hope the aircraft runs into it. After all, a moving plane hitting a moving bullet means a lot of kinetic energy behind that slug. I hope some of that lead falls back onto their bastard heads.

The tactic is frighteningly successful. Both engines catch on fire and the Bronco falls like rock. My heart damn near falls with it as we can only watch in horror as the plane slams into the ground and skids along the dirt. She comes to an abrupt stop at the ravine, nose tilting down before ramming into the bank. Already the raiders are up and advancing on the wreck as Hayes runs down the stairs.

Given the fact that we might have to leave in a hurry, I had the security team set up ropes at various points so that we can quickly egress from the top of the wall.

This is one time I wish I had a camera. Like a hero out of a damn movie, I damn near leap off the wall as I grab the rope and quickly slide down. Ms. Hayes opens the gate just enough for me to get through.

While the lieutenant uses the gate for cover, I run out it with a growl, making for the wreck of the Bronco. I make the raiders trying to converge on wreck find out that they made a very bad decision. My AK-47 barks out thirty caliber rounds, forcing them to scatter when one of their men goes down.

The beast has taken over. When they stop and drop, returning fire, I'm operating on zero fear. As bullets whiz past me, I continue running while pumping round after round their direction. A couple of them break in panic and run away. Because really, what kind of lunatic would run, solo, into enemy fire?

Breathing hard, I dive behind one of the abandoned raider vehicles and fire on the enemy. I put a bullet in the heads of two of them while dirt kicks up all around me and rounds ping into metal. Bastards are still rushing up fast, a couple practically on top of the wreck already.

As I engage two men coming around the front of the plane, I see Pete's shadowy form struggling to climb out of the shattered cockpit. I tag one, putting three bullets across his chest. He jerks and falls face first into the dirt. The other man gets to cover behind the crumpled nose and fires a few shots before disappearing. Taking the opportunity, I lay down suppressive fire against the rest of the group before rushing in to help Pete.

You'd better be alive, you Army bastard!

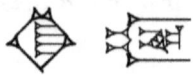

Chapter Twenty-One

Fuck me!

With a groan, I crawl out of the plane and try to get my bearings. Bullets ping off the body of the aircraft, a couple even punching into the canopy. That crash really roughed me up and I'm trying to recover my wits and get some cover between me and the assholes shooting my direction.

The cover part is actually easy. When the nose hit the bank of the ravine, the poor plane slid sideways. I've now got the natural depression and the wrecked aircraft between me and them. The big problem is that my rifle is in the back seat. That's when my situation goes from bad to worse.

A bandit dashes around the front of the craft. I think initially he doesn't realize I'm here, because he drops behind the nose and fires a couple rounds from his rifle. Then he stops and turns. That slow, lecherous smile I always get from these bastards forms on his face. He strolls up to loom over me.

What the fuck? Like, it's the middle of a firefight yet they have plenty of time to size up the female? Seriously, I need my rifle, stat!

"Well, lookee what I found? A nice, sweet piece of tail."

"Up yours!"

The bandit chuckles darkly. "You first. Now let's get..."

Someone comes up behind him and shoves a long blade right through his neck. I watch in a combination of shock and joy as the body falls to reveal Beast. My Beast! He stares back at me with equal shock. Then he gives me a quiet smile.

"Is it just me, my lady? Or is this becoming a common theme for us?"

Scrambling to my feet, I launch myself into his arms and our lips meet. He holds me tightly to him, kissing me back with such fervor that I can taste just how much he has missed me. I can't help but moan into his mouth as tears of joy fall down my cheeks.

When we finally come up for air, I drop to my feet and take a deep breath. Then I deck him. Really deck him. So hard it fucking hurts my hand and I have to shake it off. He recoils and grabs his chin. Bullets are still flying, but fortunately there is some covering fire coming from the base. I'm a roiling mess of emotions as he composes himself and looks at me angrily.

"What was that for!?"

"For not coming straight to us," I yell back while the firefight continues. "I thought you were dead. I spent five weeks wanting to kill myself. I had to give birth to our daughter without you. And I've had to become a leader to dozens of people, something I'm not good at! Then, when I finally think I'm going to be okay, I start getting messages that you're still alive! And your body wasn't THERE!"

Teeth bare as he growls at me. I know he's angry, but that sound still makes my insides clench because it's such an exciting noise. Stepping right up to me, he glares down, blue eyes locked with mine.

"I didn't have a ch... wait, what? Daughter, what?"

"Yeah, daughter. Clearly you still shoot straight in more ways than one."

I'm not exactly sure how he's taking this. It looks like his brain has just stopped as his brow creases and his mouth drops open. Here we are, middle of combat with bullets zipping back and forth and all he does is stand there, staring at me, eyes blinking.

Then this slow smile begins to tug at his lips before he throws his arms around me, lifting me up with an ecstatic yell that is so infectious that all I can do is laugh as he twirls me around.

"Chloe, I love you," he shouts, like he's proclaiming this to the whole world.

Sliding down his body, I'm already breathless when he brings his lips to mine once more. It's a slow, passionate kiss that makes my heart race as I slip a hand into his hair and make a fist, desperate to hold him to me. I'm so afraid that this is all another dream and when I wake up, he'll be gone again.

He stops for a moment, puzzled. "What happened to Pete? And when did you learn to fly?"

"Pete was wounded, but I think he'll be fine. And I learned to fly in my old life, thought I could be a pilot some day when my other career was over."

Holding me tightly, he kisses me again like I'm a miracle. What should be obvious is that he's the miracle, come back to life. For so many months, I've been struggling to keep going, my life almost nothing but black and white. Now he's alive and my world is full of color once more.

"My lady," he whispers against my lips. "We need to retreat back to the base."

"So long as you have a bed there, it's a deal."

Once more he growls at me, and this time it's a seductive one. My body shudders and I damn near come on the spot. Pulling off the extra M-4 he is carrying, he hands it to me before moving to the plane's nose and firing a few shots. I settle the pack I'm wearing a little tighter. I've put trauma plates around the breast pump, because, damn it, do you know how hard it is to find one these days? I'm not losing it, not to a rotten bunch of raiders.

"Ready, my Angel of Death?"

"Yes! Let's go get 'em, my Beast."

"Go!"

I break into a run as his AK-47 goes full auto and sounds like the end of the world. Shortly thereafter he's running and quickly catches up to me. We both run nearly at full speed, although from time to time he falls back and fires at the enemy before catching up once more. We both dive through the barely open gate as a hail of bullets rains about us. I can't even explain how good it feels to be a team again.

Beast lands on top of me, partly to shield me from harm, but I don't care. Being in such close proximity, looking into his eyes, his heavy breathing that sounds like an animal; that has caused my breathing to stop.

"Breathe, my lady," he whispers as multiple pairs of boots run up.

"Are you both alright?" Some woman yells with obvious concern, hovering over us. "Are you hit?"

With a grunt, Beast rolls over onto his back. "Only my pride, Lieutenant Hayes. I'm going to need a new trauma plate, I think."

Getting help from the various soldiers surrounding us, we get to our feet. The shooting has stopped and everything is quiet. Although the lieutenant is looking at me like I'm the enemy that has just walked in uninvited, reached into her fridge and took the last beer.

"Who is this? Sir."

Beast puts an arm around me and I smile. "This is my lady, Ms. Hayes. Pete had been wounded, so she took his place."

"Ma'am," the lieutenant says with a slight frown.

I feel his arm hold me a little tighter to him. "Tell the Major I'll give my report in an hour. Or two."

When I look at him, his eyes lock with mine. The way he gazes at me robs the breath from my lungs and my pulse quickens. A wolfish smile graves his lips and all I can think of is that I want them kissing me right now. Immediately. Where is this bed he's promised me?

"In fact," he states while still lost in my eyes. "Better make that four."

Four hours?

Heat flushes through my body as he picks me up and carries me off. My heartbeat is so loud in my ears that I can barely hear her acknowledge him as I'm cradled in the protective embrace of the man who owns my heart and soul.

Chapter Twenty-Two

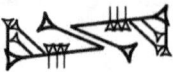

Once again I find myself taken aback at Chloe's beauty, which to me, is far more than just how she looks. It's her passion for learning everything. The fearlessness she has every time we fight side by side. Her laugh which makes me smile, regardless of how angry or feral I become. Finally her intelligence, and how she constantly catches me by surprise.

Damn, the woman's a pilot, and she never thought it important enough to mention? All these things add up to make her a lady that is completely and utterly irresistible. I never had a chance of saying no to this woman and I can't figure out how I was able to resist her for as long as I did.

Her breathing is erratic as she bites her lower lip, my body pressing her against the closest wall. Kicking the door shut, I take her hands and hold them up above her head as the animal within me struggles to be free of its cage. If I let him out now, this will be over far too quickly, and I have missed this woman something fierce. She doesn't wriggle or look afraid, but wraps her legs around me to press herself closer. *Damn.*

Chloe has been my lifeline, my every thought that has gotten me through the days and months that followed my resurrection. Getting the job done and getting back to her has been the mantra I have continually chanted like a prayer. Now that she is here in front of me, wrapped around me. I plan to worship this amazing woman and give her pleasure beyond any human definition.

A single tear slides down her cheek and I capture it with my lips, sucking it in. She whimpers and I don't leave her hanging. Taking her lips in mine, I pour damn near a year of frustration and longing into a kiss that takes both our breath away.

Chloe moans into my mouth, her body grinding against mine and heating my blood. My fingers itch to tear her clothes off and take her right here, right now. This is what she does to me, taxes my discipline and makes it difficult for me to focus.

Tearing my lips from hers, I plant soft kisses all the way up her jaw line as her hands flex, wanting to be free of my grasp. Letting her hands go, I wrap my lips around her ear lobe and suck gently before biting softly. With a gasp, she grips my shoulders, holding me to her as I whisper hotly into her ear.

"I love you, my precious Chloe."

"Oh, Beast," she cries out, tears still falling, and sobbing into my shoulder. "You were dead, and I'm so afraid this is a dream—terrified."

I refuse to let any kind of sadness overtake her and flex my hips against hers while kissing once more. Hands find their way into my hair, fisting and keeping me to her. There's a desperation in her kiss as she moans into my mouth.

We begin ripping each other's clothes off. Gear and clothing—and weapons—fall to the floor in heaps and we are both naked in record time. My hands travel across her beautiful, brown skin and then grab her ass as we continue kissing with wild abandon. Picking her up, I carry her over to the bed as she continues to kiss me as if her life depends on it.

"Don't leave me," she cries as I start to kiss down her body and the pain in her voice tears at my heart, "don't ever leave me again."

I look her right in the eyes, brushing her tears away. "Never, my lady."

When I lean down, I give her a kiss that affirms my statement. Flinging her arms around me, she damn near crushes me into her. I can only imagine the pain and anguish she's had to go through alone. It feels like it's radiating out of her and it tears at my soul.

"Shhhhh," I croon softly. "I'm right here and I'm not going anywhere."

"It's been so hard," she chokes out, unable to finish the sentence.

"I know, baby. I know."

Beautiful brown eyes, wet with tears, look up at me with fear and disbelief. In many ways I'm feeling the same, wondering if this is another dream I'll wake up from, once more feeling devastated.

"Love me," she begs me. "Please?"

"As you wish."

Once more I begin the process of kissing down her body. She twists and writhes beneath me as I turn her body into my altar. My lips kiss and suck at her nipples, teeth pulling gently at them and causing her to cry out. To say that I am surprised when milk begins to flow would be an understatement. What the-? She laughs and tells me it's okay. I can see in her eyes that she hopes I'm not too freaked out. I take a moment to consider, shrug and continue. After giving her a sweet eternity of my ministrations, I start heading further south.

She is panting and ready, and normally I'd tease her, prolong the anticipation. But she needs me as much as I need her. Without warning, I unleash my tongue against her clit. Chloe lets out a strangled cry as she shudders and grinds, helpless but to react. I take no prisoners, seeking

95

her release as I swirl and flick my tongue, reminding her that I still know my ABC's.

Goddess, I love watching her come!

I can feel her inner thighs start to tremble, telling me she's close. I push her over the edge by slipping two fingers into her and massage just the right spots. An ecstatic scream rips through the room, echoing off the walls as a powerful orgasm causes her back to arch off the bed as both her hands grasp my head.

Chapter Twenty-Three

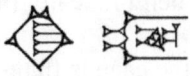

Holy. Fucking. Shit!

As my sanity returns, my breathing slows in time with my racing pulse. Beast is still between my legs, delivering small kisses to the inside of my thighs as lovely little aftershocks tremble through me, causing me to whimper and moan. Oh, I love this man. I am still trembling from my orgasm, and he never stops loving me, wanting me to have more.

This is what he does to me. Makes me feel venerated and worshipped, like I am his goddess and he is my zealot. Every time we are together, we travel to a blissful heaven of white light that obliterates all the ugly shit that plagues the world. When we bond, it's just him and I. Such a thought causes tears to fall again and in an instant, Beast is at my side. Softly he kisses the tears away as he croons. It's easy to tell that he's worried.

"It's alright, baby," he speaks softly. "I'm here. Are you ok?"

All I can do is nod and smile. "I'm just really happy right now. Please tell me this is real. Don't leave me again."

Beast answers me the best way he knows how, silencing my fears with a kiss as he slides his body on top of mine. Our hips grind together, his erection pressing against me. I moan into his mouth as he growls into mine. Fuck, it's such a sexy sound and I wrap my arms and legs around him, pressing against him in a silent and urgent plea to take me.

Slowly, ever so slowly, he eases into me and shudders as I cry out. Filling me, inch by blessed inch. I close my eyes at the intense sensations that surge through my mind as his possession claims me. *Fuck! It's been so long.*

Beast moves in and out of me at a leisurely pace that makes me gasp and purr, his weight pressing against me and our chests getting slick as my body releases milk again. I revel in our coupling as I cling to him. He's not afraid of any part of me. I was worried my milk production would freak him out, but he just went with it. He moves at such an easy pace, moving in and out slowly, like he's savoring me, loving me.

It's so good I lose track of time as I tilt my pelvis up to meet him, hoping to motivate him to pick up the pace. The lovely, sweet pressure is building, but I want more. When I rake my fingers across his back, that's when the intensity changes.

With a shuddering growl, the cage is flung open and the pace begins to quicken as he really starts to move. It's a relentless, pounding rhythm. All the time he grunts like an animal as he ravages me, lips sucking and teeth nipping at my neck. My whole body begins to tighten as he doesn't stop. *Oh fuck!*

It is just what I need, and I shriek as I explode around him as he continues to slam into me over and over, never missing a beat. Such an unrelenting fucking sends my orgasm into multiple climaxes so powerful I damn near pass out as I continue coming from his delicious punishment.

My nails dig in, hanging on for dear life and feeling completely consumed by our passion. With a roar, head thrown back, he spills himself into me as he buries himself deep within my body. His whole body shudders, teeth clenched as his growls and ecstatic breathing fill my ears.

Beast's sweaty body collapses on top of me, and I hold him tightly as he pants, his breathing slowing and normalizing. I can't help the tears of joy that stream down my face and I know he's back with me when he starts kissing them away.

"Are you all right?" His voice is hoarse.

I look into his blue eyes and smile. "Oh, so much better than all right, my love. I'm overjoyed! I got you back today. How could I not be blissfully happy?"

Slipping out of me, I can't help but wince. He rolls onto his back and I take his proffered arm and snuggle into the crook of his shoulder and rest my head on his chest. Immediately he runs his fingers through my hair and I purr with contentment.

Joy and happiness has returned to my life, but given all that I've been through, I have to wonder how long it will last. Life has a nasty habit of ripping my happiness right out of my grasp and leaving me broken and bereft. Such dark thoughts make me sigh, and I roll a little to look up at him.

"How are you alive?"

Fingers stop playing with my hair, and stroking my back, and after a moment he finally looks down. "I don't know if you're going to believe me. I still don't believe it myself."

"Tell me."

A painful sigh escapes him. "I was resurrected by my patron deity."

"No shit. Really?"

He nods to me. Somehow his story already sounds true to me, for reasons I can't explain. Under normal circumstances, there's no way I would or could have believed it. But this world is no longer normal, and just telling me stirs an inkling of a memory that I can't quite grasp. Besides, I have no reason to not believe him. My man has never lied to me. The wicked scar on his neck is a reminder of the fatal wound he took.

"Who is your deity?"

"Inanna," he replies. "Sumerian goddess of love and war."

I can't help but grin at him. "And suddenly it makes sense why you are so good at combat *and* driving me crazy in bed."

Oh, he grins at me. It's that wolfish smile that makes my heart race. More importantly, it warms my heart to see him smiling. We've both been through far too much, been subjected to far too many nightmares. If any two people deserve some happiness in this world, it's us.

"So," he speaks while still sporting a grin. "A daughter?"

I laugh. "Yes. I hope you don't mind, but I named her Leona Katherine. Leona for my mother, Katherine for… your Katie. I call her Leah for short."

This is one part of the conversation I was dreading. There a definite flash of pain in his eyes and I can see a single tear start the slide down his cheek. Taking a page from his book, I kiss it away before caressing his cheek.

"What does she look like?"

"She has your eyes," I state proudly. "And my hair."

I get a warm smile in return. "So, Leah, eh?"

"I found a book that had the names of your family in it, and almost used Katie, your mom was Katherine, too. But I wanted to honor my mother as well, so…"

He chuckles slightly. "Even though I was dead, you still considered what I would want. You amaze me." Then he pulls back a bit to stare at me accusingly. "So, you can fly?"

"Yes," I reply with a giggle to his shocked question. "Why so surprised?"

"You just didn't strike me as a pilot," he states with a smile.

"I was getting close to retiring," I say factually. "I didn't want to do porn forever. One of my friends mentioned becoming a commercial pilot. Most people never see your face and so there's less chance of being discriminated against."

"How do you mean?"

"Being in porn carried a stigma." I grow a little sad. "Many ladies try to get out of the business, go into something else, only to be fired simply because they used to be an adult entertainment actress. It was bullshit

99

discrimination, but it did make me find something I could do where my past might not affect me. So, I started learning how to fly. I'd just gotten my private pilot's license a few months before everything fell apart."

"Once again, my beautiful angel," he states with pride. "You amaze me."

My heart melts, but inside I'm dreading what I have to tell him next. I know he was dead, but now that he's alive, I feel like I've been unfaithful to him with Liz. Maybe it seems stupid, but this whole crazy episode has really screwed me up.

"I have something else to tell you," my voice is a mere whisper. "I've been unfaithful to you."

"What!?" Beast looks at me like I'm crazy. "I was dead, woman! I would never, ever want you to be unhappy. If I'm gone, you should be able to find someone to make you happy."

"Oh Beast," I cry, happy with his reply, but go on, "I can't really say I've been happy, though I did try to find a certain contentment. All I wanted was you, but you wanted me to survive. So it became my job."

"Do you love him?"

I can't help it and laugh. "You mean her?"

Beast's eyebrows shoot up. "Oh really?"

"Yes," I reply with a chuckle. "I saved Liz from a fate like you rescued me from. We helped each other get through the winter and she helped me get through the pregnancy. Do I love her? Yes, but not in the same way I love you. You own me heart and soul."

Pushing up, I kiss him passionately and he quickly reciprocates, his rough hands gliding up and down my body. I moan into his mouth as his tongue parts my lips and dances with mine. I can already feel him getting hard against my hip.

"If anyone owns anyone, my lady," he whispers against my lips. "It is you who owns me. I did come back from the dead for you, after all."

While I laugh, I also thump him on the chest for being morbid. "That's nothing to joke about. Please don't die on me again. I don't think I could bear it a second time."

"Death cannot stop true love, my lady. I can only delay it for a while. Besides, I was only mostly dead."

I pummel him hard for that comment and all he does is laugh. His mirth is so infectious that it's not long before I'm laughing as well. *Oh god, I love him so much!* He's come to mean so much to me, even when he's being a pain in the ass.

Grabbing my face, he kisses me soundly and I whimper before sliding my body onto his. He did such a lovely job worshipping me, I think it's time I returned the favor. I kiss him deeply and passionately before starting down his body with little kisses.

100

A low moan escapes him as I follow his happy trail towards my ultimate goal. Being on top of him, he's already hard and ready for round two, silently saying just how much he's missed me. As soon as I take his erection into my hands, his whole body shudders.

Like him, I don't take prisoners. Sucking his cock into my mouth, I swirl my tongue around as I suck on his shaft. And remember, I used to do porn, so I do know what I'm doing. With a growl through gritted teeth, he looks at me and I bat my eyelashes at him. As his head falls back onto the bed with a groan, he flexes his hips.

Beast really is a nice size. Not small, but not so huge I want to run away screaming either. He's just big enough that he's hard to deep throat. Still, I do my best to take him all the way in and get close enough that he lets out a louder growl, telling me I'm doing a really good job. It's such a sexy sound that I do it again, getting a similar result.

While he's pleased me so well today that I wouldn't mind having him come in my mouth, I'm not through with him yet. I have needs that only my man can provide for. I stop and straddle his thighs as he looks up at me, pupils dilated from my ministrations. Once I've got him properly positioned, I drop onto him, all the way to the hilt.

Fuck! He's so deep.

I throw my head back with a cry and that sweet feeling of being filled mixes with the soreness of the love we'd made not long ago. He groans as his hands grasp my hips, holding me in place.
My breathing is ragged as I look into his eyes, ready and waiting for some sweet friction as I try to move my hips.

Finally letting go, his hands travel up to my breasts, and briefly I wonder if he's noticed that my body has changed, I mean, more than just the milk production. It doesn't seem like it, but then it becomes difficult to think anymore as he gyrates his hips, twirling his cock inside me and making me cry out again. I move up and down while he continues to gyrate. *Oh fuck, it's so good!* I'm so swamped with passion that I have to put my hands on his chest, gasping, as I continue to ride him.

Our breathing becomes a panting, practically in perfect time with each other. My moans and cries fill the air as he growls with me. More than once his body shudders and I know he's trying to last as long as possible. Always aiming to please me, and that thought makes me so happy.

Laying my body against is, I bite at his ear lobe. "Take my from behind, my lord."

This low rumble of a growl is all I get as his blue eyes blaze with a passionate fire meant solely for me. My hearts hammers in my ears as I slip off of him and get into position. My Beast wastes no time and once at the edge of the bed and behind me, he slams into me. Such a quick thrust makes me cry out before he settles into a fast, hard rhythm.

Fingers dig into my flesh as he holds my hips firmly. My body tingles as I feel myself preparing to come again. I become a willing slave to his relentless pounding.

Then he gathers up my hair, wrapping it around his wrist before pulling my head back so that he has access to my neck—*Holy shit!*—Beast slamming into me, never missing a beat. His lips and teeth moving along my neck as he kisses, sucks and nips. One hand moving all along my body, teasing my nipples and then rubbing my clit. The other hand pulling at my hair, the sweet pain mingling with the pleasure. It's too much and my body begin to tighten as my climax approaches and I begin to see stars. When that long, low growl rumbles through him, I know that he's close as well and that thought sends me into orbit.

We climax together, his animalistic roar mixed with my screams as he twitches and spills himself into me. My body explodes around him like it's the Fourth of fucking July and my orgasm is so intense I am totally lost, collapsing onto the mattress.

Beast falls onto the mattress right beside me, and I barely have the strength to curl my sweaty body up against his. His breathing is harsh and fast, a panting the likes of which you'd expect an animal to have. As it starts to slow and he comes back to me, his arm settles around my shoulders and I relax, heart slowing, delightful tingles still coursing through my body. And with that, I slip into a warm pleasant slumber.

Chapter Twenty-Four

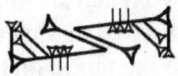

When I wake, Chloe is curled up right beside me. *Goddess, she looks so damn sexy!* My knees are aching from being draped over the edge of the narrow bed. Carefully I slip my arm out from under her and sit up. I've worn her out. And I must admit I've also worn myself out. Running, jumping, combat and then a couple rounds of sex? Hell, so long as Chloe is snuggled next to me, I could hibernate until next year. But not in this bed.

As I get up with a slight groan, I gently pull the rumpled sheet and cover my beautiful lady. Whimpering at my absence, she clutches it tightly to her, one hand searching for me. I bend down and softly kiss her cheek, then stroke her lovely, dark hair. She sighs into deeper sleep and relaxes her grip, making me smile.

Quietly I make my way into the bathroom and do my business. I really should wake her as well. She should clean up before too long in order to avoid any adverse health effects. It's never ceased to amaze me how well the human body was designed, and yet how easily some things were overlooked. The Gods must have had the engineers doing a rush job on some things.

I start the shower to clean up before my briefing with the Major. One of the luxuries the base has is a water collection and recycling plant, some of that technology courtesy of the Biosphere Two operation. This allows the water supply to be recycled with great efficiency. In fact, there were hardcopy notes on the system which I packed in with the critical supplies. I don't see how we could replicate it, but knowledge is power.

According to my watch, it's fifteen minutes before sixteen hundred hours. I'll be a quarter of an hour ahead of schedule. Or at least I thought I would be, until a brown pair of arms wrap around me from behind.

"Hello," Chloe purrs against my back. "You weren't in bed with me. I missed you."

I laugh and turn around. "I needed to clean up before talking to the Major."

It would be so easy to get lost in those brown eyes again and forget the meeting with the base commander. The feeling of her wet body pressed against mine does things to me. When she moves against my growing erection, I know she's well aware of that fact. With a smile, she traces a single finger along the lines of the tattoo on my chest.

"I missed you." she repeats with that sultry voice that put fire in my blood.

"As did I, my lady."

With a giggle, she presses her body against me again, accentuating the differences between us, making me growl. "I can tell. So what are you going to do about it?"

"What I'm going to do is drop to my knees and torture you with my tongue until you come, screaming," I growl, "and when you can move again, I'm going to let you do the same to me."

Her lips part slightly, her eyes dancing with expectant passion as I lean down and kiss her. I love her so much it hurts. With equal fervor, she kisses me back, her hands fisting into my hair as our lips and tongues dance together.

As I begin my journey down her wet body, I can already hear her ragged breathing. Putting my hands on her lovely ass, I push her up against the wall and rest her thighs on my shoulders. Then I go to work, relishing every ecstatic moan, cry and scream that pours forth from my beautiful angel.

I march into Major Drummond's office, tired but very, very happy. So happy I can't get the grin off my face as I deliver a crisp salute, which he returns. He begins to smile himself, and hands me a glass of bourbon.

"I hear that your woman made the flight in Pete's place," he states with his typical southern drawl. "I assume she's all right from that crash landing, given that damn smile on your face."

Choking back a laugh, I respond. "Yes sir. She's fine."

"Where is she? Do we know about the airfield status and Pete?"

"She's—sleeping it off, sir," I reply before taking a drink. "And I already debriefed her."

"I know that, son!" The Major rolls his eyes. "The grin on your face says that quite plainly. What about Pete?"

"Healing, sir. When the bandits shot at him on takeoff, he took a bullet to the leg. Wasn't able to completely stop the bleeding, but they got him to a doctor when he landed. He's going to be fine, with a little luck and some of the antibiotics we're bringing in."

104

"Well thank God for small favors," the Major exclaims before taking a drink. "What about the airfield?"

"Pete say's it may be tricky, but he thinks we just have enough length to land on."

"Then the plan is a go?"

"Yes sir. I've already got ground crews getting both planes ready for takeoff."

"What about our surprise?"

This is the conversation I've been dreading. With a sigh, I pull a radio out of my pocket, red tape resting over the transmit button. This single radio is already set to a frequency that our detonators are on.

"Here you are," I reply while handing it over. "Turn it on and press the talk button and that's all she wrote."

"Good. Can your lady fly a C-130?"

"She was going to be a commercial pilot before the Collapse," I reply with a nod. "But I'll make sure she's up to speed on the differences."

"Excellent." Sitting back in his chair, he looks lost in thought for a moment. "Issue an order for everyone to meet in Hangar A this evening. It's time I made that promotion final."

"Sir," I exclaim with a sigh. "You could come with us?"

He shakes his head. "No chance in Hell. This is my last command, and I'm not runnin' with my tail between my legs. And I'm certainly not going to burden the few decent people left in this world. I'll make sure you guys get out of here and keep them from anything left behind. Besides, I've been missing my wife a long time. It's time for me to find my way to her."

Shit, I could understand that sentiment more than anyone. In a way it could be said that I came back from the dead for Chloe. I'd move Heaven and Hell just to protect her and keep her safe. I certainly died for her. That's what any real man does for the woman he loves.

"Yes sir." Regret hangs heavy in my voice. I have really grown to like him.

"Now there's one other thing," he tells me brusquely as he gets to his feet.

Picking up a large, impact resistant case, he pulls a key from around his neck and unlocks it. Spinning it around, I can see what's inside. It appears to be two laptop computers, in a case designed for them.

"These may be the only two working laptops left in existence that can access our eyes in the sky."

As he explains to me what they are, he pulls a tough looking laptop from its seat within high density foam. It's clear that they are both very well protected while in the case, but this is a system that looks like I could beat someone to death with it and it wouldn't care.

"I have left a note underneath to top layer of foam with the login name and password," he explains while handing me one. "This can give you an idea of what's going on in the world so long as nothing happens to those computers. The satellites have enough fuel to stay in orbit for at least fifty years."

"How many are there?"

"The network is a little over nine hundred strong," he says while sitting back down. "There's an app that can allow you to tap into the civilian ones as well, and that will give you another two hundred, give or take. Technology on those will vary of course."

"Understood, sir."

"I highly recommend you put that case with the plane that has the least chance of crashing."

With a laugh, I nod to him. "That will have to be her, sir."

"Well then, you have your choice. Here's the key."

I catch the key he tosses and put it around my neck before tucking it under my fatigues. I close the laptop and stow it. Then I close and latch the lid before setting the case on the floor. I can lock it after I've shown Chloe.

"Anything else, sir?"

"That'll be all for now, son. See you tonight."

"Yes sir. Thank you, sir." I give a crisp salute.

The Major returns it, and for a moment, I see something in his eyes. Something emotional passes between us, but we are men, and the moment passes with nothing more than a nod. I need to get back to Chloe and update her. There is a lot to say and we haven't actually talked much. And, I need to get the Major's order out to the entire base for tonight's meeting. So much to do and so little time.

Chapter Twenty-Five

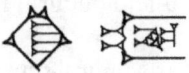

If I wasn't so sore in such a delicate place, I would think I am dreaming. But my joy is real. My Beast is alive, and I feel reborn. I can't help but feel overjoyed at this turn of events. Sure, I have my bruises and hurts, but I am in such a state of bliss, I barely feel them.

I am astonished that he hasn't seemed to notice the mess my body has become over the past year. I mean, giving birth in a modern hospital with surgeons on call would be one thing, but I had no one but Liz and Nena and I feel much different down there than I did before. But he didn't even notice! My stretch marks still look like maps of the fjords of Norway, and he hasn't even seen them. My boobs are milky and much less perky, and he still wants them and me. God I love this man! I sigh in contentment and look around me.

I'm seated next to Beast, and we are in a large hangar filled with people, including a number of children. I am beginning to see why it was so important that he come here. To leave these kids at the predations of the bandits beyond the wall would have been criminal.

For the first time in a long time, I also feel completely safe and whole. His arm is around my shoulders, and he has me pulled into him. I can't help but rest my head on his shoulder and put one hand over his heart as we wait for Major Drummond to give a speech.

I got to meet the major as we were getting ready to leave our room. Dropping in, he wanted to say hello and thank me for saving Pete. I told him it was the least I can do, especially when he was delivering a message from my beloved Beast.

Using the world "beloved" certainly gets my man's attention. He gives me one of his rare smiles. He then tells the major he's briefed me about the laptops since I'm his second in command.

Excuse me? Who's in command?

I decide to save that debate for later. Oh, maybe much later. I really am more than a little sore as I adjust in my seat. While I would love to use my fine motor sexing skills on him, maybe I need to wait a day.

My movement certainly causes him to give me a wolfish smile that tells me he knows exactly why I'm shifting around. While I try to give him a censorious glare, I can't help but grin in return. We are both far too happy right now to be angry.

The hangar becomes quiet as Major Drummond clambers onto the back of an open bed Humvee and motions for silence. All eyes are on him as Lieutenant Hayes hands up a bullhorn. Pulling the handset off the back, he smiles before addressing the crowd.

"Thank you all for coming," he speaks with that southern drawl I noticed earlier. "It's been a long and difficult time for us. We've lost family, comrades and good friends. But, finally, we have a ray of hope on the horizon."

There is some murmuring before he motions for silence once more. "Tomorrow morning, you will all board two planes and head for a place in Colorado. There will be running water all year round, land capable of growing crops and shelter. It'll be a real home."

Everyone cheers, yells and claps as a wave of buoyant happiness moves through the building. I look at Beast and he's smiling, as well. Our small family in Colorado is about to get much larger. We are going to have to plant a lot more crops. I hope we have enough seed to feed everyone.

"Now, I do have a little bit of bad news," the major continues. "I will not being going with you."

Shocked gasps and cries fill the air and he quickly silences the crowd. "No, listen! I have stage four lung cancer. We don't have the drugs required to treat it, not that it could help me at this point anyway. I don't want you to feel sorry for me. I plan to stay behind and ensure you get away. We don't want to leave those bastards with anything we can't take with us. And I wouldn't mind takin' a few of them with me."

Oh dear. There are many wet eyes in the crowd, and the children who are old enough to know what that means are crying. The major has kept these people alive, turned them into a family. Now, 'daddy' is going to die and leave them behind. I know this pain far too well. We all do, really.

"Please," he calls out. "Do not despair. I have gotten you all as far as I can. Now, it is time for someone else to take my place and get you the rest of the way. Chief! Get yer ass up here!"

"Fuck," Beast mutters under his breath, shooting me a frown.

Everyone watches him approach the major and deliver a crisp salute, which is smartly returned by the commanding officer. Dropping down onto the concrete floor, Drummond walks up and shakes my man's hand before continuing.

"In recognition of your initiative and bravery as well as helping to band our team together into an effective fighting force and giving us hope and a new home, I hereby promote you to the Navy rank of lieutenant commander. I want you to lead these people and get them to safety."

Oh, I can feel the utter reluctance of my poor Beast as he slowly takes the collar devices that the major offers. I can picture his grim expression as he realizes the weight now pressing on his shoulders. My man stands stoically while the new rank insignias are pinned to his collar, one and then the other. Major Drummond gives Beast a salute, which is quickly returned. Beast then marches back to me and sits down.

He notices I have a few tears in my eyes—tears of pride and love. He glances at me, concerned. I smile reassuringly and squeeze his shoulder. I know he's not comfortable with this. It doesn't take me much to spot his uneasiness anymore. This is far too much civilization for him, and he's been surrounded by it for months. I'm amazed he was able to hold out for as long as he did.

I'm also surprised that he has even been speaking to people while training them; whole conversations with the commander. Lucky people got his voice. I had to make do with gestures and grunts. Not that I mind at this point. But this is not his happy place. He is not fond of being amongst people, but now they are all going to be looking to him. I will need to help with that, I can see it already.

Getting him home to Colorado will help, I think. I can sequester him in the bunker. Most of our people don't even know it exists. I've kept its secret on purpose, partly because I'm selfish and don't want to share what he was giving me. Of those that do know, I've only shown the first layer. Only Liz, Mike, Nena and I know how to get into the deeper sections. I didn't get this far by being foolish and blindly trusting. Trust is something that is earned, not given.

Next, the major calls on Lieutenant Hayes and promotes her to captain. Ah yes, the woman who has a crush on my man. Not that I can blame her. In some ways, I envy her. For the entire time he's been here, she's gotten to work with him and fight by his side. That should have been my job.

In hindsight, though, it's probably better that I wasn't by his side. After all, I was pregnant. Going into serious action would have meant putting our unborn daughter in harm's way. The powers that be knew this, so I figure that's why he was sent here while I had to stay in Colorado. I don't know that such a realization makes all our pain worth it, but I try to think so.

"Chloe," the major calls out, commanding my attention. "Please come forward."

Puzzled, I look at Beast, he shrugs his shoulders. I get to my feet and approach the major. All eyes are on me, making me feel exposed, so I do what I've always done when I feel that way. I lift up my chin, walk with purpose and meet the major's eyes as I close the distance and stop in front of him.

"In recognition of your deeds saving McBride and flying here to deliver much needed intelligence, I hereby conscript you in the Armed Forces and award you the rank of captain."

Wait. What???

I can see Ms. Hayes face, and she is as shocked as I am. Since I'm wearing my fatigues, the Major pins the proper devices to my collar and then gives me a firm salute. I try to return it properly, but I have no clue if I'm even close.

"You may return to your seat, good lady," Drummond whispers just loud enough that I can hear.

I nod and make my way back to Beast, who looks as surprised as I feel as people clap and cheer. Sitting down, he wraps one arm around me. Putting a finger underneath my collar, he inspects the devices while smiling at me. He looks so proud that joy swells within my chest.

"Listen up," Major Drummond calls out, silencing the room. "As this is our last night here, I think it's only fair we have a bit of a celebration with what little booze we have left."

Just about the whole crowd stands up and hollers as a couple soldiers wheel out a stack of coolers. They immediately start passing out cans or bottles of various beers and soft drinks. With a grin, I rush over to snag two Corona bottles. As I return to my man, people pat me on the back and shower me with praise. Maybe I've been hanging around Beast too long, but suddenly all these people make me feel claustrophobic. Back within the safety of his arms, I hand over a cold bottle.

"Thank you," he replies softly.

"You are quite welcome, my Beast. Can we get out of here?"

"Yes, please."

We wait for a few minutes, accept congratulations and greet people Beast knows; but finally the party takes on a life of its own. While everyone celebrates, we slip out, I think unnoticed.

Outside, it's still on the cold side, but the night sky is beautiful. The stars are out in full force and we stroll along, enjoying the kind of frosty cold beer I never thought I would have again. I better enjoy it, for this may be one of the last good beers left on earth.

Since I am following Beast, I really am not paying attention. I don't know the base well and find that instead of taking me back to his room, he has guided me to one of the big cargo planes already sitting on the runway.

110

"Where are we going?"

"I need to show you the controls for tomorrow, make sure you can fly this thing."

"Of course I can. Thanks to a shortage, I was going to be one of the backup pilots for the Spurs, and this isn't far off from one of the models I trained on."

"Of course you did. You will never cease to be a miracle, my love."

I smile brightly and look at him sideways. "What do we do after that?"

Beast stops, a sly grin on his face. "After that, I'm going to carry my angel back to the room. Strip all her clothes off and slip into bed with her. Then, I am going to hold her tightly while I run my fingers through her hair until she falls asleep. And, I promise not to let her go until morning."

"Oh, you had me at Happy Birthday." I can't help but swoon.

He pulls me close and my breathing stops as he leans in, his lips upon mine. My heart races as I feel his warm breath wash against my face. His eyes lock with mine, desire for me quite evident within those blue rings, dark against the fall of night.

"You had me at, 'You know how to kill. I need that kind of training, so I don't end up like this again.'"

Without giving me time to think about the first words I ever said to him, he brings his lips to mine and kisses me with fervor. Standing there on the tarmac, we hold each other tightly as we kiss in the soft moonlight.

Chapter Twenty-Six

As I wake, I realize I am in a warm bed with my naked Beast curled up behind me. His arms are wrapped around me, keeping me so close that I can feel his chest expand against my back when he inhales. I match my breathing to his and relax into him to keep him from waking up.

I can barely see the clock, telling me there are only eleven minutes left before the alarm will sound. I want to enjoy every last second of this feeling. I'm safe and warm in the arms of the man I love. A man who loves me back with equal intensity. He worships me like I'm the only woman on the face on the planet, and I adore him completely.

It isn't the only reason I love him, but it's at the top of the list. To him, I'm not an object to have, a possession he can own. I'm his partner and his equal. He respects me and my opinion and shows me by his actions. Hell, the man even died for me and then came back from the dead to fight by my side once more. If that isn't a declaration of true love, I don't know what is.

Soon, we will get dressed, get into airplanes and fly for home. *Home!* Dear God, how that very idea brings tears to my eyes. What was an impossibility before is now totally possible. I get to walk into the bunker with him and share that which he had been wanting to give me. It was the whole reason we left L.A., so that I could be safe.

"Hey," he murmurs, letting me know he's awake. "What's wrong, beautiful?"

I shake my head and crane back to give him a bright smile. "I just can't believe it. We're going home."

Turning me in his arms, he tenderly kisses away each tear. When that task is accomplished, his lips find mine and we embrace tightly. Part of me that is still terrified that this is all a dream that I will wake from at any moment.

Beast's arms tighten around me and I revel in his warmth and closeness as he entwines himself around me. Being so much taller and broader, I feel cocooned in warmth and safety. God, I wish we could just stay like this forever, but we have work to do and people to evacuate.

And we have a beautiful baby daughter to get back to. I'm sure she's been angry the entire time mommy's been gone. My breasts are sore from milk production, and I really need to pump again or I will be in agony.

The alarm goes off and startles us both, and we laugh. "Come on, beautiful," he murmurs softly. "Let's get dressed and get home?"

"Yes sir!" Giving him a mock salute, he rolls his eyes and smacks me playfully on the ass before rolling out of bed. "And, I need to find my bag so I can release the floodgates."

Stopping, he turns and looks at me oddly. All I can do is shake my head at him. He'll see. Living with a lactating woman is not all fun and games all the time. There's no doubt in my mind that he's fighting hard to keep his amorous side at bay just as much as I am.

As I move out of bed, my body reminds me of our glorious sexual collision upon being reunited. When we get home, I tell myself. He'll get to see Leah, we'll have a good meal, and then I'll let him take me on those satin sheets that I had stowed away.

We take a quick shower together, and we are careful to make it fast. We towel off and slip into our gear. One of the things I had been given yesterday was a real flight suit! It's even in my size. Climbing into the olive green jumpsuit, I throw my tactical gear over it. Once everything is on, I grab the M-4 Beast gave me yesterday, and we head out the door.

The closer we get to those big planes, the faster my heart beats, mostly from excitement, but there's some fear, as well. I shake it off as we approach the rear hatch, which is down as people rush to finish boarding. The airmen nearby come to attention and salute. I'm no good at military protocol, but fortunately Beast is and shows me what to do when he salutes back.

Looking into the cargo area, I see pallets stacked in the center, from front to back. Seats are arranged against the walls, mostly women and kids sitting in them. I've got the most precious cargo of all. Along with the children, I have almost all the medical personnel, medical supplies, food and various other gear. There is also a Humvee, which is an ambulance version, and word is they stuffed it with all the medical gear they could.

"Ma'am," the cargo master states while coming to attention and giving a salute.

He almost looks like one of the kids, but I know he's an adult because he is in uniform and has a name tag sewn on his flight suit that reads, "Nolan." Sandy brown hair and blue eyes on a freckled boy who can't be more than nineteen.

"Nolan, do me a favor?"

"Yes ma'am."

"Don't salute me," I state back with a smile. "I may have been given rank, but I've never been military, and I don't want to insult you by doing it wrong."

Beast chokes back a laugh and Nolan grins. "Yes ma'am. All cargo is fastened down and double checked. At last count, all passengers are aboard and counted for."

"Thank you. I presume you've loaded this crate so the weight is evenly distributed?"

Nolan nods in the affirmative, and I think he's impressed that I know what his job is. I am just grateful they covered situations like this in flight school. Weight distribution is important in a plane, otherwise it screws with your performance and can even cause you to crash.

Beast waves me forward and we head to the cockpit. Once there, I try to control my hammering heart and recall everything he told me last night. While I may have flown before, it's been a while, and I haven't taken one of these on more than a couple runs a lifetime ago.

"You ready, beautiful?"

Oh, I love it when he calls me that. The way he says it, as if it were my name.

"Yes, my lord." I grin at him.

He grins back. "Just remember what I showed you. You'll do fine. You always do."

Such praise makes me lift my chin and grin with pride. It's time to go, so I launch myself at him and give him a kiss to remember me by for the next two hours or so. When he growls into my mouth, I desperately want to rip his clothes off. With a mutual gasp, we break contact.

"When we get home, my lady," he whispers deliciously low and growly. "I am going to tie you to the bed and pleasure you to the best of my ability."

I think my heart just stopped.

His blue eyes gaze at me with dark and lascivious intent, making my mouth go dry. I know what he's doing. The objective is to prolong the anticipation and stoke the fire. Well, two can play at that game. Deliberately, I lick my lips slowly, and then bite my lower lip while looking at him innocently.

Oh yeah, that did it. I see his pupils dilate right before he presses his body against me and growls once more. Feeling frisky and mischievous, I growl back while standing my ground. Fuck, it's hot in here!

I think he's going to do something, when an explosion outside rudely interrupts our foreplay. *Fucking bandits!* In an instant, my playful Beast is gone, replaced with the side of him that is going to get some killing done.

"Raiders are attacking the south gate," someone yells through his radio.

"This is Beast," he barks with a commanding voice. "All security personnel, stand your ground. Be ready for rapid evac on my order."

"Yes sir," a number of people respond in rapid fire.

"My lady," he states in his calm yet loving way. "Start your plane and taxi for takeoff. I will be right behind you."

"You'd better be," I warn before grabbing his vest and giving him one last kiss.

I let him go, and he runs off as I get into the seat and start up the engines as I carefully go through pre-flight. Finally, the engines start up with a roar, propellers get up to speed. It's my job, I know what to do, but I can't help but worry about my man out there without me by his side.

Chapter Twenty-Seven

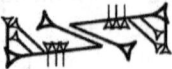

I can barely hear the ramp closing over the sound of the engines starting up on Chloe's plane. When I look to the direction of the south gate, black smoke can be seen rising up beyond the wall. Then, there is another explosion at the north gate. Evidently, this is the attack we've been waiting for. They must have spotted the planes somehow and don't want us making a run for it.

Quickly dashing into my plane, I leap over Airmen Jackson and Burnett as they lay prone on the deck, machine guns at the ready. I'd made sure the night before that all the cargo was secure. With all the munitions I'm carrying, last thing I need is a container coming loose and killing us all. Chloe might be just a tad angry with me if I die. Again.

"Deploy the mortars," I order sternly into the radio as I strap into the pilot's seat. "Hayes, get your ass to the plane!"

"Yes sir!"

As I get settled in, I spot Chloe taxiing towards the end of the runway. Slipping my headset on, I keep one ear off so that I can still hear the walkie talkie. I run my preflight at top speed. We need to leave and fast! A series of smaller explosions go off all over the place, and that tells me the team deployed the mortar rounds.

Of the many things the Army was storing here, there were two dozen sixty millimeter mortars and a good number of rounds. The problem was that the only person with any experience in using them is myself and we did not have enough time to train properly.

What we did have was some rather effective improvised grenades. The rounds for the sixty are not unlike a grenade. Pull the pin to arm the fuse, and it's ready to rock. Instead of dropping it down a tube, toss it over the wall and let gravity do the rest. That much shrapnel would play hell on the raiders.

The squealing of tires signals Ms. Hayes coming to a stop. She piles out of the vehicle, along with three other airmen and they rush onto the plane. As she comes into the cockpit, I turn and look at her.

116

"Open the side door, make sure you are strapped in, and have one of the machine guns at the ready to provide cover fire."

"Yes sir!"

Once she ducks out, I start up the engines one by one and watch as the props start getting up to speed. That's when I spot a small figure break through the fence beyond the end of the runway. *What the hell?* I confirm with the others that there are no missing personnel. I finish my rushed preflight check, when an insistent inner voice and a burning in my tattoo tells me to stop, wait, go see who that is.

With a growl, I again jump from my seat, stride back to the closed hatch of the aircraft and open it a crack. Whoever the small form is has made good speed across the tarmac, darting quickly back and forth to evade enemy fire. The enemy of my enemy, and all that, right? I yell at the person to hurry, for as he gets closer, I see it is just a kid. He dashes the final few yards to the plane and jumps, grasps my waiting hand, and I haul him in.

The kid is light, but older than I first thought, maybe eight or nine, but he's very small. He's also bruised from head to toe from what I see under his rags. Dirty and bleeding in a few places, he looks at me with huge brown eyes that are streaming with tears.

"Please, take me with you. I swear, I don't eat much. My mom died and… and I gotta get out of here. Don't leave me."

At that, he bursts into tears. What can I do? Besides, Chloe would kill me if I left him to the tender mercies of the raiders. With a growl, I hand him off to one of the airman who has medical knowledge, and the kid goes with no complaint.

As if I don't have enough to do. I dash back up to the cockpit. Only a few minutes have passed, but already I see that Chloe is in position and ready to make her run. On cue, I hear her over the radio.

"Tower, this is Mother One. Ready for takeoff."

The major replies. "Mother One, you are clear for takeoff. Safe flying."

"Roger that," she replies with enthusiasm.

I pick up the walkie as she starts to move down the runway. White plumes from the JATO fill the air, along with an added roar that mixes with the drone of the turboprops. Thanks to the rocket assist, she's picking up speed quickly.

"All security personnel to the end of the runway, on the double!"

I toss the radio into the co-pilot's seat and slip the headset completely on. Pushing the throttle forward I begin my taxi to the end of the runway as Chloe gains speed for takeoff. As she gets close, I pull out an extra walkie in my vest pouch and hit the button.

My final parting gift is thanks to some construction material. There was a stack of plumbing pipe slightly larger than sixty millimeter. I set up an array of them at every gate, and wired them to a switch. The voltage would set off the base charge and fire the round. And that's exactly what happens. The series of improvised mortars go off, blanketing the areas near the gates with multiple explosions. Chloe then sails over the wall and gains altitude.

"I'm up," she cheers through the radio, making me smile. "I'm up!"

"Be right with you, baby."

"You'd better be," she warns and I laugh.

"This is Papa One, taxing for takeoff," I report as I see Humvees converging at the end of the runway.

"Papa One, you have clearance for takeoff," the major reports. "Best make it quick, son. *Hannibal ad portas*. The hordes are at the gates."

I curse because we are cutting things way too close. I had hoped the mortars would keep their heads down for a time, but I guess they don't care about dying. This Father Roberts must have quite the charisma to whip them into such a frenzy.

"They are breaking through the south gate," Drummond reports. "Best get a move on."

The sound of controlled machine gun fire tells me shit's about to get real. I can't give the security team a lot of time, so they have to run to get on board as I start swinging the plane around and lining up the runway. I only hope we don't miss anyone.

"This is Papa One," I report. "Lining up for takeoff. Godspeed, Major Drummond."

"Thank you, son. Tower out."

I switch to intercom. "This is your captain speaking. On behalf of the flight crew, let me welcome you aboard Air Force Flight Two to Crested Butte, Colorado. We should touchdown in Crested Butte at approximately ten fifty three local time, assuming we don't get shot down. So, please buckle up and hold onto your helmets."

The long, concrete strip is laid out ahead of me as I slide the plane into perfect position and slam the throttle all the way before hitting the JATO button. The propellers churn in the cold morning air as rockets flare to life. She lurches forward and starts gaining speed—fast.

Fuck, I hope the men had enough time to get on.

Reaching over, I hit the button for the back hatch, and it starts closing as a few bullets ping against the hull. As we begin to really pick up speed, I'm pressed back into my seat from the extra thrust.

That funny sinking feeling you get in the pit of your stomach when the plane lifts up hits me. I pull back a little more, gaining altitude and clear the wall. There are dead bodies littered all over from the mortar shells, but there are still a large number shooting at us. When I hear a machine gun open up, I know Ms. Hayes has still got the door open.

A couple more rounds hit us as we continue climbing as we leave Nellis behind with a swarm of angry ants pouring through its wrecked gates. I've just started banking right when the base goes up in a huge series of explosions. Flame, smoke and debris are thrust high into the sky as all the remaining ordnance and fuel detonates in a fiery cataclysm.

Goodbye, major. I hope you took a good number of those assholes with you.

"Baby, are you there?"

I smile at the sweet sound of Chloe's worried voice. "This is Papa One. We are airborne on a heading of zero-six-three degrees, over."

"Oh, thank God," she exclaims. "Is everyone okay?"

"I don't know yet, baby. I'll find out. The base is gone, over."

"Dear God, have mercy on his soul."

"Amen, over."

"Can you see me yet? I've dropped my speed so you can catch up."

I scan ahead, looking for her plane. "Beautiful, what's your altimeter say?"

"A little over eight thousand feet," she purrs through the headset.

I'm at six and still climbing, so I start looking up and that's when I spot her—still a ways off, but I should be able to catch up quickly. I increase my rate of climb, heading for the same altitude.

"Angels eight, understood. I should be pulling alongside you in a few minutes."

As I climb, I marvel at how peaceful the world looks from up here. You can't see any of the shit or scumbags that infest the land down below. It's just us, alone in our own private bubble for a while. At least until the fuel runs out or we land.

Captain Hayes comes into the cockpit and takes a seat in the co-pilot's chair. She looks a combination of exhausted and depressed. This feeling in the pit of my gut tells me I'm going to hear something I'm not going to like.

"Spit it out, Captain."

She sighs painfully. "Three of our men didn't make it aboard in time."

Fuck!

I turn on the intercom. "Goddess, I ask you for salvation of those we lost today. Please save the souls of those who have perished against the face of evil. I pray in accordance to your will. Please bless the lives of those they greatly sacrificed for, so that their loss is not in vain. Your will be done. Amen."

Ms. Hayes begins crying as I switch the intercom off. This family has lost four good men today, all because of assholes who had to take from others instead of learning to do for themselves. I can only hope that massive explosion killed them all, because they all had it coming.

Chapter Twenty-Eight

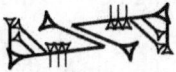

I pull my aircraft alongside Chloe's and we look at each other and smile. Even from here, her grin is brighter than the sun. Giving me an enthusiastic wave, I can't help but laugh at her before activating the radio.

"Hello, beautiful," I say smoothly. "Now I know for sure you're an angel, because you've got such lovely wings."

Her laugh comes in over the headset. "You just like me for the size of my propellers."

My turn to laugh. "And the shape of your fuselage."

"You are so bad," she purrs. "But, I still love you."

"I love you more." I take a quick glance ahead before continuing. "Let's climb to angels twelve."

"Roger that, handsome. Climbing to twelve thousand."

Slowly, her plane starts gaining altitude, and I match her, lagging only a little behind so that I can see if she took any damage. As we continue, I move underneath and around to the other side, continuing to look for anything bad. So far, I don't see any obvious damage and as we level out, I shoot her a smile.

"Your plane looks to be okay, beautiful."

As she starts to respond, she glances to the rear of mine and frowns. "Yours not so much."

"What do you see?"

"The tank under the wing is leaking."

I nod. "Take a look and see if I have any other damage as I pass over you."

"All right."

Carefully, I climb and then slowly pass over her before leveling out on her starboard wing once more. Even from this distance I can see the frown that graces her lovely face as she shakes her head.

"Don't look at me in that tone of voice," I say jokingly. "What's the assessment?"

"Baby, you have bullet holes all over your plane," she replies with obvious worry.

"Anything leaking or smoking beyond the starboard fuel tank?"

"No."

"All right," I reply with a grateful exhale. "It's just extra fuel, beautiful. I still have more than enough to get there on."

"Why the extra then?"

Planning long term is something she's still not gotten the hang of yet. I will need to teach her my prepper ways so we can be on the same page. As intelligent as she is, she'll probably come up with things I wouldn't have thought of. She's already given me an earful about maternity clothes, or rather the lack of them in the bunker.

"In case we need them for later," I reply. "I've got two qualified pilots, so having some aircraft at our disposal couldn't hurt."

"I wish you were in this plane," she murmurs through the headset.

Fuck, what this woman does to me.

I smile as my heart goes into double-time. "I could walk across the wings and hop in."

"No," she exclaims with a laugh. "I've already lost you once. I'm certainly not going to lose you a second time. Especially to a stupid stunt. I'll wait impatiently, thank you."

"Yes ma'am."

I give her a salute before paying attention ahead. It's a great day for flying. Clear skies with scattered clumps of dark clouds. Golden rays of sunshine spill across a pale blue sky as the land slowly rolls by. I can't help but feel touched by the hand of the goddess again.

As we continue, I start balancing my fuel and make sure my main tanks are full before jettisoning the wing tanks. Otherwise I'll just keep leaking fuel all over the damn place. Once that's accomplished, I eject the tanks.

"What was that?" Chloe's voice practically shouts over the radio.

"Just dropping the tanks, baby. I can't keep that leaky one, or I'll just keep losing fuel."

"All right," she replies, sounding relieved. "You got enough to make it the rest of the way?"

"More than enough, angel. Don't worry, I'll make it there. I have a promise to keep to you."

"Damn right you do," she growls back. "And, you'd better deliver this time."

I can't help but laugh as I look forward to being able to keep my original promise to her. The bunker is mostly for survival, but I've stocked it with a few luxuries. Once we have the time, I plan on sharing those surprises with her to see just which ones put a twinkle in her eyes.

"How's the bunker?"

"Fine," she replies with a smile I can easily hear. "Most of our people don't know it's even there. The few that do, don't know how big it is. It felt right to keep that to myself, even though at times I feel selfish."

"I don't see anything selfish in that. You can't be totally trusting, especially these days."

"Agreed. We control everything from roughly a mile south of the bunker, all the way to Crested Butte."

"Really?"

She laughs at the shocked tone of my reply. "When the worst of winter was over, people started showing up. I took them in, and we started taking over the area. There were a few survivors that remained in Crested Butte and a few in Gunnison after the Collapse. "

"Good people?"

"None have given me reason to mistrust them," she states proudly. "Even the people you sent from Green River seem to be working out so far."

I can't help but smile at my beautiful angel who said that she's bad at leading people. It sounds like she's done a pretty damn good job. Taking people in, keeping parts of your base hidden and making sure they are taken care of anyway. Sounds like solid leadership decisions to me.

I can't wait to see all she has accomplished. I know she's done more than she wants to take credit for. Sometimes, I think she doesn't put enough faith in her decisions. I wonder if that's an estrogen thing, or if our society undermined our girls into making them think that way so the men would feel more important.

One thing is certain, I'm going to back every play she makes. I firmly believe that is part of a real man's job, to be a true partner. Not the boss, not the lone decision maker. You build your woman up, help her to be strong. Sometimes that means sacrificing your pride, but never your principles. Win her respect and understand her. And in Chloe's case, I started by helping her become the best killer of bad men in the world, even better than me. I don't mind if she is, because a real man isn't threatened by the success of his woman.

Hell, I think the only way I could be threatened by Chloe is if she's coming after me with a weapon in hand. I'd like to say that I'd have to do something extremely stupid for that to happen. But, I am a guy and definitely suffer from testosterone poisoning, so it's not impossible. I laugh to myself as I remember our sweet reunion. She kisses me first, sure. Then she clocks me one that leaves a mark.

Goddess, I love that woman!

As we close in on home, I start thinking about what we are going to do with all the extra people. Water is easy to take care of, but keeping them fed is an entirely different matter. Sure, we have food supplies in both planes, but I'm unsure that will make us all the way to harvest. We will need to plant more than enough crops. Extra food can be traded, and if it goes bad, it is always better than empty bellies trying to make it days or weeks until another source of food is found. Nothing brings down morale faster than people not being able to eat. Nothing makes them more content than having a job and bread on the table.

Of course, I'll have to see if Chloe has thought of anything. She may be ahead of me, because she's had boots on the ground there. Together, we'll keep our tiny area of the world safe and beat back the savages. I hope she knows she is my equal in this. Having her there for the past year has tortured me near to distraction, but now I can see the wisdom in the Goddess' plan. She was safe to have our child, and I was able to find just the help the valley needs—the able bodies of children, men and women, all healthy survivors eager for a new home and to help build the new world.

I need to think about keeping Chloe strong, letting her plan and guiding her steps. And, for that matter, letting her guide mine. Just because I came back to life doesn't mean I'm still not two steps closer to the grave than she is. Keeping her strong is important to getting her through life, especially after I'm finally gone for good.

Chapter Twenty-Nine

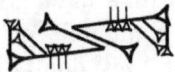

The flight lasts a little more than two hours before we climb over the mountains that make up the west wall of Crested Butte's valley. Chloe and I talk the entire flight. In between, I make sure Captain Hayes is all right.

She's lost good friends today, and does not appear to be weathering it well. For the most of the flight, she has sat in the co-pilot's seat looking out the windows in a melancholy state. Her knees are up, and she appears withdrawn.

"Snap out of it, Captain."

Her head jerks toward me. "Sir?"

"Don't, 'sir' me. Quit moping. You lost people, there's nothing you can do but learn from it. Say your goodbyes, and move on. We've got quite a few people that still need you on your game."

She starts to open her mouth, but then closes it and appears lost in thought before responding. "I just… Major Drummond pulled us together. Kept us going. Now he's gone."

"But not forgotten," I quickly add. "You have to keep his momentum going. Keep that memory of him alive while keeping our people alive."

"Yes sir." She smiles slightly.

"Good. Because I can't handle all these people on my own. You're going to have to pull your weight, provided I don't kill us all on this upcoming landing."

That gets a laugh, not a big one, but it's a start. There's a bit more life in her eyes now. Ms. Hayes doesn't understand just how important she is. I'm Beast. People are afraid of me, but fear can only motivate people so far. Women like her and Chloe need to have the leadership skills to build and maintain loyalty and morale. While I'm the stick, they're offering the carrot.

"Baby," I state over the radio while throttling back a little. "You land first and then taxi off the runway. Once you are out of the way, I'll make my approach."

Chloe detects the uncertainty in my voice. "Are you going to be able to do this?"

"Got no choice," I tell her with a slight grin. "I don't think we have a ladder tall enough for Pete to climb in."

She laughs over the headset. "Just don't kill yourself. Please."

There's a note of desperation in her voice that is hard to miss. It's bad enough she lost me once, ripped from her grasp by an asshole. I'd hate to think the impact on her psyche if I die again.

"Most that happens is that I break the plane, baby." I give her a reassuring tone to help assuage her fears. "I'll get us on the ground safely."

"You'd better," she growls in a way that makes my heart race with sweet promises yet to come. "Making my approach now."

"Safe landing, beautiful."

I pull into a holding pattern, making a constant turn so that I can watch as she approaches the local landing strip. With the smooth precision of a pro, she sets her plane down and brings it to a stop just before the end of the runway.

"I'm down and taxing off," she reports with unbridled glee.

It's hard not to laugh. "As usual, you do an amazing job."

"Your turn," she replies. "And don't screw it up."

Finishing my turn, I line up the runway and go through the motions— flaps down, throttle back and drop the landing gear. I'm approaching the concrete runway at a little over seventy knots, which is a tad over eighty miles an hour.

While each plane has its own unique characteristics, the basics of flight is easy for anyone to understand. Even taking off is a breeze once you get up to speed and lift off the runway. Landing is a different matter altogether. There's a "feel" to it that can only be learned by experience. And in that, I have none. Simulators are well and good, but actual landings are the only experience that matters.

My rate of descent is too steep, and I slam onto the deck like I'm an F-14 pilot trying to catch the first arresting wire. The C-130 does not approve of this, and the port landing gear strut snaps off. That shifting of weight and stress causes the right to follow shortly thereafter, but not before putting the plane into a spin—and the nose gear shears off.

All we can do is hang on as the plane skids along the length of the runway in a slow spin before we finally run out of road and into the soft, damp earth. Jerking to a stop, I quickly look out both sides and check to see if the engines are on fire. I'm relieved to see they are not and hit the switch for the intercom.

"This is your captain speaking. We have successfully come to a stop. If you will, please exit the plane in a calm and orderly fashion before we catch fire and then explode. Thank you."

"Are you serious?" Captain Hayes sounds freaked.

"No," I state with a chuckle. "But take command and get everyone funneled out and away while I shut everything down."

"Yes sir."

Clambering out of the chair, she's gone in a flash, and I can hear the door open as she orders everyone to leave the plane. I start shutting everything down, killing the power to help prevent any kind of electrical fire from starting. We have far too many important supplies to have them go up in smoke.

Once that is complete, I exit the plane to see Chloe running my direction, with a number of people in tow. There are a couple fire extinguishers being carried, as well. As I watch my lady, she runs full bore before flinging herself at me.

I can't help but grunt and stagger back as her limbs wrap around me while I struggle to remain standing. Holding her tightly, I kiss her hair and physically let her know that I'm here and safe. I can only imagine the horrible thoughts that must have been going through her mind as I skidded across the runway.

"Hey, it's okay," I whisper softly. "I'm right here. I'm okay."

Pulling her head back to look at me, she drops her feet to the ground and then punches me square in the jaw. Second time this week. I'm on a roll. Shaking my head, we can't help but grin stupidly at each other, her eyes wet with unshed tears.

"Don't you dare think that just because I've got this damn grin that I'm not pissed at you. Don't ever scare me like that again!"

Ignoring the pain from my jaw, I gently grab both sides or her face and kiss her eyes, kissing away her tears in the process. Then, I bring my lips to hers and we stand there, people rushing all around us, and kiss passionately.

When we finally come up for air, I look her dead in the eyes. "I love you, Chloe. Not even death has kept me from you. Don't ever forget that."

"Okay, fine. You're forgiven," she nods breathlessly. "Come on, let's get away from this plane just in case it blows up from you plowing it into the runway."

"Hey now!" I'm quite hurt over the comment. "I think for my first landing that was pretty good."

Looking back, the poor aircraft is lying nose first into the soft, damp earth. The landing gear are scattered along the length of the runway, shiny bits of metal and debris littering the length. The propellers on one

127

engine are bent and useless. At least there's no smoke or fire. I don't see any leaking fuel either.

Chloe looks at the same damage before shooting me a wry grin. "Yeah, looks like an amazing landing."

"Woman," I growl just loud enough for her to hear. "Get us home so I can see our daughter and then make good on a promise that is long overdue."

Fire dances in my lady's eyes as she presses her body up against me and purrs. The animal side of me wants to rip her clothes off and take her right here on the runway. Instead of shocking everyone around us, she grabs my hand and leads me across the runway to where Truck sits by the field office.

Chapter Thirty

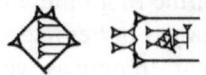

Introducing these people into a new culture has taken some time. Doc, for instance, had to meet the new medical personnel and be reassured that nobody was taking over and that he now has new resources. His gruffness and irritability aside, I think he's happy for the help. In fact, I think he's going to try to weasel back into his veterinarian job now that we have more experienced people on hand. I wouldn't blame him one bit.

Pete is much improved from the last time I saw him a few days ago. He and Beast are better friends than I realized. When we entered his room, the pilot's face split in a grin when he saw who I had with me. I must say, I'd never seen my man with a friendly expression on his face for anyone but me before this. It was a new experience, and I greatly enjoyed it.

Mike and Liz already have places for everyone to stay, not that I've seen Liz at all since landing. They'd been charged with finding room for at least a hundred and fifty people, so they've had their hands full figuring out where everyone could go until we get things more organized. From what we understand, they have places in Crested Butte, Gunnison and, of course, our enclave near the bunker.

Decisions needed to be made about who would stay in town and who would come out to the enclave. I reassured Lieutenant Hayes that we had several mobile homes available, as well as a few barracks buildings we'd put in for newcomers a few months ago. They're just shipping containers with bunks and some kind of heating. They are buried in dirt on three sides for insulation. While it's not much, it's better than nothing. When you've been on the road for a while, a place like that feels like a fortress of safety. Many people were grateful, and I got the distinct impression that they were going to be happy so long as they were where Beast was.

Finally we are able to disentangle ourselves from all of the people that need our attention, and we've figured out who goes where. Beast and I are going home. I get word from Mike that Liz has moved to a place in Crested Butte, and though I am saddened, I accept her decision.

Once Beast is in, I start up Truck and drive out, heading towards the bunker. A part of me still can't believe he's here, that he's with me and about to see our daughter for the first time. I can't help but wonder what he will notice first. Her blue eyes or her happy smile? Unbridled joy swells in my chest, growing in strength as we get closer to our destination.

He starts laughing and I shoot him a quick, curious glance. "What?"

"Baby," he says to me with a warm, loving smile. "For someone who said she is not good at being a leader, you seem to be doing a rather fantastic job at it."

I feel my cheeks heat at his praise. "I had to figure it out. You weren't here. The problem is, I find I don't like being around a lot of people anymore. Maybe it's a side effect of the Collapse, or maybe I was hanging around with you too long."

"It happens," he states mournfully. "It's hard to get close to people after losing so many. And the more you lose, the harder it gets."

"Is that why you can't stand being around people?"

My mind is reeling over this conversation. I can hardly believe he's being so open with me, talking so freely. I guess death really does change a man.

"That's part of it." He nods slightly. "When Anna and Katie were murdered, I lost a good portion of my humanity. Everyone calls me Beast for a reason, and that's because I became an animal."

"You're no animal," I exclaim. "Stone cold killer of bad men? Sure. But, you aren't an animal. Well, except in bed."

Beast shoots me a lascivious grin that makes me breathless. Then, on purpose, he licks his lips like a wolf about to eat a meal. The lower half of my body warms in a rather pleasant way as I think about what I'd like that tongue to be doing. Instead, I focus on driving before I get us both killed and ruin the promise he's given me.

Fortunately, our destination is just up ahead, and I pull off the road. As we get closer, he sees the half-dozen small homes that we've parked and/or built around the bunker entrance. At the sight of it, he looks at me curiously.

"You put structures at the bunker site?"

"Yeah," I reply with a grin. "I towed and parked one of the small homes damn near right over it. That way it stays hidden. Our place, this valley, it's been named The Enclave."

"Very good idea, my lady. You continue to amaze me."

I can't help but beam a smile at him in return of the proud tone in his compliment. God, I love this man. I can't think of a single time when he has not had my back and kept driving me to be better. He's always making me feel like my input matters.

130

Stopping Truck, we get out and I wave at those who are nearby. Already, Nena is coming out of the house that camouflages the bunker entrance. A very unhappy Leah is crying up a storm in her arms, and I rush up, taking my daughter carefully. I am so sorry to see her crying this way, I hold her tightly to me and rock her.

"Hey, my beautiful girl," I croon. "It's okay. Mommy's here."

My sweet girl quiets almost instantly and looks up at me, still hiccoughing, with wet, blue eyes. A smile forms and she wiggles in my embrace. I can't help but laugh as Beast comes up beside me to take his first look at our bundle of joy.

"Leah," I state softly, "meet daddy."

Our baby girl looks up with wide eyes, utterly silent. I wrap her in her blanket more securely and carefully hand her to him. Leah has an adorable look of shocked amazement as Beast cradles her in his arms. He has such a lovely, fatherly smile. I can't help but be overjoyed at the scene as he rubs his nose against hers. Leah giggles and plays with his beard, making him laugh. This moment makes everything I've gone through completely worth it.

Nena looks just as happy as I am. "And, all is right with the world. The child has both her parents, and the bond of love is restored."

"You knew this would happen?" I can't hide the shock in my voice.

"Of course I did," she replies seriously.

"Why didn't you tell me?"

Nena shakes her head. "I did, but you could not hear me. Some miracles can only be believed when we experience them."

She has a point. When Dan put the revolver in my hand, I couldn't believe that Beast was alive. Even when Pete delivered his message, there was still a part of me that could not believe it was true. It was such an impossibility. Yet here I am, blessed with the most impossible of miracles. My only wish granted.

"Beast," I call out to him. "I'd like you to meet Nena."

Tearing his gaze from our daughter, he carries Leah over with a brilliant smile gracing his face. "Hello, Nena."

"Good day, Beast," she replies with a sure voice. "I am so happy for Angel that you have been returned to us."

My man doesn't seem to be affected by the cryptic nature of her words. In fact, they share the same kind of smile. As if they know something I don't. I'm left wondering what knowledge he gleaned in being resurrected?

"Well, Nena, if you do not mind, I'd like to take my wife downstairs and get some much needed rest."

Wife? I swoon.

131

"Of course." She kisses Leah once more, then exits to go to her home next door to ours.

While holding Leah, cradled carefully in one arm, he offers his other to me. My daughter and I giggle simultaneously. While I want to wonder just what kind of a connection she and I seem to share, I'm too enraptured with *my husband* as we make our way into the bunker. While father and daughter get acquainted, I rush into the bedroom and quickly rip the current sheets off the bed. In the closet, I find the dark maroon, satin sheets that have never been used and slip them on. Already, anticipation spikes in my blood stream as I feel the soft, silky texture against my fingers.

As I finish making the bed, soft, dulcet tones of a classical piece drift through the air. Then, I begin to hear Leah giggling up a storm. I can't help my curiosity and silently move up to the doorway and take a peek. What I see fills my heart with such joy.

Beast has her firmly cradled on one arm, her hand clutching a finger of his other hand as he leads her around the living room in a waltz. Our daughter giggles and smiles at her loving father as they dance in circles. He spins her around and makes her squeal. When she does, he laughs back at her, and it's all such a lovely sound.

I can't help but compare her immediate adoration of her father to her rejection of Liz. I sigh and shake of that depressing thought, hoping, for the last time, that Liz will be okay. I turn my thoughts instead to the perfect picture before me.

Carefully, I join in the dance. Beast and I hold her gently between us as we continue to waltz about the living room. When Leah giggle-yawns, that's our cue telling us that she's ready for bed. It's been an exciting day for her, after all. Mommy came back and brought daddy with her. Way too much excitement for such a little one.

"Here, let me take her. I need to feed her, and then you can burp her."

He's surprised, but he hands our daughter over and we settle into a rocking chair I traded for in Gunnison. Beast is transfixed by the sight of me nursing our baby, but soon he excuses himself to the bathroom for a while. When he comes out he's freshly washed, and I am done with Leah, so I hand her to him.

Making sure to keep a firm hold, Beast drapes her sleepy form over his shoulder and pats gently on her back until the air bubbles are gone. Then, he carries her over to the crib and lays our little angel down. She yawns once more, letting out a little squeak of happiness. I join him at the side of the crib, smiling down at her. Beast stuns me into silence when he starts singing to Leah.

My Beast can sing? Yes, he can, and it is a beautiful, rich baritone.

132

Goodnight, my angel
Time to close your eyes
And save these questions for another day
I think I know what you've been asking me
I think you know what I've been trying to say
I promised I would never leave you
And you should always know
Wherever you may go,
No matter where you are
I never will be far away
Goodnight my angel,
Now it's time to sleep
And still so many things I want to say
Remember all the songs you sang for me
When we went sailing on an emerald bay
And like a boat out on the ocean
I'm rocking you to sleep
The water's dark
And deep, inside this ancient heart
You'll always be a part of me
Goodnight my angel,
Now it's time to dream
And dream how wonderful your life will be
Someday your child may cry,
And if you sing this lullaby
Then in your heart
There will always be a part of me
Someday, we'll all be gone
But lullabies go on and on...
They never die
That's how you
And I
Will be.*

And just like that, our daughter is sound asleep, and I've fallen for
Beast all over again. I know he had a daughter before, but I'm still
surprised by his tenderness with ours. My poor Beast had lost so much
when they were murdered.

When he turns and looks at me, the air leaves my lungs. Even with the
mask, he looks like a man on a mission. Taking my hand, he leads me
into the bedroom, and my pulse begins racing through my veins.

* Lullaby by Billy Joel

Chapter Thirty-One

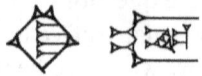

Once we are in the bedroom, Beast closes the door softly. Turning to face me, he looks at me like I'm his sole reason for living. I feel treasured and safe as he presses his body against mine, folding me into his warm embrace. I've been subjected to a roller-coaster of emotions in the past few days that the tears begin to flow. Again. How can I help it?

I hug him back fiercely, never wanting to let go. A part of me still dreads that this has all been just a dream, and I'll wake up alone again. I silently offer a prayer of thanks to the heavens for this miracle. For giving him back to me. I don't know how I have managed without him.

"Hey, beautiful," he whispers softly. "It's okay."

I look up with wet eyes. "It's been awful. I hope you know that. I mean, not *all* of it, and I'm not trying to blame you. There's Leah, and I had Liz, but I wanted you so much. And I really wanted to die. But I promised you, and there was Leah to think of." I give a teary laugh. "I've, I've *dreamed* this. You being here, and I want to trust it, for it to be real. But I'm so afraid."

Instead of saying anything, he kisses me passionately. I hold on tightly while fisting one hand into his hair, making him growl, low and deep. Oh, how I love that sound. My heart stutters as his tongue wiggles into my mouth and enters into a dance with mine.

When our lips finally part, I'm breathless. Blue eyes gaze at me hungrily as he continues to hold me. It feels like he is drinking me in. Like every line and detail of me is being burned into his mind. Yet again, I feel like I'm being worshipped by this man.

"I have a surprise for you," he speaks softly.

My heart is racing. "I know. I've been waiting for it."

With a lascivious grin, he walks over to the bed and reaches under the overhanging at the foot of it. I hear a latch click, and then he pulls the bed up to reveal a number of toys—a LOT of toys.

All this time, I had no idea that there was a storage area under the bed. My heart is now going like a galloping race horse as he pulls out a black, eyeless mask, a flogger and two pairs of leather cuffs before putting the bed back down.

Holy shit! My mouth drops open.

"Just what do you plan to do with those?"

Beast advances toward me like he's stalking prey and my breathing runs ragged as I swallow. While we played with handcuffs a little, this is something totally new. While he can be quite the animal, I never pictured him as a dominant. Not that I mind it. Just the idea is sending all kinds of erotic thoughts flashing through my head.

"I plan on tying your hands to the bed, putting this mask over your eyes, and then pleasuring you to the best of my ability. With your consent, of course."

My brain stops, and I can't formulate a response. All I can do is nod. His irresistible grin sends my pulse skyrocketing as he reaches out and takes my hand, leading me to the bed. This promise has been a long time coming, and right now, I feel a little lightheaded as heat flushes through my body.

"First things first," he says with a provocative smile. "We need to divest you of all this clothing."

Nope, still can't talk. I nod once more, my eyes fixated on his.

I'm facing a side of Beast I've never met before, and I love it. When it's come to sex, either he's been a wild animal, ravaging me with sweet, savage abandon. Or, there's the soft side of him, loving me slowly until we finally unravel in each other's arms. This change is so invigorating.

At a leisurely pace, my man undresses me. He slowly pulls down the zipper of my jumpsuit, my skin is unveiled, and he delivers soft kisses upon me. Oh, he's teasing me mercilessly, making me moan and whimper as my flight suit finally slides down my legs and pools at my feet.

I stand before him in just my bra and panties. My hands cover my belly, more importantly, my stretch marks. I still can't believe he hasn't said anything. Surely he's noticed the changes my body has been through? Without surgery, my career in my old life would have been over. So, every time I look in the mirror, that's all I can see. It makes me feel shy in front of him.

"Step towards me, my lady."

Trying to put my shyness aside, I do as I'm bidden. Taking my hands, he guides me as I step out of the clothing at my feet. The anticipation is driving me crazy as he continues to smile enticingly at me. Holding up the mask, he makes his next move quite clear to me, and I nod.

In all the times we've made love, I've come to realize that consent is important to him. Right now, it's even more so, because we are about to enter into some bondage, and it's critical that both lovers are on the same page. While I trust this man with my life, I still feel cherished because he seeks my consent in this.

When the mask slides over my eyes, my breathing spikes. You don't know how erotic this is until you try it, preferably with someone you trust. All your other senses are amplified in an effort to make up for the loss of sight. When his body presses against mine and his hands grab my ass, I whimper.

"Do you trust me, my lady?"

"Always."

His lips touch my neck and I moan as he sucks and bites gently while holding me against him. Beast is so much taller than myself, and I feel enveloped by his body as he worships me. I can't help but gasp when he picks me up and lays me on the satin sheets.

Once again, I want to cover my nakedness, especially my still-jiggly stomach, but he doesn't let me. Instead, his fingers roam up and down my body, all while delivering little kisses that leave me awash with desire, wanting more. When his lips wander back up to my ear, he whispers hotly.

"Give me a safe word, my precious Chloe."

The word "precious" reverberates through my head over and over. "Precious," I whisper hoarsely.

I swear I can feel his smile against my neck. "Good choice. Now lie still."

A whimper escapes me as he takes my trembling arm and gently fastens the first leather cuff on me. My mind races, wondering what he will do to me as I hear him clasp the cuff to the bedpost.

I tug softly to discover my limits. Then he clasps my other arm, my wrists straining against soft leather as I tremble on the soft sheets with need.

"Oh, please," I cry out.

He growls close to my ear, making me squirm. "All in due time, my lady."

I pull against the restraints, wanting to feel his touch. Then, I freeze as I feel the soft suede strands on the flogger dragging across my skin. As they dance along my body, it sends little arcs of electricity through me. I sigh, then moan, as the flogger skates over my breasts and belly, hips and thighs. My breath catches when he drags it back up my pussy.

"Do you have any idea how amazingly sexy you are?" His voice is hoarse, telling me that he wants me badly. *Oh, yes.*

"Beast, please!" I cry out. "I want you!"

Taking me by surprise, his lips are close to my ear and he whispers hotly. "And I want you, my lady. To cum over and over and over again. I think it's time we started with that."

The flogger is replaced by his lips and his hair. As he rains kisses upon my body, his hair and beard provide extra sources of stimulation. Slowly, ever so slowly, he trails down my throat and across my breasts, worshiping me as he goes.

Anticipation builds as he inches closer and closer to his ultimate goal. I'm writhing with need, panting as I flex my hips in an effort to get him closer. Settling between my legs, Beast prolongs the torture by kissing the insides of my thighs. When he slides two fingers inside me, I can't help but gasp. As that wonderful tongue is unleashed, my body damn near launches off the bed. *Oh fuck!*

Oh, that tongue! I can feel every bit of it as he swirls it around, flicks and he even sucks on me. My sweet torture doesn't last long. My insides begin to tighten and I know he's aware of it. His hands snake around and grasp my hips, holding me down. I want to slip my hands into his hair, hold him to me, but I'm cuffed to the bed. That adds another desperate layer to the desire I already feel.

I pant and quake, and when I can't hold back any longer, I explode, my body lifting off the bed. Once again, he wrings a draining orgasm from me that is so powerful, I can barely even register the sound of my own ecstatic screams as the world disappears.

Chapter Thirty-Two

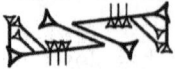

Chloe lies in my arms, both of our bodies sweaty from the exertion of our lovemaking. Her head rests on my chest as our breathing begins to match. I run my fingers through her hair, making her purr as she dances a fingernail along my chest.

It certainly was nice to deliver my promise. By the time we finally climaxed together, I had drawn six, beautiful orgasms out of her. There's no greater a spectacle than watching my lady cum, that sweet voice filling the air. *Goddess, I love this woman.*

One moment of hilarity came when Chloe's cries of passion woke our daughter. Our daughter! I still can't believe it. She is so tiny, so perfect. When Leah woke, I left my lovely woman tied to the bed and comforted our sleepy girl until she fell back to sleep. Meanwhile, her mother giggled helplessly, trying to loosen herself. Unsuccessfully, I might add. While my wife was slightly annoyed, I made it up to her with my tongue.

We've come a long way to be in this spot, both figuratively and literally. We both had to endure so much pain and anguish. I'm grateful to be here now and have her in my arms, but am admittedly a bit miffed over the fact that I could not be here to see my daughter born. In hindsight, maybe that's not such a bad thing. I remember how I was with my first wife. A total fucking mess. That's the problem with being medically trained. Everything that could go wrong in a pregnancy is like a checklist in your head. I'm sure I would have driven Chloe absolutely nuts—and not in the good way.

Maybe my death and our brief separation did do some good. She was here, safe and sound, though admittedly suffering. I can only imagine that had I been here, we would have gone looking for bandits that needed killing. She has told me that she did while I wasn't here, I can only imagine how much more we would have done before realizing she was pregnant. Keeping her safe meant keeping the baby safe. Leaving her behind while I went to hunt raiders alone would have been a mistake, as well.

Am I being petty in not admitting my Goddess was right?

My tattoo tingles, and I get the feeling that's supposed to be a yes. With a sigh, I kiss the top of Chloe's head, and she snuggles tightly against me and lets out a contented sigh. Smiling warmly, I crane my head a little closer.

"I love you," I whisper softly.

She looks up at me, her softened expression showing nothing but joy. "I love you more."

In a way, this relationship is still new for the both of us. While saying those three words to her, and showing it with one's actions are something one does every day, it still has an extra special impact at the beginning of the relationship. When you tell her that you love her, you can see her heart melt in her eyes as she looks at you with such wonder as would move a man of stone.

"Can I ask you a question?" Her voice is soft, and full of concern.

"Of course."

The expression on her face worries me. There's indecision in her eyes. With everything my baby has been through, indecision is not something she does much of anymore. She's become damn near as fearless as myself.

"I, well," she sighs. "I... my body. I mean, it changed a lot after Leah. Am I... do you honestly still think I'm beautiful? Or do you just- just call me that to make me feel better?"

When you hear a question like this from a woman, you know there's something wrong. Such a situation requires tact and understanding. Don't ever leave a woman hanging when she asks you something like this. She's seeking reassurance, and she needs to be loved.

"Oh, Chloe," I exclaim. "Of course you're beautiful! Why would you think otherwise?"

She looks away from me, appearing ashamed. "The pregnancy changed me. I've got stretch marks. My boobs are already sagging. I'm- I'm not the same, Beast. And I... sometimes I feel ugly."

Oh, hell no!

Putting two fingers under her chin, I lift her eyes up to mine. I give her the most serious expression I can muster, because, right now, I'm fighting a demon. This is a demon inside her head and it needs to be vanquished. My lady should never, ever feel the way she does right now. And I'll be damned if I'm not going to do my best to slay it.

"You are the most beautiful woman in the world. To me, you are magic and make miracles happen. Our daughter is a testament to that. What I see when I look at you is the most perfect, golden angel on the face of the earth. I love you, not only for how you look to me, but for who you are as a person. Your tenacity, intelligence and even sense of humor are all part of what make you attractive. If anyone is ugly, it's me. Don't you ever forget that."

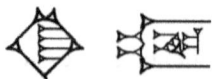

There is not a hint of guile in Beast's eyes as he tells me that I'm beautiful, only certainty. All my new flaws don't seem to matter to him at all. I do believe him, but I still don't like the jiggly bits. Of course, it's not like I could invest in plastic surgery, even if I wanted to, which I don't. I have to think about this.

My husband sees my thoughtful expression and strokes my hair, holding me loosely to him. As a younger, attractive woman, I never gave it much thought, to be honest. I worked out, sure, and enjoyed the body God gave me. I had a career that hinged on my looks and flexibility, in more ways than one.

But did I ever once imagine what it would be like to not be at the top of my game? Well, sort of. I imagined I would "lose my looks," whatever that means, and would gracefully retire to a pilot's life. Very glamorous, right? Of course, the Collapse halted that life for good. I doubt it will ever be back, to be honest. The only reason I have even the simplest luxuries is because my brilliant man thought ahead enough to invest in this bunker and land. Now, we're trying to build a civilization of sorts, and I wonder how well the values of that old life really fit into this new world.

A new feeling rushes through me. This civilization is what we make it. Why in hell would we base our values on something as shallow as looks? A jiggly belly from having a baby is the least of my worries. I am a strong woman, and I've been lucky enough to find like-minded individuals that have the same dream of peaceful civilization that my man and I do.

I do care how I look, I do. I'm still a creature born of the old world, but this really is the smallest of worries I could possibly have. My husband loves me how I am, for who I am. What more do I want or need? I'm not getting younger, and this is a hard new life. We're lucky to have the medical resources we have, the weapons and good people we have. Life has become much more valuable, and I'll be damned if I let the old world's esthetic ruin it for me.

Peace flows through me. My sense of shame, or whatever was infecting me since my daughter's birth, melts away, as I gaze into the blue eyes that see me as nothing but the angel he loves and adores.

"Oh Beast," I sigh and hug him tightly. "I love you."

"My lovely angel," he murmurs softly and kisses the top of my head.

Resting my head on his chest, I close my eyes and breathe in his scent. It's the best scent in the world and relaxes me like nothing else. My man loves me without question. I'm not only the luckiest, but also the happiest woman in the world. My smile lingers as I peacefully fall to sleep.

Chapter Thirty-Three

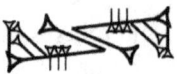

The morning comes too soon and brings its share of battles. Leah, however, is a joy. I'm finding she's rarely even fussy unless wet or hungry. My woman cares for her endlessly, as if she were an extension of her own body, which is impressive. She makes it look so easy, carrying Leah around in a body-wrap, sling kind of arrangement. Mother and child both seem utterly content with this.

But there is trouble in the Enclave, and it's partly my own fault. I had imagined everyone from the base coming and helping to build a civilization. What I hadn't realized is that Chloe, with the help of Mike and Liz, has already done that. She has fields ready and fields being planted, gardens already burgeoning with life, and now dozens and dozens of extraneous personnel from Nellis show up and try to take over.

With a little effort, we manage to cool the hot heads in the group and give everyone a job. I send teams of airmen out to search for more mobile homes and trailers so we can put them up nearby to house the extra numbers comfortably. A couple of the locals go with them to help locate what they need.

Chloe and I meet with all the managers and figure out what needs to be done first, and we send the rest of the airmen to work on that. I even send some of the middle school kids out to help with the planting; they're going to need to pull their weight, too. The little school Chloe had set up is nowhere near the size of what we're going to need now.

In the afternoon of the first day, I came upon Chloe and Liz in the middle of an argument. Liz was looming over my woman and the beast in me took over. I strode over and pushed Liz off my lady before I knew I'd done it. Chloe shouted at me to back off and took off after Liz, leaving me standing there feeling like an ass.

Later, Chloe told me it pretty much broke the tenuous and strained relationship she and Liz had once Chloe had learned I was still alive. Poor woman. I can really feel for her, because I can imagine only too well how I would feel if Chloe left me for someone she'd known in her former life.

But, for the most part, things seem to be working well. The Enclave is well designed with the wall and moat, the guards and defenses, the planting fields and gardens. My woman is better at this than she realizes, though she brushes it off and says she got all of the ideas from the books in the shelter. I still think she is a miracle, and my heart feels light because the work I thought we had ahead of us is already half done.

As I oversee the work going on, the one thing I do notice is that there's no more of the stupid, old world issues. We've got a group of human beings working together, and skin color no longer matters. The only thing that matters is survival. Each day is filled with faces who have become one big family.

My nights are glorious, though we have learned we have to hold down the noise or our daughter wants to join in the screaming and yelling. There is a lot of muffling of sounds with pillows and laughing, and overall, I couldn't be a happier man.

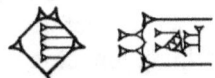

Beast has been back a week, and already I feel the weight of the burden lifting from my shoulders. Oh, he hasn't taken over for me, but now, with his help, it's like ten times as much is getting done that needed doing. I suppose all the airmen are part of that. We have a lot more manpower now, and he knows how to keep them busy.

The farmers and other refugees that have made this valley their home see how busy the airmen are, and I think they feel challenged, because now they're also working twice as hard! The people from Green Valley were happy to see Beast and cheered upon seeing him. That made him uncomfortable, but he greeted them anyway—especially Dan, who was near to tears at shaking hands with him.

Leah loves her father. She always reaches for him as soon as she sees him, and he delights in her company. It warms my heart. How sweetly it soothes the pain of the last year. Every time I see them together, their resemblance is more apparent, and I love it. Nena is still there for us so we can have some alone time now and then, but Liz has distanced herself.

Liz. Liz. What could I have done differently for her? I care about her still, want her to be happy, but not at the expense of my own heart. I see her watching my Beast sometimes with such loathing. I wish he hadn't intervened that time I'd finally gotten her to talk to me. I thought I'd been making progress, softening her to him, and then he came in all protective of me, and Liz was gone.

She won't speak to me at all anymore and keeps to herself in Crested Butte most of the time. I worry for her, I don't want her to hurt herself— or anyone else. But there is an anger now that I've never seen in her before. I don't know what to do about it, though Beast and Nena both have told me this is her life to live, and she has to choose whether to live in anger or in love and forgiveness. I know Liz has a good heart, I just hope she listens to that side and not the rage.

Part of me is actually relieved that I don't have to continue to try. I honestly hadn't realized how much work I had put into loving her, when it should be easy and effortless, the way it is with Beast. That, too, makes me sad. I hope she finds love or a purpose of some sort soon; I worry about her.

Our valley is blooming with life. We have a better schoolhouse now, made from a prefab home the airmen put up. There's a boy I want to talk to Beast about. His name is Jimmy, and he was on Beast's plane with him. I guess Beast pulled him aboard before leaving the base.

Captain Hayes has been helping him along, but he needs more. He has been through a lot. He was captured by the Reverend's men when they killed most of his family, but they kept him and his mother as their playthings. He fled them when his mother died. I shudder to think what's happened to him.

I have thought long and hard, and my heart tells me we need him in our family. I want to adopt him. I think Beast will feel the same way. Jimmy needs a good role model like Beast to help him fight those dark battles that I know will be ahead of him.

Each day, I see a lot more work ahead, but every day has been a joy, challenging or not. Every night I sleep in the arms of my man with our baby girl in the next room. Every day is full of work and laughter and so much wonder at what a few good men and women put to good work can accomplish. I have a lot of hope for the future now. As I snuggle into Beast's arms at night, I feel happy and content.

He's told me how he came back, and I can't help but believe. He was dead. I know dead, and he was definitely gone. How do I believe in something like this, though? I was raised Catholic! But, as they say, you can't argue with results, and the result is here with me, working by my side every day. If the facts have changed, I must change my thinking to reflect that reality.

Who could have imagined miracles were real? Not me, even after the birth of my beautiful daughter. That was wonderful and miraculous, but in an everyday human being kind of way. This? A whole other ball game.

I also can't help but remember the missing body at the travel center. Besides Beast's, I mean. I almost want to go back to reconfirm, but we're too busy for that. Its spring and there is too much to do. Still, it sends an unsettled feeling through me whenever I remember that Kane's body was gone.

When that happens, I take a good long look at my husband and my daughter, and walk out my door to see the civilization we're building, and I feel much better. There is a saying: living well is the best revenge. That will have to do.

Epilogue

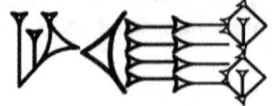

I limp away from the burning wreckage of Nellis Air Force Base with the help of some of my followers. I must have lost at least half my flock when all the explosives went off around the base. To make matters worse, those devils in uniform got away in two planes. Possibly the last two working planes in existence.

What a fucking mess!

Limping into the living room of a nearby abandoned house, two men set me down on the couch. With a groan, I lean back and close my eyes, trying to will away the pain of my burns and scrapes.

"Father Roberts. What are we gonna do?"

That's William, one of the youngest of my flock. The blonde-haired boy had been in prison for simply having a bag of marijuana. Locked in a jail with vicious, hardened criminals for something as simple as that. The old world was corrupt and decadent, run by faithless politicians that bound the people to them with greed and wickedness.

"I have communed with the Lord," I tell him consolingly. "We will have an angel sent to us. Just be patient."

"Yes, father," William replies. "Can I get you anything?"

I exhale painfully. "See if Doc Amos survived, please? I need attention."

"Yes, father."

William runs out of the house after the doctor, and I lay my head back and close my eyes once more. *Dear Lord, please send me an angel of vengeance to do Your will. Our reward has been robbed from us. We can no longer escape to the Promised Land as You told me. My flock needs Your help more than ever. Your will be done, amen.*

There are no words to describe the righteous anger that surges through me. The aircraft there and the crews were supposed to get my flock to the fertile fields of Denver. Fertile fields for growing crops, plenty of running water and a huge city to scavenge supplies from. We'd have everything we need to start a new community run by God's will.

Instead, we were stopped by a devil in a white mask. White mask!? Only the devil would be so bold as to stop God's plans while pretending to be the Lone Ranger! Such a heretic should be burned at the stake for his insolence.

While I know my Lord is supposed to handle any revenge, I feel a burning need for it, so it must be a righteous need. So many of my flock have perished at the hands of those devils from the old world. Corrupt men and woman keeping me from doing my Lord's will. I want to punish them personally, to hear them scream in torment as I lash them with the rod. I find myself praying for that opportunity, sinful though it may be.

Now, I am at a loss. I know the Lord is on our side, yet still we failed. The food and water we needed to survive was destroyed with the base. The transportation. The weapons. It's all gone. I doubt we will find anything of any use after the explosions. If they had the sense to booby trap the base, then clearly they were doing it to deny us that which we needed.

Bastards!

Brother Fred brings me a canteen of water, for which I am grateful. I give him a smile, but I have no kind words. I am so angry that were I to speak, nothing gracious would flow from my mouth. Unscrewing the cap, I take a long drink of cool water.

Water. There is still snow on the ground. We must begin collecting it at once. We will need all the water we can collect. Somehow, we must also scrounge up transportation. The road to Denver will be long and difficult. Who knows what bandits and devils may lie in wait on our path. Still, we must strive to do our best, as God has intended.

"Father Roberts," William yells from outside as he comes running in. "There is a man here to see you. He says you asked for him."

I look up at the child, confused. "You mean Doc Amos?"

"No sir." He shakes his head vigorously. "I don't- I don't recognize him." William is shaken.

Now I am confused. Who could this possibly be? I have asked for no one, save the doctor to check my wounds. Of course, I need reports confirming how many we have lost and what supplies we have remaining. But it's too soon for that information to have been compiled, given the chaos of the base's destruction.

"Send him in," I state tiredly.

Readying my trusty Colt 1911, I make sure a round is in the chamber and the hammer is cocked. I am a man of God, but I haven't survived this long by being stupid. I slide the pistol between two cushions, hidden but within easy reach should I need to shoot this stranger. Brother Fred sees my actions and makes sure his rifle is ready, as well.

147

William is right. I do not recognize the man that is brought before me. Bald, muscular, and with a hard edge. This man must be in his forties, but the way he carries himself, you'd think he was much younger.

"Father Roberts," he states respectfully and bows. "You asked for me."

I shake my head. "How could I ask for you when I do not know you?"

For some reason, I am nervous. Something doesn't feel right, and I slowly slide my hand down between the cushions. The feel of wood grips, and the steel is comforting in my palm as he looks at me and smiles.

"Of course you do not know me. But you asked God to send you an angel of vengeance. So here I am, as you asked, ready and willing to do your bidding."

All the air leaves my lungs, my eyes widen as he gives words to my inner thoughts just moments ago. No one could know them except me and the Almighty himself. How could this man know... unless he is what he says he is?

"How...?"

"You will not have need of your pistol with me," the stranger remarks with a warm smile. "I am your servant, sent by God himself. You and your flock have been wronged, and I am here to help see your plan to fruition; even help you get revenge on the devil who denied you that which you so desperately needed."

I am stunned, awestruck even, at the miracle that stands before me. Clearly, the Lord does work in mysterious ways. Slowly, I smile. I had not thought I could do that again after the treachery that has befallen us.

"Yes," I reply with a shaky voice. "We are in need of salvation. Everything we needed was just ripped from our grasp when we were so close. A devil in a white mask murdered many of my children."

This man, no, this angel, smiles the kind of smile that tells me we will have our vengeance. Without words, it speaks volumes about how we will cut out that heart of evil and burn it from this world, a world that shall belong only to the righteous who follow me.

"That is what I am here for, father. I can help you and your flock seek vengeance upon thine enemy for their heresy. You will fall upon them and deliver the Lord's will, smite them with bullet, arrow and rock if need be. You shall purge them with fire. You shall wipe the land free of their pestilence. And when that is done, you will find yourselves in paradise."

I drink in every word like it is sweet wine as he continues, holding up a finger. "And in that paradise, you will find they have women. Women which your flock will need to repopulate the Earth."

Brother Fred and William both grin lecherously. While I would normally preach against such sin, children are the future. Those women in league with the devil should be punished, yet will also be useful in rearing our future progeny. *Yes, so it shall be.*

"Thank you." I am breathless with the Lord's generosity. "What shall we call you?"

The man smiles wickedly. "Kane, father. You may call me Kane."

Fire

Chapter One

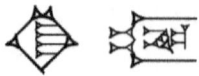

Another winter is behind us. The snows have finally melted, and it is a relief to be outside more often. This winter was perhaps only slightly as hard as the last, but this time we had the greenhouses all ready for the cold season, so we've had fresh vegetables. Nothing can beat a wonderful, ripe tomato soup on a cold winter night. And, I can testify that homemade tomato soup made by my man tastes a million times better than the canned stuff used to taste.

At first, I was worried about how long we could live in the bunker. My husband relieved my fears by teaching me all about our home. The solar power system, designed by Tesla, should last us at least two decades before starting to seriously fail. A ramada up the hill, across from the river, provides solar with a combination large panels and roof tiles that are also solar cells. It's all set up to look like a picnic area and not the power station for a hidden bunker.

This power is fed to nickel-iron batteries made by Iron Edison. According to him, they are far superior to lead acid and safer than lithium. Bonus is that they should last at least two decades, as well. Light bulbs are all LED, daylight rated, and they've got a life of roughly nine years minimum. On top of that, Beast has spare parts, bulbs and equipment for the critical things. The hope is that the bunker will outlive us and continue to protect our children long after we are gone.

Speaking of Beast, he and I have settled in together as if we'd never been apart. Yet, every day is a new miracle for me, because I can't ever take him for granted again. Leah is over a year old now. And Jimmy, sweet Jimmy. He's her best protector and favorite person in the world.

That poor boy moved in with us shortly after we got all the people from Nellis settled. He had constant nightmares as soon as he fell asleep. Beast and I were at his bedside most every night, soothing him every way we could imagine: songs, stories and simple rocking while he cried. Those bastards in Las Vegas used him in very bad ways.

I think the worst of it is behind him now. He rarely has those dreams anymore, but knows that if he's upset, we are right here for him. That's probably half the battle. And, he has Leah. Caring for her opened something up in him. He thought he was unworthy, unlovable and ruined. But we allowed him to help us with Leah, and when he saw our trust in him, he simply sat down and cried. He thought he was broken, but we trusted him with our precious daughter. Now, he is her biggest protector and is better than any big brother she could ever have had.

At only eight years old, he's already in fourth grade at our little school. Well ahead of any other kid his age. We couldn't be prouder if he was our own child. When school is out he rushes home to do homework and play with Leah. She recently said her first word, and it was Immy.

Beast has also taken the boy under his wing. Evidently, to my man, eight years old is an important age, because that is when you should start teaching children proper gun safety. This has included target shooting and hunting, to which Jimmy proudly brought home two rabbits. Or, at least, he was proud until learning how to clean them.

Today we're plowing the fields, so Beast is out there working with one of the tractors which we're still able to do, thanks to the ingenious efforts of some of our people. They figured out how to make diesel using plastic from landfills, among other things. We have a mining operation at the local dump to pull out enough plastics. You would not believe some of the stuff they've come up with. I still can't fathom how much people had in the old world that they just threw away. Our gain, I guess.

Right now, I'm on my way to a meeting with Mike and Captain Hayes—April—as she's told me to call her. She was not my number one fan at the beginning, but now that she's seen my husband and I together with our family, well, she understands there was never a real chance for her. She's okay and has been dating others on and off.

I've fed my daughter and am leaving her with Nena. Lovely, wonderful Nena, who always knows just when I need her. I so love that woman.

"Don't be late today, Angel. There is bad news." She states calmly while picking up my toddler and settling her on her shoulder to rock. Leah settles in and blinks at me.

"What? What do you mean?" Nena always knows before something happens, good or bad, but I have a chill building up inside me today.

"Don't waste time, hurry."

Shooing me out the door of her little house, I run toward the meeting place. It's one of the many tiny houses we found in a tiny-house village at Crested Butte. It's perfect for meetings, because we can't fit too many people inside at once, which is kind of the point. It sits right next to a trading post. Yes, a real trading post, where you have to trade for what you want.

That's an interesting story in itself. It's run by the Corrigan brothers. One of the brothers, Walt, was in the Air Force. He was stationed at

Nellis before the Collapse. The other, Barry, was living in Denver with his family, wife and two kids. They had been in Crested Butte on vacation when everything fell apart.

When we flew in from Nellis, Barry was helping Doc Calvo and discovered his brother on Beast's plane. It was quite a reunion. The two of them, with permission, started the trading post, and they built it out of logs they cleared themselves. It's one of our happier stories, considering all of the broken families and orphans we have now.

I arrive just as a truck comes barreling toward the gate. Screeching to a halt, two men leap out. The gate is open most days, but people know not to just drive on through because there's a lot of foot traffic. Some days, it takes too long to get through with a vehicle. One of the men spots me and hurries over to the meeting room as Mike and Captain Hayes are climbing the steps.

"Captain Hayes, Captain, um, Chloe, we've got news. And, it's bad." Of course it is. Just as Nena predicted. I need a drink. Is it too early for a drink?

"Come in and sit down, let's not freak everyone out, shall we?" I herd the two men in after Mike and April. Walking in myself, I close the door behind me. All the while, I'm trying to push down the feeling of dread that's welling up in my chest.

Chapter Two

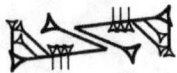

I'm just about finished with the field I'm working on when I spot a truck driving too fast on the main road toward the Enclave gate. *Shit.* Something's up, and I should be there. Finishing off the row, I turn the tractor over to my replacement who had been waiting at the end of the field. She's seen the truck too and anticipated that I'm going to need to be at headquarters. I toss her my gloves and take off toward the main camp.

Perhaps two handfuls of minutes later, I'm just getting my second wind and slow down so I don't worry anyone. I nod to people as I pass, noting that they are friendly, but still a little afraid of me. They know I'm the stick and Chloe and Captain Hayes are the carrots. I feel like the vice principal of a middle school sometimes, but at least it keeps most of them away from me, which is the way I like it.

They've taken to calling us "Founder." By that, I mean, Sir Founder and Lady or Madam Founder. It beats the hell out of me why they need us to have other names than just Beast and Chloe, but people are strange. At this point, it almost seems natural, so we've decided to just go with it. If they don't want to call me Beast, that doesn't mean they don't know who I am. I have a hard enough time keeping the animal side leashed with so many people around, which is why I enjoy my time out working the fields and other remote jobs. It feeds my need for solitude and everyone seems content with Chloe as the face of our team here, and Captain Hayes in Crested Butte.

As I approach the building we've been using for meetings, I get a prickle across my tattoo that I haven't felt in a while. Something is definitely up. I can't help but wonder if it has to do with Liz. My tattoo suddenly burns at the thought.

Liz disappeared at the end of last summer. We, at the Enclave, assumed she was in town, and the group at Crested Butte assumed she was out here. She didn't show up for a meeting and a full search began. She left no trace behind, just a pistol that Chloe had given her back when she'd been rescued. That told Chloe everything. Liz had found my presence and the loss of Chloe too difficult, and she'd moved on. Chloe has put word out that she wants any information anyone has, but no one has come forward.

I glance inside the window as I approach and see Chloe's shocked expression, telling me this does have something to do with Liz. I step up and open the door to see an entire collection of unhappy faces. Closing the door behind me, I stand in the already-crowded room, waiting to hear the news. Every head turns, but the only face I am locked onto is Chloe's. She has a look about her: anger, pain, determination. Somehow, I already know what's happening just from gazing at my lady's countenance, but I let them tell me anyway.

Mike takes a deep breath and relates the details. "We've got trouble, Sir Founder." *No shit, Mike.* "There is a horde of raiders, an army, heading here from Cortez, and we've got evidence that Liz is involved."

One of the two men hands me a tablet with a few dozen photos queued up. Looks like one of the UAV pilots, so I trust he hasn't shown this to anyone else. Those guys know how to keep their own counsel.

We knew we would have trouble with raiders as we got successful. So we brought all the remote UAV (drone) equipment from the Grand Junction National Guard depot to help keep an eye out. Funny thing is, it wasn't intentional.

We went to Grand Junction hoping to raid the depot, to pull out anything useful that we could find. Grand Junction had mostly survived the Collapse, but not without hardships. With the Colorado River flowing through it, they had water. Problem was that it was not as easily defendable as the Crested Butte valley was.

Raiders hit them constantly, stealing food and murdering people. The surviving population of a little over three hundred had dwindled down to seventy-nine. By the time we arrived, they were living in the depot area, growing food on the roof, and hand-pumping water from a well.

Initial talks were touchy to say the least, but we we're able to get them to realize that we were friendly and had a much better place to live. Our most convincing voice was Kim Thermopoli, an airman from Nellis who showed great promise on our special team, the Reapers. Somehow, that tiny woman was able to gain their confidence, and they let her in. After a few hours of talks, they were convinced.

So, we rounded everyone up, along with everything we could take and pulled them out. You, of course, know what I did with what little we had to leave behind. Oh yeah—boom.

Our drone pilots are Steven Cornell and Larry Sanlin. Their drone detachment was in Grand Junction assisting the DEA. While marijuana was legal in Colorado, farms operating without a license were not. The other two members of their team left when shit hit the fan, trying to get home to family. That left them with four drones—they insist they are UAVs, not drones—and no real reason to use them.

These guys are the best, though, and we have gotten loads of reconnaissance on small groups of raiders and refugees, as well as herds of elk and deer to help feed our people. Any attacking raiders have been turned back, unless they insisted on volunteering for our marksmen. The refugees are taken in, given some time to heal and rest, and are shown where they can settle. Then, we wait until they prove themselves before allowing free movement. The system has worked well enough so far, and now I am glad we've put this system in place.

I can see from the images that this army is at least a thousand strong, probably more. The force is on foot for the most part, but they're well organized. They certainly look like the typical raiders because of their makeshift armor. The unhappy faces of the only women and children, who are kept to the rear of the group, don't look like they are marching by choice. That certainly helps cement the judgment.

Their supplies and portable shelter appear to be transported by truck. There are teams that put it up each day and take it down each morning so as to keep the rest of the army on the march. Too organized for my liking. We have some close-ups of some of the leaders in the trucks. One of them is Liz, hanging on the arm of a man whose face I know too well. My tattoo burns, and I glance up at Chloe. She has fear in her eyes. It's Kane. The bandit leader in Phoenix who simply could not allow us to move on with our lives once we escaped him in Arizona. I look at her and she at me. We are thinking the same thing.

She killed Kane. He was the leader of that same team of Phoenix bandits that had ambushed us at the truck stop. He was the asshole responsible for killing me, and Chloe was very clear about how she gutted him with my sword. She shakes her head at me, begging me with her eyes not to mention it to these people, not until we've talked it over. Then, she nods at the tablet and I keep scrolling.

Aside from the two leaders we know too well, there is one more who is held in highest esteem. He's wearing a minister's collar, and must be the Reverend who led the raiders back in Vegas. So, like a cloud of locusts, they pillage Las Vegas, move on to take everything they can. And now they want the valley.

I realize a low growl is coming from me as I say in a low voice, "Over my dead body."

157

Chapter Three

Two hours later we are still in the meeting room. The two UAV-pilots have been sent back to their station with orders to keep this stuff classified, keep an eye on the incoming army and report back regularly. I also remind myself to access any overhead satellites later, just to see if I can spot anything that's been missed.

The meeting room has now turned into a command center. The shades are drawn, and we have maps and printed images from the tablets the pilots brought in. We're getting ready to have the yellow flags raised at all compounds, but are waiting for families to be together this evening to break the news.

We're not unprepared. Remember, more than half of our people were military, so we have more than a few surprises in case of such an emergency. I've taken my core security team from Nellis—with a few additions—and continued training throughout this past year. Taking them on sniper missions and training them in all kinds of weather, in ghillie suits, and even in water. I have a team I can trust to get in and out of situations with little to no detection. They may not be SEALs, but I think they'd still make my old team proud with as far as they've come.

Most of this meeting has been setting up our long-term and short-term strategies. We have a gauntlet along the roads from Montrose to Gunnison, and Liz knows nothing about that. Much as it pained Chloe to admit it, she knew Liz could be a key player should she go over to or be captured by hostile forces. So, we've prepared for that by planting some of the explosives we took from Nellis when we left. Among other things.

When we started making soap, the glycerin byproduct gave me ideas. After some consultation with the right people, we set up a soap-making operation, which is also an explosives lab with no one the wiser but those closely involved. Surprise, we can now make nitroglycerin, and thus, dynamite and gel explosives.

For safety, we have our mad chemists located at a distance from the rest of the camp, just in case. They're careful, of course, not wanting to blow themselves up, and they are ready to prepare what we need when we say go.

Our lead chemist is Mike Ruane. The man actually used to work for Dupont. With the pay he earned as a chemist, he not only bought land in the Crested Butte area, but was able to retire early. He was working as a part-time teacher for the school system when things went to hell.

In fact, it was his idea to make fertilizer bombs. The ammonium nitrate we need for this project has been fairly easy to come by, as well—farm supply stores, some of the instant cold-packs Nellis had and other sources. I don't believe Liz knew any of this before she disappeared. Call me paranoid, but I try to keep tactical knowledge compartmentalized to need-to-know only.

Thanks to all of this, we've identified key places we can set up ambushes, IEDs, and we are even ready to blow up bridges, though we really don't want to. While there is not much traffic from that direction, there are a small number of people living in Montrose, and we were able to talk them into relocating to Gunnison in an emergency. The promise of proper security alone made it an easy sell and, fortunately, they've already been radioed. We also have some farm homesteads that we are nurturing. As population expands, they will need that land further east. This is why we don't want to destroy the bridges.

Now, the meeting is winding down. We've discussed this to death and figure the Reverend's army can be here in less than a week. The last UAV report shows them marching out of Vernal, about seventy miles from Gunnison. That means we have a week at best. It's time to put the contingency plans into action. Immediately.

My lovely wife is looking a little frayed around the edges, and I want to get her away from this for a while so we can talk. I don't think she's going to like me very much, though. I see in her eyes that she knows what I am going to ask, but I can't tell how hard she is going to fight me.

"Okay, I think we've figured out our base plan. Let's go get the other command centers loaded up, and we'll—"

At that moment someone starts pounding on the door frantically. I frown and get up to answer it since I'm closest. It's one of the middle school kids, apparently on farm duty, because he's in one of the vests we make the kids wear when they're helping in the field. He looks terrified, but more frantic than scared.

"What?" I growl, a little more harshly than I intended.

The kid gulps and stammers out, "Mr., um Sir Founder, sir, Thomas got a blade in the foot, and they said I should get you 'cause you're medic-trained, and he's bleeding an awful lot, so please, um—"

By this point, I've already grabbed the medkit by the door and am out and running toward the fields. "Catch up, kid, you have to show me where he is!"

The kid sprints to catch me and then runs off in the direction I need to go. *Good. I was sick of that meeting anyway.*

Chapter Four

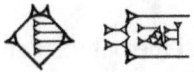

Beast thinks he's going to keep me here, I know it. I see that look, and he thinks I am going to fucking stay behind like a civilian. By god, if he thinks for one moment that I am willing to be some little woman and hide with the rest of them, he has got another think coming.

Don't get me wrong, I know he thinks he's doing the right thing. He'd still better come to the realization that we are far better together than apart, or I will fucking read him the riot act.

The damn meeting lasted too long, and now I won't get to have words until later tonight, if he gets back tonight. He might end up taking the hurt kid to the hospital in Crested Butte, and I don't know how long that will take. Or when he'll be back. *Fuck.*

I fume and go to pick up my daughter from Nena. It's clearly time to begin weaning her. She's already gone to one milk feeding a day, and is mostly on solid foods, so it won't be that bad. In the meantime, I need to take care of a few things, in case he thinks he can bully me.

"Your daughter is a jewel, Angel. You must wean her, though. It is time." Nena's soft voice confirms again what I was thinking, the way she always does. "She sleeps through the night now, yes?"

"Oh, yes, she's fine. In fact, I've been waking her to feed her, but she is losing interest. I think I'm done. It's going to be painful, isn't it?"

"Oh, not too bad. You've been taking the birth control?"

A few months ago, Nena had gotten hold of a few years' supply of birth control pills for me. Well, not just for me, but for any woman in our group that was ready to wean their child. I'd started taking them on her advice, so I give her a nod.

"The birth control pills will help. They've already slowed your supply. But I've also made you these." She holds up a bottle of grey-green capsules.

I look at them with a wrinkled brow. "What is this?"

"Nothing frightening, dear. It's dried sage. You are to take this three times a day. If your breasts are too engorged, pump, but not too much. It will be a little painful for a day or two, but you will be fine."

I take the capsules and hug Nena. She is like a mother to me after all this time, and I am so grateful to her for her help. "I love you, lady. Thank you for all you do."

Nena nods and pats me and the baby. "I am glad to be useful again. I am glad I knew to find you. And you are right, Angel. You and Sir Founder are far better together than apart."

I shake my head as I take Leah back home. That woman is too good at reading my mind. Or, whatever it is she does. But regardless, I trust her. I don't think I could do without her at this point. I'm also counting on her to care for my daughter while I fight the raiders at my man's side.

A few hours later, the yellow flags have gone up at the towns of Crested Butte, Gunnison and the Enclave. Everyone knows that raiders are on their way. There is much less fear than I thought there would be. More anticipation, if anything. The children are all excited, as if there is an adventure afoot, but I don't think they realize how dangerous this army is.

Damn it, I want them to take this seriously, but I guess I am happy they're not terrified. We are getting everyone who is not combat-approved ready to evacuate, and everyone has a job. Even the little kids have a job, because we figured it would be better for everyone to work together. It keeps them focused and occupied.

This all reminds me of when Beast told me that we should consider adopting something of a British colonial ideal. Children to be raised not only with school learning but also military skills. This is no longer the old world with its illusions of safety. We need to raise children that can survive in the harsh world we live in now. I didn't want to agree, but now that I've given it some thought, I know he's right.

Leah and Jimmy are happily playing, and he's telling her a story about how he is going to take care of her while they go camping. She is laughing and happy to be with him, as she always is. It is such a joy to behold the both of them untroubled by current events. Leah may be our little girl, but as far as we are concerned, Jimmy has become our little man, as well.

The evac location is something we only recently came up with. There used to be coal mines up near Crested Butte, but there were accidents and explosions, and they'd been closed down for decades. But there is also an old rail line that stretches from Crested Butte to Gunnison, and we've uncovered it, repairing damaged sections. We have carts in the proper gauge that travel the line very well when pulled by a couple of mules, or using the old, man-powered pusher carts.

When one of the locals found a cavern near one of the old mine sites years ago and told us about it, we realized what it could be used for. It is now our fallback and evac site. We've stocked it with all the MREs we

162

had left, quite a few actually, and have cleaned it out and prepared for people to live there for at least two weeks. Possibly longer, if we have time to move some of the greenhouse facilities. There is a water source inside the mountain, not pure, but we have ways to purify it. It is perfect for our purposes, and we've commandeered an old bank vault to act as an inner door into the cave. The outer door is made to look like part of the mountainside.

Everyone has go-bags. Everyone has a job. But, I never thought to give myself one. Now, I feel at a loss, not sure what to do to help. I've spent a good part of the day taking care of the few things I needed to, in case Beast thinks he's going to evacuate me, and now I am at a loss. When is he going to get back? I need him!

This shit with Liz has made me emotional. I feel edgy and uncertain, and I'm questioning my judgment. *How could I be so wrong about her?* I need Beast. I need his arms around me. I need him to make me feel like everything is going to be all right. When he's gone, I feel like half of me is missing. Right now, that's a bad thing. My man is my rock, my balance, my anchor. And, just now I need that more than ever.

"Come on, kids, let's go take a walk." I figure we can check on the mood of the people and keep spirits up. If nothing else, keep me occupied.

"Yaay!" Jimmy says to Leah, making her giggle happily. "We're going to take a walk Leah!"

She seems happy to go wherever he goes. He turns to me and asks if he can take a kite with us since the wind has picked up. I agree and get coats for everyone. I let Jimmy carry Leah outside, her dark head of hair close to his blonde head. I smile at the sweetness of the two of them. I will fight and kill to protect them, god help me.

Chapter Five

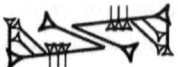

We had to take the kid, Thomas, to the Crested Butte hospital. Doc Calvo is still around, but he is happily ensconced in the animal hospital a couple blocks down the street. Now that we're invested in livestock, horses, mules, cows, steers, goats and the like, he's back in practice as a veterinarian. The medical staff we brought with us from Nellis is more practiced than he is on humans, and that's the way he likes it.

Lieutenant Fraser is red haired and fiery tempered, but capable. She'd gone to med school on the Army's dollar and was on leave in Las Vegas at the time of the Collapse. She was smart enough to retreat to the Air Force base when things started to get rough. Of course, she was thrown into deep water and has kept her head above the surface, barely, ever since.

She has competent help in two nurses she took with her from Mountain View Hospital when she fled the city. There had been at least two dozen medical personnel at the hospital when everything fell apart, but only nine of them have survived thus far. She's also training two people that show promise so that we can expand our pool of doctors.

We don't use the ambulance very often. This occasion called for it though. The kid had nicked an artery and he needs surgery. I got the bleeding under control, and we got an IV in him before we transported.

Not much traffic these days. Only takes a few minutes, and then we've got him into a sterile environment. Fraser is prepping for surgery. She's got an anatomy book open on the table as she scrubs up. This does not inspire confidence. She blushes, looks up at me and sticks out her chin.

"Hey, I never got to complete internship. This stuff is complicated, as I'm sure you know."

"I know you got this, Lieutenant."

My vote of confidence seems to assuage her mood, and she smiles slightly. I get out of the way, and the other medical personnel swarm around my patient and wheel him into the operating room. He's out now and blissfully unaware. He'll be fine.

I don't need to watch the surgery; I know it's well in hand. As I am leaving, I am waylaid by a lab technician. Colleen, it says on her name tag. I have to rack my brain to remember her last name is Gilmore. I'm told in no uncertain terms that my daughter is due for her immunization boosters.

"Already? Have you told Chloe?"

She glares at me and informs me that fathers are parents too, and if I know what's what I'll care just as much as the child's mother when it comes to communicable diseases. I am clearly in too deep and backtrack by saying that I will have my daughter in for her shots as soon as this emergency is past us, and beat a hasty retreat.

As I am leaving, I run into Ben Waters, the other medic in our special team. He's in to observe the surgery, so I tell him to hurry before he misses it. He salutes and asks if he'll see me later. I assure him he will.

I head outside to clean up and restock the ambulance. The driver is already there, so I help him and we're done quickly. The boy can't be older than twenty and seems nervous around me, but as long as he doesn't pester me with questions, that's fine.

"Uh, Sir Founder, sir?"

Shit. He wants to talk. I glare at him, and he subsides for a moment, but gathers his courage and presses on.

"Uh, is it true that raiders are coming?"

"Who told you that?" I growl at him, and vow to have words with whoever can't keep his mouth shut.

"Oh, no, no one, sir. But you and the others were in that meeting this morning a long time, and those UAV guys were in and back to work so fast, so we figured..." He's babbling, so I hold up a hand to stop him.

"We're not going to keep it from anyone. We have had drills and exercises this last year for a reason, and we expect everyone to be prepared. We're making an announcement soon. Got that?"

He looks gratified that he got information and is about to go on, but I hold up my hand again. "You got a duty station, son?"

"Ah, uh, yes sir, Sir Founder, I'm..."

"No, no. You don't need to tell me. You keep your mouth shut, though, until the announcement is made. Got that?"

"Y-yes sir."

"Good. You do your job when the time comes. I'll do mine."

"Right, yes. Yes sir."

He can barely keep from grinning, kid that he is. Like all youth, he seems to think that raiders are going to bring excitement and glory. But in this day and age, he should know better. *Damn sheltered kids.* I sigh.

"Now you get this crate back to the Enclave, I'm going to hitch a ride back later." I close the back door of the ambulance and clap the kid on the back. "What's your name again?"

"Perry, sir, Perry. I'm—" The kid takes a look at my face, gulps, and gets into the ambulance. "See you later, sir!"

He starts up the Humvee and idles there, like he's waiting for something. I roll my eyes and pound the top of the ambulance. He grins and takes off.

Kids.

I've been meaning to visit town anyway, so this is as good an excuse as any. I want to check on my team and get any fresh intel from the UAV guys. And, a quick tour of the fallback site would be a good idea, too. Before I can take more than a few steps, however, I am blocked by Mayor Johnson of Crested Butte, a slight but strong woman with a will of granite. *Shit.*

"Mr. Founder, I am so glad I caught you. I would like a word before you are off on whatever errand you're here on."

I inwardly groan but put on a polite expression, give a bow and follow her as she leads me down the street into her office. Not that it would matter if I wasn't polite. Betsy is one of the few people that isn't afraid of me.

"I thought we could have a little lunch while we talk. I've had my husband, David, gather a few others that are interested in recent events."

When she gives me a pointed glance, I know she is aware of the approaching raiders. *Shit! My intelligence network leaks like a sieve.* This is why I rarely leave the valley. Already, I'm pissed and in even less of a mood to talk.

It's a three minute walk from the medical center to the town offices, which is basically the city hall. I hope I am not in for the full council meeting. I'm told they used to hold meetings twice a month, but I don't think anyone has time for that kind of loafing these days. We have too much to do to keep ourselves alive.

Chloe, Captain Hayes, Sergeant Mike and I are invited to every meeting, but we rarely attend unless it has something to do with the Enclave. We had some rowdy teenagers messing with someone's sheep last autumn, for instance, and had to enforce the community service sentence that was inflicted on them. I thought it was appropriate: watching the sheep over the winter, caring for them, feeding them. The kids learned a little respect for life, and I appreciate a punishment that fits the crime.

That's the arrangement, though. Crested Butte and Gunnison run themselves—within reason. The Enclave sits in the middle and acts as the core holding it all together and enforcing what few laws we have.

They look to us to provide the framework for overall leadership as well as protection. After all, I've got all the soldiers under my command.

Yeah, I know what you're thinking. Isn't that creating a police state? Actually, no. Because everyone is armed. If that raider army actually makes it to the wall, every man and woman capable of shooting will be fighting them back. That's part of the deal. The original meaning of the second amendment was that all able-bodied civilians should be armed to defend against any aggressor—be it a criminal or an invading army.

At the same time, my responsibility is holding our actual army together, training and directing them—thanks to my promotion from Major Drummond, Goddess bless his soul.

Now we're entering the building and there are far too many people running around for my liking. I realize I've let out a low growl only when Mayor Johnson shoots me a censorious look. I inhale, close my eyes for a moment to gather myself, and go inside.

There is no power most days. They have solar cells, but they can only do so much. Today, however, there are some lights burning, and I see a few people busily typing at computers. I glance at Mayor Johnson as if to ask what's up, but she just keeps walking until we enter the meeting hall.

Yes, it is filled with people. I curse my fate and try to hold it together. These are not my enemies. I am filled with an urge to bolt, but push it down and continue calmly into the room.

Mayor Johnson leads me to the head of the table and seats me at the end, in the corner. I think Chloe has talked to her about this, but I don't care. It gives me a little peace to have the wall at my back. The other six council members are also present. They nod at me and pass the plate of flatbread sandwiches down. I can't say that I'm really hungry, but a soldier always eats.

The mayor's husband, David, has their son Braiden at the table with him. Babysitters are few and hard to find these days, and I note a number of other children in the room, as well. Braiden looks to be about Jimmy's age. I hope the boys will live through this encounter with the raiders and get the chance to grow up.

But that is a distraction. They are calling the meeting to order and informing the attendees of the recent intelligence. I am relieved to hear that Captain Hayes, not a rumor, has informed Mayor Johnson of the incoming raiders. We had planned it this way, but I hadn't realized I'd spent so much time at the hospital. Mike is likewise informing the Gunnison people, and since their town is in the path of the incoming raiders, they have to be calling a similar meeting there.

We've had flags made to inform people when we have incoming hostiles. Yellow is danger incoming. Red is retreat to safety/go to battle stations. Black, with an angel of death logo, which was my idea, is to say

167

battle forthcoming. I hope it strikes fear into the hearts of invaders, but if that doesn't, we will.

At this moment, yellow banners are going up all over the settlements in our valley. People know it is time to prepare to flee, or to do whatever task they are set for incoming raiders. Our little group is not a bunch of sitting ducks like so many other towns have been.

Now Mayor Johnson has turned the meeting over to me. That was not unexpected, and I'm still not thrilled. Nevertheless, I stand and brief the crowd on what I feel they need to know. They seem gratified once I sit down, so I finish my sandwich, and get the fuck out of there! I have work to do and so do they.

Chapter Six

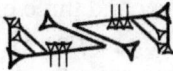

Finally, my time is my own, so I head to the apartment complex most of my team stays at when they're in town. It's a half-hour walk, but I need the solitude. I turn down three offers for rides, mostly in horse-driven carriages of some kind.

Five of the team are there when I arrive. We've got six from Nellis, two from Grand Junction, a few ex-military, and one unique individual named Vivyayna.

This enigma of a woman came from the west, walking out of a blizzard wearing wolf skins last winter. She walked right through Gunnison and kept walking until she arrived at the Enclave. There, she waited at the gate ignoring everyone, until I showed up to ask her what the hell she wanted. At that point, she drew twin axes, did a couple of fancy spins with them and threw them. At me. They buried into the wall, on either side of my head.

Some of the guards were ready to take her down, but I got a peculiar prickle in my tattoo and motioned for them to hold off. That's when she finally spoke.

"I didn't have to miss."

"I don't doubt that."

"I want to fight on your team."

"Okay. Guys, let the lady in."

The rest is pretty much history. She and Chloe hit it off right away, as deadly women sometimes do. Viv hasn't opened up, so we don't know much about her, but you have to respect a woman who can wield two axes the way she can. Certainly has allowed me to hone my skill with a tomahawk. She's taught us a few things about knives, as well.

Viv and four others—Seth Rawlins, Jakob Kawalski, Shawn Roche and Tess Nalwani—are in the fitness center of the apartment complex. I know they're expecting me, because when I walk in they all nod and stand at attention.

"We ready?"

"Yep."

169

That's Seth, our second in command. Being an ex-marine staff-sergeant, he knows his stuff. He's also a damn good hunter. Last winter, he brought in two good size deer and three elk. Seth and I are the main two people who alternate hunting parties. However, more are getting trained, as Chloe hates me being gone for days to a week at a time.

"Where are the others?"

"Airmen Grant and Thermopoli are out checking the fall-back site. Louis and McIntyre went to the armory to load up. They should be back soon. I've got the mortar teams making sure their equipment is ready to go. They are also making sure your catapults all have ammo stacked next to them."

The way he says *your catapults* makes me shake my head. Seth is a modern-day warrior. The old tricks don't quite compute to him. Mortars are something he can understand, but flinging a rock doesn't make sense because it doesn't go boom. I told him to trust me, because a boulder rolling over people is still an effective way of killing someone. And, we can also hurl things that *do* go boom.

At that, the door opens and four more of my Reapers, as I've deemed them, walk in the door—the aforementioned Mace Grant, Kim Thermopoli, Dale Louis and Paul McIntyre.

"I'm glad you're here. We need to discuss the new intel."

Leading the team into the old apartment manager's office, I lay out the most recent printouts. Quickly, I start pointing out areas that need work, getting them up to speed.

Thermopoli has a sly sense of humor, and I don't notice immediately that she is parallel to me at another desk mimicking my every movement in sync with me. Once I notice, I stop, glance over to see her grin, and the whole place breaks up. Yeah, she's hilarious. Yeah, I laugh too.

"Come on, enough. Who's up to work with Gunnison for their surprise while the rest of us delay the army?" Louis and McIntyre raise their hands so they get the job.

"Great. Now, Nalwani, you and Roche will be on vehicles: you driving, Roche servicing." At the group's laugh, I clear my throat, glare and continue. "Waters, you will be my opposite. If I'm in the field, you will be at camp. We need one medic on site at all times. And you'll need to fill in with the UAV screens whenever you're not busy 'servicing' our needs." They laugh again. Children.

Seth Rawlins speaks up, "Boss, looks like we have some night recon first thing, who's doing that?"

"The best at night ops, which means you, me and Nalwani. We'll accompany Kawalski and Grant to their special duty."

We go over plans in more detail for a while, then have some freshly-brewed beers Kawalski has been working on. It's a barley beer, but it really does go down nice when you haven't really had any others since the end of civilization. We finish up by toasting our success and Grant makes a special toast to Kawalski.

"To my new best friend, who's found a way for me to have a cold one again. Now, for someone to come up with Monday Night Football."

We all toast to that and wind up the meeting.

"Everyone be ready, we're going to meet at the Enclave tomorrow afternoon. Rawlins, I want us loaded for bear. Issue a LAW to each person, as well as a claymore and stick of cee-four."

"We're golden, boss."

"Tell Chloe I can't wait to fight at her side." That's Viv. She has been itching for a real fight, so this must be her lucky day.

"You got it, Viv. Want to drive me back so you can tell her yourself?"

"No, I've got stuff to sharpen." She gives a predatory grin and leaves the room.

Seth tosses me a set of keys. "Take my bike. I'll pick it up when we come down tomorrow."

Seth's Harley is his prize, his baby. He treats that bike the same way I treat Chloe, Leah or Jimmy. So, needless to say, he must be happy about the situation and ready to mix it up with the raiders, as well.

"Thanks man. See you all tomorrow." I bow and make my exit. They salute. *Nerds.*

I really want to get back to the Enclave before dark. Chloe is no doubt going through an emotional moment. On top of that, my lady and I need to have a talk. In all honesty, I'm dreading it. I'd rather she be coming at me, knife in hand, with deadly intent than have the discussion we need to have.

Chapter Seven

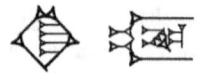

I'm glad I took the kids out to play. People have seen the yellow flags and they know what that means. We've drilled and drilled, and that's been fun, I guess, like when kids have a fire drill and get a break, but now it's serious. People are more nervous than I'd realized. A lot of these people are non-combatants and will be evacuated. The kids and I being out with them has helped.

Jimmy got some of the other kids interested in the kite, and a few more joined in until there were a half-a-dozen kites dancing in the sky. The mess hall upped the ante and served spaghetti with meatballs.

I know what you are thinking. Mess hall? Actually, it was Beast's idea, and a good one at that. When we first started, food was at a premium and needed to be rationed. So, we assigned people who were good at cooking to run cafeterias for each location. This has allowed us to centralize stockpiles and use what we have efficiently.

There are some things people keep in their homes: baked goods, preserves and the like. But, we encourage everyone to have two of three meals at the local mess hall. This also helps foster a community spirit. While my man still likes to cook for me, we too go there quite often.

Now, we are snugly ensconced in the bunker. It is empty at the moment, save for our little family. The children are quietly playing together in the common area, and that frees my mind. I can't help but let my thoughts turn to Liz.

I saved her life, or at least saved her from an unknown period of torture at the hands of raiders in Gunnison. She was so terrified. Even as I freed her from captivity, she never questioned anything I wanted to do, and I know that must have been PTSD. It took some time to give her the confidence to want to fight back.

I know I shouldn't, but I compare myself to her. When Beast freed me, I wanted to fight back immediately. I wanted to learn how to protect myself from being taken advantage of again. I can't comprehend how Liz fought the idea. She simply wanted to be near me and wanted me to protect her. I was the one who had to insist she learn weapons skills so she would never have to be a prisoner again.

Today's intel photos have shaken me deeply. She is now with the raiders from Las Vegas, and she is with Kane, who I *know* I gutted after Beast died. My head spins. I fear some dark entity has brought him back, the way our Goddess brought Beast back.

He's told me everything from the time he was reborn, and he mentioned the possibility of a door being opened for something bad to happen. This must be why and how Kane is up and dangerous again. The reason he is coming after us. Coming after me? Could it be he is simply that driven because we once bested him? Can the world be so small that he can't just find a kingdom and live there, but has to come after the only two that got away?

None of that explains Liz. Could she have gone to them willingly? It's like a punch to the gut. I feel pain and sickness in the pit of my stomach over the idea of her helping them. But why? Why would she jeopardize a safe and beautiful place that brings hope and security to so many? A place she helped to build.

Is it because I was no longer her lover and personal protector? Was she worried about rank, and worried that she would be replaced as a leader with Beast in the picture? Why didn't she come to me? Why did she have to do this? Why?

I just don't understand. No promises were made to her. I was careful only to promise what I knew I could provide. I never said I loved her, but I did tell her I cared, and I trusted her more than any other friend. And she's betrayed us. Betrayed me. Fuck, it hurts!

This kind of betrayal can't go unnoticed or unpunished. I feel a dragging heaviness in my heart that now I will have to take care of Liz, once and for all, and the idea makes me sick. I still care about her and what happens to her. Of course I do, she was here for me during one of the most difficult times of my life. I was grieving over my Beast and had discovered I was carrying his child. Liz was here to help me give birth, for god's sake, and she was the one person I trusted with every secret I had. And now this.

I realize tears are flowing freely. I don't want to frighten the kids, so I push the thoughts away and blow my nose. I want Beast here, damn it! I hope he isn't staying in town, because we need to talk. A happy screech from Leah's room draws my attention, and I quietly walk to the doorway to watch.

Jimmy is playing peekaboo with her. He has given her a blanket and she lifts it up to her face. When she pulls it down, Jimmy mugs a startled expression and she laughs. They look so content, so happy. I can't believe we are going to have to be separated from them while we deal with more asshole predators that would take all this joy away.

I have to wipe my eyes again before I can go in and start getting everyone ready for bed. Jimmy can tell I've been crying, though, and clings to me extra long for a hug. I hug him back and tell him to go get his pjs on so we can get a good night's sleep.

He nods and darts away, calling back, "And brush my teeth, I know. Can we have stories?"

"Yes, of course. I'll read you two books tonight. You pick."

As usual, he speeds through his tooth-brushing, and I have to make him go do it again. I chuckle over his exuberance over being read to. It's our nightly ritual.

Finally, all the hubbub is over and I sit beside Jimmy's bed in a rocking chair with Leah in my lap. She doesn't seem to want to nurse, so this helps me with my determination to wean her. I read two picture books and then tuck Jimmy in. He looks happy and warm, and Leah has fallen asleep while I read, so I tuck her into her crib. I hear them murmuring to each other after I leave the room, and it warms me. I tiptoe out and go to the front portion of the Bunker, waiting for Beast. He is still keeping me waiting, and I don't know how much longer before I need to go hunt him down. I am sharpening my short sword, the one that used to be his before the Goddess gave him a longer one.

Finally, I hear his footsteps in the house above. He walks into the entrance of the bunker, which I've left open for him, and notices me waiting.

"Love." It's all he says, and I run into his arms, all my fears and worries clear on my face. "I'm sorry it took so long to get back. I had to attend meetings." He growls this last part, and I laugh at him.

"That's what you get when you show your face in town. How's Thomas?"

"He'll be fine. I left when he went into surgery. Lieutenant Fraser fixed him up. He'll have a scar. I hear chicks dig scars."

Then he kisses me and all my cares fall away. Lifting me up, I wrap my arms and legs around him to help him keep balance as he closes and locks the bunker door and then carries me back to our bedroom.

I nestle my face into his neck and breathe in his scent—musky, male, outdoorsy, pine and some other aroma that is all him. As always happens with him, a spear of desire pulses through me, and I kiss his neck in little pecks and an occasional bite.

"Woman," he warns while closing our bedroom door. "We need to talk."

That cools my ardor, and I know he is trying to contain himself, physical reactions aside. I slide down him, making certain he feels my every curve on the way down. I take his hand, and we sit on the bed together. He takes a deep breath. I fear I know what he is going to say, but I keep my peace, waiting for it. Taking both my hands in his, I brace myself.

"Chloe, this past year, we have become a family. It's not just you and me anymore. We have Leah, Jimmy and others we care about, too. Nena, Mike Wayne and Captain Hayes. So many to look out for."

I nod calmly, waiting for him to tell me I need to stay behind to take care of them. While he looks tired beyond his years, outrage still burns in my chest. I think this shows on my face because he gazes at me quellingly, and I repress the words that want to bubble forth.

"And, I know how you care for every single person we've brought to this place. I don't even remember half their names. They make me want to run and hide in a cave. I can't comprehend how you care for so many and seem to get strength and joy from it. But, I am glad you do, because you know how I feel about people." He takes another fortifying breath, and I am kind of glad he is finding this difficult. He has no idea.

"So now that we have actual raiders incoming, I want to ask you to do something very hard," he pauses, then goes on in a rush, "and come with me anyway."

Wait, what did he say? I'm shocked, and can't quite process what he's just said. My mouth drops open as he continues.

"I know how much you need these people and care about them. I know how worried you will be about Leah and Jimmy and all the others, but babe, I need you. I need you to fight by my side and watch my back. We need to be a team again. And Goddess knows things aren't the same, but if you can stand it..."

His voice breaks off as I burst into laughter, sprinkled with happy tears. His face is a study in bafflement as I try to contain myself.

"What... is so funny?" He is growling again, and I love it when he does that. I climb up onto his lap and bring his stubborn face to mine in a long and lingering kiss.

"You idiot." I finally reply, still giggling. "I was worried you were going to ask me to stay behind with the civilians. And, I will not stand for that. I thought I was going to have to fight you about this, because there is no way in hell you are going anywhere into battle without your Angel of Death."

His relief is palpable. His features relax into a smile and he looks at me with a puzzled expression and asks, "You really thought I would make you stay behind?"

"I hid my weapons and gear in case I had to follow you into battle without your permission." I laugh again. "My lord, you and I are perfectly matched. Both of us were worried that I was going to stay behind."

175

"Life is too short," he sighs, content. "I will take care of you as you take care of me. The Goddess has made it clear we work better together. Besides, I'm going to make Captain Hayes be in charge of the civilians. No easy task, plus she will be the last line of defense, if it is necessary."

I've had enough talking now, and pull my man down to lie with me. He is still for a long moment while I stroke his face, at least what I can touch of it around that mask of his. Then, I snuggle up next to him and press my lips to his collarbone, then his neck, and I work my way up his face to his lips. Mmm. Softly, I kiss, loving the taste of him, and he allows me to minister to him, for now anyway, and so I do.

His impatience grows and he growls into my kiss. At that, my mouth goes dry. He flips me over, strips off his shirt and follows up by pulling my jeans and t-shirt off my willing limbs. I help him with his pants and soon we are tumbled in a happy pile of naked skin. He rolls me over and over until my head spins, and then kisses me again until I see stars. Helpless to do anything but cling to him and moan in delicious pleasure, he kisses his way down my body to my very center.

Beast tortures me by pressing his hands to my hips and holding me still as he uses his tongue on my thighs and belly, slowly circling with caresses, nips of his teeth, and kisses, all driving me wild. Finally, with a growl, he pounces on my center, and I gasp and writhe. He breaks down all my defenses until I am lost in a sea of bliss. I have learned I cannot shriek the way I want to, or I'll scare the children, so I try to muffle my cries of pleasure and stifle my gasps and moans. It is not an easy task, but it is easier than dealing with a crying baby while in an erotic state of mind.

I gasp and try to pull myself back together as Beast strokes me gently, allowing me a moment of respite. But, I don't want to wait for long. I need my man desperately, and I intend to have him.

"Baby, I need you inside me." I am pleading because I know him, and he wants to go have more fun tormenting me, but I add, "Please?"

At that, he opens his eyes and moves up my body as if he is stalking me. As soon as he is close enough I wrap my arms around his neck and kiss him, still tasting my moisture on his lips. God, he is sexy. He holds me tightly and rolls, allowing me to place myself astride him. Now, I can do a little torture of my own. I swing my hips and saddle up, letting him ease into me slowly, though I know he wants to plunge deep. I roll my hips, and he groans. When he tries to thrust, I pull back, and he subsides with a gasp, waiting for me, just as I wanted him to.

I grin and lean back then rotate my hips again as I seat myself more firmly. He grabs my hips and I lean down, brushing my nipples on his chest hair, and kiss him deeply. I press into him, then rise again, and allow a slow, lingering thrust before leaning in for another kiss. Rinse, repeat, until he can't take anymore and rolls, throwing me on my back. Taking one of my knees and crossing it in front of his torso, he thrusts the way he wants to.

This new angle of attack quickly sends me to the moon, and while I am trying to control my sounds, Beast is getting close, as well. I wrap both my ankles around his neck and that sends him over the edge, with me following right behind. Oh god, it is always so good.

Eventually, we are entwined and at peace, wrapped up in each other and utterly relaxed. The moment is so real, so good. I can't help it as tears leak in pure emotion. He holds me tight and lets me weep for joy.

Chapter Eight

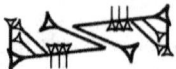

The morning comes too soon for my liking. Chloe is very uncomfortable because she's weaning Leah. The kids are awake earlier than usual, so I take care of their morning needs because my wife is putting compresses on her breasts so the pain will be minimized.

I am not thrilled by anything that causes her pain, but I understand this is probably for the best. Leah is almost a year and a half old, and if we're going to be separated from her for a week or more, this is the better plan.

Quickly, I get the kids dressed and take them to the kitchen for breakfast. There are plenty of eggs from the chickens, so I make eggs and toast. There is fresh milk in a sippy cup for Leah and a regular cup for Jimmy. By the time Chloe comes out, they've made short work of the eggs and are starting on mandarin oranges from a can.

For my wife, I've prepared a ham and cheese omelet with chives sprinkled on top. She beams at me and swallows a couple of painkillers with her mug of coffee.

"That bad, huh?" I sit down with her to eat my omelet.

She winces. "Nena said it would be painful for the first few days, but would ease up after that. I would have to go through it eventually, anyway. Besides, it's not that bad. Thank you for breakfast, baby."

"Any time, beautiful."

Once everyone is done eating, I carefully wipe the face of my beautiful daughter as she calmly smiles up at me. Then she pops out with a word.

"Da." She looks quite pleased with herself.

"Yep, I'm your Dad."

"Da, da, da, da. Immy." She points at Jimmy as she speaks his name, and he grins at her.

"Clearly, your daughter only cares for men because she still hasn't said mama." Chloe complains with a smile. "Come on, sweet girl, say mama. Mama? Ma-ma?"

"Da, da, da. Immy." We all laugh, and Chloe shakes her head at Leah as she scoops her up and rubs noses with her.

"It's okay, sweetie, you're still my favorite girl." She puts a sweater on over Leah's clothing and tells Jimmy to get ready for school.

"What? But there are raiders coming, and I've got stuff to do."

He and the other grade-schoolers are tasked with helping to load the train carts we've rigged up. The older kids and adults are carrying the heavy stuff, but there are always lighter things that need to be tucked in amongst the heavy items, and the grade school kids are very excited that they get to help. We've only done one complete run-through, a few months ago when ice was still on the tracks. It went fairly well and allowed us to work out some of the bugs. We don't need to worry about ice now, though, so it should go well enough.

"School first," I tell him. "We're running the first loads out this evening, so you'll need to be ready as soon as class is over. You are getting pretty strong. I expect you'll be a lot of help."

The kid has grown a few inches at least in the past year. He is a far cry from that skinny, abused waif that begged to be let onto the aircraft back at Nellis.

Jimmy looks proud and pleased as he rushes off to get his backpack and jacket. Chloe exits with the two of them, pausing to kiss me first. When I squeeze her waist, I notice she is carrying at least one pistol. She notices me noticing and pulls the walkie-talkie out of her pocket.

All the team leaders have these and in a yellow alert they are required to carry them. I nod. Then, she looks pointedly at her boot, and I see a small knife tucked away in an inner pocket. I approve.

"You going to meet with the Reapers this morning?" she asks softly.

"Yep. They're all going to be here by ten, so try and make it back from martial arts training by then if you can. We're meeting in the back room of the Trading Post."

"Yeah, I figured. You all want some of that bacon they just brought in, don't you?"

"You know me so well," I laugh, and steal another kiss before she is out of my sight.

Strange that being with people is irritating, but being with my family is soothing. I hear Chloe saying "Ma-ma? Ma-ma?" as they exit the bunker, and I smile. Babies always say da-da first. The real surprise was the "Immy" she uttered before anything else. We knew Jimmy belonged with us when Leah went straight to him, young as she was, and nestled her head in the crook of his shoulder and fell asleep. He looked worried, his skinny arms careful not to hold her too tight, but Chloe had him carry Leah to bed.

That was the day we moved him in with us. He was a little scared of being underground, and awed at the extent of the bunker, which he called a hideout. He got an excited expression and said it was like the bat cave

179

and that I must be Batman. *Damn kid, almost made me cry.* Chloe had no resistance to the cute. She cried her eyes out once we'd tucked him in and he was asleep.

Not that he slept for long before the bad men came out of the dark. For that first month, hell, the first six weeks, he woke most every night with nightmares. I was there every time, holding him and letting him sob out his terror. In a sad way, he reminded me of Chloe after I first rescued her from that asshole gang that had been holding her, naked, as their sex slave. *Goddess, grant we make assholes extinct in my lifetime, amen.*

Now, I need to prepare for the upcoming mission. I have one of the areas of the bunker set aside as my armory. It is extensive, what with all the weapons Chloe and I have accumulated, as well as the other really good gear. It's damn near the Enclave armory, while Crested Butte and Gunnison have their own satellite armories. We even have a small armory topside, but it's more for show with some shotguns, bolt or lever action weapons and a small amount of ammo.

In the bunker, there's a reloading station with all the die sizes a reloader could hope for. The supplies of gunpowder and lead are holding out okay so far, and we carefully collect and recycle our brass. Still, I foresee we will need to learn to make smokeless gunpowder eventually. There's a reason I have black powder weapons in the inventory, and it's just because black powder is easier to make than modern gunpowder.

Being alive and with Chloe has meant a few bonuses, like having my G3 back. Tossing a suppressor onto it, I've got a great, hard-hitting platform that has quite the range. Loading the fifty round drum in, I make sure my vest is kitted out with fully loaded magazines. I follow up with my Kimber race gun, Steyr GB and Webley. I have my sword on my hip, a combat knife and other gear, and I'm set.

Since Chloe is out, I go ahead and set up her kit that she brought back from hiding this morning. Since she has gotten very good with the Tavor, I go with that. A fifty round drum and loaded magazines will keep her going for a while. This is backed up with an FN FNX and a Glock 19. Finally, I include her favorite combat knife and my old short sword, which she keeps with her because it makes her feel like I'm right there with her.

Once everything is packed, I take the two duffels out of the bunker and lock it. Of course we had to change the numbered code once Liz disappeared.

Making it to the trading post, I set up in the back room. When they were building it, I asked them to add this room for meetings with my team. They were glad to do it. I like it because it's separated from the rest of the building by a thick log wall. It has its own fireplace, and that is what kept us going during the colder winter months. This has been our meeting place and the rest of the Enclave somehow knows to avoid it. Maybe the fact that the dozen most dangerous people they know frequent it regularly.

Viv is already there, which is no big shock. Any time there's adventure in the offing, she's where we plan on meeting and always early. Sitting in a chair, she runs one of her axe blades along a sharpening stone and grins at me. Yeah, she's scary like that.

I have almost an hour before I can expect everyone else, so I put the duffels inside and ask Barry Corrigan to see about food for the group. And, I ask him to make sure the food includes some of that bacon we just got in from Gunnison. He grins and gives me a thumbs up.

With that done, I take off for the fields, because I want to check on a mare who just foaled twins. Viv follows along, armed to the teeth. Yeah, I'm getting domestic, but I can still kill as fast as ever, so don't get any ideas.

The foals are in good shape, but the mother is looking peakèd, so I go find a book about equine medicine. I discover the mother needs a richer diet, especially when she's nursing twins. I find the stable manager, a nearby rancher who's been helping out. He's been giving the mother ten pounds of grain a day, and I think she needs more. We're discussing it and the mare's condition when I hear a squawk on my walkie-talkie.

"Beast." It's Chloe. She's in trouble, I can hear the tone of her voice, and I know it. But that's all there is.

I hear a roar and realize it's me. I am searching the stable for a likely horse, spot a stallion I am familiar with, a Morgan named Rapscallion. I leap onto his back. Then, I look over to Vivyayna.

"Give me one of your axes," I damn near yell.

To her credit, she doesn't look affronted or upset that I'm asking for one of her prized babies. With a graceful toss, it arcs up and I catch it. I start galloping toward the bunker, and I try to get someone on the radio as we fly. Mike is there, and he's got a youngster who saw some men put a bag over Chloe's head and take off with her.

I don't realize I am kicking Rapscallion for more speed until he takes off like we'd been standing still. We race to the little house near the bunker, and I leap off, looking for signs of Chloe. I find her radio and pistol on the ground. I let out another roar as I realize she's gone.

Chapter Nine

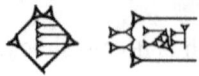

I've been taking Aikido twice a week, along with Kim Thermopoli and Tess Nalwani. There is an instructor, Maria, who lived in Gunnison. Ex-military, a staff-sergeant in the Air Force, she was stationed in Korea and Japan as a chef. She got interested in martial arts, and after her stint she stayed in Japan for a few years, working as a chef at the Officer's Club and taking different classes every morning.

She finally had to come home when her mother got sick, and after the Collapse was one of very few who not only survived, but thrived. Pam, the woman with the daughters who I saved at the same time I rescued Liz, turned to Maria and has been training herself and her children since that incident. They are no longer easy prey. The whole Gunnison contingent kind of hoarded Maria and her ninja skills until they finally realized that all of us strong is better than one pocket of well-trained people. Now, she teaches two mornings a week here, and two evenings at the Enclave. The rest of the time she is in Gunnison as the primary cook at their mess hall.

Aikido is basically mixed martial arts. Fighting with any weapon one can grab or with a specific weapon. It also includes fighting groups—one-on-one, two-on-two, anything and everything. It's been very helpful keeping me fit and sharp. It also gives me an edge on my husband, as he's not adept against it. More than once my new skill allowed me to get the upper hand while wrestling in the bedroom.

After class and after chatting with Kim and Tess for a few minutes, I head back to the bunker to change so I can get to the meeting with the Reapers. Nena has Leah, and they are going to go work in the gardens, which basically means Leah screeching her input while Nena and the others gossip. Sounds like a jolly good time, but there are raiders that need killing, and I am anxious to get started.

As I open the door of the house above the bunker, I hear a creak on the floorboard inside. Is Beast in there? Huh. Not like him. The hairs on the back of my neck prickle, and I pull out my walkie-talkie. I press the button to call Beast, and as I do, a heavy black bag is shoved over my head. I get out one shrieked word—Beast!—before the radio is snatched from me and strong hands have grabbed my arms and legs and are carrying me away. As they lift me, I feel my pistol slip out of my holster and thud to the ground.

Fuck! How am I going to get out of this?

Of course I struggle, I'm not going to make this easy for them, but it doesn't seem to matter. They're running with me and my strongest efforts don't seem to slow them down. My weight is hanging down with one person to a limb, and that is a damn awkward position to do anything. I realize I need to hold still, pull myself together, and wait for my chance.

How did they slip past our guards? Damn it.

They keep jogging, carrying me through the wooded section. I feel the sun on then off my body. I know this terrain. They are most likely unfamiliar with it. I hear the river and know they will soon come to a small plank bridge. It is too narrow for them to cross over carrying me the way they have been. They're going to have to shift me, and when they do, I have to be ready.

My muscles, which were nicely warmed up by my exercise earlier, are freezing up and cramping the farther I'm carried, but I know I have to try. If Beast heard my last transmission, he will know there is something wrong when he can't reach me.

The sound of running water is getting louder. I remember that the path follows alongside for a while before it crosses. Just as I thought they would do, my captors slow as they approach the bridge.

It is a long piece of metal about eight inches wide, and it bounces slightly as one crosses single file. As soon as my captors begin to shift my weight for one of them to carry me over his shoulder, I make my move, using all of my limbs to strike out.

What actually happens is that three of them drop me, while one holds onto my leg. I fall heavily to the ground, jarring my left shoulder and making my already numbed arm go dead. The right leg is still being held, but my right hand is free. I swing out with it blindly, and strike someone, but I think it's only a glancing blow.

The men are grasping and grappling for my limbs again, and the one holding my leg jerks hard, trying to pull me upside down so I am helpless once more. I kick at the one person whose location I know and for what I think might be the region of his genitals and finally score. He gives a grunt as his hold loosens just enough for me to kick free of him, pushing him backward. When I hear a splash, I know he's fallen into the water.

"Grab her, damn you," he shouts from the river.

I catch the sound of him clambering up the riverbank, but I have gotten to my feet and am trying to get the hood off my head and shoulders. I keep backing up until I feel the trunk of a tree behind me, yanking the hood free. What I see when I am finally able to is hardly promising.

Three of my captors encircle me, faces grim. I could handle grinning lecherous faces better because those can be manipulated. These guys don't seem to care about me as a woman, but prize me as a captive instead. Behind them, their friend is clambering up the muddy bank of the river and does not look happy.

"Quit fucking around and grab her!"

I take a second and pull my knife from my boot, and feel only a little better. It is a small blade. But my Aikido lessons are fresh in my mind, and I have practiced fighting several combatants at once. I wave my knife in front of me and grin. They look none-too-pleased by my confidence.

The one in the center lunges forward and back, as if testing me, but I don't fall for it. I'm sure the other two were going to lunge for me if I'd attacked, so I wait. Then, before I end up with four against one, I throw my knife at the fourth thug, just as Viv has shown me, and it hits him cleanly in the throat. He goes down with a gurgle. I grin again, get into a stance and encourage one of the men to come at me.

They glance at each other, and this time the one in the center does not feint, he just charges. I slide to the side and use his momentum to slam his head into the tree behind me. He staggers back, dazed for a moment, so I trip him. He falls heavily to the ground and struggles to stand.

The other two come at once. I grab the closer one as he approaches and yank him toward me, putting him off balance. Falling to my back, I plant my feet on his chest and fling him over my head. Sure, a few rocks dig into my skin, but this is an acceptable injury considering the guy cracks his head open on some larger rocks behind me.

Two left, though one is still struggling to get up. The last guy is angry, but he is not going to chance getting too close again. He pulls out a pistol and points it at my head. I suspect he has been told to take me alive, but he's probably pissed off at my success against his buddies that he might just shoot me. *Damn it.* I put up my hands and wait. He comes closer and motions for me to turn around, hands behind my back.

As I turn around, I recall some of my training to use for just such an occasion. He comes up behind me, gun in one hand and zip ties in the other. He's going to have to put the gun down if he wants to zip tie my hands, but instead, he puts them in my hands, expecting me to bind myself. *Like hell.*

Instead, I grab his gun hand from behind me and yank it toward me, hard. The gun goes flying ahead of me. Unfortunately, I lose track of it as he comes forward, so I yank again, then plant my elbow in his face. I

184

hear bones crunch and I yank once more. All he does is stumble forward, bleeding. I circle him, still holding on to that hand. Pulling his arm behind his back, I kick him forward with my knee to trip him while pulling his arm into an arm-lock.

He's screaming now, and oddly, I hear a beating sound. Like a horse galloping? I have a good hold on this guy, and his elbow is taut, almost ready to snap. What I don't notice is that from behind me, the first guy I rammed into the tree grabs me by the throat.

I've got enough sense to keep hold of his friend. I hear his arm snap as I am pulled backward. Hell, everyone within a hundred feet could probably hear it. When he howls, I let go, trying to focus on this new threat.

I am choking, he has a good grip on me, but I know what to do. Dropping to my knees, he is now off-balance, and as he folds over, his hands loosen. Now, he's in perfect position, and I fling him over me.

Surprisingly, he tucks and rolls, bouncing up to his feet again. *Damn it!* The guy with the broken arm is trying to crawl away, probably to go find his pistol. But now, I am faced with someone who has some sort of training, slow as he has been to use it.

He does not make his first mistake again by lunging. Instead, he crouches low, and we circle each other, each waiting for the other to leave an opening. The sound of pounding hooves is louder now. Trying to make out what it is, I make a mistake. I am inattentive for just a second, but he takes his chance and kicks. He catches me full in the chest and I fall backward, gasping for air like a fish.

I am helpless on the ground, trying to remember the taste of air in my lungs. All I can do is watch with dread for his next move. Suddenly, an axe sprouts out of his forehead. He falls backward, dead, and I lie there, gasping for just one taste of air when I hear Beast roar, "CHLOE!"

Okay, since becoming a woman of action, I detest the idea of being a damsel in distress. But in this instance, I'm not going to complain as I watch my Beast ride up on a horse to save me. It's such a damned glorious sight.

I can't even twitch or flail yet. I'm helpless to tell him I am okay, just winded. Finally, a tiny trickle of air starts to feed my starving lungs. Vainly, I try to hold up a hand to let him know I'm here.

I gasp in that first delicious breath and manage to croak, "I'm okay..." as pulls me into his arms. Without a word, he covers me in safety and warmth. A smile forms as I revel in the wonderful feeling.

I gasp again, trying to capture more precious air and manage to get out, "There's one more. He had a pistol..."

Beast places me carefully behind him, and I cling to his waist as I recover my strength and breathe. With the quiet grace of a panther, he

185

stalks the last of my attackers. We reach the asshole just before he puts his good hand on the missing gun. Beast picks it up, hands it to me, and drags the crippled man by the collar over to the horse. Quickly, he ties my attacker's arms and legs together under the horse's barrel. There is a lot of screaming in agony as this is accomplished, but ask me if I care.

When that is done, Beast turns to me and pulls me into his arms once more. He holds me tight, as tight as I can stand, and I cling to him just as hard. When his lips fall onto mine, he kisses me ferociously until finally coming back up for air.

"Did you just come riding up on a horse to save me?" I ask, looking up at him with a smile.

"Damn right I did. Got here just in time, too, looks like."

"Hey, I already took out two others. Four to one is poor odds when all one has is a boot knife."

He frowns, then looks around and spots the other two bodies. "Well done, my lady. But, I'm still glad I came to rescue you. I always wanted to see how well those axes of Viv's work."

"That's the only reason?" I sputter, and he laughs and kisses me again.

"Of course not, my love. I can't live without you."

"That's more like it."

I hold him tightly, and begin to feel all the small scrapes and pain from this last round of fighting. As I find my calm, we begin to hear voices in the distance.

"Sounds like half the camp is coming after us. On the bright side, that will make taking care of these bodies easier."

Beast pulls out his walkie-talkie and tells everyone where to find us. It doesn't take long for them to catch up, and we've piled the other three bodies together and gone through their things. I find them remarkably under armed. Only the one pistol and a few knives. What, did they think they were ninjas or something? Dumbasses!

Beast is yanking Viv's axe out of the forehead of one of the raiders, when the owner of that weapon shows up, grinning wildly. She reaches for the weapon from my man, and he bows while handing it to her. Taking a cloth, she wipes the blood all over the blade before cleaning it off.

She catches me watching and grins, "It likes a good taste of blood, you see. Makes it more ready to fight."

I have retrieved my knife from the first guy's throat and have already cleaned it. I tuck it back into its sheath in my boot, and give my own smile back at her.

"Thanks for the knife throwing lessons, Viv. Saved my ass just now."

"You responsible for all this damage?"

"Yep. Except for the axe, but you have to let the boys get a few licks in now and then. Keeps 'em happy." We smile at each other, and the other Reapers shake their heads at us.

"Bloodthirsty bitches," says Kim Thermopoli. "I want to be like you when I grow up."

"I think you're as tall as you're ever going to get, sweetie," says Viv, "but you are just as bloodthirsty as the rest of us. We'll leave the knees and ankles to you, yeah?" The rest of the group laughs at their banter. We gather up the corpses to burn. Beast makes sure to let the injured raider on the horse watch us as we gather wood for a bonfire and set fire to the bodies.

Leaving a couple of the Reapers behind to tend to the fire, the rest of us make our way back to our now-delayed meeting. Beast and I lead the horse with the cursing and crying raider tied to its back. There will be some questions he needs to answer.

Chapter Ten

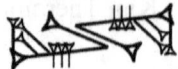

We left Louis and Kawalski behind to deal with the bodies of the raiders. I also order them to go look in on our guards. What happened that they didn't manage to see the incoming men? I hope they're not dead, but if they're not, they're going to wish they were after I'm done with them.

The whole ride while looking for Chloe was a blur. Time had dilated, and every sight and sound was intense, yet instantly forgotten. My mind was searching, hoping I was going the right way, looking for signs and finding nothing, but thinking they had to have gone along the river. If I had been given the task to kidnap one of the leaders, this is the way I would have entered, under the cover of trees, using an obvious landmark like the river so that I couldn't easily get lost.

Then, I hear a scream followed by more sounds of rage and pain. It is a siren's lure, pulling me faster in the right direction. That's when I see them. My heart is pounding, and I am ready to burn the world down to get Chloe back.

I ride up to see one of those assholes kick my wife in the chest. I can't stop seeing the image of Chloe at the hands of that asshole. He kicked her. In the chest. The sight of her flying through the air and landing hard keeps replaying through my mind, and if I hadn't thrown that axe and killed him, I would have enjoyed killing him again.

It's funny, even with the training Viv has given us, I never once thought about aiming or doubted where that axe was going to land. I just threw and it went right where it was supposed to.

Chloe is coming down from the adrenaline. I can tell. A pained expression has developed on her face, so I cut the asshole raider from the horse and put her on it. Tying a rope around his neck, I make him walk the rest of the way. I don't care how much he hurts. He should have taken that into account before he and his friends dared to come here and try to kidnap my wife.

When we are a few minutes away from the Enclave, Airman Louis and Private Kawalski show up on one of the ATVs the guards use to get to their posts. There are two bodies on the back, so that answers that.

The raiders knew where the guards were posted and took them out. Then, they knew where to find Chloe and waited until she was alone before they took her. I glance up at my lady. There's a sick expression on her face that tells me she knows how they got this information. It had to be Liz.

And then, we hear Leah screaming. I give Sergeant Rawlins the rope I've tied to the raider, leap on the horse behind Chloe, and ride toward the bunker at top speed. When we get there, Nena is standing outside our house holding Leah, who is struggling to be free. Our daughter is flinging her body recklessly around as only a child can do.

As soon as she sees Chloe, she calms down to simple crying, holding her hands out and crying, "Mama! Mama!"

My lady slides off the horse and breaks into a dead run to Nena and our daughter. I'm not far behind her as she takes our baby girl, rocking and soothing her. Leah calms down a little, but still crying and holding on to her mother.

"What happened?" I ask Nena. The woman is beaming at me, Chloe and Leah.

"We were in the garden. I was weeding, the child was playing, and then she just stopped. When I looked at her, she let out a shriek and started crying, "Mama." She hasn't stopped since. Shortly after she began screaming, you rode by on that horse."

I look over at Leah and she is still sobbing into Chloe's neck. I get a chill, then my tattoo burns. I realize our daughter has... something. A gift from Goddess? My wife has told me that when she was upset, our daughter would become upset, but I didn't realize she meant it like this. Our daughter knew when Chloe was in danger, somehow. Then, she could only be soothed by her presence.

Leah is clearly exhausted by all of this, because she's sobbing and hiccupping at this point. Chloe hands Leah back to Nena, and she goes willingly, nodding sleepily. My lady joins me beside the horse as Nena, rocking our daughter, goes into her house. Leah is draped limply over her shoulder.

By the time we get to the trading post, the whole team is together. We are a silent and serious dozen, because we allowed the enemy to get in. I blame myself, and the others seem just as unhappy. The unhappiest person here has got to be our prisoner, though. He has stopped howling his pain and now looks to be in shock. First thing is to cure him—before we kill him.

There are good reasons for this. The only reward he will get today for talking is the choice of dying quickly or dying slowly. Chloe on the other hand, also has injuries, but she will get any needed medicines the asshole will not. We just want him to survive long enough to answer our questions. Or longer if he won't.

I take Chloe to the side and start checking her out. Ben Waters was a Navy corpsman as well, so he takes our captive to the other side of the room and starts by putting his shoulder back in its socket. The screams are not pretty, but I tune them out as I take a look at Chloe's damage.

My lady has a few cuts on her back she says are from rocks, and she has quite a few bruises. The worst is the one on her stomach, right below her breasts, where she was kicked. Nena has provided us with arnica compresses and witch hazel to disinfect with. It does no harm, and the arnica seems to help bruises heal better. I also give her more anti-inflammatory. Her breasts are still sore from weaning Leah, and she says that hurts more than anything. Damn. Women are tougher than any men I know.

Now Corpsman Waters is setting our captive's broken arm. It's the humerus, a big bone, so it takes a few minutes of wrestling and screaming to get it right. Our captive passes out, which is a mercy to the rest of us.

I finish with some scrapes on Chloe's hands that she doesn't remember getting. That's how it is in a fight, though. You'd be surprised what all you can't remember, especially when your life is on the line. I put a salve on the scrapes, and she thanks me with her brightest smile.

Next, I have them strap our volunteer to a side table, and we adjourn our meeting at the main table and enjoy a late lunch. There is bacon after all.

Three hours later we have a lot more intel and a dead raider. Not one of the Reapers got sick, either… well, except Senior Airman Nalwani. Her dark skin turned ashy and her eyes got big, but she hung tough. Not one of the other Reapers teased her about it, either. Not even Thermopoli, who is a bit of a joker.

Now, we know the exact size of the incoming army, just a little over a thousand soldiers at last count. With support staff there is almost eleven hundred. They've been picking up men about as fast as others die or desert, so there will likely be just that number by the time they get here.

Unless we have something to say about it.

190

Given their speed, we figure they are going to start running into our pre-planned diversions by tomorrow evening. We want to make sure they feel welcome, after all. So, the plan is to move out tonight. We can make better time than their army ever could.

We have a few ideas that require sabotage from the inside. These are our men: Jakob Kawalski, one of our team members from Gunnison. He's a biker and all-around tough guy that has a black belt in tae kwon do. He looks like a badass with the long hair, tattoos and mutton-chop sideburns. He has three teenage daughters, two sons and his wife, Pam, in Gunnison. Those were the girls Chloe rescued from Gunnison the night she met Liz. The other is Airman Mace Grant. He's black. Very black. Bald head, grim expression. I don't know how the Marines didn't catch him, but he ended up in the Air Force. He's quiet and dangerous looking. I think he'll do.

We have enough stupid looking raider armor to set them up and they look rough enough to fit the job. We're sending them with poison we've distilled from Oleander leaves. We've made enough to make anyone who drinks water or eats food laced with this poison sick and miserable, maybe even dead.

Mace once worked in a cafeteria, so no doubt they'll put him to work slaving away to feed the troops. Whatever they have our guys doing, we will have inside men who only know their part of the plans and who've been told to cause chaos internally.

Kawalski and Grant leave as soon as we get everything we want out of the raider. We can't tell them what we're up to anyway, what they don't know can't be tortured out of them. They head to Gunnison, to Kawalski's house so he can say his farewells. We will pick them up there later tonight.

Once they're gone, the rest of us pull out a map of Interstate 50, the only real route the raiders can use to get at us. Sure, there are side roads here and there, but they are distractions and rough country. They need the interstate to make the time they want to. They have a lot of men on foot. They are scavenging as they go, but they've got to have massive supplies, or they couldn't be feeding an army. I can't help but wonder who they killed to get the supplies they have. Bastards.

While the Reapers are a total of sixteen people, only a dozen of us will head out. We have vehicles to carry what we need, but they have no way of knowing we've already set up defenses along the route. While we have modern armaments, I've also taken some clues from the tactics of the Romans, the Crusaders, the Viet Cong and Sun Tzu, among others. There are more than a few nasty surprises the raiders will not be expecting.

191

Now, it's time to let everyone get their gear together, check the vehicle and take care of loose ends. Chloe is going to have to say goodbye to Leah and Jimmy, and I am not looking forward to that myself. But this is what we do, and, now, we have that much more to fight for.

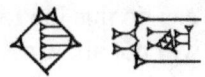

It is hard to say goodbye to the kids. I know what we're doing is the right thing, but I am finding it very difficult to let go of their little hands. Beast is right. This is difficult. I trust Nena, and I trust Mike and Captain Hayes, but damn, I have to choke back my emotions, because I don't want to scare Leah. Thankfully, they don't cry.

Jimmy sees it as he and Nena and Leah going on an adventure. He is excited. The red alert flags will go up first thing tomorrow in Gunnison. Then when Gunnison is clear, it will be the Enclave, followed by Crested Butte. We have a dozen mule trains to pull the carts to the evac point. I know they will be safe there for a good long time. I know it mentally, but emotionally, I am a little strung out.

Finally, Beast and I give our last kisses. He talks seriously to all three of them about their responsibility to be safe, work hard, help lift everyone's spirits and to behave. Jimmy and Leah are solemn as he talks. Nena remains her calm and confident self.

After he's done, Nena speaks, and her eyes look strange. They've turned milky white and I nudge Beast and draw his attention to it. Jimmy is still holding Leah and they don't seem to notice as he tickles under her chin, probably trying to prove how capable he is.

"The road is dark, more twisted than you know. Two will be lost, but more will be saved because of their valor. We will be saved. We will be well. Trust that. But turn them back at the reservoir. And when they've turned, flee home. All. The way. Home." She emphasizes that last bit. Then, Nena's eyes refocus, and the milky look is gone. She takes a deep breath and smiles tiredly.

"Thank you, Nena," I state gladly, "for everything. For taking the babies—"

"Hey, I'm not a baby!" Jimmy caught that last comment.

"I mean *the* baby and big Jim here," I grin, slightly mollifying Jimmy. "And thank you for… for sharing your gift,"

Beast finishes for me. "We will take what you say into our planning. Thank you." He bows to her and steps back, waiting for me.

I give everyone a last big hug and turn around and walk away with my man. I don't look back, because this is harder than I thought, but it's important, too. Nobody else can do this job for me. No, I am not sending Beast out without me. No, I will not allow asshole raiders to come take over without a hell of a fight.

Beast is holding my hand as tightly as I am clinging to his, and I take a look at his face. He seems to be having just as hard a time as I am, and my heart warms. That's when the tears start. Of course, Leah also begins to cry, but I still don't look back.

Before we turn the corner on our way to the vehicle, I hear Jimmy's piping voice say, "Don't worry, Leah. Mom and dad will be back before you know it. And until then, I'll protect you."

I choke up completely and as soon as we round the corner, Beast and I hug tightly. When we pull apart, I see by his face that he is more shaken than he would like me to know. And, I figure he is remembering Anna and Katie, his first wife and his other daughter, both dead at the hands of raiders back in the early days of the Collapse.

"They'll be fine. You heard Nena. I believe her."

"I know." He growls, squeezes me again, and then takes my hand as we walk toward our transportation.

We considered several vehicles, but this will work best for our needs, and it will keep the team together. It's a Stryker LAV. A stripped-down SWAT version that was part of the Gunnison Police department. It seats eleven, so I get to sit on Beast's lap once we pick up Kawalski and Grant. I don't think this is going to bother him too much. If my head bumps on the ceiling, though, I'm sitting with Tess.

When we get to the Stryker, Jackson and Burton are standing there, grinning at the rest of us. When we come around to the front, we see why. They have been busy with stencils and black paint and have named our vehicle, "The Saucy Goose." All we can do is smile at that.

"Now," Jackson states while grinning at me, "we were going to have you christen this fine vessel with a bottle of champagne, but there is none to be found."

"But," adds Burton, "We did find a bottle of Bud Light we were willing to sacrifice to make this official."

Burton takes said bottle—a towel wrapped around its neck—out from behind his back and hands it to me with great ceremony. Laughing and shaking my head, we move to the front of the Saucy Goose.

"Whack it good, Angel!" This is Shawn Roche. I don't need any more encouragement.

With as much pomp as I can manage, I pronounce, "I christen thee... the Saucy Goose!"

Smashing the bottle on the front fender, it breaks quite easily. The skunky smell of old beer invades our nostrils, and I add, as an aside to Beast, "Don't think this beer was any big sacrifice, it reeks."

"Just go with it," he whispers before we turn around, beaming. "We all ready to go, Rawlins?"

Seth steps forward and salutes. "Sir, yes sir." He barks. "The troops are ready to go, if these assholes are done fucking around." He glares at Jackson and Burton who are still grinning as they head back to the main gate in preparation for our departure. They stay behind to help with the evac. Their poor luck to be off rotation right now. Or their good luck. I haven't decided yet.

We load up and it is as tight as we remember. But settled onto my Beast's lap is probably more comfortable than I have any right to expect. He holds me carefully, and when we begin to pull out, my heart skips in anticipation.

Two hours later, we're almost where we want to be on the other side of the Blue Mesa reservoir. We have made arrangements with some of the farmers outside Gunnison, and they've delivered some of what we wanted. Viv and Airman Thermopoli have also been here and back with some of the specialty products from our soap makers. We've also been hauling big rocks this way for half a year.

Of course, Seth is annoyed by the low-tech siege weapons. He wants all tech all the time, but he also knows that won't last forever. The days of big-government spending and unlimited supplies are over. He still glares at the catapults and trebuchets as though they have personally insulted his mother. We drop off Airman Louis and Staff Sergeant McIntyre to get things put together here, and the rest of us continue on toward Cimarron.

We pass people evacuating from the Blue Creek Ranch. There aren't many living out this far, but they're completely unprotected, and we've promised them safety behind our walls in exchange for food and seed. Waving as we go by, they have two wagons pulled by horses. I estimate they will probably make Gunnison before nightfall. There are cowboys in the hills moving livestock, and they'll probably be in town before morning.

The rest of us continue on in the Stryker. We want to get Kawalski and Airman Grant closer to their end point, an abandoned trailer park north of the ranch. We rescued most of the RVs, trailers, fifth wheels and tiny houses from this place in the past years to provide housing for people in the Enclave. There were a few that were too dilapidated or fragile to move, and we've stocked them with a raider's bounty of food, and have planned to let the oncoming army "discover" our two team members.

The backstory is that they found this place and are, basically, highwaymen, taking what they can from passersby by threat of their lives. They have typical raider weapons: a couple of machetes, a shotgun and a pistol, but they only have ammo for the shotgun and not much at that. The working ranch, the reservoir, the towns of Gunnison and Cimarron, and the fact that this is the only road connecting these places makes their story plausible.

In fact, there were raiders here doing this very thing before we took them out of the picture. Most travelers simply took it as a toll they had to pay to pass, but getting rid of them certainly didn't hurt anyone's feelings. Now Kawalski and Grant will take their place. They will be there without radios, without any instructions other than to poison the army's food and water, and to cause as much havoc as they can without getting caught. Then, they are to separate from the group past the reservoir and return via whatever means they can after that—together or individually.

We hope they won't be found out. The two of them look tough enough, have mean faces and know their odds. We can't change course now, though I worry for them. They are grownups with just as much at stake as the rest of us.

Leaving the highway north of Fitzpatrick Mesa, I'm glad I am no longer on Beast's lap. I would definitely hit my head at this point. It's a bumpy ride. We park the Saucy Goose behind the mesa, off the road and in a highly treed area near Stumpy Creek, which is still flowing this time of year. This will help cover any incidental noises we make, though we will observe what Beast calls, "light and noise discipline." When we get out, we pull a camo net up and over the vehicle and use branches and other flotsam to decorate it.

Now, more of our team is going to split off and help insert Kawalski and Grant. Beast is going with them, and I am staying here to man the comm. We are in contact with the UAV operators in Crested Butte, so this will be our command center for awhile. We put up a ten-man tent and camouflage it well. While we are not likely to be spotted from above, there is no sense taking chances.

Inside the Stryker, I set up the comm center and check the radios of the insertion team. Beast, Seth Rawlins and Kim Thermopoli, will accompany Kawalski and Grant to the ranch. They are the best at the stealthy stuff. I really want to go, but I need time to rest and heal after my ordeal.

The ranchers were also informed to leave some supplies our two team members could "steal" and take with them to the RV park. I want them to maintain radio silence unless there is an emergency. It is unlikely that anyone would be able to tap my communications with the UAV team, but sound travels. I don't want them making any more noise than necessary.

I hug Beast tightly and tell him to stay safe. I will be here monitoring their every move via the high-flying UAV and listening in. I've got an earbud in my left ear to monitor them, while I have the UAV team in my other ear. For now, I will monitor days, Tess Nalwani has nights. Ben Waters will cover for either of us, as necessary, while the others are on guard duty. He's a light sleeper and grabs hours as needed, so we're not worried about him. It is almost 5:00 p.m.—1700 hours I mean. I even have the watch set to 24-hour time, but it's still just 5:00 p.m. to me.

By the time they get off the mesa, it will be dark. Not much of a moon tonight, so cover will be pretty good. Still, I worry. You never know what's out there anymore in the world we live in now. Beast and the others take off, and the waiting begins.

Chapter Twelve

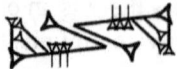

The hike to the ranch is almost too easy. We see only a few goats that must have been left to forage by the ranchers or were too wild to bring in. There is elk and deer scat, and I think I hear some kind of wild cat in the distance, but it's too far away to worry about.

We've done this trip before, three times. We wanted to know the trails, so the first two times were in daylight before doing a night run. Now it's full dark, and we have night vision goggles, if we need them. We haven't, though. Batteries, even rechargeable, are a precious commodity, and the moon gives us just enough light to find our way on this familiar trail.

We follow Stumpy Creek for a way and then turn southwest until we hit an abandoned farm house. It's beside two low-slung hills, and if one passes through the wooded valley between them, you come out at the far north side of the ranch.

We intend to go with Kawalski and Grant all the way to the ranch, but from there, they are on their own to the RV park. All the while, I pray to my Goddess that these two men succeed and get out of it with their lives.

The time is 1900 hours when we get to the abandoned house. The people here apparently starved to death or fled elsewhere. There is still a reek of death about the place. A lot of people died of starvation in the first year after the Collapse. People had maybe a week or two of food in their kitchens, and when trucks stopped delivering to the grocery stores, they didn't know where to find food. Often they would take off for the hills or plains, run out of gas and then start walking. Then, they'd starve, freeze or become prey for raiders.

Given our wartime situation, we aren't hiking for speed, but stealth. It takes longer. The valley though the two hills is wooded, so stealth involves moving slower so we make as little noise as possible. Not as easy as it sounds. We're golden though, and by 2000 hours we are at the north end of the ranch.

Rawlins is in the lead, using the scope on his rifle to see what's up. We pass fields with sprouts of newly planted alfalfa, wheat, corn and hops. As we are coming up on the outbuildings, Rawlins suddenly drops to the earth. When he does, we all do.

Quietly, he signs that there are two people ahead, in the ranch house. We spread out, high stealth mode now. I motion for Kawalski and Grant to go first, since they are supposed to be here. We are their backup. They move silently through the field, and we fan out. I'm to the right, Rawlins to the left and Thermopoli has rear guard. Rawlins and I keep fanning out so that we become the right and left flanks.

I search the bunkhouse and newly built outbuildings the ranch hands and their families live in. Rawlins and Thermopoli take the barns and lines of hay storage. Kawalski and Grant wait until we've found everything clear. All is silent. The ranchers haven't left anyone or anything behind.

We sweep back down to check the front and side yards, which are treed. No chickens are in the chicken house. The garden is plowed and most likely planted. All is still, except for the clatter inside the house. The area is clear, easy to see because light is spilling from all the windows. The solar batteries must be fully charged and these assholes are draining them by lighting the otherwise empty home.

The faint sound of drunken singing, laughter and breaking glass comes from an open window. I slide back around my side of the abode, motion that it's clear, and circle back to the front. Seth stays on his side, and Thermopoli circles to the right. We have the perimeter.

I know when Grant and Kawalski have entered because there are sounds of pandemonium. I hear yelling, the sound of fighting and only one gunshot. I wait, because I don't want anyone getting away. Eventually, Grant comes to the front door and says they've got the situation under control. When I enter, I lock the front door behind me and stride through to find out what we have.

Typical asshole-raider mess. The stock of food the ranchers left has been pillaged, but put to the side once they found the beer. Fuckwits had kicked back to get drunk with no one on watch and no cares in the world. There are two dead bodies, throats cut and bleeding out on the yellow linoleum tiles. One man is still alive, tied to a chair with a gunshot wound bleeding down his side and pattering onto the floor to join the other blood pools.

Alcohol may numb pain to a certain extent, but it also dilates your blood vessels, helping you bleed more freely. And the pain may make you sober up more quickly, but you will still bleed out faster if you don't get first aid. This guy is not getting any such thing.

"Hi, buddy," Rawlins says in a friendly voice when he enters the room. "Havin' a little party, were we?"

"I don't know who the fuck you guys think you are, but—"

His voice is cut off when I cuff him on the side of the head and growl. "No talking 'til we ask you questions, asshole."

"You are in so much trouble, and you don't even know it." He smirks.

Rawlins steps up. "You think we don't know about your little army, is that it?" The man looks startled, then shaken. "You just think you're gonna traipse on down the road and take over?" He doesn't answer, which is an answer.

"Now," I take command of the conversation, "Clearly, you are the lame-ass excuse for your idiot-army's scouts. Guys, you know what kind of army has scouts that don't post guards?"

It's a rhetorical question, but Kawalski answers it. "A pathetic, low-life, fuckwit army, sir."

"Yeah, that's right. You got anything to say for yourself, fuckwit?" I level a glare at the man.

"We have four more guys in the barn," he lies.

Rawlins makes a buzzer sound. "Wrong. We're not a half-assed army like you belong to. We already checked the barn. Want to try again?"

"Well, the army will be here in the morning," he attempts, sweating now.

"Wrong again. They left Cimarron this morning and probably got to Happy Valley this evening."

Kawalski speaks up, his baritone voice a low rumble, "I don't think he's got anything for us. Let's just kill him, nice and slow." Grant moves forward with his knife, grinning like a crazed idiot.

"No, I want to do it," says Thermopoli, grinning as she steps out from behind Grant, her eyes wild, and pins our captive's hand to the arm of the chair with a dagger.

"Wait!" the bandit screams. "I can give you numbers. Names! Caches of supplies." That last slows my people down and they look to me.

I sigh and say, "Talk."

We gave him an easy, quick death. I made sure he knew he was looking at a long slow one with that gut-shot wound, so he showed sufficient gratitude. There is a map of caches of water, food and other things they've scavenged. While I take the map, Kawalski and Grant take the two weapons the three raider scouts had, and all their ammo, which wasn't much. This along with any other useful items to complete their look.

"Keep each other safe, boys," Thermopoli tells them, "or Mrs. Kawalski says she'll kill both of you." Kawalski shakes his head with a grin, and he and Grant get ready to go.

They put the supplies the ranchers left back together and once they are set, head off down the road on bicycles. Kawalski is pulling a cart behind him, cleverly made with bicycle wheels and an old crate. Both it and the bikes had been stashed here waiting for them. I have their earbuds and anything else they had that might ruin their cover.

Now, we head back to camp. It is a faster walk because we're going over known territory and we don't have to be as cautious. We are still quieter than most, and there are just the three of us. The hike only takes us a couple of hours, and we're back to camp by 0100 hours.

We check in with the others who are seated around the dead campfire. Waters, Viv and Roche are shooting the shit, recounting past glories, I imagine. Roche is describing some medieval battle or other—he used to be a medieval recreation enthusiast—and I don't mind because we use classic battle techniques since they still work. He is getting excited, so I come stand behind them. Thermopoli and Rawlins settle in beside the others. They need wind-down time.

"Don't forget we have school tomorrow, kids." I mutter when Roche gets to a stopping point.

They all chuckle and Roche adds in, "Yeah, but we won't be the ones getting schooled." I clap him on the back and head to the small tent Chloe and I have set up downstream a little way.

She's camouflaged it with netting and branches, and if I hadn't helped set it up, I wouldn't even know it was here. She is inside, but not asleep. I pull off most of my gear before I slip in, but put it just inside the door, and crawl to her. This is the best way to wind down, here with my wife.

"Hello, handsome," she whispers. "Have a good night?"

"Roger that, beautiful. There are three fewer raiders on the face of the earth. Kawalski and Grant are in place, and now I get to sleep with my wife in my arms."

Beaming a smile at me, she scoots over as I crawl into the double sleeping bag. She winces so I stop and pull back the covers to take a look at her. No wonder she's still awake. Her breasts, still swollen and sore from weaning Leah, have a towel wrapped around them. My poor lady grimaces when she moves because of her bruises and cuts from her struggle earlier today.

"Sweet goddess, you need some salve. Hang on."

I go to her pack and pull the arnica and painkillers from the side pocket where I stashed them earlier. I also get one of the sage capsules Nena has given her, which she admits she has forgotten to take. Then I get her a canteen with water to take the pills and have her lie back so I can treat the bruises. I take my time, letting her relax and gently try to soothe what I can.

"I love you. Thank you for taking care of me."

"Baby, I've been taking care of you since the day I met you, without complaint."

Chloe scoffs. "Please! You were ready to kick me out the next damn day!"

"That was a test," I quickly reply with a grin. "One which you passed with flying colors. You've continued to amaze me non-stop ever since."

She shoots me a wry smile. "Nice save. Let's get some sleep?"

I finally cover her up and crawl in beside her. No shenanigans tonight. She is exhausted and hurt, so I cradle her in my arms in the most comfortable position she can find, and we both drift off to sleep.

Chapter Thirteen

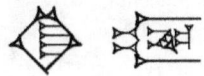

I wake to find myself alone in the tent. It is surprisingly silent outside, and I feel a raw panic as I scramble to get dressed and grab my boots. When I step outside, I slip into them, but leave off lacing.

My heart begins to race as I smell smoke. And blood. My heart is pounding in my chest and I run, boots flapping around my feet, up the bank of the creek to where the Stryker was parked.

It's gone. The tent we placed is burning, and there is blood on the ground, as if someone has been wounded. I search the area and find other places with blood trails. What happened here?

I reach for my weapons, and realize I've left them in the tent. Not a habit I have been in since I first met Beast. Turning around and around, I search for some clue as to what has happened, but there is just the burning tent and the blood.

"BEAST!" I scream, but the wind tears my voice away. The wind is strong, rocks me back on my feet.

"BEAST! Where are you? Beast!?"

My voice echoes and there is no response. Dropping to my knees, I begin sobbing. I feel utterly empty, lost. He's left me again. Why? Why? Why?

And, at that, my Beast wakes me from the nightmare. Soothing me with his touch and his softly murmured words. Warm arms pull me into his embrace, and I sob into his chest until the fear and horror leaves me.

"It's been a long time since you dreamt like this, love. Are you okay? Do you want to tell me?"

"I—you were gone when I woke up, and there was blood. Everyone was gone. The tent was on fire, and I thought you had left me again." I sob anew, and he strokes my hair, banishing my fears.

"I'm here, baby. It's okay now. Hush, it's all right."

My breathing slows, and I come back to myself. Between Beast's touch and the soothing rumble of his voice in my ears, I fall back to sleep.

Morning comes too soon, but I must have been more exhausted than I knew. Moving is difficult. My poor breasts are finally starting to feel a little better as the weaning process enters the third day. I'm hoping to feel more normal and less like a milk cow soon, and that thought is pleasant.

I don't know how Beast got up and dressed without waking me, he must have only had a few hours of sleep, but that is ever his way. Some mornings when I wake, he's already up, watching me sleep. Other times, he's holding Leah quietly so as not to wake me. He is my perfect mate and partner.

When I remember the dream, I get a chill and quickly dress myself. Grabbing my weapons and tactical gear, I lace up my boots before I step out of the tent. I smell food cooking, though, and something inside me eases. When I get to the main camp, Beast is stationed at a tiny camping stove making eggs, coffee, and blessedly, bacon.

"You talked one of the Corrigan brothers into giving you some bacon, I see. How did you manage that?"

Vivyayna laughs. "It was me. I asked Walt real nice."

"So, one axe or both?" Beast grins at my question, and the others laugh.

"He wanted me to go out with him, actually," she grins all feral-like. "And I said yes, if we both live that long and if he gave me the rest of the bacon. Barry is going to kill him, but we, my friends, will eat like queens—and kings."

Giving a half bow, she grabs the first piece of bacon. We all golf clap and then gladly line up for breakfast. It is going to be a long day.

When I'm done eating, I wash my dishes, get a fresh plate of food and take it to Tess to relieve her. With all the training camps we've had, breakfast is the one meal we all eat together and everyone attends the meeting, but I already know the plan and someone needs to be on the comm. Tess hands me her notes and takes the food.

"It was a slow night. I watched the team take out the house though. Very smooth."

"Yeah? You record it?" She looks at me like I'm crazy. Of course she did. "Thanks, Tess. Get some sleep after the meeting."

"You know it," she says around a bite of bacon.

I keep one ear and both eyes on the comm in front of me, but I still listen in. As the meeting starts, it reaffirms my thought that Beast came back different after he died and was reborn. He isn't sure, but I am. I remember all the arm waving, how he never spoke, even to our friends at Walma. Hell, he rarely even spoke to me. He'd growl, threaten and glare, with an occasional nod and bow thrown in for good measure. While he had softened some when we began to fall in love, he has never stopped wearing that mask. But when he was reborn, I think some of the pain of his former life must have been healed.

Maybe seeing his lost wife and daughter, Anna and Katie, on the other side was part of it. Perhaps, seeing them at peace and happy, he was able to let them go. Maybe just a correction of a short circuit in his heart, or something else only the Goddess knows. Whatever it is, he is different, better, more able to do the job he was returned here to do. It warms my heart to hear him lead our Reapers.

One of the drones has just taken off and is flying high. The cameras are highly sensitive, which is why I get such good images. I am also told that with the right tech, a drone can pinpoint a strike. It hovers over the target, the operator finds the exact target we want, and it points a laser at the object. That way the people on the ground can then direct their fire to the laser point. Very effective. Seth is anxious to try it, but we don't know what kind of opportunities we will have. We also don't have a lot of ordinance to waste.

Beast goes over our plans again, and I listen while sipping my coffee. I did not forget my painkillers and my sage pill this morning, so I take those, as well as my birth control pill. I wonder how the children are. They may very well be leaving the Enclave today, probably this afternoon. I hope Nena isn't having any difficulty. I think they will be fine, because Jimmy is so eager to help, to please. He is such a precious boy.

I have not gotten any information out of our Jimmy as to who his parents were or what happened to them. He says he doesn't remember. I hope that's true. I know, in children, trauma can block memory, and time, which helps to cure the physical pains, can also dim the memories of bad times. I hope he didn't have any nightmares with us gone. I say a quick prayer to whoever is listening to watch over our family and friends.

Now, Beast is handing out assignments. I am pretty much stuck here, but that's okay. We will be here a few days. The job is to set up some ambushes that won't really go into effect until the army gets closer. Camp chores are divided, and Beast wants to test some of the explosives we got from our mad scientist soap makers back at the Enclave. I think it's insane, and have a horrible notion that someone will get their hand—or something worse!—blown off messing with this stuff.

Seth and Viv have been at the forefront of chemical and explosive testing. Both of them are excited and flippant about the dangers. I can't help to yell out the doorway of the Stryker that they need to be careful with that stuff. They laugh at me.

"Okay mom," Viv taunts, "and if we shoot our eye out we won't come crying to you." Everyone laughs again.

"Real funny. But it would be best if you had Beast take care of your burns and amputations. He's better at medical stuff anyway." Another laugh. *Hilarious, guys. Ugh.*

"Nobody is going to get blown up, Chloe. We do know what we're doing." Seth calls out. "We are trained professionals."

I turn my attention back to the monitors. The UAV has already sent images from the area of the ranch and show the raiders' supply trucks are almost to the next night's camping spot. I am very interested in this. Even though there is no sound, I put both plugs in my ears and pay full attention to the monitors. The camera zooms in very well. The trucks have already driven past the RV park on their way to the next camping area. We've made bets about where they will stop.

Two of us think just south of Fitzpatrick Mesa, where we are presently, but most of us are betting they'll stop at the ranch. There is another, nicer ranch house just northwest of the ranch, but it is not easily seen from the road, so we're pretty sure they're not going to stop there. But Roche thinks they will find it, not realizing the sheer stupidity of raiders, I imagine. Just because he would have found it doesn't mean they will. He is always the optimist.

I watch the trucks slow as they approach the ranch, then stop on the highway. They are stopped for a long time. I think they might be waiting for their scouts to come out. Hmm.

"Guys, we do anything with the raiders' bodies at the ranch?" I call out.

Beast concludes the meeting and comes into the Stryker to look over my shoulder. "Why?"

"The camping vehicles stopped there to pick up the scouts, I think."

"We buried them in the back forty. No time to burn them. They're under a few feet of topsoil, so they are not going to show up for their meeting. And we cleaned up the blood. We didn't want the ranchers to have to deal with that mess when they got home."

I nod and go back to the monitor. Another few minutes pass and someone gets out of one of the trucks, walks up the long driveway and peers into the house. He walks around, kicks in the back door, disappears and then comes back out again. Walking back to the truck, he gets in and the small convoy drives up the road.

Beast walks back outside and tells Kim Thermopoli and Tess Nalwani they won. They high-five and demand the money from the pool. Of course, the money isn't worth shit anymore, but they don't care. It's really all about the bragging rights.

Shaking my head, I go back to paying attention to the road again. The UAV has flown on down the road, and now I can see the army. It looks really, really big, walking in a mass the way they are. I don't like it. The leaders of the herd are nearing the RV park, though, so I keep my eyes open. I see Kawalski and Grant ambling around the park like they own it. They have a nice little set up. Lawn chairs and a cooler with what is left of the beers.

My heart is pounding in my chest. This is the moment they live or die. I hear Beast in the background giving orders to get the day team together and on the road and for the night team to get some rest. But I am focused on the video on my screen sent from the UAV, to someone in Crested Butte, to a satellite that is still up in orbit, and then back to me.

Finally, there is action. The leaders of the walking gang of raiders see Kawalski and Grant. They get weapons up and run toward them, probably shouting. I see another few guys circling the RV park through the overgrown fields making no effort to cover themselves. They are stupidly overconfident and show it.

Now, we see Kawalski and Grant on their feet, and I feel the vehicle shift as Beast comes into the Stryker behind me. He wants to see this play out, too. I hear a few others crowd in behind, but pay them no mind. The raiders are surrounding our guys, and they seem to be checking each other out.

Then suddenly, Kawalski and Grant are on the ground and my heart stops for a moment before I realize they have assumed the position. They are searched for weapons and being questioned. The army continues to march down the road with just six or seven remaining behind to question the two men. Our guys could easily take out the six and melt into the tall grass before anyone noticed, but they have a different job to do.

One of the raiders makes my heart quail, and I don't know why. Staring at the image, taken from above and to the side, though, I cannot make out any distinct features. Yet, I feel certain this is Kane. Glancing quickly at Beast, I notice that he is rubbing his tattoo, so I feel sure I'm right. A shudder runs through me. If Kane is in communication with the dark god or goddess that resurrected him, we are through. But whoever raised him may not be as thoughtful as our Goddess, and that is all we can hope.

207

Finally, one of the raiders is helping our two teammates to their feet, shaking their hands in a parody of honor after they collect their belongings. Kawalski and Grant fall in with the marching army, now safely inserted. I note that two other members of the army have taken their bicycles and ridden off on them. Too bad. I was hoping our guys would be made into the new scouts.

I let out a breath I didn't realize I was holding and turn to give the others in the vehicle a thumbs up. A little cheer goes up and the strike force gets ready to move out. They have planted a few surprises on the road past the ranch, just to let the army know they aren't welcome here.

Chapter Fourteen

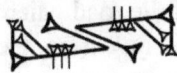

Chloe was not happy to be left behind again, but she's not willing to slow us down by coming along, injured and in pain as she is. She knows this logically, but my dark-haired vixen still longs for action. I think she'll be ready by tomorrow when we move camp. In the meantime, my team and I take a different route off the plateau than we did last night.

I take Rawlins, Viv, Roche and Thermopoli. We leave behind Nalwani and Waters with Chloe. Waters will nap once Nalwani wakes up, but until then, is on guard duty. He's also our other medic, and I try to keep the two of us separate in case an emergency happens to one team or the other.

We head southeast on the mesa until we hit an old ranch and logging camp. We'd removed the lumber a long time ago. The good stuff went back to our valley, mostly for the trading post. Some of the other logs were half rotted from lying on the ground for over two years, so we found another use for them. At present, they are on the back of a logging truck near a right angle turn on the nearby highway.

We've salted the highway a half-mile west of the logging truck with an ingenious device of Roche's invention. He's come up with something called caltrops. They are spikes that always have one point facing up no matter how they land on the ground. Ours are made with nails from the hardware store, welded together. He is overjoyed his history as a medieval reenactment enthusiast is paying dividends. He says these used to be hell on armies and their horses. Now, we'll see how effective they are against modern tires.

This is the goal. We want to slow them down, harry them, piss them off. We don't mind using medieval methods. We've salted the road with a few dozen caltrops and covered them with mulch and debris that looks like it accumulated there at the bottom of a hill over a few years of storms.

By the time we get to this part of the road, we see they've already found our surprises. There are three trucks and two motorcycles. Both motorcycles are down. Of the three trucks, two of them are down. The truck in the rear was far enough behind that it stopped before it ran into any trouble.

Roche points to the side of the road where a few people are down, having stepped on his demonic invention. He's grinning like a fool. I shake my head and motion for everyone to take their positions.

"I told you it would work."

"Roche?" I ask softly.

He shoots me a quick glance. "Yeah, boss?"

"Shush."

The man just sniggers like a six year old who just got the coolest Christmas present ever. I've noted that for a mechanic, he's a little on the bloodthirsty side. This is probably why he fits in so well.

Quietly, we take our positions. We were prepared to neutralize any posted guards. So far, there are none. They are so busy trying to get the vehicles working again and caring for their wounded they never posted any. *Amateurs.*

Our number one target is Kane, but Chloe says she spotted him with the rear of the army. Target number two is the Reverend. To our luck, he is in one of the downed trucks. He's sitting in the front seat comfortably while his minions scurry around. The window's down, and it looks like he's taking a nap.

The weapons we are carrying come in two varieties. The first is bolt action, fitted with makeshift suppressors. They're our long range, heavy hitters shooting big bullets that can reach out and throttle someone. Then, we have lighter M4s and AKs if we get into serious trouble.

We dug out a dozen emplacements on this hill some time ago, imagining scenarios with incoming raiders. Down below is where we want the raiders to camp, or rather, a little way down the road where there is a wide flat plain. We want them spread out.

In the meantime, we are going to deploy some chaos.

The truck in the rear is backing up and turning around, probably going to get some reinforcements from the rest of the army to help change and/or repair multiple truck tires. Perfect.

We are all in place. There are a little over a dozen people down below, scurrying around and not paying attention. There are five of us. Odds seem pretty good. My team is waiting on me to make the first shot. Goddess, I miss Chloe.

Sighting in on the Reverend, I aim through the open window for a head shot. I squeeze the trigger and as I do—he falls to the seat. Before I shoot him. My round punches into the headrest.

What the fuck?

At the sound of my shot, four other suppressed shots take out more of the enemy. The Reverend has not shown his face yet. The truck is armor-plated, so I can't try to tag him through the door.

I turn my attention to raiders who are looking around as their comrades fall. We get ten of them, and the other three are now hiding under the trucks, attempts to change the tires forgotten for the moment. I want to go down there and find out what happened to the Reverend, but it is time to move. The survivors are gathering nerve to start shooting back wildly.

We ghost out of the area and get ready for our next move just up the road. It is over the hill and around the right angle of the turn where we have the log truck ready and waiting. It is going to be a while, so we post Roche as rear guard and have a bite to eat while we wait.

"Hey boss?" Roche whispers over the radio.

"This is Beast. Go."

"I want permission to sneak in after the trucks have passed and salt the road again."

I don't know that I'm thrilled with the idea. He'd have no cover if he got spotted. Still, it would be rather effective since the enemy would probably think the road had been cleared by their forward group.

"Fine," I reply. "Just keep your eyes open. We can't cover you from here."

"Hey, it's me."

We all roll our eyes and then wait. A lot of time passes before we hear the sound of the third truck returning. There is a clamor of men and vehicles from over the hill but we stay under cover and continue waiting. There is some shooting at our former emplacement we think, or maybe they're killing the remnants of the team that survived, we don't know.

It takes another hour for all the new people to get the trucks up and going again. We purposefully did not hit any of their fuel tanks, though that would not have made them explode anyway. Contrary to what movies would have you believe, it's never that easy, I promise. There has to be actual fire or sparks hitting *fumes*, in case you wondered.

Finally, we hear the trucks starting up, and we assume they've taken care of the rest of the caltrops in the road and have reinforcements. We haven't seen any radios at all, just a few Radio Shack-style walkies that can't hear our military versions, so I radio Roche that he should be clear to salt the road with more caltrops, but wait to make sure he's safe, then, fall back to our rendezvous point.

Soon, the trucks are crawling down the road again, less confident about what might lie ahead. The two motorcycles we wrecked have been replaced with two guys on familiar-looking bicycles. Not Kawalski or Grant. We would know if it was them, because they have specific

211

bandanas to designate them. In fact, it was Kim that chose them—bright pink Hello Kitty pattern that gave all the guys bitter beer faces. They've been instructed to wear them so we don't accidentally kill them.

We'd found them along with more skull versions like Chloe's in an old biker shop. We requisitioned them for the team. Chloe loves the bandanas even though she teased me about being sentimental in my old age.

Soon, the trucks are in range. We don't want the bicycles, just the trucks. The logging truck has been sitting here a while. We don't know how well it will work, but it's what we have on hand, and we're going to use it. The steering wheel is tied down, so it won't turn away from the course. We want it to head straight down the hill and onto the road.

We get ready to go, when I hear Chloe's voice on the radio. "Retreat, man on the road. Tango ten o'clock in the brush. Suppressive fire."

She's not talking to us, so all we can do is to keep doing our job. Thermopoli and Viv take the chocks out of the front tires. Rawlins and I take the chocks out of the rear tires, and then take it out of park before taking off the parking brake. I jump out of the way as it groans and moves forward. We quickly retreat up and over the top of the hill.

The truck rolls down the hill, reaching a breakneck speed before crashing into the rear of the lead enemy vehicle. Lying down behind the crest of the hill, I tell Thermopoli and Rawlins to get back to the rendezvous point while Viv and I watch the fun below. I can't help but think again it should be Chloe here beside me, but shake it off as I watch the raiders. Several men get out of the second truck and start shooting up the hill at where we used to be.

I am itching to get a bullet into the Reverend, but he is nowhere to be seen, at least, not from this angle. Their truck is damaged, but not crippled. The log truck kept going after the crash with the supply truck. It went into a ditch and stopped short, spilling some of the logs across the highway. Not quite the success we wanted, but not too bad either. They are shaken and worried. Time to go.

As I start to turn, I catch sight of Roche following the last truck, hands bound and tied to the bumper, stumbling to keep up. *Fuck!* This is who Chloe was talking to. We can only watch as the truck slows and Roche comes to a stop behind it, his head hanging down.

The Reverend exits the second truck, careful to keep the vehicle between us and him. All I see is his hand as he holds it out and one of his men hands him what I think is Roche's radio. I let out a growl; I want to rip the fucker's head off. I know Viv feels the same by the way she is vibrating beside me.

With no further ado, they stand Roche up in front of a tree and line up firing squad-style. This is a show for our benefit. Why waste all those bullets otherwise? I tell Viv to get as many of them as she can, starting from the right. I've got the left, and we start firing as soon as they do. While Roche falls, so do the six members of the firing squad.

It is time to go to the next rendezvous point, and radio silence is in effect. I—we—will pay them back for this travesty. The six that we sent to Hell for Shawn is most definitely not enough. There will be more to follow.

Chapter Fifteen

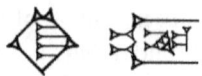

I'm in the Stryker watching on my monitors when Beast's team comes upon the downed trucks. I watch all the bodies go down. In a new camera angle, I can see the army marching ever closer to our homes and try to pick out Kawalski and Grant. It's impossible. They've melted into the mass, and that's all for the best.

We do some reconnaissance, checking for extra scouts. They must be missing the ones that were killed the night before. We see some movement near the ranch house again, but can't get anything. The leaders haven't been terribly smart that we can see, but that doesn't mean they are dumb, just careless. So far.

But then the UAV cameras start sending images of the area Beast's team took down the trucks, each telling a story as it comes in one at a time. The army has sent more troops who are getting the vehicles up and running again. When the convoy moves out, I notice they send about a half a dozen men into the brush on the west side of the road.

Time passes, and the UAV has stayed focused on that side of the road. I consider telling Beast and the team, but they are on to the next ambush, so I am not too worried. But, then I see a form dart out of hiding on the east side of the road. One of our guys. He is sowing the handmade nail caltrops on the road, presumably for the incoming army.

I get on the radio, push the button to speak, "Retreat, man on the road. Tango ten o'clock in the brush. Suppressive fire!"

And then they are all over him and it's over before he can even answer. Shit. I am guessing its Roche, those things were his idea. Damn it! Now what?

They cuff Roche, he falls to the ground, draws a pistol and takes two of them down before the others fall onto him. The operator zooms in, so the images show him throwing something. It's small, maybe a grenade? Nothing explodes, so I guess not. The next image is him on his belly, and they are kicking him.

This is killing me. I want to say something but they may have his radio, and we can't show our numbers. Maybe that's what he was throwing? I am on my feet, urging him to escape somehow, though I know he can't hear me. I can't stand it.

Now, he's on his feet and they've tied him to the bumper of the truck. What, are they going to drag him now? He leg-sweeps one of his captors, it looks like. The guy is going to go after him, but someone else holds him back. They drag their dead to the ditch and take off after the truck. It's moving slowly. Maybe they aren't going to drag him after all.

I can't make out our team members over the hill, but the image pulls out and refocuses. Now, the image of the log truck at the top of the hill is clear, though it looks odd from above. It is pulling loose from the hill and careening down to meet one of the supply trucks. The images come one after another like an old-time movie showing the chaos with logs rolling off the truck and scattering as it comes to a stop in the ditch. One of the supply trucks has been impacted, but it doesn't look like it caused much harm. That's when things get worse.

All I can do is watch in horror as those assholes line up and shoot Roche. I can't tell if our people know what has happened until I see the six shooters also go down. That's my man right there. I cheer inside the Stryker, tears rolling down my face. I can't say anything on the radio or give up our numbers through Roche's radio. All the same, I am so furious with the raiders I want to reach through the monitor and bitch slap someone.

Throwing down the headphones in helpless fury, I sob for a moment. Then I reach down to pick them up, just as an arrow slices through the air where I was just sitting. Bouncing off the monitor, the impact knocks it over. Throwing myself to the floor, I draw my pistol. There is nobody in the doorway of the Stryker. Carefully easing forward, I look out the doorway for any sign of who sent that arrow, but can't see anything.

Furious with myself that someone was able to sneak up on our camp on my watch, I get the dental mirror out of my vest, grateful I remember this trick from the old days in Los Angeles. I carefully look around the right side of the Stryker, see nothing, then move to the other side and spot my prey. He's wearing camo gear, hugging the left side of the vehicle, waiting for me to show my face around the corner. I'm low, so he doesn't see my reflection.

I have a round chambered, so I snake my arm around the corner of the vehicle and start shooting. I hit him, and he lets another arrow fly wildly before I hear a heavy thud and a scream as he falls to the ground. Coming around the corner now, I wish I had Beast beside me to go high. The fucker looks so surprised when I shoot him in the face. My weapon is suppressed, so there's not a lot of sound, other than his brief scream. I drop to the ground again to make sure he doesn't have any friends with him.

215

The tent Tess is sleeping in is a few steps away, and I hear a struggle going on inside it. Shit. Where is Ben Waters? I hope they didn't kill him, too. I get a chill when I remember Nena said we would lose two. Damn it, we need all of our team!

Tess needs help, so I get there fast, checking the area as I go. I don't see anyone else, so I hope this is the only other threat. When I get there, she is pinned to the floor of the tent by another raider, also dressed in camo, though his pants are down, exposing part of his ass. He holds her hands down with one hand and has shoved a sock in her mouth. Her eyes are wide and tears are spilling down her face. When she spots me, her eyes widen, but she doesn't give me away.

The raider's last few minutes are rough. I stop the rape by stabbing the asshole in the most obvious target, his ass. Well, okay, his asshole to be precise. With a scream, he rolls, letting go of Tess and giving her the opportunity to take the knife I hand her. She makes a bloody mess of the guy before finally letting him die.

While she is having her moment of revenge, I search for Ben Waters. He's down, bleeding from a scalp wound. *Fuck!* As I rush up to check him, he begins to come-to.

"Wh- what's that sound?" He asks groggily.

"Oh. That's the raider Tess is killing. He shouldn't have put his dick where it didn't belong, I guess."

His eyes widen. "What? He-"

"He was raping her. Now, she gets to make him suffer. I don't see a problem, you?"

"Uh, no. Is she okay?"

I sigh. "I don't know. Probably not. But this might help. It helped me." I have never made my past a secret, but I haven't exactly done a dissertation either.

Now he looks angry. "Bastard snuck up on me and hit me with a rock. You think she'd let me help?"

"It might be too late by the sounds of it, but we can go check. You ready to get up?"

With a nod, I help pull him to his feet. By the time we get to the tent, Tess is pretty much done. She's cleaned up her mess as well, having taken him outside to do the major portion of her work. I don't think she'll have any problems during interrogations again.

"You okay?" I quietly ask Tess while helping Waters to sit down and clean the wound on the back of his head.

"I will be." She's angry still, as she should be.

She'd forgotten what these raiders were like, having lived, for the main part of her life since the Collapse, on Nellis, followed by a year in the Enclave among people who are not savages. Getting a shovel, she

216

starts digging a hole far enough away from the creek that it won't cause any problems downstream. Normally, we'd burn pieces of shit like this, but the smoke would give us away. Then, an epiphany hits me and I stop her.

"We have the latrine ditch. That's good enough for the likes of him and his friend." She grins evilly and puts the shovel down. "Go through his things and see what he has. His friend is on the other side of the Stryker. I know he has a crossbow, so we can take that off his hands."

I tell Waters he's going to need stitches. "Sorry, Ben, my stitching isn't as nice as Beast's, but this needs to be sewn up."

Going through the kit, I find what I need, and tell him to brace himself. We don't really have Novocain anymore. What we do have is reserved for tooth extractions and critical surgeries.

He winces as I douse the area with alcohol, something easily made and filtered, and start stitching. To his credit, he doesn't make a sound, and I soon have the wound closed. We have a little antibiotic ointment, so I use some sparingly on the wound and cover it with a bandage.

Tess has bundled up all of the raiders' possessions on a tarp she's placed on a table. Now, Waters and I help her carry the bodies to the latrine area. We take the privacy screens down, no sense leaving them up when we won't need it. The bodies make a satisfactory squelch as they land in the ditch, and we start piling the dirt over the top of them.

"From shit you have come and to shit you return, you sick pieces of shit," I intone as we bury them. "May your afterlives be unquiet and filled with torture. Amen."

"Amen," the other two repeat heartily.

I leave them to finish it up and go back to the Stryker. I need to see what's going on with my man and his team. After this little adventure, I am worried about him. So far, these bastards have shown themselves to be more effective in some ways than we thought.

I half wonder if there are two armies here. The main army of idiots with the Reverend, and the special ops army with Kane. I try to remember if the two assholes we just buried had a "K" tattoo anywhere obvious, but I just don't remember.

Picking up the monitor, I straighten my station, trying to see where the UAV's point of view is now. It's on our camp, and I soon see why. There are more tangos incoming, about a dozen of them are hiking up the side of the mesa.

Making a note of where they are, I rush to get my team. There are three of us, and that is plenty to take them out. I grab my Tavor and tac gear and get the other two so we can ambush the incoming assholes. I think they both have a bone to pick.

217

Ten minutes later, we're situated at the perfect location to ambush the raiders. They are a way up the mesa still, most of them out in the open. There's a ridge, however, with some shrubs and trees along it, and that is where the group was marching when I last saw them. The sun is high, shadows are short, they were marching pretty fast it seemed to me, as if their buddies had radioed them where to go. We have the radios they were using, nowhere near as nice as our military issue, but we haven't heard anything on them yet.

After crossing the creek, we pick a nice spot of high ground, a small rock formation where we can lie prone and take them all out. I've set a claymore at the curve where the creek and tree cover swing to the east. When we have them past that position, I will activate the remote detonator. Once it goes off, we can pick off the survivors.

Waters has been switching channels when he hears them. "Rufus, where you at, over?"

He looks at me. I shrug. We're in the trees some distance from our camp, where I think they're going to approach us. If they keep going the way they were headed, it will be easy for them to skirt the creek-bed and use the cover of the trees.

"In position." Waters states into the enemy walkie. He raises his eyebrows and shrugs back at me. "Over."

"We'll be there in about ten, you got them subdued? Over."

"Yeah, no problem. Two women. Over."

There is an evil chuckle. "Save some for us, fellas."

"Will do." Waters is also angry. "Over and out."

"Roger."

"Well, wasn't that sweet." I say softly. "They'll be here soon, so be ready. We want all of them in sight before we let loose. And like the man said, we have to save some for him."

Tess lets out a bark of laughter. "I've saved something for him, all right."

Waters nods grimly and we all settle in. We're not widely spread out, but wide enough to get a few angles. Yet, not so close that it is easy to suppress all of us with return fire or get us all with a single grenade.

"We shoot on my mark. I will take the leader. Waters, you take the rear. Tess, you just pick out whoever you want and ruin their day, yeah?"

She nods seriously. I do see a glint of tears, but this is not the time for therapy and conversation. When she glances over at me, I nod to her, sympathy and determination on my face. Tess sets her chin, nods back, and refocuses on her sights.

When the raiders finally do come, it's not all quiet and serious. It's with laughing, guffaws, crude jokes and boasts of how many times they can rape a woman before she is used up. Wrong day for that kind of humor, fellas.

A red dot is a woman's best friend. It makes your target acquisition easy and quick—provided, of course, you have battery power. This is one time I want to use it. We're at war, and that's no time for holding back.

Our targets are in position, and I activate the detonator. There's a nice loud explosion as the enemy team is enveloped in the blast. Smoke and dirt cover them, making it impossible to see them at first.

As the first of the survivors stumble out of the cloud, we open fire. They aren't prepared mentally for our ambush. I'm sure between the concussion from the blast and dust in their eyes, it's impossible for them to mount a proper offense. Most don't even have the sense to dive for cover. I can hear Tess yelling like a banshee as she lays into them, probably wasting more ammo than needed, but I'm not telling her no.

When we're done, there aren't any left to fulfill any of those boasts. Amazingly, we have one left alive to take back and question. His legs are still good, so we make him walk, dripping blood. The rest, we strip of gear and leave for the wildlife to take care of. We only buried the other two so the next group wouldn't run across them. At this point, I figure they know where we are. We're going to have to move camp.

Chapter Sixteen

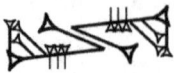

When we get to the rendezvous point, I have the unenviable job of telling everyone Roche didn't make it. There are shocked expressions, and I really don't want to talk about it now. We're still on the clock.

"Maybe he made a mistake. More than likely he just got dealt a bad fucking hand. It's that simple. Any of us can get screwed, and if we're lucky, it won't cost us our lives when we do. Let's keep moving, and respect the man by finishing the mission. The more of those assholes we take out, the better we avenge his death."

The shock eases off their faces, and grim determination takes its place. Now, we're a man down, so we all need to work a little harder. We are in position, overlooking the wide area of plain we want the raiders to camp in. It's almost ten miles from their last camp, about as far as they seem to travel in one day, especially with the problems they've had so far today. They want to get places fast, but they can't push the army too hard or they won't have one left.

We watch through our scopes as they roll on down the hill and stop. Slowly, they start unloading and setting up the food tents near an old snowplow shelter that's shaped like an igloo. Below the shelter and down the hill is an area that had once been a site for grazing cattle. We only know this because the ranchers mentioned it. Now, there's a largely unused pond in spring and early summer, and lots of nice soft grass.

They don't know we've scattered more of Roche's caltrops in the field—reasoning we can pull them later with magnets if necessary—and have placed random pit traps in the ditches. We've also trapped the nearby building, a bunkhouse for the cowboys who lived there in the summer. Nobody lives there now. The house was damaged over two long winters of snow and neglect. But, we know raiders are nosy bastards and will likely venture in, even if they're forbidden. There are trip wires in the barn and a pressure plate on the back porch of the bunkhouse.

When the troops start marching in, two familiar bandanas are in the lead group and are herded to the kitchen tent. So, as we figured, they have to work before they eat, and have been put right where we wanted them. Good news for us, bad news for the raiders.

So much of what we do is waiting. The pit traps in the ditches are deadfalls with a few tricks the Vietcong used on Americans during the Vietnam War. The bunkhouse has some explosive mines we liberated from Nellis. We don't have a lot of them, but this is the perfect time to utilize them.

We watch a little while longer, but they are where we want them. The traps will do the rest of our work for us. It's time to move out. I hope Kawalski and Grant are able to do their job and that they don't get caught doing it.

The hike back up the mountainside is quiet. Not that we're normally chatty or anything, but we are missing Roche. If he were here, he would be crowing about how well the caltrops worked, egging on Rawlins about medieval versus modern. The silence is too fucking loud, and depression is a cloud hanging over our heads. I want to know what happened, how he was caught. I can't use the radio until we set new frequencies, since we have to assume Roche's radio was captured.

If everything is going as planned, Kawalski and Grant have added their Oleander concentrate to the food or water. Or both, if we're lucky. Their army will start feeling weird, nauseated and dizzy. They might get headaches and vomit. They won't have time to make the latrines. They'll use the ditches around the field for their diarrhea. Some will die. I just hope the women and children get a different batch of food. It won't be pleasant. If we are very lucky, the Reverend and Kane will eat with the troops.

By the time we get back to camp, it isn't there. I feel a momentary panic but see a blaze on one of the trees that is a sign from Chloe that they've moved camp. We thought something like this could happen. They will be in a predetermined fall-back point, and the blaze on the tree tells me which it is. Not too far.

An hour later, we come in sight of the Stryker. Chloe has not set up camp again, they have been waiting for us. Waters looks rough, has a bandaged scalp wound. Nalwani and Chloe both look weary, but all three of them smile when they see the rest of us.

"What happened?" I ask when we get close enough.

"Raiders. We took out fifteen. You?" Chloe's eyebrow quirks. She is so competitive.

I laugh. "Twenty."

"Yeah, but there were only three of us. That's five each. Divide your kills by what, five of you?" Then, a shadow passes over her face. There are only four of us now.

"What happened? We never saw anything but Roche gunned down."

221

"They sent a half a dozen men into hiding beside the road under cover of the trucks. Roche couldn't have seen them. I warned him as soon as I saw him on the road, but it was too late. He took three of the raiders down before they got him."

I grimace. "What happened to the camp?"

"Raiders. We were so busy watching the road that we didn't notice the group that came up the way you went down last night. Admittedly, they were mostly under cover of trees, but the two scouts got the drop on Waters, and were trying to assault Tess. One almost shot me with a crossbow. We saved it, by the way, and a nice bunch of bolts to go with it. We killed the scouts and ambushed the rest of their gang, but we decided to pack up. We don't know who they told about our location. We captured one, but he was worse than useless, so we killed him, too. We will want to get off the mesa now."

I grunt. "We'll fall back to our next site in the Gunnison River forest."

We get drinks of water and energy bars, and pile into the APC. I know we are all missing Roche at this moment, but damned if I know what to say. I grimly stare into space as the Saucy Goose starts up and we start moving.

My Angel is better than I am, though. She lets us sit for a few minutes, then she brings up memories of our missing comrade. "Remember that time just a few months ago, we were out on maneuvers and Roche built himself an igloo, just to prove he could do it?"

Everyone laughs and Viv chimes in, "Fool nearly froze to death but he was going to prove it was good shelter if it killed him."

Then, she swallows, looking stricken, and Chloe reaches over to squeeze her shoulder. Yeah, it doesn't matter how hardened a combat veteran you are. You still grieve over the loss of a comrade.

Then Rawlins pipes up. "I remember when I first met Roche. The Founders here—" He motions toward Chloe and I. "—just brought me and this bunch of half-raw idiots from Nellis and damned if the cocky bastard didn't try to pick a fight with me first thing. Course, after we had it out, he bought me a beer, so I had to figure he just liked being in pain."

Everyone laughs again, and the stories about Roche begin in earnest. This is the way we will remember our dead. This is healing, this banter. It's like a mental version of stitching up a wound. I pull out my flask of vodka and pass it around, and we make sure to keep the intercom open for Nalwani and Waters to hear from the driver's seat.

I clear my throat. "Let me tell you about the first time I got Roche on a horse..."

Chapter Seventeen

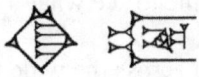

The ride to the next campsite is long. We stick to back roads...
bumpy back roads. Turns out an armored personnel carrier like the
Stryker is not known for its wonderfully comfortable suspension.
According to my husband, this is common with all military vehicles.

To be honest, I am beginning to feel a lot better. Yes, I still have
bruises, but they aren't as painful as they were. And my breasts are
beginning to feel less sore. It's almost like I am getting my old body
back. The one I had before I gave birth and turned my entire life, heart
and soul, over to my child. I know, that sounds peevish, but until you've
had a baby and lived through its first year of life, you don't get to
criticize.

I am half asleep, head resting on Beast's shoulder when we finally
reach our destination. We are in the wooded hills just south of the
Gunnison River and north of highway 50. It is a forest and on our
scouting trips, this has always been my favorite place. We won't be here
too long, the army will catch up with us sooner than we like, but we have
some surprises in store, and I can't wait to get back into action.

Setup is quick. We have semi-permanent shelters here. Just need a
tarp over the roof and we're mostly set. We also have golf carts. Yes,
golf carts. They're much quieter than ATVs, and we have solar chargers
for them. There are three fully-charged and hidden nearby. We make
sure they're all good to go.

Next, Seth Rawlins and Kim Thermopoli take off to set the remote
charges in case we have visitors. This area is a natural box canyon,
heavily treed, and there is only one obvious way in and out. We know the
charges will be there, and we have alternate routes that are not so
obvious if we need another way out. The rest of us set camp. It is much
easier than the last one since we have temporary structures in place.

Heavy clouds are gathering overhead, and I think we're going to see
some rain soon. I hope the rain mucks up the Reverend's army, as well.
As for us, we'll be warm and dry. If there's rain, we may actually get to
have a fire.

By the time Rawlins and Thermopoli are back, we're set up and I'm back at the monitor watching the army settle in for the night. Half the group is huddled up behind me to see what's going on, but there isn't that much to see.

The army has set tents all across the wide field, as we thought they might. The women and children are finally being fed, and I can't help but hope they don't get any of the poisoned food. The rest of those assholes, however, deserve anything they get.

I haven't seen Liz at all since that first UAV image they brought to the Enclave. I keep looking without really meaning to, but I never see her. Where is she? What is she doing? Surely, they're still getting information out of her. Is she with the women and children or with the main group? It's driving me quietly insane, the wondering.

Most of the tents or tarps or whatever the army's been using have been set up. Many of the men have spread out beyond the campsite, exploring, poking around, just as we knew they would. They don't generally build latrines, just leave a mess wherever they've stayed like the savages they are.

I don't see signs of any sickness yet. Maybe there wasn't enough of the poison in the food. I don't know what I thought I would see, though. It will take some time to work through their systems, and that is only if our guys got the poison in the food. They may not have had an opportunity.

The evening wears on. It's certainly boring work, sitting in front of a monitor and waiting for something to happen. It is dusk when I notice a squad of men investigating the further reaches of the field.

"Guys, guys, look. We got some takers on the bunkhouse." Rawlins crowds too close and I swat him back. "Looks like at least a dozen. And, wait for it..."

Everyone seems to hold their breath as we watch impatiently. Half of the group stops, waits for others to catch up. They head to the barn. Now, it's a larger group of several dozen in the barn and another dozen at the old farm house. The interior of the Stryker is so quiet that I probably could hear a pin drop.

"The suspense is killing me," Viv exclaims and everyone shushes her.

More of the army are heading toward the barn, some of them lugging barrels. Others have boxes or small wooden crates. Maybe some kind of party is going on? Good, the more of them the better.

"Come on!" Rawlins bursts out, scaring me half to death.

I punch him, and the others all pummel him, as well. We are so distracted that we almost miss the bloom of an explosion when the bunkhouse goes up. This is quickly followed by the barn. *Oh yeah.*

The cheer from my team could probably be heard miles away at the Reverend's camp, if they weren't all deaf from the detonation. Detonations. The rest of the team leaves the Stryker, and I finally get some breathing room. I will keep an eye on it a little longer, then leave it to Tess for the night. Tomorrow, I will go with my man to take out the trucks. I am looking forward to it.

When it finally gets dark, Tess has woken from her late nap. Her sleep earlier was disturbed by an attempted rape, and I am impressed she was able to get any sleep at all. But killing the rapist might have been good therapy because she looks rested. I, on the other hand, am looking forward to a little quality time with Beast.

Handing her the headphones and a thermos of coffee, I give her a smile. I also left her some of the sort-of-pemmican, sort-of-granola-bar stuff the Corrigan brothers came up with. It's not the best tasting food, but it is nutritious and filling. It actually tastes mostly like honey to me, and fruit, but I am told there is lots of protein in there, too. Not bad.

Tess smiles back and takes the headphones. I ask her, "Are you okay? It's been a very hard day."

She smiles brightly. "I'm fine, Chloe. I got to kill that bastard, and then we got his friends."

I keep looking at her, and she sighs when she sees I haven't totally bought it. "Okay, fine. I'm still a little upset but nothing to worry over now. We're not letting those bastards into our valley. We will wear away and wear away at them until there is nothing left but bones and blood." The new smile she gives me is fierce.

"That's the spirit. You call me if you need a break, I won't mind."

"No, you sleep. Ben owes me."

I chuckle and offer to sit with her a while, but Kim Thermopoli shows up to keep Tess company for awhile. They were closer with Roche than the rest of us, and I think they want to talk privately. I hug both of them and exit into the dusk.

Taking a few steps in the right direction, I am struck into stillness by the beauty of the night. The stars are so bright these days, and I can't help but look up in admiration at the gorgeousness around me. I hear a step behind me, and I breathe in, inhaling the scent of the woods, the night and the smell of my man as he wraps his arms around me. I sigh again and lean back into his embrace.

"Were you waiting for me?"

"Of course. Don't want to miss a second with you."

I know exactly what he means. We could die here, doing what we do, or in the next week, as the army comes closer to our world. Sighing with contentment, I close my eyes and turn in his arms to face him, reaching up for the kiss I know he will give me. He does not disappoint. *Ah, I love this man.*

Soon, he scoops me up and carries me off like a caveman with his prize. I giggle softly as we approach our cabin, the only real cabin at this campsite. We think it used to belong to park rangers, and we've done some work to spruce it up. The solar panels on the roof are used to charge the golf carts, not for anything special inside.

It's a basic square room with a fireplace, a bed, a cupboard and a table with two chairs. I smell smoke as we approach, and I take him to task for starting a fire. We were not to have any hot food or fires!

"Hush, woman. It's cold, the smell will dissipate before morning, and the raiders are upwind of us. Besides, I have plans for you beside the fire." He grins wolfishly at me as he opens the door and carries me inside.

I am going to argue, but the heat feels so good I decide not to. Anyway, it's too late now. "What about the others? Do they get fires?"

"I told them small fires, in a pit, tonight only. It is very unlikely the raiders have scouts skilled enough to find this place."

I am still not quite convinced, but I slide down his body to discover he's made up our bed before the fireplace, and the blankets look toasty and warm. I hug him tightly, and he returns my embrace, then kisses me again with more passion this time.

Then, he draws back a little, though I know he wants to go on. Holding my face in his hands, he looks a question at me. It's easy for me to see what he is saying. How long were we together with him barely speaking a word? He wants to know if I am okay, how I feel, and do I want to do this? His expressive face tells me everything, all his concern, and, also, all of his desire. Amazing for a man who won't take off that damned mask.

To answer his question, I pull off my jacket and lay it on the chair. Then, I lift an eyebrow and gesture to him, *it's your turn.* A sly smile graces his face, and he pulls off his jacket, laying it beside mine.

Slowly, I begin to unbutton my blouse, eyebrows waggling suggestively. I turn before the blouse comes off, though. Letting him see me peeping over my shoulder at him, I draw it off and lay it atop the jacket on the chair. I wink over my shoulder, and he growls at me.

Closing in fast, he spins me around to face him as he devours my mouth with his. Oh fuck, he makes me dizzy as we kiss.

"Impatient, are we?" I ask when he lets me have a moment to breathe.

"It's been days..." he growls into my neck, making me shiver. I love the way he growls and his insistence. Suddenly, I am eager, too.

I unbutton his shirt in record time, and we quickly skin each other's clothes off, scattering them as we make our way to the bed. He lifts me to kiss more deeply, so I wrap my legs around him and cling to his body as we kiss, all of my minor hurts and pains forgotten in my need for him.

The warmth of the fire is no match for this. He sinks onto the bed with me still wrapped around him, and he leans back onto the pillows taking me with him. *Oh, yes.*

Now, I have him before me like a feast. I kiss my way down his throat, chest, and have reached his belly before he realizes what I am up to and pulls me back up to his lips.

"Not so fast, my love. You come first. You always come first to me."

He grins again and flips me onto my back. Now, he begins his tortuous way down my body, kissing my breasts lightly to avoid any pain, and softly caressing me where there are no bruises. I was about to protest, but now I am lost in sensations. Damn. He knows very well that he can have his way if I am distracted by his touch.

His hands wrap around my hips, and I tremble in anticipation of the ecstasy he is about to bestow upon me. He buries his face in my belly, the belly I was so self-conscious about a short year ago, and which is now touched and loved as if it were perfect. He caresses my thighs, the slightly jiggly part no longer gives me a second thought. Because he finds me perfect, treats me as his goddess, I feel like one. I am perfect to him, and that is enough for me.

He lowers his face to my core, and I catch my breath as his clever tongue goes to work. Half of his battle is won because I know his skill will bring me quickly to climax. I am already so turned on it won't take long at all.

I orgasm so deeply, I wonder for a split second if I will survive the ecstasy. I am a melted candle, a pool of deep and utterly fathomless water, an entire moon, revolving around my world, my man.

He looks very pleased with himself as I begin to come back to reality, shuddering and gleaming with sweat, glowing with pleasure. He continues the sensations flowing through me by caressing my hips, teasing little kisses where I am too sensitive, and pressure where I am not. I want to pleasure him, but am still limp, as he very well knows, as he pulls himself up my body.

Those blue eyes seek mine, and all I can feel is the love, the desire, the pleasure that comes with loving him. I embrace him, and open my legs to let him in, wanting more, wanting his pleasure too, wanting this to never end, this dance we do so well.

He leans into me, and I taste myself on his lips as we kiss. Our tongues dance, and he presses himself at my entrance where he slides easily into place. I gasp, as always, the pleasure increased, and he groans as he settles, waiting for me to accommodate him.

"Fuck," he hisses through gritted teeth as his body shudders.

Our movements are smooth and perfect, my legs wrap around his hips to help provide more friction, urging more depth and speed. He groans again, settling into a rhythm. The firelight flickers against his face, and the fire in his eyes heats me further. I am ready to climax again, but I want him to come with me, so I resist the urge to let go.

Caressing his back, I slide my hands to his buttocks, and pull him more forcefully into me. His eyes darken, and I know he is close. Our breathing is rougher, more frantic, and before he lets go, I feel him begin to tighten against me, and that sends me spinning once more into ecstasy...

I awaken hours later, tangled in the sheets, reaching for my Beast, but he isn't there. I sit up in bed, muzzy-headed to see him standing beside the door, clad in only a blanket. He is talking to someone. When he glances back at me, he nods to say all is well before going back to his quiet conversation.

Once done, he closes the door softly and returns to the bed. I pull him in beside me to warm him and ask what that was about.

"It was Waters. He and Nalwani were watching the monitors and saw a couple of raiders coming up the road toward our camp."

Alarmed, I sit up, but he pulls me back down beside him.

"Relax. Rawlins' traps got them. Made quite a mess of the road, though. Good thing we have the Stryker to get around that, or we'd be screwed." After a moment he adds, "And not the good way."

As I giggle, he pulls me into him and we spoon together, his body cocooning me in warmth and safety. We slowly drift back to sleep.

Chapter Eighteen

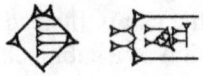

The sound of a watch alarm forces me to consciousness. I groan in baffled weariness, and Beast stirs behind me, slipping out of the bed before turning it off. I crack open my eyes to check the time. *Two thirty!?* My weary mind insists this is some mistake.

"Morning, beautiful," he whispers.

There's a soft glow coming from the fire, which has been reduced to red coals. A green glow stick sits on the table. When I turn my gaze to my husband, he is slipping into his fatigues.

"What's wrong?"

He shakes his head. "Nothing. How are you feeling?"

"Tired, but better."

"Come with me then."

I shoot him a confused expression. "What? Where?"

"To get Roche's body," he growls softly. "Just you and me. Like the old days."

"Fuck, yes," I growl right back and practically jump out of bed.

No, I haven't had a lot of sleep, but I am so excited that I get dressed in record time. When I've slipped my tac vest on, my husband is ready and waiting. The sight of him makes my mouth go dry. His face is shrouded in shadow, accentuating the feral expression he's wearing. I slip on my death's-head bandana and sling on my Tavor, and we're out the door.

Waters is still on duty when we leave the camp. When we tell him what we are up to, all he does is grin in agreement. I doubt any one of us would argue. The only thing they might do is request to go along. Not this time. This is something Beast and I do well.

We know this terrain, so moving quickly, yet quietly, is easily done. We take one of our golf carts along a back trail near to where the old camp was then go the rest of the way on foot.

As we move across the terrain, we find no one until we get to our recently abandoned campsite. It makes me sick to see the enemy sitting there, but we will soon see about resolving that.

There are three men, two of whom are asleep. Like most of these idiots, he's not even really paying attention or walking a patrol. Instead, he's sitting on a log and poking the fire with a stick.

Beast left his G3 back at the camp. Instead, he's carrying a Kriss Vector. It's a semi-auto version of a submachine gun design. It's also got a longer barrel in order to be a legal, civilian version. With some work, he was able to thread the barrel in order to put an oil filter suppressor on it. The other weapon he's carrying is the crossbow we recently acquired.

Silently, my man moves into position while I cover with the Tavor. There's a soft twang and then a bolt appears in the man's head. The body drops, and we wait to see if the other two wake or someone we didn't see yells an alarm. Nothing happens, and they don't stir. Too bad for them.

My husband gives me a nod as he slings the crossbow and readies the Vector. With a grim smile, I sneak forward with my knife in hand. I'm sure some would say it's a cowardly way to kill someone this way, and sure, we could make a show and have some sort of fair battle. But, let's be honest. These raider pieces of shit don't deserve good deaths. And, as they say, all's fair in love and war. This is war.

One at a time, I cover my volunteer's mouth and sink my blade into his neck. I lock eyes with each one, letting him see the face of the Angel of Death that sends them straight to Hell. When I'm done, we do a quick check of anything useful before moving on.

Moving quickly, we get to the location where the logging truck had been stationed. Like the finely-honed team we are, we make little noise as we slip through the trees and brush, closing in on our destination.

Stopping at the place the truck had been parked, we drop prone. While Beast pulls out some rope, I glass the area. My Tavor has the night vision scope, so I'm able to see the entire area in green-tinted light. I don't spot anyone obvious. There certainly isn't anyone on the stretch of highway where they executed Shawn.

My heart breaks when I spot a dark shadow on the side of the road that is probably him. Fucking hell! Since I don't find any raiders, I shoot a quick glance at Beast and nod.

He gives me a me a quick nod back, and we start moving down the hillside using the rope that he was preparing for our descent. It's slow going but, finally, we get down to the road and start moving towards Shawn's body.

I'm near to tears when we approach our fallen comrade. Beast pulls out a glow stick holder and rotates it to allow light out. Soft, greenish illumination spills onto Shawn's peaceful, blood-stained face. Twisting the holder shut, Beast gets ready to pick him up, and that's when we hear voices.

Cursing this turn of events, we stealthily retreat to the hillside end of the road, choked with brush and not far from our rope. Then, we wait in darkness to see just who is coming towards us, and I listen intently.

"Do we really need to be getting another dead body?" The voice is low and gruff. "The guy was just some random asshole. Let the crows have him."

"Kane said we go get it. That means we go get it. Remember what happened to Lewis when he disobeyed orders?"

"Yeah, I remember," the man grumbles. "I'm just not feeling well."

The second voice snorts. "Me neither. But Kane wants the body to send a message. After that fucking trap that killed Tony and John, I agree with him!"

Beast is starting to growl, so I elbow him lightly. He stops just as the two men approach. One is stocky, the other is skinny. Mr. Stringbean is carrying a makeshift torch, spreading a small amount of firelight about them. They've got their backs to us now as they look down at Shawn.

"Is this the piece of shit?" Chubby asks in a disgusted tone.

Stringbean nods. "Yep, this is him."

We stalk them silently as the two continue their conversation. I've got my knife in hand. From the corner of my eye, I catch sight of Beast with his hand on his sword, ready to draw.

Mr. Chubby spits on Shawn. "What do you think Kane is going to do with him?"

"I don't know, and I don't care," his friend scoffs. "Desecrate the body in some way? Better him than me. Pick him up so we can get this done. I think I'm coming down with something. My stomach is killing me!"

Oh no, it's not your stomach that's going to kill you, fucker!

With expert stealth, I slip up behind Mr. Stringbean. One hand clamps over his mouth while the other slips my knife into his neck. A scream tries to escape from between my fingers but, instead, it's just a muffled gurgle. It is, however, loud enough to catch his friend's attention.

Mr. Chubby turns and his eyes go wide when he finds himself face-to-face with The Beast. Hesitation seizes him, and it's his death sentence. With a flash of my husband's sword, the raider's throat is cut open. All he can do is clutch fruitlessly at his neck, gasping as blood flows copiously around his fingers.

As the raider expires, we pay him no mind. Instead, Beast is moving and picking up Shawn. With a grunt, he rolls onto his feet, carrying our fallen friend in a fireman's carry. Then, we move as quickly as we can while we still have the cover of night.

The rest of it is relatively easy. We get him back to the golf cart and carry him safely back to his friends. All-in-all, it only takes us a few hours. By the time we get to camp, the rest of the crew is up waiting. We lay him on the picnic table they've covered with canvas, and we stand beside him for a few minutes.

Kim had some candles with her, and she's placed them at his head and feet. Viv and Tess made a circle around the table with smooth white river stones. We all take our time to say goodbye. Eventually, each one of us touches his face, his hand, while saying a word to him. Beast takes out his flask, and we each have a sip, toasting Shawn Roche in turn.

Finally, Beast approaches and says softly, "Go now, my friend, to greet the lady of heaven, and save a place for us there. We were honored to be called your friends in this life." Then, he pulls up the edges of the canvas and starts stitching it closed making it a shroud.

We stand for a while as he does his work, but the service, such as it is, has ended. The spell is broken, and everyone makes their way back to what they were doing before. We still have time to get a few hours of sleep.

I wait for my man to finish, and walk with him back to the cabin. We undress again and lie soberly next to the fire.

"He was a good man." I say thoughtfully. "He shouldn't have died so young. I feel like it is my fault. I should have warn-"

My husband cuts my words with a kiss. "No, my angel, the raiders did this. It's their fault. We can't see everything, be everywhere. He was told to be careful, watch for raiders, to only go out when it was safe."

"But, he didn't know it wasn't safe. *I* saw them hide, and *I* didn't tell you. I should have said something, but I didn't. He didn't have to die. I could have saved him by speaking up. It's my fault."

"Chloe, it's not. It happens. It's war. We can't control everything. Loss is part of life. And you were doing what you thought was best, right?"

I nod, numbly.

"So, let it go. We don't have the time or energy to tear ourselves up." He kisses me again. "Now sleep. We have a lot to do, and we need to be in top form."

"Yes, my lord."

"Goodnight, my lady."

Chapter Nineteen

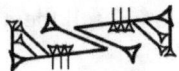

Chloe is still sleeping when I get up. I cover her with the blankets and she doesn't stir, even when I get dressed and lay out fresh clothes for her. Not surprising given our extra-curricular activities last night. Hell, I wish I could go on sleeping with her, but there's too much to do.

My angel looks like one, her hair spread on the pillow and a sweet look of peace on her face. I gather our gear as quietly as I can and go to start breakfast for the group. We still have bacon, and I don't intend to let that go to waste.

Heading into the camp, I stop by the Stryker to find Waters still watching the monitors. Thermopoli is waiting on him to start her shift.

"Anything going on?"

"Thermopoli just asked me that, and I told her we should wait for everyone, but that's up to you, boss."

I raise my eyebrow. Waters grins and gives me a quick rundown. The two from last night were not coming down with something. Our men did manage to poison the food and water at the raider's camp. What, with the poison, the explosion in the bunkhouse/barn and the pit traps, the raider camp is in shambles this morning. They never dug latrines, figuring they would leave the mess behind them when they moved on.

Locusts is all they are. Now, they are likely regretting that decision, as nausea, vomiting, diarrhea and unconsciousness are all some of the typical symptoms. I imagine sick people vomiting, defecating and passing out all over the place, falling into a pit and being helpless to get out; more falling in with them. I grin and rub my hands together. The other two smile at me, and Waters stands, stretches and hands the monitor duty over to Thermopoli. She sits down and intently watches the monitors, looking for screenshots to print for our morning briefing.

By the time I have breakfast in hand, more of the group is trickling in. I have made sure we don't have people off alone so they aren't prey to kidnapping, as Chloe was. I feel a twinge of worry before I look around and see my angel walking up the slight incline toward the rest of the group with Viv.

233

Once everyone is here, I brief them on how well Rawlins' road traps worked the night before. Everyone gives a little cheer, and Rawlins suggests he and someone else go scout it out to make sure everyone is taken care of. Viv volunteers, and I tell them they can go once we are done with the briefing.

Thermopoli brings out prints of some of the havoc we discovered at the Reverend's camp this morning, and we go through the pictures together. When we get near the end of the stack, she points out one that she's tabbed in red.

"I think we might have got the Reverend. I don't know what he looks like, but they are swarming around this one truck."

She shows the photograph, then moves on. "And look at this one. Doesn't that look like it might be him?"

We are shown a grainy, blown-up picture of a man on a stretcher surrounded by numerous raiders. Black clothing with what might be a preacher's collar graces his throat.

We all take a look and finally agree that it is impossible to tell. By then, breakfast is finished, so we go through our duties for the day. We will wait to see if the army intends to move, what with all the sickness they've been experiencing and the possibility that the Reverend might be down. Either way, the strike team will move down and split into two positions along the ridge for better coverage. Thermopoli, Nalwani and Waters will stay behind—one to monitor and communicate, one on guard duty, one to nap—but the rest of us have our tasks.

We have changed the channels and scrambled our radios, so we are secure again, even if the Reverend does have Roche's old radio. We also have a plan if another radio is captured. Everyone knows the new frequencies and codes, so we won't be incommunicado again.

Regardless of whether or not the army moves, we need to be in place before they make a decision. If they decide not to move, we'll have a practice run. If they do, we need to be there well ahead of time.

We have a daisy chain of IEDs along a slot of road that runs between two bluffs. We will be a safe distance away, but well able to see when to set off the explosives. Now is the time to cripple their army, when so many of the soldiers have food poisoning—well, poison-poisoning.

We take two of the golf carts and extra batteries for each. Taking alternate routes to the main road, we zip down the pavement, bold as brass. We also have the M60 in one and the M249 in the other. Chloe is my gunner with the 249, Rawlins is Viv's. Parking the vehicles along a forested road, we cover them with tarps and hike into the area we want. It is just south and west of a hairpin curve in the freeway.

The hike is a familiar one, Rawlins has run ahead—the man is a monster—to make sure the connections are still good. He is to rejoin us in short order. In the meantime, we get settled at two points on the bluffs, south and north. Chloe and I have the south end where we can be aware of any incoming scouts, as well. The army has shown it likes to use scouts and there are more of them than we realized, so we need to stay aware.

The area is tricky, though, unless you are familiar with it, which we are. There are plenty of dead ends and rock falls that make it a pain to travel through. We've set a few traps too, for good measure. Trip wires with surprises, things like that. Kawalski was the mastermind of most of that, but we know where all the traps are, and they are not set in the direction we come from anyway.

We get a call from Thermopoli confirming that the trucks are on the move. *Damn, eager are we?* I shake my head and radio Rawlins to get up off the road. We will have trucks within the hour, but we don't know if scouts are headed this way. Thermopoli has not located any yet, but will keep an eye open.

She reports the army looks like someone kicked an anthill. All the shelters are gone, loaded onto the trucks. There are quite a few people still lying in the field, either dead or still unconscious. We don't think there was food served, and the women and children are also milling about the field. They won't be following along for a while. They know their next meal and all their shelter just drove away, so they will need to catch up before night falls, or they won't be fed.

Then she reports there is a squad formed around one leader; we suspect it's Kane. He's rounding people up and getting them organized. Clearly, the army will march, and he's the one pushing them forward. Hopefully, that's going to wear them further down.

Rawlins scrambles to get into position and, after that, it's a waiting game. We get updates from Thermopoli every ten minutes, but she doesn't need to tell us when the trucks are approaching. There is a rumble that breaks the stillness for miles.

We see them round the corner into our narrow alley of road, but they are moving slowly. When I look through my scope, I see the trucks are overloaded with both supplies and some of the sick. We don't see any women or children, though, I do spot the Reverend—sitting up, head lolling—through one of the windows. *Yes!*

We have set the IEDs a few feet apart, six of them in a row, something called a daisy chain. They are disguised by the usual clutter—leaves, sticks, rocks. When the first truck approaches the first IED in the chain—the one furthest north—we will be ready. Rawlins will punch it, and that IED will go, hopefully taking the lead truck with it. The rest of the explosives will follow in a chain reaction, taking the other two trucks if we're lucky.

To be honest, I'm not convinced. These aren't military-grade explosives we are using. The detonation speed isn't going to be serious enough to blow up the trucks. Still, it might shred tires and definitely cause casualties.

The trucks crawl so slowly I am ready to growl, but Chloe's presence helps keep me calm. She is scanning the area watching for tangos that could come up on us, as is Viv. Rawlins and I are in charge of the IEDs.

In what feels like a fucking eternity, the trucks are almost in position. It looks like the perfect setup, so, of course, I don't trust it. I hate it when things look perfect. Something is bound to go wrong because you should never expect the enemy to participate in your dream engagement.

"Steady," I whisper into my radio, "Steady, almost there. And, ready.... FIRE-FIRE-FIRE!"

The women know the signal and duck behind cover. Rawlins and I are in prone position already and duck our heads briefly while each explosion goes off in succession, just as we had planned. We are far enough away that it should be okay, but it's a good habit to keep when setting off explosives.

When the explosions are done and the dust begins to clear, I check the road. I see all three trucks are damaged and undriveable. Two of them have shredded tires and are dripping fuel. The lead vehicle amazingly has most of the rear axle sheared off, though the front, oddly, looks okay. There is glass and metal debris everywhere and more than a few bodies.

In my radio, I hear Thermopoli cheering, "You guys, that was so awesome from above, I can't even..." I tell her to calm herself and look for raiders in the rocks, and she gets serious once more.

Chloe and Viv are watching for tangos again at our sides, so Rawlins and I watch at the road, scanning for any movement. We have two angles of attack, so when I see someone crawling out from under one of the trucks, I take him. I also hear Rawlins' suppressed shots through my headset.

We wait for ten more minutes to see if there are any more takers, but we don't have any more volunteering to die. It's time to go, and Thermopoli radios that we are clear, so we book it back to our vehicles. This time, we stick to back roads since we're not in such a hurry to get in place.

Chloe and I look at each other, wondering why we are uncomfortable. Finally she speaks what we're both thinking.

"That was too easy."

"Right?"

"Yeah, now I'm waiting for..."

"The other shoe?"

"Yeah."

We drive in silence for a while, but I have decided we should just try to be happy with our success, yet wary for anything new. As I am thinking these happy thoughts, Thermopoli breaks into my reverie.

"Tangos on the road ahead."

"Roger that," I say softly into the radio. "Landmarks."

"A rock shaped like Snoopy and overhanging trees, roughly twenty meters ahead of your position."

"Snoopy, seriously?"

"From here it does!" she insists.

"Rawlins, you got that?"

"Roger, will circle around, boss."

He steers off the trail and moves around some heavy brush nearby. I am glad we're in relatively quiet vehicles. You want to stay alive in a hostile environment? Silence is your best tool for that.

Chloe and I slow and park our golf cart behind some brush, and get our weapons ready to discover what is waiting for us. My lady covers the cart with its tarp and sets up the solar charger, as long as we've stopped anyway. I ask Thermopoli if they are waiting or walking. They're waiting. They could be waiting for us or for friends. We need to find out which it is. Rawlins and Viv are on the trail ahead by now, so it's up to us to move in and find out more.

We may be familiar with this area, but we don't know every rock and stone. Thermopoli says a rock shaped like Snoopy, but it might just look that way from her angle. From mine, it could look like Angelina Jolie, for all I know. Ahead, I do see an outcropping of stone, so we will pretend that's it.

Slipping off the road—well, it's more of a trail—we move up a dry wash, moving as silently as we're able. I motion for Chloe to move while I cover her, then she does the same for me. In this way, we flank the raiders.

Thermopoli tells us when we're even with the men. We are near what was a pond earlier in the year, but is now drying up. There's a small ridge to climb, and I remember the area now. I had noted it would be a great place for an ambush, because the trail continues through two ridges of rock, so the person on the trail could be a sitting duck to parties waiting above. We cautiously climb this side of the ridge, listening intently.

I am surprised by what I finally hear. A screeching yowl comes from below, followed muffled laughter. Then voices: one protesting, two others carrying on. I have no idea what I've heard. Once we're at the top, we have a limited view of the cleft below, so we move to one side until we get a better perspective.

I mouth softly into my headset, "Rawlins, report."

"Five tangos tormenting something on the road."

"Got a good angle on them?"

Viv replies, "Oh yes."

"At my shot, you go. We take the south, you take the north."

"Roger." Rawlins again.

At that, there is another shout of laughter and another shrieking yowl from the road. I hear Viv's snarl, then a burst of suppressed gunfire that isn't mine. *Shit.*

Chloe raises her eyebrows and glances at me, then we focus on the raiders below. Viv's caught two of them, but the other three have ducked for cover behind an outcropping. We have a good angle on two of them, one is too far south. I motion to Chloe to stay put and fire when I take my shot, and take off back down the ridge to look for a better angle.

The raiders are now firing back at Rawlins and Viv, and I hope they have cover. Finally, I get to a point where I can see my target. Quietly and cautiously, I position myself. Taking aim, I pull the trigger.

I don't get a clean head-shot, but the bullet gets him in the neck. Chloe's shots follow up, and I hear her say she's got her tangos. I tell her to wait, but Viv is rushing in. Goddess, take all fools and bleeding hearts, I fire again and luckily get a head shot.

"Thermopoli, any others?"

"None that I can see. You get the ones on the trail?"

"Checking now. Rawlins, you want to get control of your team." It's not a question, it's an order. My voice is icy, I know Viv can hear, but she should fucking know better.

Viv answers, "Sorry boss. I—Just get down here."

"Angel, cover me as I backtrack."

"Yes, my Beast." My lady moves to position. She covers me, Rawlins and the idiot we normally call Viv, who is already on the trail.

I head back down the ridge, checking for any others and for any traps they might have placed. Fortunately, I find nothing and no one. Then I head up the other ridge, much easier to walk as it's not as high or as brushy. When I am positive the area is clear, I tell Chloe to meet me on the road. I stalk down to see what got Viv so upset she forgot what she was supposed to do.

This had better be good.

Chapter Twenty

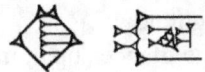

Beast might still be mad, but I don't blame Viv for one instant once I see what's happened. The raiders had been torturing a mother cat, and her three kittens are huddled around the mother's still-breathing body.

Viv is kneeling on the road, openly weeping. I have never seen her like this before. It is sort of shocking, and yet also reassuring in a way. Viv has always been the most coldly brutal one of us ladies, especially when it comes to asshole humans. Now, to see her so overwhelmed is, well, disquieting and terrible.

Beast strides up, and I can tell he is furious, but he falters when he catches sight of Viv. She's never been openly emotional with any of us. I've seen through her tough veneer a few times, but never like this. Rawlins is completely put off by this situation and is, for want of a better description, guarding the roadway where she kneels.

In a colder voice than I could have managed, Beast grates. "Do you want to explain just what is going on here, Viv?"

She's choked up, but wipes her face, stands and replies in a strangled voice. "Sorry, sir. It won't happen again." Then, she gets a wild, desperate look in her eye and goes on, "But I had to. They were going to kill the babies, too." She turns to me, tears streaking down her face harder than ever. "I had to..."

I take her in my arms and let her sob. The kittens' mewling is breaking my heart a little. Beast sighs, casts his eyes to heaven and pats Viv on the shoulder awkwardly. The raiders are dead, but he's still not happy.

He and Rawlins go through the raiders' packs and carry the bodies off the path. To where, I don't know, nor do I give a damn. They can feed the wildlife here for all I care. Viv and I kneel down to see if anything can be done for the mother cat.

The poor thing is gasping, burn wounds on her neck and torso, one eye burned out. Gods, I think they even cut off a portion of her tail! Even with such grievous wounds, she is pathetically trying to lick one of her babies.

"God damnit, what is wrong with them?" Now, I'm crying, too.

"We got them this time. We got them." Viv is muttering to herself, and I am slightly worried. Her eyes are fierce and dilated, and I don't know if she's still with us right now.

"Viv, hon, you okay?" She glances up at me blankly, then seems to bring herself back to the present. She shakes it off and nods slowly.

"We're not leaving them here. They'll die."

She is as fiercely determined as I've ever seen her. She puts her hand out to the mother cat, who hisses, even as injured as she is. Trying to rise and drag herself away. The kittens continue to mewl, circling the mother, who shudders, lies down and gasps, then expires.

Viv bursts into tears again, and this time I don't know what to do, so I end up patting her shoulder as awkwardly as Beast was doing earlier.

"Um. Viv, we've got to keep moving."

The scene is heartbreaking. She has picked up the mother cat, a larger animal than I had realized, and is holding it to her, stroking it softly. After a moment of mourning, she picks up each kitten and hands them to me. Then carries the mother to the side of the road, where she digs out a shallow area. Reverently, she starts placing stones over the little, torn body.

I am crying anew at this point, both from Viv's obvious grief, and because these babies are now motherless. I can't help but imagine my own babies without their mother. Frankly, we are a mess.

Beast and Rawlins take one look at the two of us, the cat funeral and then look at each other. My man motions to me that they will go get the vehicles while we finish what we're doing. I try my best to dry my eyes, but I think I need to just cry this out for the moment. I have put the three kittens inside my shirt in case I need to use my rifle, but feel sort of foolish with a moving, mewing blouse.

One of the babies is medium brown while the other two are gold colored. All three are marked with dark brown spots, especially on the limbs. They all have white fur on their chests, bellies and on the insides of their legs. I also notice they have short tails and seem kind of large, but I don't dwell on it. They are so adorably cute; and scratchy on the inside of my blouse. I take them out and hand two of them to Viv.

By the time the men return, Viv and I have pulled ourselves back together. She thinks the kittens are about six weeks old, about the right age to be weaned anyway, but I am concerned about what they will eat. How are we supposed to care for these baby creatures while making war on the incoming army?

When Beast and Seth Rawlins return, Beast makes it clear that the kittens are now Viv's responsibility, and that if they endanger our mission for one second, they will be left behind. She prickles at that.

"So, what? You're trying to punish me now?"

"Why, yes. I am. You good with that?"

Viv nods and takes the third kitten from me. She pulls a canvas bag off the pile of goods retrieved from the dead raiders and puts the kittens inside, then carries them to the golf cart, tied in and secured. They are already trying to clamber out, but the sides are too high, so they mew. She gazes defiantly at Beast, who lifts an eyebrow at her, then nods. Yes, Viv is scary, but Beast is the only thing that apparently scares her.

As we walk back to our golf cart, I notice the kittens have learned to use their claws to climb the sides of the canvas sack. I giggle, point this out to Viv, and she curses and closes the sack before there are any more escape attempts.

Beast reports in to Thermopoli and gets Waters instead. "How's our route now?"

"Clear."

"What's happening on the road?"

"No movement. Fires burning. The army has begun marching, they're leaving some behind. We saw a few groups of escapees as well, probably deserters. Most are heading away from our area."

"Good. We'll see you soon."

"Roger. Will keep you informed."

The rest of the trip back to camp is uneventful, at least as far as raiders go. Seth and Viv seem to be getting into it, but I am sure they will work it out. Strong personalities clash sometimes. Especially when you have a team of nothing but alphas and one of them disobeyed orders.

I am surprised when, after we arrive at camp, Seth stomps off into the trees as soon as the vehicle has stopped. I help Viv hook up the charger while Beast hooks up ours.

"What just happened?"

"He's an asshole."

"Well, yeah, so?"

Viv sighs. "He thinks I'm an idiot, and he's probably right. I just can't stand to see a helpless creature hurt. He can't see why I have no problem killing people, yet lose my shit over animals. He got all dominant and heartless and... Well, you know?"

"It's not something that is hardwired into most men, I guess. Especially in the culture they have been raised in. I mean, the younger guys? They were raised to be a little more caring. Most of these older men were punished for having feelings while growing up. Given what's happened to our world, I'm starting to see why."

"It's not just that, though, I know what you mean." Viv has opened the bag now, and has handed me the brown kitten again. "I have no moral compunction about killing a person. None. If they deserve it, I am happy to pull the trigger or throw the knife; or throttle them with my bare hands if necessary." She grins ferociously. "But, animals are truly innocent. People should not be fucking them up. I won't stand for that. I will die trying to save them."

I notice out of the corner of my eye that Beast is casually cleaning up, but has not left the area. He's eavesdropping on our conversation, and I don't blame him. Viv has been a mystery to us for some time.

I try to keep her talking. "Did someone—what happened to you to make you feel so strongly?"

Her rueful smile tells me there is a bigger story here, but she just says, "Let's just say I have raiders to blame for it." Pulling the kitten away from me, she puts it back in the sack with the other two and turns. "I know you're here still, boss, and I don't care if you know this stuff."

Beast nods at her again. "You know what you're going to feed those creatures?"

Viv smiles and says, "Going to go hunt it now. We might share with you if I catch something big." Then, she turns and walks into the forest, mewing bag slung over her shoulder.

Beast wraps me in his arms as she strolls away, whistling. I lean back into him and relax for a moment. Given the roller-coaster of emotions that I just went through, it's nice to have a moment's peace.

"What's next on our itinerary, oh, glorious leader?"

"Itinerary? Do we have one right now, beyond me holding you, wife?"

"Mmm. No, but..."

He buries his face in my neck and inhales. I melt a little and turn in his arms for a kiss. He gratifies me and sends my pulse racing until I hear someone clearing their throat nearby.

"Uh, boss?" It's Ben Waters.

"What?" Beast answers curtly.

"You're going to want to come see this." Beast sighs and releases me, then takes my hand as we follow Ben back to camp.

The situation is—interesting. The monitors show an army divided, a stream of men marching our way and another stream of deserters marching back the way they've come. About a half mile up the road, around a blind turn, is what can best be described as an execution squad—those men deserting are being shot on sight.

This is all good news for us. They're killing their own men. Of course, some of the deserters have taken to hill and field, but now they are policing their own men. I would guess they've lost at least a quarter of their troops through illness, desertion or execution, and it's only been two days.

Chloe points to one area where there is a straggling line of bodies heading into the wilderness north of the reservoir. They don't look like the typical raiders, it looks more like some of the women and even a few kids. More power to them. I hope they make it.

On the other monitor is the scene we left the army to find, the ruined trucks and scattered provisions. The remaining army is approaching and will soon come upon their erstwhile support. The troops are being led by a man on a motorcycle, presumably Kane. We watch, fascinated, as he comes around the corner to the ravine with the damaged trucks.

His bike stops. The men stop. There is a long moment where nobody moves. Then, we see the motorcycle speed up the road, the men shambling after it. When the cycle arrives at the wrecked trucks, it screeches to a halt spilling the bike. The rider leaps off in time to avoid decapitation as it spins under one of the wrecks. Then, the man is seen to be searching the vehicles.

Finally, as the army catches up to him, he has uncovered a body in one of the trucks. He's laid it out on the pavement, careless of broken glass, shredded metal and rubber. The men who have caught up encircle the man and the body.

The cameras are zoomed in. We can see everything with no sound. The men stand around the body as if it were a holy relic. When the body moves, Beast lets out a stream of curses. I believe the Reverend has survived. *Fuck.*

With the Reverend still alive, the troops somehow allow themselves to be mustered. We don't know if they are radioing each other or what, but with his survival, the wreckage of the army pulls itself back together. We watch as the execution squads turn most of the army back toward our valley and our homes. Even though they've lost a quarter of their troops through the various deaths we helped cause, it's still not enough.

On the bright side, the army has to carry its own supplies now. This will slow them down. Wear them down. Yet, they still have their figurehead alive to push them forward. We don't know what condition the Reverend is in, but I, for one, hope he is suffering. We watch as they set up a travois to carry him. The men appear to take turns like it is some kind of honor.

With the three trucks being a total loss, that means, tonight, there will be no food-tent feeding the men. They will have to set up their own camps and fix their own rations after carrying tents and equipment all day. We'll see how well that works for them.

There are still hundreds that are too sick to move on. There was an armed guard at last night's campground, rousing people or hauling dead ones off to a nearby ditch. That's got to be unpleasant.

Viv returns late with a small deer. She's already gutted it out and prepped it, so we will have venison steaks for dinner. The kittens seem happy with their new mama, purring and content to stay with her; though, the brown one with white feet visits Beast and I at dinner time, cadging bites of our venison. The kitten reminds me of a woman I used to work with, so I start calling her Mimi, which catches on.

The other two Viv names Bee-ghoul and Tree-ghoul—Bygul and Trjegul in Old Norse—after the Goddess Freja's two kitties that pull her chariot. I tease Viv that they probably won't get that big, but she points out to me the size of their feet and that there are white spots on the backs of their ears, so they are at least part wildcat of some sort. The mother was kind of large for a house cat, so now I'm wondering.

We will be leaving here in the morning. Once more we will leave some surprises on the road, but we have more work to do on the other side of the dam. I look forward to a nice long evening with my man, in privacy. Chances are we won't have too much of that in the next week or so.

Seth Rawlins has already reset the traps down below, should more scouts come our way, and the UAV pilots have done a very good job keeping us apprised of our situation. There are only four of them, the two that we started with and two more they've trained. They manage full coverage for us 24/7. Of course, Beast made Pete the Commander, Air Group for all our air assets, so he runs an effective department.

The night shift comes on, and the rest of us head to our respective beds. Beast and I walk hand-in-hand to our cabin, discussing the day and Viv's kittens. He is still upset that she was so easily manipulated into moving when she shouldn't have. That could have gotten one or more of us killed.

I hadn't seen it that way before. I understood that she had a visceral need to rescue the innocent animals, but you can't let your enemy use your weaknesses against you. We stop by Viv's small shelter to talk, but she isn't there. Beast gives a snort, and we move on to our cabin. There's only one thing that will calm him down, and I look forward to it, because it will make me a very happy woman.

Chapter Twenty-one

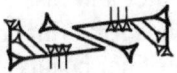

The fire is already going. I saw to that before everyone settled in at dinner. I wanted the cabin nice and warm for what I have planned for my lovely wife. She sighs as we open the door and warmth floods out. I bar the door behind us after we enter, and I am rewarded with her squeal of delight when she sees what is waiting.

"Oh! Is that a bath?" She is referring to the small tub of water I have warming near the fire. "You think of everything, my love!"

Spinning around, she kisses me until I forget about the bath, about the cabin, even the world. It's just her and I, locked in an ardent embrace within our own little paradise. At least until she pulls away, bringing me back to reality.

It is a pretty nice reality, as she takes off her boots and begins a slow, half-humorous strip-tease, hurling her heavy shirt my direction. This is followed by her thick woolen socks. She may think she's being funny, but I think she is all delightful curves and luscious warm skin. There are still bruises easily noticeable under her brown skin. Those will take some time to go away, but I notice her breasts are nowhere near as swollen and painful looking. She must be feeling much better.

So am I. Simply observing her delight as she climbs delicately into the small metal tub eases my frustrations almost instantly. I'd found the tub and buckets behind the building in a crude storage cabinet. She will have to sit up, but it is workable. The pioneers managed, so will we.

"It's actually kind of warm!" she exclaims, settling in, knees poking up out of the water. She grabs a small cloth and soap I've placed within reach and begins to lather up.

A kettle of hot water stands ready and a bucket of cool water will be used to help wash her hair. She is no blushing flower, no delicate creature. Chloe is my strong, beautiful and capable woman. But she does enjoy her creature comforts. And, I enjoy helping her partake of them.

I warm the small tub of cooling water with the hot water from the kettle. Carefully, I begin pouring the freshly warmed water over my lady, vicariously enjoying her pleasure. Then, I help her lather her hair and rinse. When water spills over the top of the tub, we both laugh as it disappears into the cracks between the floorboards and causes some small creature below us to chatter and fuss.

When she is clean, she stands for a final rinse, and I drink in the sight, saving it as a special memory of her beauty. I try to contain my impatience when she steps out of the tub into a towel I have waiting. But rather than leading me to the bed, she insists that she now give me the same treatment.

Quickly, I shrug off my clothes and step into the tub. The water is still fairly clean, but I am not going to be able to sit in the tub as she did, so I do much of the work while she assists from a perch on a small stool. She is deliberate, perfunctory, but has a secret smile as she washes me and lingers. There is not much warm water left, and though she chides me for using it all on her, she makes good use of what remains.

Soon, we are both warm and dry and lying content in the bed. I had to move it away from the fire so I could set up the tubs, but the room is small and we are both still warm. I can tell she is as excited as I am; we both seem to be of a mood to take things slowly.

We lie nestled into each other, watching the fire crackle and burn. Holding her this way, listening to her steady breaths, I realize how lucky we are. We've been blessed, personally, by a goddess. I figure one reason must be to help take out this army the Reverend has amassed, but also to make a seedling of civilization before all humankind turns to savagery and pillage and there are no decent people remaining.

I think of our daughter, safely ensconced inside the mountain with the other evacuees. Jimmy, watching over her so steadfastly. I think of the ones close to us, Nena and the other leaders and fighters we left behind to organize and prepare. My angel, here, makes life worth it, but the others make it all a civilization.

I roll slightly, turning her in my arms to kiss her. Chloe's arms snake up around my neck, and the warmth of her returning embrace heats my blood again. I hold her tightly, and she squirms in my grasp, loosening my hold so she can climb on top of me. Her kisses soothe my brow. Her fingers loosen the ridge of concentration and make me relax. She smooths tired muscles and helps me truly unwind, as I never do with anyone but her.

My beautiful Chloe is my home, my peace, my contentment. She is all that is soft and smooth and kind. She is my family, my mate, my reason for existence, my life.

She turns her lips loose on me now, and her teasing is becoming more difficult to bear. I want to take over, but my Chloe can have what she wishes, and I can tell she really wishes to be in charge right now. So I endure, only an occasional gasp or groan escapes me.

I can hardly think straight when she straddles me, cowgirl style. Grabbing her hips as she lowers herself onto me and oh, what a view I have. I pull her hips backward until I have that sweet spot in my sights, and, as she takes me between, I begin to work on her.

Finally, when I am at the edge of my control, I feel her thighs begin to clench and ensure she slips over the edge. It would be easy to let go and come with her as she cries out, but I am not done giving her pleasure yet. She is breathing hard, and seats herself as deeply as she can, shuddering, and finally relaxing atop me in a position of absolute release. I continue to caress her thighs, back and delicious ass as she shudders, and when she begins to come back to herself, I draw her to me, up my body, then I flip her to her back and position myself at her cleft.

She wraps her legs around me, her eyes dilated with passion. "Please, my Beast..."

I ease inside her slowly so she can adjust. Her breathing quickens again and she moves against me, pulling me deeper inside. I can't hold back any longer, and growl into her mouth as we kiss. When she gasps, I know she is going to cum again for me, and it sets me off as well. We breathe each other in and melt together, a warm pile of entangled limbs. My angel has tears in her eyes, and I kiss them away. Holding her close, I stroke her hair and, slowly, we drift into sleep.

When I wake in the morning, it's still dark. Chloe's raven hair is spread over the pillow, her arms flung out the way she does. She looks warm and comfortable, but I need to get up. Too much to do, my mind won't let me rest when I want to take care of things. I am careful and quiet, though I could probably drive a herd of elephants through the room and she wouldn't wake. Strange to say, she wakes immediately at the slightest peep from Leah or Jimmy.

I get dressed, stoke the fire, add another log and then clean up the water from the bath. Now, it's time to pack up. I get all our gear loaded, leaving some clothes for Chloe, and deposit the bags just inside the door.

It's a quick walk to the main camp, and I check in with Thermopoli, who's on duty watching the monitors. Surprisingly, Ben Waters is with her. I hope it's not guilt. They seem okay, though, so I go through the prep for breakfast.

I get the fire pit going and gather ingredients for the morning meal. This is the last of the fresh eggs and bacon, at least until we get back over the dam. We've all lived on worse, we'll be fine. But I want to use the good stuff as long as we can.

Coffee is going when I go to the cooler to get the eggs. That's when I find something I thought I would never see again. It's been well over three years since the Collapse. Most of the ready food and drink disappeared long ago. But there in the cooler, practically shining like the fucking Holy Grail is a bottle of Dr. Pepper. It has my name on it. No, really, *Beast* is written on a piece of paper stuck to the side.

I need to take a moment.

"Oh, Dr. Pepper. Caffeine thou art in our drink, hallowed be Your name. Your rush will come. Your will be done, on Earth as it is in Heaven. Give us this day our daily twitch, and forgive us our withdrawals, as we also show mercy for those who are Jonesing. And lead us not into temptation, but deliver us from Mr. Pibb. For Yours is the true rush, the power and the glory forever. Amen."

I hold it up as I speak, and kiss the bottle. Now, though, do I save it? Hoard my precious treasure? Or, do I drink it now before anyone else catches sight of it?

I hear a sound behind me. It's Viv. She's grinning like a fool, kittens stationed mostly inside a bag at her side, small paws making random escape attempts. I won't admit it aloud, but they are cute little buggers, and I don't think they are house cats. She's grinning from ear to ear as I hold the bottle.

"Do you think this is going to make up for your blatant breach yesterday?"

"I think it's a good start." She grins even bigger and adds, "And, I know where the rest of the six pack is."

"Goddess." I take a breath. "Don't do it again. I need a promise this time."

"Jeez, fine. I just got mad. I will stay under control in the future."

"You don't want the enemy to be able to manipulate you, Viv. I'm serious. You could have gotten any of us killed. You could have been killed. And, we still need you. Your life is worth more than an animal's. I'm sorry, but it's true."

"Okay, I get it. I know. I'm sorry. I swear to you on my life. I won't do it again." I let her sweat a moment. "Are we okay?"

I wait a minute, staring at her until she sighs and nods. Then, I nod at her and return to breakfast. There may be more, but this bottle I will save for a special occasion. As I start cooking, I watch as Viv takes care of the little ones.

In all honesty, I don't want to be too hard on her. While she's hasn't told anyone else, I know she's a devout follower of Freyja. It's why she magically knew to hunt me down and join up. We are both followers of old gods in a world gone mad. Only makes sense that we should be allies in the same fight. It's one of the reasons why she gets along so well with

Chloe and me. Watching her care for the cats, I smile only briefly and continue cooking for the team. Soon, we'll need to move and fight once more for our homes.

Chapter Twenty-two

I wake and I'm in the bunker. *What the fuck?* Rolling in the tangled sheets, I try to pull my head together. I hear Leah fussing in her crib. My brows furrow, and I try to figure out what is happening. Beast was back. I flew to Las Vegas and crashed the plane and then we flew two C-130s back to the Valley. And Kane and his army were approaching, so we were engaging the enemy and...

Liz walks into the room carrying Leah. I am sputtering and trying to gather my wits. Leah is about the age she was when we left the Enclave a few days earlier. Where's Jimmy? Right, he's in Vegas with Beast. A Beast who doesn't really exist? Tears spring to my eyes at the thought. What is happening to me?

"Hey, babe!" Liz states happily, plopping my daughter down on the bed with me.

Leah sees me and comes to me immediately, and I hold on to her, inhaling her sweet scent, trying to smell my Beast on her. Her blue eyes, her father's eyes, look up at me and fill with tears.

"Want daddy. Want daddy. Immy!" She begins crying and clings to me, sobbing.

Liz begins looking at us with concern and puzzlement when Nena comes through the door, her face a mask of worry.

"Why are you here? This is not where you belong, Angel. You need to wake up."

"Wha- what are you talking about?" Liz's voice is plaintive. She glances back and forth between me and Nena before growing angry. "Get out, old woman, you're going to ruin everything!"

"I will not." There's a strength in Nena's voice, and she seems to stand up straighter. "Be gone, demon."

Liz hisses. "I have every right to be here! I helped to build this place long before you showed up, hag!"

"Liz, what are you saying?" I am shocked by her words but not surprised anymore. "Liz, if only you could stop hating my husband. I love him! All I want is for you to be happy."

250

"I can't be happy unless you love me!" Liz comes closer and slaps me. "Snap out of it, Chloe, he's dead. You belong to me now."

"No, Liz. He's not dead, he's not!"

Suddenly, I'm beginning to doubt myself, and it's terrifying me. Did I dream his resurrection and return? Has my loss and grief started to make me insane? I seek reassurance from Nena's eyes.

"Angel. Be strong. This isn't..."

My fright changes into abject terror as Kane walks up from behind Nena and casually slits her throat. Blood sprays across the wall in huge gouts as I scream, and Leah joins me. All I can do is sit there, whimpering as the poor old woman drops to the floor, gurgling with wide eyes.

"There is no escape," Kane states darkly. "You belong to us now."

Liz joins him as they both begin to reach for me. "Yes. To us."

"No," I moan in pure anguish and shake my head violently.

There's a rasp from Nena, who looks me right in the eye. "Wake up, Angel. Wake up."

My terror subsides slightly as Kane recoils and hisses at Nena's crumpled form. Even Liz appears uncertain, through her eyes flash with anger I've not seen from her before.

"Beast is waiting for me to wake up." I proclaim while holding my crying baby girl close for one more minute, stroking her dark hair as I whisper, "It's time to wake up!"

I wake to tapping on the door, and sit bolt upright with pistol in hand. It takes a few moments to gather my bearings. I shudder as I recall the awful dream. It's all or nothing with her and always has been. There is no in-between, no reconciliation. I knew that, really, and seeing her with the army made it real. I know I will see her again, eventually, unless the poison killed her, and when I do, I have to be strong. Whatever we once had is dead, killed by her jealousy and hate.

The person outside taps again, and I finally get up to open the door, wrapping a sheet around myself as I go. The room is still warm. My Beast must have put another log on the fire. I swear that man spoils me, even when we're on the warpath. I peek outside, gun in my hand—old habits die hard—and see Tess Nalwani. I let her in. She's here to get me up and going, and with the clothes Beast left out, I am ready in no time. I douse the fire. Tess and I carry the packs to the main campsite where breakfast is waiting. The meeting this morning is supposed to be brief.

The reconnaissance shows our luck is holding out. The army has slowed considerably. After we wrecked their trucks, the enemy managed to move a short way down the road to an old storage facility that turns off the main highway near a hairpin turn on the road. They trickled in through the night, set up their campsites haphazardly, and some of the slowest not arriving until well after dark. There seems to have been a mess tent of sorts, but they didn't have to carry it far from the wrecked truck.

Ben Waters and Beast think our men on the inside were able to poison the food again. There appears to be many people down, but it could still be residual from the night before. It is well past morning, but the army shows no sign of leaving their campsite. Then, I realize today is Sunday and bring that point up. With the Reverend injured and it being Sunday, I think they may be taking a day of rest.

This means we have more time to come up with horrible things for them to suffer. This does not bother me a bit. We brainstorm for quite some time, trying to determine our best course of action. We will leave camp today so we can get far enough ahead of the army so they don't trap us behind the reservoir. That would mean a long detour around, and we can't lose that time.

Besides, Beast reminds us that our options are starting to dwindle. Laying traps is all well and good, but we are going to have to be more careful. Chances are, all our traps will do is slow them down. While making them potentially weary, we probably won't cull their numbers much more in that way.

By the time we're done, we have all had our say, and we're all comfortable with our tasks. Some of the things we plan are hardcore, sniping at the troops and a few random road traps, for instance. Some of the things are meant to demoralize; some are meant to slowly cut away at their health and strength. All of these things aren't huge, but taken together we hope they make a difference.

We pack up camp. Most of the work is done, but we clean up behind us and leave a few surprises in the cabins. Just in case the raiders find this place. We'll be back if we win. If not, well, anyone who comes along will just have to take their chances. It's become a dangerous world.

We will head to our next location in the Stryker. We will also take all the golf carts. We're not leaving them behind for someone else to use against us. They only move about twelve miles per hour, so the three carts go first. Seth Rawlins and Viv, then Tess Nalwani with Ben Waters, and finally Kim Thermopoli alone. She was supposed to travel with Shawn, but we try not to dwell on our missing comrade. While they all travel together, Beast and I will follow in about an hour in the Stryker.

We want them to stay together to watch each other's backs, as Beast and I will do as we follow along. The two of us complete the shutdown of the camp. No scrap of information about us is left behind, not a footprint, scrap of fabric, stick or twig of firewood, nothing that could comfort the enemy.

It is easy to camouflage the site since we've done this before. Fallen leaves, broken glass, dust, rocks and bones make the camp look like a relic that was deserted long before the Collapse. The half-cabins have removable doors we hide under the foundations. They look like skeletons, but become surprisingly secure when they are covered over with the proper canvas.

The only problem is the ranger's cabin, which we don't want to deconstruct or destroy, and the solar panels on its roof. Those we cover with another ratty tarp, and then half-bury the cabin with fallen, rotting tree limbs, and scatter skunk droppings and decaying animal remains.

That job complete, we disguise our tracks, and I slowly drive the Saucy Goose with Beast following behind me in the dusty road taking care of tire tracks. Once I reach pavement, he climbs in.

Clouds have been gathering all day. I hope it rains enough in the camp to literally muddy the situation even further. Of course, rain will hurt the raiders too, slowing and discouraging them, even if they don't move today. It's not at all pleasant to be sick, but in the rain and mud it's even worse.

As if answering my prayers, it does start to rain. Better cover for us, more suffering for the enemy army. We make it to the next rendezvous site in plenty of time to still get some work done today. By now, word has come that they only took a half-day off. No rest for the wicked, apparently, because the army is marching once more. Which makes our work more important.

So, while half the team led by Beast take posts alongside the highway to snipe randomly and intermittently at the raiders, the rest of us have other work to do.

We gather at the other abandoned RV/trailer park between Blue Mesa Point and Pine Creek, near the reservoir. The trailers are mostly duds though a few are still okay, just unfit to be moved, which explains why we haven't moved them to the Enclave. While we don't do anything obvious, we make sure every water tank is still full and put some of the oleander poison in.

We have contact poisons our chemists have come up with that will make people break into hives or blisters after limited exposure. The couches, chairs, beds, everything left behind has a liberal sprinkling of this substance.

We hide charcoal briquettes that seem like they are just remainders from before the Collapse, which they are. But, we've infused them with a poison that, if inhaled, will make the users sick.

Finally, Ben Waters and Kim Thermopoli are at the creek, hiding stakes where people might walk. They are having way too much fun, splashing around. Rawlins and a team had already put traps, pitfalls and explosives in the nearby fields earlier this year for practice, so we stay clear and remove the "Danger-Minefield" signs.

Then we move out. But not before leaving leaflets telling the raiders that only death awaits ahead; that there is no good reason to follow the Reverend and Kane; that they are failures and will only lead their followers to death. It's dumb, but we understand it can put ideas into weak minds.

"These are not the droids you're looking for," states Walters as we load up to leave. "Move along."

"You're such a geek."

That's Kim Thermopoli. But she's grinning, too. She found an unopened bag of cat chow that still looks good in one of the trailers and is looking forward to bargaining with Viv. She's heard about the Dr. Pepper, I imagine.

At the end of the day, we hope we've done more damage to the morale of the army. From our camp, on the other side of the reservoir, we watch them approach the trailer park. After the day they've had, on their feet with snipers continuously shooting at them, they are stupidly eager to find shelter.

The army is no longer able to make the ten or more miles per day they have been. They're down to five, if they are lucky, checking everything at a snail's pace. The caltrops have them shuffling their feet until they get to an area with trip wires. Now, they are cautious every step of the way. This is a victory of sorts.

The leaders, along with the sick and wounded, take the trailers, as we'd hoped. To be honest, we can't believe our luck. But it is raining and they are weak and exhausted. We figure they are incapable of making good decisions at this point.

We catch a glimpse of the Reverend on his stretcher being taken to shelter. Good. The rest of the army trickles in with the usual casualties with the traps and pits in the fields. They've put together a field kitchen of sorts. With any luck, our two plants—Kawalski and Grant—are still working it, sickening and weakening the army even more. They have instructions to detach and rejoin us once they're near the reservoir, but that's up to them. They need to decide whether to move on or try to continue undermining the army.

To be honest, I worry about them. Perhaps it would be better if they broke off sooner, rather than later. I fear the longer they are there, the more they are pushing their luck. I know Nena said we'd lose two, but losing Roche still stings, and I don't want to lose any other members of my family.

We're nearer to Gunnison, but it's safer to trek back and forth across the bridge to harass the raiders. On the road from where the raiders are camped and Gunnison, there are two major bridges over the reservoir, and one minor one. Rawlins wanted to blow the bridges, but there were enough people telling him "No" that he finally had to listen. Besides, it would be impossible to build bridges like this again, at least for a long while, and we still want to have trade with the outside world.

For now, we are set up behind the tree line once more, off the beaten path, and have been reunited with Paul McIntyre and Dale Louis, who have been busy on this side of the reservoir. They've been working closely with the town of Gunnison to get the final barriers set up for the incoming army and have been calibrating our siege weapons. They are the crew Shawn Roche trained on the catapults and trebuchets we had made last fall. Seth Rawlins is still disdainful of them, but is prepared to help load them with explosives, among other things, when necessary. Especially now that Roche is gone.

Beast has taken a note from "The Art of War" by Sun Tzu, which he made me read early on after his return from the dead. I didn't see what was so important about the book at the time, but I am beginning to understand now.

One of the ideas he's using is to make the enemy chase you for the purpose of luring them into a trap. To do that, one needs bait. Now that the raiders have become so much more footsore, in some very real and painful ways, and their trucks are history, we know they would like nothing better than to replace those trucks, or at least one for their leaders and their sick. Heck, maybe even just for their traveling soup kitchen.

We've got just what they want. It's a canvas covered truck with a fuel trailer. Yeah, perfect. Too perfect, but we still think desperation will win out, and they'll take the bait. Tomorrow we plan on baiting the hook by "rescuing" this truck just in sight of their troops. They will give chase, and they will fail to catch it. But, they will see it again on the third bridge over the reservoir, supposedly broken down, but in actuality, undriveable and loaded with enough fuel to explode with the right hit from artillery.

What they don't know is that there is a nice place for artillery on the hill on the other side of the bridge. The thought makes me grin madly with glee as we get ready.

Chapter Twenty-three

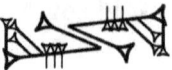

We're in a wooded camp, and there isn't much privacy, crowded as we are. Chloe and I have our tent set up as far away as possible, which isn't very far.

I'm not complaining, but the cabin from last night was a five-star hotel in comparison. Our evening meal is in close quarters, as well. We're in a secure area, but it doesn't have tons of square footage. Good news is that we have water, and we have the high ground, should we need it.

The ravine is another box canyon, though small, and we decided that even with close quarters, it's preferable to possibly being spotted by the enemy. You ask, why would you put your team in a box canyon with no escape? A good general puts his team in a position that the only way out is through, another little something from my reading.

Today, breakfast is cold and fast, we have a lot to do and miles to cover. The briefing is just as quick, but everyone knows their tasks. It's still dark when we get out from under the cover of the trees. We leave our remote team in the Stryker, holding down the fort and watching our backs.

We have to cross the reservoir with an old, POS pickup to carry our teams and gear to the other side. Our task is two-fold, so we have two tactics today. We don't want the army to cross at all, so we're going to try one last time to convince them to leave. If that doesn't work, we have bait they can't resist, and when they come after it, they're not going to like what happens.

We get a message from Nalwani. It seems the raider army has split again. They've sent a few squads of soldiers tracking the side roads we've been using. They may be taking the long way around to reach the reservoir. I think they're trying a pincer attack. We all grin at each other. We prepared for just such a contingency without the expectation they would walk into that particular trap, but now we get to make more things go boom. Oh, darn.

Once we get over the reservoir, we hitch a trailer to the back of the truck. In brilliant red paint that doesn't look too fake, I swear, is the word

"FUEL" in all capital letters. We do, indeed, have fuel sloshing around in there, half-bad gasoline mixed with some dregs of propane siphoned from a few dozen wrecks. And we have a few trucks and buses at the Sapinero Trading Post just past the first bridge over the reservoir, all, sadly, *without* fuel. There are five of them, made to carry lots of people and their belongings. Just what the footsore army wants. No spark plugs in any of them, but they look good.

But first, their final warning. Dawn is breaking, and I want us to be in place well before the army arrives at our display. It will be a little bit Wizard of Oz and a little bit Scarface. So kill me, it's going to be a show. Chloe and the Reapers all have their skull-faced balaclavas, while I, of course, am recognizable because of the white mask.

On spikes across the road are the heads of a good half-dozen of their scouts taken from various parties. Rawlins and I have been quietly collecting them, and just before we went over the reservoir last night, put them here to get some seasoning. They look sufficiently gory.

We uncover a long and extended trench in the road in front of us. It wraps around, surrounding us and cutting off an easy approach. It has been covered with metal plates like those used when road work was ongoing, and has allowed us free access. Now, with the plates removed, the pitch and oil is visible.

We are ready to light them as soon as we have word the army is close. The plates are lined up on our side of the trench forming a sort of half wall. The plates will get hot once we light the trench, thus restricting the oncoming army even further.

Of course they could go around if we give them time, but we aren't going to do that. They aren't going to see us. They're going to be too busy watching the fire. We will be on the south side of the road and on the high ground.

The fire wall goes all the way down to the water, but the army will be focused on the scarecrow figures we have set up beyond the firewall. They look okay, but will look better once we get the extra balaclavas and a duplicate mask on them. They look pretty good now, if I do say so. Not perfect, but the flames and smoke will help. And we have set up a remote loudspeaker behind the scarecrows.

We made them taller and bigger than we are in real life. We should have made them shoot fire out of their asses, but we didn't have enough time. It will still work. We send Thermopoli back to the truck to wait and have it ready to go, as well as keep an eye out on our rear. Viv, Chloe and I climb the ridge to our blind. We are missing Roche, he should be here, too, but we will make it work without him.

We are comfortably in place for the hour or so it takes for the army to get off their butts and get to this point. Nalwani keeps us apprised of

257

their progress, and when they're within about a half a klick, we light up the firewall. She informs us when the plume of smoke goes up and the army begins to run toward us. Good, we want the strongest and fastest. Nalwani also tells us there are leaders trying to get them to slow down, so we presume Kane is trying to show a little discretion. It doesn't stop our newest volunteers from running right into our scenario.

When they arrive, they are barreling around the corner and catch sight of our little show. They slow, then stop, bodies crowding in after them. They're angry, sick of being preyed on, actually physically sick to boot, and ready to make fools of themselves. We intend to let them.

"Hold it right there, assholes." My voice is loud, amplified, coming from behind the scarecrows. We have their attention.

The army shouts with rage, and quite a few of them ready their weapons. Nalwani's voice is in our ears that the leaders are closing in and catching up.

"Afraid to try something now that you're face-to-face with your worst nightmare? That's what we thought." I take a breath and nod to Angel, at my right and then to Viv at my left. The three of us are locked and loaded. I feel like Fezzik from the Princess Bride. This is awesome.

"Run away, little children. You're not ready for us. The Angel of Death and her Beast are here for your souls."

At that, Chloe grins at me. I wink at her. The Reverend's army lets out a scream of rage and begins firing at the simulacrums. With grim smiles, we begin firing at them.

Chapter Twenty-four

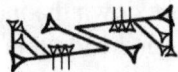

For once, I finally get to use the M60 that we had picked up back in Blythe. I'm one of the few that's rated to use an MG, so we don't use them much. It's not like we have replacement barrels lying around either.

That's something a lot of people don't understand. You can't just "open up" with a fully automatic weapon. The barrel heats up and will deform if you fire it too much. Recoil is another reason why you also want short, controlled bursts.

Chloe and Viv are also ready to rumble. My lady is still sporting the Tavor, which she likes immensely. That and the P-90s are her two favorite weapons of choice. Given her small frame, the lighter recoil is a better choice.

Viv, on the other hand, is a bit taller and likes a heavier recoil. As such, she's carrying the AK that I obtained at the travel center. Like Chloe, she's got the rifle loaded with a drum, and she loves it!

In most cases, our bullets rip through multiple people. I don't know what's better, watching the assholes get cut down or watching their faces change as our scarecrows remain standing under their fire. I let out a laugh, as menacing and threatening as I can, while continuing to shoot. It is difficult not to laugh, in all sincerity.

In the meantime, Nalwani tells us the pincer action failed because we are not where we are supposed to be. They are running down the road toward their friends here at the reservoir and are not paying proper attention.

They are in such a rush that they run into one of our Claymores, and we're told they go up with it. Over the shooting, we can barely hear the sound of a distant boom that informs us of that fact. Nalwani tells us there are a few survivors, but they are not headed toward the battle any longer.

Here and now, the surviving volunteers are panicking as their brethren fall around them. They try to back up, only to be held in place by the weight of incoming bodies and the dead. The shrieking of the panicked and wounded is like music to our ears.

The panic is so bad they have even dropped their weapons, and the press of the army is finally beginning to reverse and spill outward toward the side of the road. A few slide down the incline toward the water. Others run madly in blind fear and end up in the fire, their screams adding to the chaos.

Our weapons continue to chatter, taking their toll. Piles of bodies litter the road, and the terror of those in the front is spreading to panic in the remainder of the army. But, as long as there are bodies in range, we continue our fire, and I continue my loud bellowing laughter. I put in a few "Run for your lives!" and "We are your doom!" and "Say hello to hell!" while I'm at it.

As soon as the majority of live targets are beyond the curve in the road and out of range, we get ready to move out. Before I go, I hand Viv an incendiary grenade. With glee, she lobs toward the pile of dead and wounded. It goes off roughly in the middle of the pile of dead and dying bodies. They begin burning merrily as I laugh into the microphone and exit, stage right.

We advance in stages, one person covering the other two, then switching out. Once we get to the truck, we can hardly see anything behind us, thanks to the smoke and flames. It's lasting better than I thought it would.

We arrive at the truck just in time to see a struggle going on. Thermopoli is in the truck, head back and on the ground. Beside the vehicle are three bodies in a life-or-death struggle.

"What the fuck is this shit?!"

I realize I am still on loudspeaker when the words leave my mouth. I rip the microphone away and throw it to the ground as I close in with the scuffling men. Grabbing one by the back of his jacket, I pull him up.

It's Mace Grant, bleeding from a wound to his abdomen. He moves to fight me, sees who it is, then pulls back. Quickly, he grabs one of the other two men by the ankles and pulls him away from the body beneath, Jakob Kawalski.

Both of my men are wounded. The raider who's caused all this damage has a long knife in each hand. He comes up swinging both of them. Before we can react, Viv puts an axe in his head, and he drops. Taking a breath, the three of us assess the damage.

Grant speaks up first, his deep baritone raspy voice with disuse. "We took the chance to make our getaway when we saw the smoke. We figured it was you." He coughs, and I see blood dripping from his wounded side. I get a trauma pack out and start bandaging him.

"This asshole saw us leave and thought he'd better see what we were up to. He circled around and got here ahead of us." Kawalski is out of breath and has wrapped a rag around the wound in his forearm, which I think is going to need stitches.

At that point I hear Chloe's voice in a loud denial. "No! No-no-no-no!"

I turn to see her bent over Thermopoli in the truck. Chloe's hands are at Thermopoli's throat, and at first it looks as if she's throttling her, but the blood spills past my angel's fingers, and continues to flow, barely unchecked. *Fuck.*

Immediately I rush over to assess the situation. It's as hopeless as I feared. Chloe looks at me with tear-filled eyes, and I slowly shake my head. I don't even have any morphine to give in order to ease her passing. Hell, in a situation like this, I might even deliver an overdose in order to make it mercifully quick.

"Kim, you're going to be fine, sweetie, just relax," Chloe mutters while holding onto Thermopoli, who is weakly thrashing and struggling to breathe.

My wife is covered with the woman's blood and holds her hands to reassure her. Viv and I stand helplessly to the side, realizing that this will be over all too soon. Yet, not soon enough.

It ends quickly, and the five of us are left looking at the remains of our friend in the driver's seat of the truck. The damned silence is painfully deafening.

My still-weeping Chloe speaks up. "We have to move out. Thermopoli—Kim—wouldn't want us to die, too."

At that, Viv and I lift our fallen sister up and put her in the back of the truck with the covered motorcycles. Grant and Kawalski get in the back with her. Chloe has done her best to clear the seat of blood, but there is no way to avoid it. She and Viv get in the front, and I take the driver's seat.

The army will either be deterred or will come after us as soon as some of the fire has gone out. It was already burning low when we left a few minutes ago. We have to behave as if they are going to come after us. In my ear, Nalwani is asking what has happened. Viv glances over and briefs her. There is a shocked silence in our ears as we get into place before the second bridge and in clear sight of the army.

Finally, Nalwani starts updating us again with the army's movement. Seems Kane caught up to the shit-show and made order of the mess. The few remainders of the group who were trying for a pincer action finally caught up and charged in when they saw the smoke. Thinking they were slaughtering us, they managed to kill a few of their own before Kane stopped them. Were it not due to the fact that I was sitting in Thermopoli's blood, I'd laugh.

The lake provided enough water for them to put out the fire, and they've spotted our truck near the bridge. We have it rigged to billow smoke from the engine compartment when we flip a switch. The army is getting ready to come after us, so I flip the switch now.

On seeing it, the army lets out a roar and comes after us again, and I don't rush to keep us moving—driving in fits and starts, drawing them forward and letting them edge ever closer but staying out of range of their weapons.

It takes most of the day, playing crippled. I'm driving for a while then stopping to "frantically" attempt repairs, rushing down to the water to scoop buckets-full for the engine, stuff like that. What we're really doing is cleaning up the blood, and putting stitches in Grant and Kawalski. We have the two men stay low, the army doesn't need to know their erstwhile raiders were our spies. At least, not yet. If necessary, we can save them for a special surprise.

Finally we drive off, as if we're fine. When we stop this time, we are well out of sight of their men, and we get the motorcycles unloaded and get ready to go. We've stopped in the middle of the third bridge over the reservoir, a good distance from them. It will give us plenty of time to get out of here.

The problem is Thermopoli. We're not leaving her on the truck. But, all we have are the three motorcycles to evacuate. When it was four of us, Thermopoli and Viv were on their own cycles, and Chloe was riding with me. Now, we have Grant and Kawalski, which is fine, but how does one ride with a dead body?

Viv solves the problem by rigging a harness for Thermopoli to ride behind her. Grant and Kawalski will ride double and so will Chloe and I. Not the way we wanted to go, but our plans are already proceeding, and we can't leave our dead behind.

We turn the smoke machine on high, and the oncoming army lets out a cheer we can hear at this distance. Ben Waters is online with Nalwani off shift, and he tells us the army has gathered itself and is making a rush for the bridge. They are so eager for a victory they are pushing themselves to reach us before we can "fix" the truck again.

I have Grant and Kawalski make a run back toward the army so they can be seen before turning around and running. I don't know what they say, but a roar goes up from the army as our two men book it away from them. Gunfire erupts as they go, but Kawalski is driving, and he has moves they don't teach in driver's safety class. They take off past us, and I send Viv on her way. Chloe and I pour gasoline into the truck bed and into the front seat. We want fumes, lots of fumes.

263

We get on our bike and wave toward the hills on the north side of the reservoir. When we see a flash, Operation Firestorm is a go. The army is approaching the curve that leads to the bridge, and when they see us riding off, they let out another roar, this one of rage.

We take off before the army comes into sight. We've set up the truck and fuel trailer in a "C" blocking the road. We know they want it, and we know they will do anything to get it. By the time we get to our rendezvous point, they've surrounded the truck. We have binoculars, but Waters on the radio helps us know what's going on.

"They're at the truck. They're surrounding it. It's like that scene from *Space: 2001* where the apes find the obelisk..."

We can see the army gathering, even from this distance. The bridge isn't high or wide, just two lanes of concrete with a two-foot high railing.

Then, there is a hubbub of some sort. Waters comes in again. "I think it's the Reverend. He's walking on his own now; that poison did NOT kill him."

Chloe and I glance at each other. What are they doing? We look back out over the water, trying to catch sight of what Waters is describing.

"Now they're leading him to the truck. They're putting him in the driver's seat."

Chloe looks over and I pull the key to the truck out of my pocket. With a grin, she nods, and then goes back to her binoculars. I can't help but do the same.

Apparently, someone is doing something to the truck, hot-wiring it, no doubt. It starts up, and the entire army cheers. That's when the tracer bullets start streaking out from the bluff across from the bridge, aiming for both the truck and the trailer half-full of fuel.

Remember when I said bullets won't cause a gas tank to explode? While I was right, there is a caveat. A tracer projectile is constructed with a hollow base filled with a pyrotechnic flare material. This is made of a mixture of a very finely ground metallic fuel, oxidizer and a small amount of organic fuel. Metallic fuels include magnesium, aluminum and, occasionally, zirconium. The oxidizer is a salt molecule which contains oxygen combined with a specific element responsible for the desired color output. While it creates a streak of light, it's also burning when it does it. Thus, it can cause flammable materials to catch fire. And, you can guess what happens next.

When the gas tank blows, it takes out most of the people surrounding the vehicle. There is no way the Reverend survived that. At least fifty of the Reverend's closest followers went with him, straight to hell where they will be introduced to the Goddess's special treatment for rapists and murderers. Some men on fire fly off the bridge and into the water.

264

"That one's for Kim Thermopoli, you son of a bitch." Chloe's voice is bitter.

Then, as a special bonus, the catapult flings some of our special explosive on the army further away on the bridge. It is already aflame as it's thrown, but nobody notices it until it's too late.

"And that one's for Shawn Roche, you filthy animals." My voice sounds just as bitter.

There is a great deal of satisfaction in this destruction. The next few shots from the catapult are perfectly placed further and further along the bridge, effectively chasing the raiders from it. If this doesn't make our point clear, nothing will. One thing is for certain, if these idiots dare to press on, they will pay dearly for it.

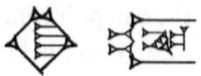

Since finding Kim bleeding out, I have felt numb, floating above it. The endless trek across the reservoir has seemed dreamlike. I have done everything necessary to play out this charade, watching myself fetch water, play panic and drive across the fucking water until I felt I was the one lying dead in the back of the truck.

Beast could see my state and had looked askance at me every now and then. I just smiled and nodded, and we continued with our play on wheels until the trap was well set. All the while, I could imagine the blood slowly drying on Kim's body and wondering if blowflies would find us even here. I imagine never hearing her quiet chuckle and quick wit ever again.

I tell myself there will be time to grieve later, but I am grieving already. Beast holds me, and I feel a moment's relief before I remember Kim will never be held again. She will never kiss anyone again, never fall in love and never know a moment of looking at her newborn child with awe-dewed eyes. It feels like I am breaking and that terrifies me a little, when that thought can push its way through the numbness.

Now, watching the well-placed bullets igniting the fuel trailer and truck and sending the Reverend and some of his followers to hell, all I can feel is relief. It's finally a chance to have a respite and get Kim's body somewhere away from all this ugliness.

The catapult shots add insult to injury, and the bridge is a mass of flame. More than a few of the raiders have jumped into the water, but our compound is not easily extinguished. We like to call it Greek Fire. Shawn Roche would have been so proud.

I don't know what we're going to do now, and I lean against Beast while he watches the flames on the bridge. I simply have no will to move, act, do... anything. I just want to lie down where we are and curl into a ball and weep.

My Beast can see this is affecting me. I know he sees the depression and hopelessness in my eyes, and he sees I am crumbling. As always, he is my rock, my steadfast shelter, my safe harbor. That, too, makes me want to weep. I have no strength as he leads me back to the motorcycle, and I cling to him as we drive back to our rendezvous point, our late camp, and I don't care. I don't want to talk to anyone about what has happened. I don't want to explain how I had to wash the blood off of my hands and how there is still Kim's blood soaked in my jeans that will never come out. I don't want it to come out. I want to feel the pain of it, of feeling the life slip away from her panic-stricken eyes.

I start to sob, clinging madly to my husband as he wends his way along the route to the campsite. My tears stream away in the wind of our passage, melting into my hair like Kim's blood melted down her strong neck and pooled in any hollow and crevice on her body.

The bike is slowing, and, through tear-filled eyes, I look up and around in puzzlement at the roadside turnaround area where we've stopped. Why are we here? We need to get back to camp. My sorrow-induced haze is not ready to lift yet, and when Beast gets off the bike, I would have toppled over if he hadn't been prepared to catch me.

He turns me in his arms and holds me to him tightly so I can cry in the shelter of his embrace. There is no need for words, he knows me. He strokes my hair and murmurs endearments, and I grieve over the loss of a good friend.

When we are once more on our way back to camp, I feel a little better. Before we got back on the bike, Beast and I talked a little, we both shed some tears, and I think we found a little composure to now be strong for the others, to be able to handle our responsibilities without falling apart.

Beast held me for a long time before he spoke. When he did talk, he said, "You can be told that a number of your people are going to die. It doesn't make their loss any easier." It's so true.

We left the Enclave so full of ourselves, even with the warning ringing in our ears that we would lose two. But, it didn't mean anything at the time. Now, it is all too real and all too terrible.

Before we start back again, Beast reminds me that, after the reservoir, Nena had told us we were to flee home. I had forgotten that little bit of advice in my shock, but he hadn't. So, he called ahead and told our crew to keep an eye out and to pack up. We're moving out tonight.

The radios have been very quiet since the explosions on the bridge. This was as far as we've ever gotten in our planning, besides our fall-back plans and what we've helped the Gunnison people come up with. Once Beast gives his orders, things get livelier. Not cheerful or anything, but everyone has a task now, and that is helping.

The camp is packed and ready to go when we arrive. Even the catapult has been disassembled and is in place atop the Stryker. Solemn faces surround us, and tears spring to my already sore eyes, but I am not in such a state as I was. At this point, we have several golf carts, three motorcycles and the Stryker.

All our gear is packed away, so we'll hide the golf carts and remove their batteries. Rawlins, Viv and Waters will ride the motorcycles, while the rest of us go along in the Stryker. We are all connected via radio, and we have no need for radio silence.

It was going to be Kim's turn on the UAVs, so I take over while we're still stationary. Our other two remaining operators are busy. Waters is on a cycle, and Nalwani is driving the Stryker. Kim's body is in a plastic shroud on a stretcher on the floor of the Stryker. I put the headphones on and hear one of our remote pilots urgently hailing me.

"This is Angel, what's the problem?"

"Thank god, ma'am, the raiders. They're moving again."

"Okay, so what's wrong with that? They will need to camp tonight, and they're likely waiting for the fire—"

"No, ma'am, they're coming your way."

"What?"

"They are coming up the road that leads to your camp. You need to get out, stat!"

"Roger that." I take off one of the headphones, turn in my seat and speak through my radio to all of our people. "We have tangos headed our way. We will take the alternate route out, and we're going hot. Everyone copy?"

Once I hear back from everyone, I go back to the monitor to make sure we're going to be clear when we get to the alternate road. It looks like we have plenty of time to get out of the box canyon we've been in, but getting to the side road might be a bit dicey. We're going to have to use all speed, and that's not going to be fun on this bumpy road. But it will be better than being trapped by Kane and his army.

The UAV team will be able to reach us without images once we're moving, so I will keep that earbud live. The motorcycles are our advance scouts, and they are already on their way when we get started. The calm voice of the drone pilot is steady and reassuring, but he urges more speed. We make the turn up the dry creek bed we had chosen as our alternate route, but I see torchlight reflected off the walls of the canyon below as the raiders close in.

The Stryker groans and bumps at a steep angle, and we all seem to hold our breath as we climb. We've tried this in a Humvee but not in the APC. I see Beast clenching his fists. I suspect he would rather be outside, pushing. He restrains himself and checks in on the three cyclists.

Rawlins has sent the other two ahead and has been fiddling with some rather large boulders that overhang the road. He still has some explosives he is itching to use. I hope he doesn't blow his fool head off, and tell him so.

"Don't worry, grandma. I'm going to try one last time to dissuade the raiders from coming any further." At that, I hear a grunt and a whoop from him, then the sound of him gunning his bike. "I'm coming hot after you, I would appreciate it if you could move it just a little bit faster!"

Not a handful of seconds later, a low rumble vibrates throughout the vehicle, and a muffled *whump* is heard over the noise of my radios and the sound of the vehicle.

Tess Nalwani lets out a string of curses, shifts gears and keeps going. Then, she curses again, and there is a sharp turn. Then, we are on more level ground.

"Tess? What's going on?"

"Um. I think we lost Seth. Um, Rawlins."

"What?!" Beast comes to my side, and Tess keeps the vehicle moving as she speaks.

"I saw his bike go flying. I didn't see him, but where did he go then?"

All I can think is that Nena promised us only two. Only two.

"Stop the vehicle."

It's Beast yelling the command. And, though Tess looks at me with a question, she slows us down and stops. Beast opens the back hatch and stalks out into the night with the M60 in hand, belt draped over his shoulder while the vehicle tics and creaks around us.

A few long minutes later, he jogs back into the vehicle carrying Rawlins who is bloodied, but not dead. A cheer breaks out among the passengers. Viv, Waters and the UAV pilots want to know what's going on. Beast lays the man down and begins treating him, so I answer as Tess starts us moving again.

"Well, all I can say is Rawlins finally blew up more than he could handle. But it looks like he's gonna live."

Viv points out that I have been warning him about this all along, but I don't have the heart to tell him I-told-you-so. He's bleeding pretty heavily.

The upside to Seth almost blowing himself up is that the UAV pilots do inform me that the raiders have a mess on the road and won't be following along anytime soon. So, all we need to do now is get ourselves back on a more well-known route and get to Gunnison with all due haste.

There are things going on upstream from the reservoir that will need our attention soon. The pilots assure me there is a passable route, but the army will have a lot of difficulty following without air-support.

269

I heave a sigh of relief and watch my husband care for our wounded. Looks like Rawlins has a broken collarbone and some serious stone shrapnel from the boulders. He's awake and in pain. He tells Beast he had grabbed the Stryker with one hand to help him up the ravine when the blast went and he saw stars.

Kawalski holds onto him as Beast sets his bone, and Rawlins looks at me wearily when that's done, then grins wickedly and gives me a thumbs up. "Still got both hands and both eyes!"

I shake my head at him and try not to smile, but he smirks at me because he knows me too well.

As we travel through the night, a heavy rain begins to fall, and we leave the raiders far behind. Next stop, Gunnison.

Chapter Twenty-Seven

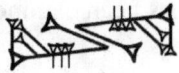

A few hours later in Gunnison, everyone is ready for the next phase of our fight against the Reverend's… well, Kane's army, now. We've been unable to stop them but, by hell, we slowed them. We've also cut them down by almost half. One of their leaders is dead, and though the remaining raiders may be the toughest, most stubborn, or the luckiest of the troops they started with, there are far fewer than there were to begin with.

All told, over five hundred of Kane's army are either dead, crippled, or have deserted. If we do the math, each of our Reapers is responsible for a minimum of fifty of Kane's fighters. We only lost two Reapers. I call that a good ratio. Chloe thinks I'm being morbid.

Although, in retrospect, Kim deserves more, and I'm hoping to honor her with that. Every one of these fuckers deserves to die. I know what you are going to say, what about Shawn? He died a good death, a man's death, and was well avenged. In all honesty, that's what men are supposed to do, be willing to die for their loved ones.

With women it's a different story. They are supposed to be part of a community's' future. But cutting a woman's throat from behind? Only assholes find that acceptable behavior, and they will pay dearly for it.

We've settled into temporary quarters for the moment. If we had more than one link to the UAVs, this might be a bit easier, but we are the only contact the Gunnison people have with air support. While we've been delaying the army, the engineers from the entire area have been working very hard on yet another nasty surprise.

The spring runoff had just begun a few weeks ago, and then we'd had one of those random spring freezes that happens occasionally in the mountains of Colorado. When the raiders made themselves known a little more than a week ago, some rock falls that we'd placed strategically were set loose. That was what Louis and McIntyre were up to while the rest of us were harrying the army.

These rock falls were the final piece of two dams on two rivers. Or rather, a creek and a river. Beaver Creek rarely has much more than a trickle until spring runoff. It has been dammed right above the highway. The other river is the Gunnison River, a much more substantial waterway that leads to the reservoir. It has been dammed at the freeway between two rises of ground.

Yes, a lot of earth had to be moved, but this is something we'd been working on for a while. The only piece of the puzzle left is the rock fall that finished the blockage. With the two rivers blocked, now we're waiting for just the right moment to blow the dams and wash the army off the face of the earth.

We have to wait for them to get in place. They tried following us through the hills for a while; but, thanks to Rawlins' amazing flying fireball—which is what we've started calling his explosion last night—and the completely fortuitous heavy rains, they finally gave up and got back on the highway.

Speaking of Rawlins, he and Grant have been evacuated, to their extreme dismay. Chloe rubbed it in a little when Rawlins started complaining.

"Damn fool and your explosives. Sure, sure, now you think you're some kind of big-time rock star, saving all our lives. What, you want us to name a school after you? Please. Go home and get some rest, war hero." She turned her back on him and nodded to the medic.

Poor Rawlins sputtered after her as he was firmly herded to the ambulance for evacuation. Grant laughed harder than the rest of them until he was put into the ambulance with Rawlins, to his chagrin. Gotta love it.

But now we're down to six, and not all of us are up to snuff. Kawalski was wounded, but he's not out of it yet. To our great surprise, when the ambulance returned, it brought Jackson and Burton back with it. They turned their duties over to Rawlins and Grant and insisted on being brought back to get, as they put it, in on some of the action.

"If this works out, there may not be any more action," I tell them in a gruff tone, though, it is good to have them.

"Now that we're here, those assholes are going to turn tail and run," Jackson boasts.

"Oh, yeah. I'm sure." That's Viv. She's grinning at the two of them and shaking her head. They look sheepish, and she goes on, "C'mon, boys, I'd like you to meet our new mascots."

Chloe comes up behind me and twines her arm around my waist. "You know she's going to get them to babysit the kittens, right?"

"Is that what she's up to?"

"Watch and learn."

But there's no time for that. We get word the explosions are imminent. We've hooked up several big screens at the command center to our feed so more people can watch. And, we know it's time, because it seems the raiders have finally got their sorry asses on the road again and are approaching their ultimate destiny. Chloe rubs her hands together in glee, and we head to the monitors to watch the show.

We've been watching them constantly, of course. Night vision on the UAVs helped with that. We were able to track the army while they were raging through the hills. When they finally gave up and went back to the road for some much-needed rest, we also tracked a few groups that splintered off to either desert or that seemingly got lost in the mountains near the reservoir. We're not really sure which, as they are still wandering as far as we can tell.

All the same, we think we know where Kane is. We are fairly certain he's been holding up the rear, and knowing him, he's shooting anyone slower than himself. The remaining army members seem very motivated, and I wonder how many he has brought from Phoenix with him. His persistent determination for revenge is really beginning to irritate me.

It wasn't enough to kill me and to try, time and again, to take my lady as his personal slave. But then, after my ferocious woman so justly killed him, he had to come back from the dead to guide this army here. Why? To destroy, out of a misplaced sense of revenge what we have spent so much time and energy building? So you must understand how much we want to wipe the fucker off the face of the earth.

We are aiming for maximum destruction of life. There was much discussion and inspection and more discussion to find an army engineer. We lucked out finding Rawlins, our demolitions expert and someone who used to work at the Hoover Dam, in Colorado Springs.

After all that, we have placed the dams strategically at locations where the road passes out of the reservoir area and where the Gunnison River is deep and swift. There is no ideal location, but this is the best we have. Especially after the strategic earth-moving we've been doing over the last year to channel water.

Everyone looks to me, and I say, "Go!" There is a tense moment before anything starts happening. The army is situated on the road, most of them well past Beaver Creek. When the first explosion happens well up-stream, the raiders stop for a moment, uncertain. Then, they slowly start moving forward again. That is until a flood of rapidly-moving water rushes toward them like a tsunami. That's when they start running. They're hemmed in by the Gunnison River to the right of them and by a bluff to the left, so they turn and run back toward the reservoir, trying to outrun the water.

That's when the other charge goes, and the water inside the Beaver Creek Dam is turned loose on Kane's army. It accomplishes much more than we had hoped. The rains last night have added to the already practically bursting dam. When we fled through the hills last night, we ended up going much further north than we had planned because of flooding behind the dam. So when it blows, it utterly finishes the army. It is a marvel to behold.

Everyone erupts into celebration, and my wife jumps into my arms, shrieking like a banshee. I squeeze her tightly, but do not take my eyes off the monitors. I want to see what's happening to Kane.

The area is a mass of confusion, white water, boulders spilling all across the road with mud, debris, and water at high velocity. It is hard to even see the people in all that mess.

One of the UAVs goes lower and zooms in for me, and I make a mental note to tell Pete to give those guys a raise. Kane is following the line of the water pushing with force toward the reservoir.

Amazingly, there are some survivors running at top speed toward higher ground and up sheer cliff faces. *Fuck.* We had hoped to exterminate all of them with just one flush of the toilet, but we have planned, of course, for any contingency.

I narrow my eyes. I am virtually certain that a cockroach like Kane will have survived. Chloe's initial joy has tempered, and she has turned to watch the monitors with me. She feels my tension and glances up at me.

"He's still out there, isn't he?"

"You know it. Let's load 'em up again."

"Roger that, my love."

She reaches up to kiss me, and then starts rounding up the troops. We're going in with more than just our Reapers, but we are keeping the core group together as advance scouts and shock troops.

"Okay, boys and girls. It's time to get back on the road. I hope you packed your extra ammo, 'cause we get to go wipe up some raiders!"

There is a rousing cheer as my wife gets everyone revved up and moving. We head back to the main building to grab our gear. I make a mental note to make sure our magazines are topped off.

All around us, the people of Gunnison are celebrating as though we've already won. They don't seem to understand that this is not over yet. I frown, and instruct everyone to stay on alert. I tell them we will be back as soon as we can, and definitely not to relax their guards yet. They nod, but they are smiling, and I don't know if they're listening to me.

I am losing patience and feel a growl building. Chloe is nowhere to be seen, and the joy of these people is pissing me off. *It's not over yet, damn it!*

I jump on a chair, then onto a table and shout, "Everyone, listen up!"

Silence descends and eyes turn to me, laughs and smiles fading as they see my face. "We are not done yet. You saw a good number of raiders

274

swept away, and that is good news. But, we aren't going to be done until the last raider is wiped out. There are still raiders at the reservoir. And, we are heading out to see what we can do about that. But we are not finished here. Is that understood?"

There are only desultory noises of agreement, but also a few offended looks in my direction. This just pisses me off further. I hear a growl and realize it's me. Again. Chloe is headed my way with concern etched on her face, but it's too late for that. Consequences be damned, they need to take this seriously. I try to moderate my tone.

"This is not the time to relax our guard. Bands of raiders could still arrive and do a lot of damage if we are unprepared. Are you willing to hand your city over after all we have accomplished?"

Shocked faces are now looking up at me, and silence reigns once more. Yeah, I have their attention now. "Keep to our plans. Watch and wait. Stand guard. Understood?"

This time there is more animation and they answer me, determination on their faces rather than disappointment and anger. That will do. Chloe and I head out.

Chapter Twenty-Eight

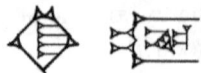

When Beast starts growling, I always worry. Unless, you know, it's private time, which is different. However, by the time I get back to his side of the room, everything seems to be okay again.

He is stepping down from the table and I take him by the arm to exit the building. The mood in the room is much more subdued, though there are still happy people. I hope my husband has impressed on them the idea that our war is far from over.

Back in the Saucy Goose—it feels more like the Saucy Goose again now that Jackson and Burton are back with us—we all take up our positions and move out.

I painfully notice there are only ten of us. Even with Burton and Jackson. So many are missing that we still have an empty seat. As I sigh, my husband knows me enough to know what I am thinking. He wraps an arm around me, and I lean my head on his shoulder.

In the meantime, the kittens have escaped from Viv's bag again, and they are playing hide and seek behind bags and boots. My tough husband smiles at them and lets me catch them before his sober demeanor returns.

Ben Waters is watching the monitors as we drive a much shorter and less complicated route than our flight of the night before. The road is clear most of the way, so it doesn't take long.

That all changes when we get past where the dam burst. The flooding made a real mess, though not as much as I had thought it would at first. The real damage begins beyond the second dam around Beaver Creek. It's still flooded. Though seeing it, that's an understatement. It would be a national disaster area if we still *had* a national anything.

"Fuck. This worked... better than I thought it would." I state in a horrified whisper. There is stunned silence as we take it all in.

Finally Beast speaks, "This is a fucking mess. But there must be survivors. Our job is to find them and kill them. Any questions?"

"No sir!" is the unanimous response.

"Good. It's going to be more complicated than we thought, but it's still the task at hand. Nalwani, you're going to want to be real careful with the vehicle. We can't see if the road is there or not with all the water coverage."

"I suggest we anchor it back here where there's solid ground," she replies with a nod. "We don't know if or where the road is washed out since everything is covered with mud and water. We risk losing it if we go much further." Beast nods back and she starts looking for a likely dry spot.

"You know, some of them could have climbed the rocks up in here," Kawalski growls. He looks grumpy, but I figure he's probably still sore from his injuries.

"There will be survivors all over the damn place," Beast agrees. "So we will all need to keep our eyes open. Wear your helmets and body armor." There is a loud groan, but everyone begins donning gear. "We are in teams of two or three; nobody goes off on their own. Nalwani and Waters will stay here—in your gear and watching out for each other. Keep us informed of the aerial surveillance, and everyone keeps their radios hot. No chatter, this is business.

"Kawalski, you will supervise McIntyre and Louis on the road. Your job is to clear the road for the incoming Hummers. We need to know where the road is out, and you will set warning flags to indicate unsafe areas." They grumble, but Beast adds, "And you will clean up any survivors you see. Obviously." That gets a grin. "I will want you on the high ground later once the Humvees get here.

"Viv. You, Jackson and Burton will take the area south of the road. Chloe and I will take the high ground with air support. Everyone good?" At the nods and assent of all involved, we anchor the vehicle and move out.

To be honest, I'm glad it's just me and Beast on the high ground for now. I don't want to risk any more of our people, and this is what we're good at. Plus, air support is such luxury. We could really have used the crap out of air support back in Los Angeles.

All our people move out professionally and I feel a surge of pride. We have Waters in our ear as Nalwani keeps a lookout at the vehicle. We've put it on high ground and staked it in, so we feel comfortable leaving them there. Now to find the bad guys.

When I said our plan had worked better than we'd hoped, that really is an understatement. The flooding was just a wash of water until it got to Beaver Creek. From up here it's obvious that some of the road has washed away. But the valley walls this side of the road are all too easy to climb, so I know we'll be hunting raiders for some time.

I am most worried about Kane and his coterie of soldiers. They were taking up the rear, but my gut is telling me they're still alive, were able to see the flood coming and get away up a canyon. We will definitely

277

keep an eye open for them, though I don't expect to see them at all. I think they've faded into back country by now, either to escape and raise another army, or to try to sneak up on us.

All around us is mud and rubble and bodies. We turn to the daunting task and start moving upward, watching out for each other and moving in turns. Waters in our ear informs us there is a clump of bodies ahead. We sidle around a ridge and see a dozen or so bodies of mixed women and girls. Oh god, I hadn't realized the camp followers had been dragged along into this, too. I falter. Beast looks over at me, concern on his face. I brace myself and keep going.

It is well above the high water mark, it looks like, but these are all unmoving bodies and the stench of death is pervasive. I can't keep my eyes off the dreadful pile of bodies, and Beast knows what—no, *who*— I'm looking for. He stands guard while I approach the bodies. In my ear, Waters murmurs something, but I don't hear him. I'm looking for Liz, and all I hear is a roaring of water. I see a tousle of blonde hair and my heart sinks, but as I begin to approach, I am abruptly pulled back by Beast.

"Chloe, wake up!" I look up at him, and he is glaring at me. I shake off my dread to actually listen to him and Waters.

"Shit." I take a deep breath. "What is it?"

"I think it's a trap. I think they planted the bodies, they're... arranged." I look over, and, of course, he's right. I sigh and grit my teeth.

"Sorry." He's still got hold of my shoulders, and he's looking at me, focusing me. I look back at him steadily. "I'm okay. I'm here. Let's go."

My man gives me a nod, and we both turn around to inspect the bodies again from a safer distance. I take a look through my scope this time instead of getting closer.

We carefully examine each of them, and I realize these people aren't dead of drowning, but have been shot. Indignant fury begins to swell in my chest. Their own people? Must be, because ours were all evacuated. I don't see the familiar face I've been looking for. The blonde I saw before was much younger than Liz, so I put the scope down.

"How do you know it's a trap?"

"They were killed and placed here, above the high water line. They didn't die here, they were laid out here. Why would they do that when they needed to survive themselves?" He looks at me. I think.

"Revenge." I quickly look over at the pile of bodies. "Now what?"

"We set it off from a safe distance, if it makes enough noise we might catch someone coming back to see their handiwork."

"Use the trap as a trap for the trappers. I like it. Let's do this."

278

A few hours later the area is as clear as we can make it, and we're beginning to get an idea of just how large this problem is going to be. The area around the road is free of any lingering raiders, and the ones that escaped the flood have vamoosed.

Aerial tells us there is quite a large group trudging west and away from the valley, which is good news, but add the numbers of dead we've found—or facilitated—to the number of escapees, we're still missing quite a few. I fear they have headed toward the Enclave.

The Humvees arrived not long after we set off the booby trap left for us, though, unfortunately, we did not catch anyone coming back to see if they got us. Kane's men are well trained. They are also well-marked. Many of the fallen raiders bear the trademark "K" tattoo of Kane's gang. Once we started looking for it, we found it again and again. And the women? They've been branded with it. Sickening.

Now we are getting ready to head back to Gunnison for the night. The engineers have arrived to try and put the road back together, and I am surprised to see an asphalt paver among the vehicles. Beast tells me there was one in a maintenance yard past the hotels outside Crested Butte. They seem to have this well in hand.

I hold my man's hand and climb up into the Saucy Goose with the rest of the crew. We're exhausted and, I think, a bit disheartened. We are all worried for our families. When I gaze at my Beast, he senses my discomfort. Clearly, reading my mind, he speaks.

"We're not stopping at Gunnison; we're going to the Enclave. We need to build it up in preparation for whatever might be coming." There are sounds of relief all around.

"Roger that, boss," states Tess, and we hit the road, leaving the repair crew behind us. I hear her confirming with our UAV crew, asking them to see what they can find using night vision.

I squeeze my husband's hand hard and breathe deeply, relieved that we are on our way home. But I am also dreading what we think is coming. The raiders that kidnapped me knew very well exactly where to go. We have to assume they will be headed there again.

But, they are on foot and we're not. And, they don't know about our fallback point. So, we have that. Maybe we can stop them before they discover our home is no longer full of soft targets and hostages.

Chapter Twenty-Nine

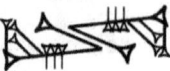

After the past week of tortuously slow-moving guerilla warfare, our trip back to the Enclave is short and all too easy. To me, it's another reminder of how vulnerable we are. I feel more awake and alert than ever, even with Chloe nestled close and comfortable under my arm.

The entire team is exhausted and weary to the bone from the week of effort, the night of running and the day of manual labor. Then, there is the soul-crunching loss of good friends. I watch them as we get closer to our gate. I want to let them rest, I really do, but this is not the time. And, letting them get too comfortable is a mistake, so I clear my throat and watch their tired eyes turn to me.

"I know you're all tired. This is not the time to relax. We need to be on our A game When we show up we have got to show the home guard that we are not relaxed and that we are ready, willing and able to kick some more bandit ass. You got me?"

Chloe is looking at me with a frown between her eyes. But she nods slowly, and the others mutter agreement. That is not good enough enthusiasm for me.

"What, have you all turned to candy-asses in the past hour? We just destroyed most of the raider army!" That gets a few more nods. "Who is it that took down ninety percent of those bastards?" I look around at their faces, their exhaustion fading as they punch each other on the arms and nod in agreement.

"And now, here we are returning to the presumed safety of the Enclave. I have to remind you, not a week ago a crack team of the Reverend's men were able to kidnap Chloe, and they knew exactly where to find her. They were able to slip in and out practically undetected. Kane is the one who sent them, so we have to assume he, too, knows everything about the area. We know Liz gave them intel, but it is old intel. They don't know half the stuff we've got going on these days. Do they?" There is a chorus of "no's," and Kawalski lets out a "hell-no!"

"Our people, though," I go on, "don't know what we know. They have got to be wondering what's been going on, hoping they don't have to fight but thinking the army is probably going to break through. We, my Reapers, are their heroes. We can't crawl home and curl up in our nice soft beds and pretend the most dangerous part of the army isn't most likely trying to sneak up on us at this very moment. We need to put the fear of Kane into their minds, and we need to put the Fifth Protocol into effect."

Chloe looks surprised. "They couldn't possibly be that close yet, could they?"

"That's just it, because what do we know? We know they sent groups out. We know there have been advance scouts and a few crack squads, one of them kidnapped you, my lady." I look back to the rest of the Reapers. "So, to be truthful, what we don't know is how many there are right now in the hills,"

There had been muttering and a few intakes of breath, exclamations. Now there is silence, but for the grumble of the engine and the wheels on the pavement.

"So, my buccos," he pauses and glances at Viv, "and buck...ettes," she nods acknowledgement with a grin, and I hear Nalwani laugh from the cab, "we are going to go back there like the big damn heroes we are, and we will not rest and fall into our soft beds. We will not accept the accolades of our people. We go back in full awareness that we are not safe yet. We will go back, ready to defend our homes and our people until we know for a fact that the last raider is dead by our hands, and then and only then, will we rest."

There is light applause that is interrupted by Nalwani. "Boss, we got some people in the road."

"What do you mean?"

"The road was clear, but a bunch of them jumped up from beside the road and now... well, look for yourself." Chloe and I peer from the back toward the small front window and see a few dozen people in the road ahead.

Ben Waters speaks up, "Yeah, the aerial folks are saying the same thing. Like, there were scattered people in the fields, but when our vehicle started up this stretch, they all kind of jumped out."

"What fresh hell..." I mutter as the vehicle slows. "What are you doing, Nalwani?" I snap, and her surprised face turns to me for a moment.

"Well, what do you want me to do, ram them? There are kids and stuff."

"Fuck! All right. Let's see what's going on."

The Stryker grinds to a halt about twenty feet in front of the roadblock of women and children. I look over at Chloe and see her searching faces. When her face goes pale with shock, I know she's found who she's looking for. Taking her hand, she squeezes mine hard, and then keeps holding on. She does not look tired now, just terrified.

"Come on." I say softly. "We're going to face her together."

Kawalski lets out a growl. "Is that Liz? How dare she show her stinkin' face here?!" He jumps to his feet and shoves past the others to open the back door.

"Jakob!" I use his first name on purpose. It gets his attention. He snaps his head around, eyes blazing.

"That fucking traitorous bitch…" he gathers himself though, closes his eyes for a moment.

"Kawalski, we're going to go talk to her. Chloe and I. You will not interfere. Just cover us. Got that?"

Kawalski doesn't like it, fists and jaws clenching in sync. Finally, he nods and opens the back hatch, bowing with a flourish to let us out. All the same, when my wife and I exit, he and Viv follow close behind. We've all got weapons ready, keeping watch for any kind of a trap.

The sudden and intense fury of the rest of the Reapers does not escape my notice. Before we walk toward the barricade of people, I stop in the doorway and look back at my team. I wait until they each meet my eyes and when they're all looking at me, I nod. Somehow, this defuses them a little. They know we will handle this.

My wife and I move around the vehicle. Everything is still except the sound of the cooling motor's ticks and sighs and the sounds of some of the few children in the crowd. At that moment, I sharply and intensely miss our daughter and Jimmy. It hits me out of nowhere. I don't like to think of myself as sentimental, but, at this moment, all I want is a normal day with them and nothing more.

Chloe's hand is tight in mine and, when I glance over, instead of the fear or pain I half expected to see on her face, I see anger, determination, strength. My Goddess, what a woman. I clasp her hand and squeeze it. She glances over and sees my utter adoration and gifts me with a little smile before hardening her face again and walking with me toward the crowd.

There is a ragged line of people who look frightened, but are bolstered by Liz, who is standing in front as if to guard them. She has her chin up, but I see utter fear in her face. She doesn't take her eyes off Chloe. As we near, I see longing, despair and desolation all make their way across her face. When we are within speaking distance, she clears her throat.

"I—" she begins, but Chloe cuts her off.

"I presume you are here to beg mercy for these innocents?" Chloe's voice is hard. Liz gulps, and then nods. "Granted."

Everyone looks surprised as the tension in the air dissipates. They become emotional: weeping, hugging each other and patting Liz, who stands there, still mute, and staring miserably at Chloe.

"You will be kept in a holding area for the duration of the war. We will interview each of you when we are good and ready. In the meantime, you will be fed and allowed facilities to clean yourselves and to rest. It will not be luxurious, but will suffice. You are not to leave the area. It will be guarded. Is this all understood?" There are sounds of assent and more tears and crying. Still, Liz stands, staring at Chloe, unmoving.

"However," my wife continues coldly, "this woman here is under arrest." She nods to Kawalski and Viv, who are all too happy to come and collect Liz.

As they pass me, Chloe mutters, "Gently."

They roll their eyes at each other, but use some forbearance when they gather up Liz and march her back to the vehicle. There are a few outraged cries from the gathered women, but not as many as Liz thought there might be, I think. She looks wounded as she glances back at her friends. They are all huddled together on the road.

I use my radio to have Nalwani summon forces from the Enclave, just a few miles away. We will wait here. I also tell everyone on their earpieces that they are not to say one word to Liz. If she tries to speak, they are to gag her. Chloe is impassively watching the group of women and children, but I see she is trembling. Wrapping my arm about her, I feel her relax slightly. She is very upset, but is hiding it well.

After what seems an eternity, but is only about twenty minutes, the trucks arrive. I am reminded of the Nazi cattle cars; but they are not going to their deaths, simply to a stock barn we have nearby. The livestock were all evacuated, the barn is clean and the stalls will be fine for camping, in the meantime. I am quite certain they have had rougher quarters with Kane's army. We get them settled and calmed, the guards are kind enough, but tough enough, that I don't worry about escapees.

The paddy wagon also arrives for Liz. She looks more hurt than ever as she is gagged and hauled away. I guess she tried to talk to the Reapers. Serves her right. Besides, she is not our concern at the moment. She will be kept safe, far from the Enclave and locked up. This is how we planned this particular contingency. Whatever kind of distraction Liz or Kane thought she and her friends might be, it's not going to go as they'd hoped. All such distractions are kept out of sight and out of mind. And, if it's not a planned distraction? Well, I don't care. She will be dealt with in good time.

By the time we finally get to the Enclave, it's after dark. Still, much as I dislike a fuss, we need to make an entrance. We know word has gotten out, because there is quite a crowd waiting for us when we finally arrive. Before we exit, though, I have one more instruction.

"We're not done yet. Don't forget. Don't let them forget. We need to remind them that the war is not over yet. Nobody is to be off their guard. Watch everyone's faces. If something seems off, it is. Trust your instincts. We are home, but it's not home until our families are safe. We all on the same page?"

"Yes, boss, we get it." It's Kawalski's dry voice. I nod solemnly at him.

"All right, let's go."

Chapter Thirty

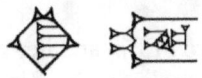

I admit it—I am still in shock and on auto-pilot. Somehow, I just knew Liz was going to show up again. I guess I still wasn't ready. And, talk about mixed feelings. One part of me was so glad to see she was still okay, another part of me was sorry for her and all those civilians. But the rest of me? Filled with white-hot rage that she presumed to bring people here after all she's done. How dare she endanger our people and bring the enemy to our doorstep? So, dealing with her and those others became quite easy. What was difficult was not opening up with my weapon despite my knowledge that they could be, for the most part, innocents.

I am very glad we had plans in place for this kind of situation. What could have been a clusterfuck is easy to deal with because this had been thought of and set up. How thankful I am for my husband who knew more than any of us what might transpire. Enemy combatants or their chattel show up? Secure prison camp or jail. This and many other contingencies have been planned and planned, so it's easy to go through the motions and just do what we know to do, and, then, I don't have to think about Liz back there with the Reapers. Liz—who I loved, though, I've never really admitted how much to myself.

Yes, I loved her, not the way she wanted me to, but it was real. I never wanted this to happen and never dreamed she would turn on us this way. But now, it's done. She's in our custody, and, when all this is over, we're going to have to execute her. Nobody has said this to me, exactly, but I know the way this works. Traitors don't get second chances.

By the time we get to the Enclave, I am beyond exhausted. But, the show must go on, they say. So, I put a smile on my face as we exit the Saucy Goose and keep my chin up during dinner with our reduced population at the mess hall, missing Jimmy and Leah intensely. Tess and Ben are still on duty watching the skies, and we put McIntyre and Louis on guard duty so more of the home guard can come to dinner.

My husband gets up in front of a whiteboard and explains all that's happened in the past week to the home guard. There are murmurs of awe, at times, and tears at our losses. Near the end, when he gets to the part about the flood, there are cheers. Beast quashes those quickly by reminding them that there are probably several large groups of raiders loose in the woods and hills north of the reservoir who are on their way here.

Then he gets to the capture of Liz and her group, and I hear mutters of rage. "She's in jail, no worries there," he states, "and the refugees are in the stock barn down the road, as we planned." At their further murmurings he adds, "We won't know until we interview them just how innocent they are. They are safely out of the action and are to remain so until this is all over." He glares at them all seriously and the mutters die away.

"In the meantime, we are to remain on guard. We have aerial superiority, but there is cover for our enemy. We are doubling the guards and have the hunting blinds ready for them. They will be much harder to spot and we will send an alert once the enemy is past our stations. Everyone is to remain in Condition Red until we know we have Kane. Once he's out of the picture, I get the feeling the rest of them will lose their eagerness."

My man takes a deep breath before continuing, "This is our home. I will be damned before I let anyone come and take what we've built here."

There is another cheer, and it does my heart good to see our peoples' enthusiasm. I am proud of my Beast. He is a good leader, a good man. More so for the fact that he doesn't seem to realize how good he is. He hates speaking in public, so when he sits down I squeeze his hand.

"I hate public speaking."

"I know. But you are good at it when you have to be." He shakes his head and calls Viv over.

"Get things rolling," he tells her. "We are done with the festivities. I don't want us off our guard a moment longer." She nods and goes to the microphone.

"Okay, playtime's over. Let's get to work. Those who are off duty for the moment, go to the secured bunkhouse, and get some rack time. Everyone else, to duty stations." There is a groan from many, but the party breaks up, and people move. Viv salutes us and several others do, as well.

"Now what?" I ask my husband. "We're supposed to be off duty now, but…"

"Yeah, I'm not up for that either. Let's do one of your walkabouts."

I smile. He knows the value of leaders being out and about among the people, though, I can rarely convince him to come along with me and the kids. Small talk is just not his thing. I take his hand and we stroll to the front gate first, talk to the guards on duty, then make our way around the rest of the Enclave. It is oddly quiet without the children and livestock, and, again, I miss Leah and Jimmy with a pang. I remind myself that is why they are safely far away from here.

One thing we haven't mentioned to the rest of the Enclave is that our radios are still live and will remain live until we know Kane and his buddies are dead. As we talk to the people we meet, we also hear the Reapers going about their activities. Most of us are getting ready to rest. Only Jackson and Burton are on duty, but will be replaced at midnight by Louis and McIntyre. The rest of us are back on at 5:00 a.m.

All of the Reapers will be sleeping in the bunker. The Reapers on duty are lurking in the houses next door to our cover house. We can only hope Kane and his team come and put their heads nicely in that noose. But, in the meantime, we do have people watching over us as we rest, which is probably the only way we *can* rest.

We're glad we're still out walking the crowd a half-hour later when we get a hit from the UAV pilots. We head over to the Stryker, which is parked in a storage area near the trading post. Waters is still at the monitor, and we look askance at him.

"What? I couldn't sleep. Who can sleep when bad guys are in the 'hood?" I shake my head at him. Beast is already up beside him and looking over his shoulder.

"What do you have?" The tone of his voice tells me how tense he's been about this. I shake my head again. Who *can* sleep when there are bad guys in the 'hood? Not my man. And, come to think of it, probably not me either.

"Movement. Not near here, which is news, because they know where we are, and they're not headed this way. We can't tell whether this is because they're stupid and lost, or because they have some other plan." Ben runs his hand through his cropped hair and looks worried, which is just how I feel.

At that moment a runner approaches us as we exit the vehicle. It's a youngster I recognize from our first days here, Kevin. He's only sixteen, but begged to be allowed to stay. He has no parents or other relations, and we decided he could stay if he followed instructions carefully and evacuated when he was told to. His bright eyes look worried. He hands me a slip of paper and moves from foot-to-foot as he waits for my reply.

Beast waits for me in that patient way he has, but grabs the slip before I drop it once I've read it. My heart is pounding, and, for a moment, I feel faint. I take a deep breath and nod at Kevin.

"We'll be right there."

Beast may seem impassive behind his mask, but I can see the glint of anger in his eyes. "You don't have to talk to her," he growls as we start toward the gate.

"I think she actually has something. I need to find out what it is."

287

Our ride to Gunnison is not long, but I ache for some rest, and the ride is over too soon. I feel like I've barely had a chance to close my eyes before we arrive at our destination—our makeshift jail.

The abandoned church is just the place. There are few windows, the walls are solid, and there are secured areas in the meeting rooms. We chose it because we figured this would be the last place the raiders would ever enter, making it perfect to contain anyone we captured. Lots of reinforced walls and small rooms with tiny windows made it perfect.

We approach the building and the guards are all over it. Once they see it's us, of course, we're allowed in. We commend them on their vigilance, and I don't hesitate as we approach Liz's cell.

There's a foam mattress on the floor, no sheets, but a warm blanket made of fragile foam that can't be used for self-harm. The guard on her door steps aside and we walk in. It's not uncomfortable or anything, we're not monsters.

When Liz lays eyes on me, hope blooms on her face for a moment, but when she sees my stony expression, it dies away. Tears stand in her eyes, and she dashes them away. Her voice is wooden when she speaks.

"Kane... he sent men to the Enclave last year, October or November. To infiltrate. They look weak, soft, but they were agents. Names were Gary and Bob."

Beast lets out a growl. He recognizes the names. "They wanted to be Reapers, but didn't have what it took," he mutters to me.

Liz sighs and continues, "So, what Kane knows, it isn't all my fault, Chloe. He found me in Kanab, Utah. I was going to... trying to go to the beach. I wanted to see the ocean again, but never made it out of Utah. Anyway, as soon as he saw me, it's like ... it's like he knew who I was. He even said I was an answered prayer, and I found out he didn't mean it in a nice way. Anyway, it felt good to be wanted. I dug it. I missed it. And when he asked where I'd been, I told him. I told him everything. I hadn't talked to anyone in a long time. That was when he sent out his men."

I nod at her, heart sinking. She really was only partly responsible for this mess. But Kane had purposefully been looking for her. That means the Goddess' opponent had been helping Kane like our patron deity had been helping us.

"Chloe, they know where your safe areas are. They know where the kids are." A look of fear flashes across her face. Even though she hates Beast, she has always adored his daughter.

"Leah." I whisper.

Liz nods, miserably. "For what it's worth, I'm sorry. I should have stayed and learned to get along without ... well, I should have stayed." Her head hangs down.

There's no time to answer. We're already on our way out. We need to get to the shelter. Now! Beast is already on his radio trying to reach whoever is online for the shelter near the mine. And, he's not able to reach anyone. Terror strikes me as we flee north toward Crested Butte.

Chapter Thirty-One

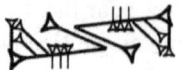

As soon as I hear Liz utter the words, *they know where the kids are,* I am ready to roar in fury. I want to break this woman and shatter her the way she has almost accomplished destroying the safety of this valley. But reason prevails, and Chloe and I leave in a flash, communicating with our seconds to get everyone's guard up.

I glare at the guard as we race past him, and I see his eyes widen with worry when he recognizes my rage. I nod toward the door, and he locks it and stands at guard once more. I am sure we will not lose our prisoner. She will pay, but Kane must pay first.

Now, I remember Nena's warning that we should flee home after the reservoir. All the way home. Not to the Enclave, in other words, but to our real home, to our family. I curse myself as a fool and we move.

The drive that seemed so swift on our way south to Gunnison has now become interminable. I am still unable to reach anyone at the evac site. But, now, we have everyone else up and on it. By the time we roll into the Enclave, the Stryker is ready to go again, and all of our Reapers are awake.

"Anyone have any news from any source about the evac site?" My lady is speaking succinctly, but there is fear in her voice, and I feel the same, even though I've been trained to push that aside. It is like a nightmare coming to life, again. I push through it and focus. We need to get there now. The best way is still the road, though, I would give much for a working Blackhawk.

Waters catches my eye, so I get over to him. "Boss, the UAVs report only unusual activity. So, either the comm is down or they've locked in."

The safe door of the inner cavern was a bitch to install, and we knew that if our people had to close it, we could be out of touch with them. We did wire the mountain, but if the cable has been pulled in—or out by other parties—we would be incommunicado. As we are.

Chloe and I look at each other. Have they locked themselves in? Or has Kane, assisted by Gary and Bob, taken them hostage? There is no movement, and if there was movement, we'd see it since we purposefully cleared the brush away from the outside of the evac site.

"Wait. Only *usual* movement? What does that mean?"

Waters first looks confused, and then gets back on line with the UAV folks. "They say... guard patrols continue making their routes, going in and coming out of the tunnel. But..." He looks troubled and looks up at us. "Then, why can't we reach them?"

"It's a signal," Chloe says firmly. "The guard patrols are almost certainly Kane's men, I'm sure of it. They could be bringing them in a few at a time under the guise of patrols doing sweeps."

I nod in agreement. "And, we can't reach them because our people had their lines cut so nobody would be alerted. Everyone just assumes the cable is down or something. When was the last contact with the evac site?"

Viv answers us from right behind Chloe. "Mayor says she spoke to her son yesterday morning."

"So, that means it's been out almost an entire day? How could we have missed this?!" Chloe is upset, and so am I, but there is nothing we can do about it now.

Viv speaks up again, "They sent Perry, the ambulance driver. He used to lay cable for one of the satellite dish companies, so he volunteered. But he didn't come back. Or at least, that's what Mayor Johnson said."

Fuck. Perry was the kid who drove the Humvee ambulance a lifetime ago before all this started last week, when Thomas got a blade in the foot. I'm already pissed we didn't see this coming, but if Kane or his men so much as touch a hair on his head... *Dammit!*

"We ready to move out?" I know my voice isn't more than a growl at this point, but everyone is ready and loaded. I nod to Nalwani, and she starts it up. This time, as we exit the Enclave, we are tailed by half of the rest of our forces. We aren't committing everyone because Kane likely has men ready to come in should we all run north toward the cavern.

We get to Crested Butte quickly, but not fast enough for my liking. Driving through the town, we pick up more trucks and a bus of fighting men and women to help us along the way. Still only half our forces from Crested Butte. Kane will not have enough men to take on all of our settlements, not if we keep them manned.

We drive north of town toward the cavern, and we're told the forces from Gunnison have caught up with the convoy. I have Waters try to hunt down Rawlins and Grant, assuming they're still at the hospital, but I'm wrong. They went out to the cavern the day they got back, thinking to reinforce what few fighting men had gone along with the families. They're idiots, but I bless them for their foresight. Now, I know I have two of my own in there... if they're still alive.

That gives me an idea, though. I get Kawalski to start trying to raise Grant and Rawlins on our secure channel, hoping they still have their radios; hoping that somehow we can get a signal. He starts working on it, but after a few minutes, he shakes his head. I tell him to keep on it, just in case our people inside find an antenna or something.

In the meantime, we've approached the outer limits of safety, at least according to the UAV pilots, who've suddenly got bodies in their sights. And, there are far more than we'd hoped, damn their black hearts to hell. At this point, we need some sort of strategy.

Once we've gathered about a few hundred of us, we stop, and I look around in the semi-dark at the faces of our defenders. I see our Reapers and the former soldiers, but some of them are just civilians that showed some promise in training. Some are old and bent, and some are kids. *Fuck me.* I can't lead them into death.

My qualms have given me pause, and I glance at my wife quickly before I freeze completely. Her eyes are shining, her smile confident, and it braces me. Taking a deep breath, I remember Leah and Jimmy, our daughter and son, locked behind a bank vault door with the raiders lined up to destroy her and the rest of the family we love. *Like hell.*

"My friends," It was already quiet, but now everyone is silent. "they still outnumber us." There are concerned looks, and I see fear, but continue. "But that doesn't matter. We live here. This is our home. They are trying to destroy our home and kill and enslave our families for personal gain. We, on the other hand, have something worth fighting for. We have each other and the peaceful home we've built. Our families, our friends, our valley. Our lives. This is worthwhile. This is worth keeping. By all that is holy, we are not going to allow them to destroy this, to destroy us."

Many nod grim-faced, but determined, as I continue. "Whatever it takes, today, we take our valley back. Today, we turn back the destroyers and reclaim our homes. We may not all survive, it's true, but I am willing to give my life for what I believe in."

"If you are not willing to do the same, there is no shame in returning now. The towns still need defenders, and I can't judge another's heart. But know now, I am going to go forward, and I will not stop until our enemy is vanquished. There will be no quarter given. Any who have come this far to despoil our homes must die. Are you with me?"

There are nods, and I see people getting ready to cheer, but I shake my head and put my finger to my lips. "Shhh. They'll never see us coming. And there is nothing like death from behind to mess up your day." I grin at them, and I see only fierce grins and fists pumping in return. They make me proud.

Ben Waters approaches and whispers something into my ear, eyes glittering with fierce joy at the information he has to share. I grin and clap him on the back, then turn back to my people.

I feel Chloe's hand squeeze mine, and I squeeze back. Her fierce eyes meet mine with a question. She wants to know my orders, so I give her, give them all, what they're waiting for.

"The UAV folks have got an added feature of the drones that are working. Spotters will assign targets for them via infrared lasers on our weapons. Those of you with goggles, put them on. You will target our heavy artillery. Ladies and gentlemen, this is called air-superiority, and it's a big deal."

I motion toward the trucks from the Enclave that have the remainder of the stuff we took from Las Vegas. No, we don't want to use it all today, but if we don't survive, there won't be a tomorrow.

"Make sure each team has at least one spotter with them. If we run out of mortars, we go with hand grenades. If we run out of hand grenades?" I bare my teeth in a vicious grin. "We use rocks."

My people are fierce, and I see nods and bared grins all around me. I dread the thought of losing, but my people have heart, and we have trained them as well as we could. It's time to get organized and get busy. I take my Reapers to the side and give them their orders.

"I am in the main force with Chloe. The other Reapers will be with our flanking forces. Kawalski, you take your Gunnison group now to get around the rear of the army. Nalwani, you go with him to communicate with Waters and the UAV forces.

"Vivyayna, McIntyre. You take the left flank. Louis, Jackson and Burton, you take the right flank. It is closer to the cavern, so I want your team more heavily loaded than the other two to break through their lines and protect the cavern.

"Everyone, get into your teams and move out in ten. Kawalski, you go now and make haste. Remember. We may be thinly spread, but we have surprise on our side. Move out."

Everyone is ready and organized, and, too soon, we are marching the last few miles toward the army. I quickly pray to the goddess of love and war to help us fight for our families and our home. And, in return, I feel a warm glow in the tattoo over my heart. Maybe I'll die today, but at least I know someone is watching over me.

Chapter Thirty-Two

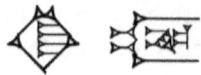

The trip north passed in a blur. Beast's speech was a brief high point, and, now, we are on to yet another battle. I find my fear for my children has numbed me, changed me, and I don't like the change. I need to find myself before we go into combat. So, for the first time, really, I pray to Beast's Goddess. Our Goddess, I know, but she was his first. I have faint memories of her claiming me, but those were dreams. Now, I need to find my center, and when I look there, I see her. So, I pray to Inanna.

I am incoherent at first, not sure what to say. So I feel. I feel the fear for my home and my family. I feel the dread of perhaps losing them. Somewhere inside me, I find a prayer.

Please help us. You stand for war and also love. We are fighting for those we love. Let us succeed, please?

Then, I feel a warm glow that becomes an intense burning on my chest on the left side. With a flash, I recall with deep clarity the dream I had of Inanna back when the Knick and Knack dreams were still tormenting me. I vividly remember how she marked me then, even though it didn't show when I woke. Now, the burning is intense, and I gasp.

Beast looks over at me with a frown. I take in our surroundings and see we are creeping through a field. Stopping for a moment, I crouch and open my tac vest and shirt. There, glowing for moment to highlight it, is the mark of the Goddess, a matching tattoo like my husband's. He sees it too, and beholds me with a brief, fierce look of love. He squeezes my hand.

"C'mon, my love," I whisper. "We have some war to make."

He grins at me, and we continue through the field. I have a calm surety inside me now. A sweet peace and certainty fills me, and that is all I needed. I am ready.

Of course, real war doesn't really allow for calm. It looks all careful and plotted on a table in a room when you're discussing strategy with your friends laughing around you, but, in reality, it's a messy clusterfuck! You only manage to stay alive by remembering your training, pushing your overriding emotions aside, and doing your best to kill the bad guys.

Our first encounter is with a mass of men gathered beyond a stream. We are lying low in the grass and muddy reeds, and there are too many to take on one-on-one. So, we wait. We have ordered everyone to stop once we encounter the enemy, and then only to go when everyone is in position.

The exception is Kawalski's team. They are to guard the rear so nobody gets away, and only to attack when ordered or when they see something. We trust his judgment, and he knows it. But they aren't in position yet, so we wait.

We get to know all the small life that fills the muddy field—small rodents and insects. A line of ants begins making its way across my arm, and I gently shake them off. They re-route. Finally, we get word that Kawalski's in place. Everyone's in place. We get to start, and when the others hear our shot, they go too. All is ready.

I have the night vision goggles. Beast is softly on the line to our M224 mortar crew, whose names have slipped my mind. I sight him in on the group of enemy whose warm bodies glow ahead of me and to the right.

Kane's men are huddled together, talking quietly, though we can't hear what they're saying until they all burst into a whoop with only one word audible. *Ka-ane! Ka-ane! Ka-ane!* Son of a bitch. I wonder briefly if this is the group he's with, but brush it aside. It is go time.

"You got your target?" I mutter to my husband.

He nods and orders into the radio. "Target sighted and… go, go, go."

The mortar is way behind us, but well within range of the enemy. Their placement ensures that they can't easily be counter attacked. We watch as the shell lands right where it's supposed to. I throw myself face down, close my eyes to the extreme bloom of heat and block my ears with my hands. The shockwave is in the air as the round goes off. It moves through the ground and my body.

The explosion deafens us momentarily, but not so much that we don't get ready to attack. I look at our team, my Beast our two team members. Paul and Jeff, I suddenly remember, grateful I don't have to go into battle without knowing their names. A different laser is in another area altogether, farther away to the left, and I see a follow-up flash and hear a boom a few seconds later. I don't think that was a mortar.

"Remind me to give those UAV guys a raise," my husband mutters as we sight in on our target and call it in to the mortar crew.

Soon, I throw myself down again, brace for it, and we fire again. Now, we get word the remaining troops are retreating toward a center that is not far from the cavern. It's near the end of the rail line we had been using to transport our people.

After that, everything is chaos. I hand my goggles to the woman, Angie, I suddenly remember. Her partner is Ben. We get one more person who takes the radio, and then Beast and I lead the charge.

The remainder of the army is fleeing, but a few of them peel off every so often to guard the rear. They're our bread and butter.

Beast and I are in our element. At first, we lay into those fleeing with our rifles. When the mag runs dry, we keep fighting with gun in one hand, sword in the other. We plow through the flood of soldiers like so many dominoes.

We try not to get too far ahead of our troops, but things happen when a person is in the heat of the moment. We find ourselves alone in the woods, stalking a group of three raiders.

I motion to Beast that I will be the bait. He nods and melts back into the brush. I walk forward a few steps and look around for something to help with the situation. I spy a nest of twigs a few steps to the left. I step over and stomp on them. The large crack reverberates through the clearing, and I look up to see the three raiders heading in my direction.

"Oh no!" I cry, "They see me!"

I let out a girlish squeal and hide behind a tree, but not before I see the lust darkening their features. I wait with my pistol ready and look over to see Beast hiding nearby.

I smell the men before I hear them. Haven't they ever heard of bathing? I mean, they followed a river upstream, oh my Goddess.

By the time the first one rounds the tree, I'm more than ready to put them out of their misery. About this time, I note more of our troops have caught up to our position. Beast has kept them from walking into the situation, and we let it unfold.

The first volunteer reaches around the tree to grab me, but I pin his hand to the tree with my knife. His screams alert his friends, but it's too late for them when Beast shoots them in the head. I shoot my raider, too, and retrieve my knife before we move on.

This is when I hear on the radio that our pilots can't target any more bad guys because our troops have infiltrated too closely. They wish us luck and tell us they'll keep us updated on movements. The one good thing for us is that our radios light up on their monitors. We hear Kane and his army are loosely encircled by our troops. This is just what we wanted. With a flare of hope, we continue forward.

Of course, when they find out they're cornered, it's not going to be pretty.

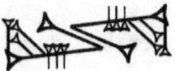

Now that we have the enemy surrounded, one might think they would grow some brains and surrender. But this is Kane's army now, his core group that he probably went back to Phoenix to find. Yeah, he got the band back together.

Every man we've killed on our way toward this final confrontation has had a prominent "K" tattoo somewhere visible on his person—on hands, arms, even on necks and faces. I don't know if Chloe has noticed, but I wouldn't put it past her. My lady is sharp.

Now, we've surrounded them, and we slowly tighten the noose, watching them mill around a flat place near the end of the rail line. We've taken the higher ground along ridges and in the trees, and any who dare to escape are shot. There is a circle of dead around the perimeter that is slowly closing.

That's when things start to change. They all straighten up, appearing more disciplined. I can hear someone talking, and I think I know who it is. *Oh, hell no.*

I quickly call into my radio. "Anyone have any mortar rounds left?"

Getting two affirmatives, I tell everyone to retreat back behind the ridge, and I ask for two rounds in the middle of that group of men. Before they can, the men in the clearing turn. Performing an about-face, and, like the army for the British in the Revolutionary War, the first row kneels and the second row stands and they aim all their weapons out toward us.

"GET DOWN," I bellow as Kane's guns roar almost simultaneously.

The only thing that saved most of us was the command to retreat behind the ridge given only a few moments before. We do suffer some injuries and losses, but not as many as we might have.

Not a minute later, the first mortar hits that packed-in mass of bodies. I'd like to say it's a beautiful sight, and it might be true, but it's also carnage like most of my people have never seen before. The second mortar hits before anyone has recovered from the first.

We wait a few minutes longer, and I send my voice down into the clearing. "We can do this all day, Kane. Time to give up and throw down your weapons."

Kane's voice comes back over the groans and coughs of the dying, "Go fuck yourself."

"You think because you came back once, you can come back again? That it? Because I can guarantee that if you get up again, we're going to put you back down. Again and again, and as many times as it takes. You got that?"

"Blah, blah, blah. Words. You want to do this right? Let's fight, you and me. Right now, one-on-one, and to the victor go the spoils."

So far, I haven't seen him. So, to draw him out, I yell, "Show yourself."

"You first."

Chloe's face is alarmed as I consider this. Her face relaxes as my laugh falls down among the dying army. This idiot really thinks he's got some kind of advantage?

"You don't hold any cards, Kane. You've lost already. You're just too stupid to know it."

I motion toward my cohorts to laugh, and a wave of amusement rolls over the hill and down toward the clearing. This is the ploy that finally works.

Enraged, Kane pushes his way through the men surrounding him. He's surprisingly fit, for a dead man. Not that I really have anything to say in my own defense.

"You don't get to win," he shouts. "You don't get to ..."

A shot rings out barely missing his foot, and I look over to see Viv, rifle smoking, getting ready to shoot again. She grins at me and takes aim, but she holds off.

"Too late, Kane. It's over."

I am about to motion our people forward to accept the army's orderly surrender when all hell breaks loose. I hear a bugle's tinny wail from the valley below, and all of Kane's surviving people, who we thought we'd trapped so neatly, charge forward in every direction.

They don't run in straight lines, but dash all over the place like so many quarterbacks lining up a toss. My people want to charge, and I'm glad for the drilled-in discipline. A few start forward. They're grabbed by their compatriots and are held back, and a good thing, too.

At a loud signal from the middle of the valley, all the fighters drop to the ground in a duck-and-cover type position. I begin shouting for my people to get back, get over the ridge, but it's too late for some of them.

In the center of the clearing, where it had been hidden from sight by the press of bodies, is something I did not expect: a fucking PK machine-gun.

Where the hell did they get one of those?

The question is moot as we scramble backward and behind the ridge. The ordinance roars over the heads of the crouching army below us, and too many of our people aren't fast enough to get out of the line of fire. I note a few of their own weren't fast enough either, and have to be satisfied with that.

Chloe is breathing hard beside me, tears streaking her face. I am concerned, but she shakes her head to say she isn't hurt and points down the hill. I realize the sky has lightened, because I don't have to strain to see what, or rather, who, she's pointing at.

Searching to see what's happened, it doesn't take me long to see Mike Wayne, prone and with blood covering his face. Dear Goddess, he couldn't have survived that.

Suddenly, there's a shriek from the left flank, and shots ring out. It's Viv, and she is in a fury. Opening fire, she amazingly takes out the machine-gunner. She doesn't stop there and begins mowing down as many of the rest of the army as she can.

This is our moment. I get on the radio and tell our mortar gunner to fire the last round and to take out the machine gun nest before someone else mans it. I hear the thump at almost the same time I get the affirmative. Then the shell hits, sending assholes flying.

I stand and yell, "CHARGE!"

Our people enthusiastically run screaming down the hill at our enemy, who are still mostly prone. They are still struggling to get to their feet when we pour over them, fighting with all the weapons at our disposal: hand-to-hand, small arms, anything and everything. Thanks to the Collapse, an abundance of ammunition and magazines are rather lacking. It doesn't take long before the shooting dies out, and it devolves into a bloody melee.

I catch one of the farmers I sent to the Enclave from Green River attacking, to great effect, with a hand scythe. An airman from Nellis has a Colt Python in one hand and a machete in the other, screaming as he fights, not apparently realizing that blood is streaming from his semi-detached ear. A young woman from Gunnison—dear Goddess, is it one of Kawalski's daughters?— she's kneeling in a pool of blood sawing someone's head off.

Chloe and I run toward Mike's body and find Viv has draped herself over him, sobbing. We exchange a glance as we work our way forward. Neither of us had any idea she felt this way about him. I don't think Mike knew either. *Shit.*

Unfortunately, we don't have time to sort it out. Our end goal is Kane. He cannot be allowed to survive this day. Our people know where we're going, and they have to get us there. Too many have fallen to do it, but we can't think about that, we just have to do our job.

We continue to do what we do best, and the blood flows. Don't ask me to explain, war is an adrenaline-filled, blurry nightmare of killing. The enemy cannot touch us, though, for my lady and I are a perfectly matched team.

When we finally reach the center, the raider army is on its last legs. Kane is at the center, fighting with a cold efficiency, but he looks as tired as I feel.

Chloe gasps for breath beside me, her face spattered with blood. For an instant, I recall the time at the university when I painted her to appear like an Angel of Death. Her heart and bravery make me proud.

As we get ready to charge, the half-dozen men that are left rush in. They yell, they bellow, hell, I think one even gibbers like he's on some kind of drug. All in an effort to scare us, which doesn't work.

While we lay into them with more skill than they have, the push separates us. I have to maneuver to put my back against the hillside as they push her in the opposite direction. I've got to pay attention to the assholes in front of me, so I have no time to look for her or Kane.

I'm breathing hard, my arm beginning to feel like rubber as I parry axes or machetes. One man has already fallen to my sword; another is wounded, but too crazed to stop fighting. Not being at my lady's side brings the animal out of me.

With a hiss I barely recognize, I find renewed strength. Parrying the incoming machete, I quickly sidestep an axe blow. Bringing my sword down, I nearly chop off the arm holding the axe. The man screams and falls back, clutching a dangling arm that's spurting blood.

That distraction allows the man with the machete to get under my guard. The blade hits my shoulder. Thanks to my reflexes, it's not as bad as it could have been. Still hurts, and that makes me roar at the man with anger.

My attacker is startled, his brown eyes going wide as he involuntarily steps back. I'm in too feral a mood to give any quarter. Launching my attack, all he can do is fall back as I level a flurry of blows at him. Batting his weapon away, the tip of my blade finds his throat, and he goes down gurgling.

As I spin, looking for Chloe or an opponent, a bullet hits my side followed quickly by the roar of a gunshot. The impact sends me flying. Well, not really, but it feels like it as I fall backwards. Hitting the ground, I raise my eyes to see Kane approaching, smoking gun in hand.

"I told you," he yells maniacally. "You don't get to win!"

Clutching my bleeding side, I push myself back against the hillside. With nowhere to go, I watch as he closes in and starts to aim. All I can do is pray that Chloe and our little corner of civilization make it through this as I wait for the flash.

Chapter Thirty-Four

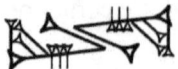

There's a joke that caliber size doubles when pointed at you. Well I'm staring down the barrel of a .45, held by a resurrected mad man. I've already been sliced and shot, I'm tired and bleeding with my back against a hillside, waiting as my soon to be murderer pulls the trigger. It's clear he wants to gloat though, all while the sounds of combat continue around us.

"This time I'm going to kill you, and you're going to stay dead. Then, I'm going to take your woman."

I can't help but laugh. "Clearly, you don't know Chloe. She'll fucking kill you. Again."

"Not once I get that door open and have her daughter," he retorts. "If she doesn't do exactly what I..."

Kane never gets to finish his sentence. A short sword juts through his neck and he briefly looks down at the blade, blood dripping copiously off the tip. The pistol falls from his hand as he reaches up to the wound. His eyes roll up into the back of his head, and he collapses to the ground, revealing my angel of death.

"I think you're right," she grins grimly. "This is becoming a common theme for us."

An exhale of relief escapes me, and I rest my head against the hillside. I'm wounded and tired. Add the emotional rollercoaster on top of that, and you could say I'm utterly exhausted.

My lady is at my side in an instant. "Baby, are you okay?"

"Woman," I grumble. "Is there any way to get you to shut up?"

Fire flashes in her eyes as she gives me something between a frown and a grin. Grabbing my tactical vest in both hands, she pulls me up to within perhaps an inch of her face.

"Yeah, there is."

Our lips clash so hard it hurts. I wrap my good arm around her as we embrace in a moment of passion. The sounds of fighting have died out dramatically, but I still keep my ears open as we kiss for what seems like an eternity. When we finally come up for air, we are both laughing.

"I love you," she whispers.

I rub my nose against hers. "I love you more."

Before she can respond, we hear Viv shriek, "Medic!"

"Shit," I groan. "Get me to my feet, my lady."

"Are you sure?"

I give her a nod. "Yeah. People need help."

"So do you."

The glare I get makes me sigh. I'm a corpsman, and my duty is saving lives. Many before me gained the Medal of Honor posthumously by putting the needs of their patients' wounds before their own. Of course, none of them had their wife with them on the battlefield.

"Then, you need to bandage me while I take care of them."

Fortunately, she chooses not to argue. Giving me a nod, she helps me to my feet. Quickly, we find Viv and she's still kneeling over Mike. Frantically, she waves us over.

He's alive? I check his pulse and sure enough, he is. I quickly clean the blood from his forehead. I'm both relieved and terrified to see that a bullet simply creased his forehead. I pray that he survives the concussion as I get the bleeding under control.

As I treat Mike, others are being brought to us. Chloe is also bandaging me as I work. She does an admirable job of working around me, barely slowing me down as I treat wound after wound. You can't even imagine how much blood there is in a battlefield environment. In a situation like this, you just can't think about it. There are lives to save, and that requires strict focus and attention.

Then, there's the triage portion of field medicine. It's the least fun of the process. Identifying what the wound is, if it can be treated… the unenviable decision-making process of deciding who lives and who dies. It breaks my heart that there are a few that fall into the latter category.

The medical teams show up with the ambulance as I'm issuing orders to make the dying as comfortable as possible. More importantly, making sure they don't die alone. At that, Chloe insists that I sit my ass down before she puts me on the ground.

I can't argue. I'm totally drained. Once the team finally gets to me, I've had enough of a break that I have something of a second wind, especially after resting in my angel's arms. Besides, we've still got to check on our kids, and I'm not going out on a stretcher until we've made sure they are all right.

There were moments over the past few days when I believed we were all going to die, and Kane and his army would win. But now, Kane is dead, and what's left of his army is being hunted down and slaughtered to the last man. The ones that surrender? Great. We'll take it. But we're going to kill them later. Call it execution. Whatever. They've done too much to us to let a single one of them escape with their lives to potentially have them come back later for revenge.

As we arrive at the vault door, we realize that we didn't think to arrange a signal, or at least not that I know of. Mike might know, but he was shot. Unfortunately, he's out cold thanks to the large caliber bullet that bounced off his hard noggin at just the right angle, lucky son of bitch. What surprises me is that Viv hasn't left his side. That still doesn't solve our problem as I gaze at my worried wife.

Chapter Thirty-Five

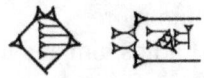

Captain Hayes is on her way. She has reported to us over the radio that she doesn't know of a special signal. Beast and I are standing in front of the vault door. I have hammered on it to no effect. Beast even tried pounding on it, but nobody's answered yet. They must assume the army is still out here trying to get in. *Fuck.*

No one is answering by radio, but then between the mountain and the door, maybe the signal isn't getting through. At least that's my hope, because, right now, all manner of nightmares are dancing in my head.

Ben Waters was also wounded, but he's still on top of the mountain above the cavern. The objective is to try and get a wire through so we can communicate. Beast is on the radio with him, trying to see how it's going, when the door unlatches. Just like that. I dive for the opening, but my husband holds me back.

"Angel, we don't know who's in there."

"Our children are in there!"

"I know. Just wait a second, okay."

It's killing me, but I do as he says, quivering a little. A multitude of guns are pointed at the entrance. Eventually, an eternity later, the door swings open further. Nena's sweet face peers around the corner.

"Mama! Mama!"

I hear my daughter's screams, and nobody can hold me back at this point. Swiftly, yet gently, I gather my little girl up into my arms and bawl my silly head off while holding her. Jimmy is right behind Nena and Leah, and he looks worried.

Beast carefully scoops up. "What's wrong, little man?"

Jimmy's face is serious, and he's staring at Beast's face. "Are you bleeding? Did you get hurt?"

"Nothing serious. We're just fine."

Beast and I shoot a quick glance at each other, and I realize we are more than just a little blood-spattered. *Damn it.* Not really the best state for our children to see us in.

"I thought that's why mama was crying, and I was worried." His face scrunches up and he sobs into Beast's shoulder, getting some of the gore on himself, which frightens him more.

With a pained grunt, Beast holds him and takes me by the arm to get me out of the doorway so more of our people can escape the vault. Then, he embraces Leah, Nena and myself. We all hug together in the brilliant morning light.

Later, we have a chance to find out what happened in the cavern. I thank the Goddess that Seth Rawlins and Mace Grant were there. Yes, they were wounded. But, they saw immediately that Bob and Gary were up to something.

They were separated, tied up and questioned privately. Then, Seth and Mace locked everyone inside. If they hadn't done that, who knows what could have happened—my worst nightmare, probably.

Of course, now that everyone is safe and the raiders are dead or soon to be executed, we can start cleaning up this hell of a mess they've left us with. My husband has recommended using a water truck from a construction yard. Fill it up, and slowly drive over the battlefield, helping to break up the blood and waste. Fortunately, the site isn't near a major river, so we don't have to worry about any contamination.

The crews in Gunnison are mostly going to work on the reservoir and make sure there are no surviving bandits in the area. Once things are back to normal in Crested Butte and at The Enclave, we'll send additional teams to help.

We have a lot of wounded and a lot of dead. It breaks my heart to see families that had either survived or come together after the Collapse, suffering once more at the hands of bad people. Still, we saved more than we lost. One of those lost is Barry Corrigan, one of the brothers who run the trading post. Barry's wife, Melody, will take over where Barry left off. Walt was wounded, but will survive.

Mike is still unconscious at the hospital in Crested Butte. Viv has not left his side, and if you try asking her to, she damn near gets feral. He is going to wake up one surprised man, I imagine. We have the promises of the nurses to get a play-by-play when that finally happens.

I haven't mentioned her, but Liz still has to be dealt with. The raiders were easy. We know they came here to destroy us and take what we have. Liz is the one who led them here. Much as it hurts me to do it, we will have to execute her. Beast insists that it has to be me. At first, I disagreed.

306

"Why do I have to do it?"

I'm practically yelling at Beast as tears stream down my face. He pulls me to him and holds me tightly. I know he doesn't want to cause me any pain, but fuck this hurts.

"If you don't, one of the Reapers will. And chances are they won't show Liz any mercy, where you would."

All I can do is cry in response as he holds me tightly, trying to soothe my grief.

"Besides, if she's to have any real forgiveness, it needs to be done by someone who has it in their heart to forgive her. You are the only one with that capacity. When the rest of us look at her, all we see is the people who died because of her actions."

I know he's right, but that doesn't make it any easier. In my heart, I'm dreading the next few days.

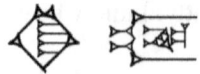
It's a week later, and it's the day I've been dreading ever since I saw Liz's face in that UAV image—the day of her execution. Although, at first, I worried it wouldn't happen. While Beast didn't like it, he acquiesced to requests for a trial. Mayor Johnson was quite insistent that an execution not happen without proper due process of the law.

In all honesty, I didn't much care for it, either. Everyone knew she was guilty. Liz didn't even try to fight it. She looked like a broken woman, sitting on the stand and confessing to her crimes. As hard as I tried, I couldn't sit through her entire testimony.

While we have no true judge, Betsy had a law degree and has been acting as such. When she handed down the verdict, there were no surprises in it. Beast didn't allow the court to go any further, though.

Oh, there were arguments, but my husband made sure it was understood that Liz was once Enclave. Since she betrayed us, she was our responsibility. I had to step in to calm everyone down, for fear they would come to blows. Fortunately, I was able to get Betsy to agree that we gave her the trial. It was time for her to understand that this is not the old world. We don't have the resources for life imprisonment these days, there is only death. We are too close to the edge to have to feed and house people who add nothing to what we are building here. Maybe someday we will be allowed to have that luxury again, but now is not that time. Finally, she agreed, and Liz was taken away by the waiting Reapers.

Beast and I wake at 4:00 a.m. and silently get dressed. We slip out of the bunker, as Nena sleeps in one of the spare beds in our section. She'll take care of our precious children until we get back.

After collecting part of our team and Liz, we take the ski-lift to the top of Crested Butte Mountain. There are a few buildings left behind up here since the Collapse. Most people had survival on their minds more than skiing. According to the locals, the tourists and much of the hotel staff fled, trying to get back to homes and families, no time spared for looting.

The Lodge was sturdily built, and the ski-lift survived. A small ranger station collapsed last year after a particularly harsh winter, but we were able to pull out anything salvageable. The ski lodge itself sits at the peak of Mt. Crested Butte and has a panoramic view of the surrounding area. These days, it's staffed by a dozen people, two of whom are Reapers. They pull a week-long rotation before coming back down to the town.

It's still dark as the procession makes its way to the peak, flashlights lighting the way, though, I see a glimmer of light in the east. Sunrise is an appropriate time for an execution.

Beast is right beside me, and Liz marches solemnly ahead of us. Around her are our four comrades: Mike, who is recovering nicely from his concussion, Vivyayna, who is sticking close to him, Kawalski and Rawlins. They all look at Liz like she's the devil herself. Their expressions make me realize that Beast is right. They all blame Liz, and not unfairly, for the losses we had to go through. Had she not thrown in with Kane and told him about our defenses, we could have avoided at least some of what happened. Maybe Shawn and Kim would still be alive.

That realization does not assuage the feeling of dread that's rising in my chest. My sweaty palms require me to grip the pistol tightly. Yes, Liz betrayed us—me. But, that doesn't change the fact that she had been there for me during a very bad time in my life. She helped me get through my daughter's birth. All that is not exactly something I can forget. Shawn's brutal execution, and Kim dying in my arms, her blood everywhere… these thoughts help to shore up my waning confidence. So, too, does my husband's presence. We reach the top of the peak, and I take a deep breath. Mike pushes Liz roughly to her knees, and she collapses with a cry.

"That's enough," Beast growls.

Liz slowly looks up at me with tear-stained cheeks, and I feel my heart break a little more. I have to steel myself. Goddess, I wish I didn't have to do this. How I wish things could have been different, that Liz hadn't betrayed us. So much death is on her hands, though. So much pain.

Without a word, she slowly turns around to watch the glow of the sunrise, her last. I see the moment she realizes this, and she drops back to her knees. I do my best to hold myself steady, force the tears back.

I make sure the pistol, just a .22, is loaded, and I ready myself. We all watch as the sun crests the horizon and a sweet rosy glow begins to suffuse the world, golden rays heralding the start of a new day. The air is still cold as a slight breeze rustles the branches of the surrounding trees.

Taking aim, I hear Liz crying and my tears spill down my own cheeks. "I forgive you, Liz."

Gritting my teeth, I pull the trigger. The pistol's report is slight, yet I still jump. There is no spray of blood, no horrific damage caused by the bullet. Liz's last breath escapes her, and she pitches forward, her body now limp and lifeless.

I can't help myself. I break down and cry. Beast wraps me up in his embrace, helping to soothe my pain. The Reapers simply nod their satisfaction with grim smiles.

"It's over," Beast states in a solemn tone while holding me tightly. "Liz has paid for her betrayal with her life. With her death, she has lost everything she had and everything she could have had. Yet with her death, she has earned forgiveness. She will be given a proper funeral, and that will be the end of it. I will hear nothing more said of her, especially in the negative. Is that understood?"

All the Reapers become serious, even a little shocked. "Yes Sir."

"Good. Go ahead back to town without us and made sure everyone else knows. Chloe and I will take care of the funeral pyre. Dismissed."

Most of them salute and start back down the path, as Beast continues to hold me comfortingly. Turning in his arms, I sob into his chest. It's hard to say for sure how long it takes, but the sun is well above the horizon when I am finally cried out.

"Hey, my angel," Beast murmurs softly. "Better now?"

I smile weakly. "A little."

"Let's get Liz taken care of, shall we?"

With a nod, I help carry her to the clearing where a number of logs have already been set up. I am grateful to my husband, who treats her body with respect as we lay her out on the pyre. Then, he takes up a torch and lights it before handing to me. With a heavy sigh, I take it and gaze at her body one last time.

Liz lies peacefully on the woodpile. She looks younger, more at peace than I have ever seen her, even in sleep. Has the woman known a moment's peace in her life? I sigh and shake my head, dropping the torch into the pile. Once more, I am reduced to tears. I sob and fall back into Beast's embrace.

The fire takes, and we step back, sun rising at our backs while the pyre slowly burns into a pile of ashes. All the while, my man simply holds me, keeping the demons at bay and soothing my pain.

Chapter Thirty-Seven

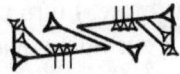

It's been two weeks since Liz's execution. Chloe and I have gathered the surviving Reapers in the bunker's kitchen. The death of Liz is behind us, and a party like this is sorely needed. Not only because we've lost good friends, but my lady needs some serious cheering up. This issue has been an emotional rollercoaster ride, and she needs smiling faces, laughter and good company to take her mind off it.

Normally, this is something I would have planned within a few days of the loss of a comrade. Unfortunately, this isn't the military. Everyone has to pull their weight, and it's unfair to change watch schedules at the last minute just for a get together. I've given Viv special permission to come down off the mountain to be here. Tomorrow, she goes back to finish out her punishment.

A party is exactly what I've provided, though. Everyone is at the table as we enjoy a little of the best of what we have available. There's a spread laden with various fruits and vegetables. We have a roast of pig as well as some chicken. Thanks to proper engineering, there is even decent beer and wine to drink.

My lady shares stories about Kim with Viv, who is seated next to Mike. He's looking better, and, I think, out of the woods as far as a concussion goes. While he joins in conversations, he's also helping Viv juggle kittens.

The other conversation of interest is at the other end of the table. Rawlins and Grant are retelling their heroic story of how they ferreted out the plants and captured them. The rest listen on, often while rolling their eyes as each man tells the story slightly differently, with one being the hero while the other was quaking with fear. We all know they both pulled their weight, but it makes for great humor nonetheless.

As everyone continues their conversations, I start placing a shot glass in front of each person. Into the glass, I pour a shot of my best vodka, Chopin. Once I'm done, I'm back at the head of the table and stand behind my lady.

"Oy," I yell in my best drill instructor voice. "Listen up!"

The talking stops and all eyes are on me. Taking a moment, I savor the silence as I set down the bottle and pick up my own glass. Gazing at the clear liquid for a few moments more, I turn my attention to the team.

"We are here today to honor our fallen dead. Their deaths have been avenged. Our sworn duty to protect our people is completed. So, we hope they rest easy."

I have to take a deep breath and reign in my emotions. Losing a comrade, a brother or sister in arms, is never an easy thing. People you've fought with, shed blood and tears with, become like family. Just like family, losing them is a highly emotional event.

"They say that no one comes home from war. There are wounds that never heal. Ghosts and demons that always plague us. But, it is up to us to try, because we owe it to our friends to do so. They lost everything, sacrificing their lives to protect this home. Our home. We have to live for them so as to remember them."

I raise my glass. "Here's to two of the finest soldiers I ever had the honor of working with. And, that's saying something coming from a former Navy SEAL. To Shawn and Kim."

"To Shawn and Kim," everyone barks back clearly, more than one set of eyes full of tears.

We all down our shot and a reverent silence settles over the room. When I sit back down next to my lady, I pull her close. With a painful sigh, she snuggles into my embrace.

The party continues into the wee hours of the morning, and, eventually, all of our family has either disbursed to their homes or are sleeping it off in the forward sections of the bunker.

My lady and I settle into our quarters after checking with Nena, who is watching the children tonight. We lock up and are in each other's arms, just the way we want to be. With all that's happened, we haven't had any alone time in quite a while. Which is why Nena volunteered to take the kids, and I insisted that we accept.

We both had a little to drink, but not enough to slow us down, now that we are alone. I'm well on the road to recovery, and my lady's bruises and hurts are healed. She is more beautiful to me at this moment than she has ever been. Yes, I am eager, but I really want her to sing for me.

Laying her down on our bed, I worship her with my mind, my body, my soul. When she is at a fever pitch, I take her carefully into ecstasy. Goddess, how I love her.

Her back arches, and I pull her to me, growling into her neck, which always seems to drive her wild. I can only imagine, because she knows that with that sound, her immense pleasure is soon the follow.

"Love me, my Beast!" she cries, wrapping her legs around me and urging me closer.

I am happy to comply, being crazy for her, and bury myself in her to our mutual delight. With no children in the next room, my lady sings sweetly for me, just as I had hoped she would.

Chapter Thirty-Eight

My mind swims in a fog between the black void of sleep and the world of dreams. Slowly, a vision coalesces and I find myself back on the battlefield, fighting the last of Kane's men.

The ground is soaked with blood, turning the earthen brown color far darker. Green grass is now a dark red, looking diseased and unhealthy. Then, there's the stench of the dead, which is pervasive and inescapable.

I gag, fighting back the body's natural reaction to vomit as my heart races. Looking around, I can see nothing but the bodies of dead raiders. No one else is there, not even Chloe. The fact that she isn't at my side evokes a deep sense of loneliness that I can't completely push away.

Nature doesn't seem to care about the dead and stench. Birds sing sweetly and I can even hear the song of crickets, as well. Looking up, the blue sky is lightly dotted with sparse, white clouds.

When the birds and insects quit their songs, the hairs on the back of my neck stand up. Ducking behind a brush, it's not long before I spy a woman walk towards the battlefield from the far side of the nearest hill. Woman may be a strong word.

Black hair frames the face of a crone, features etched in anger. Wings are tucked in behind her back, with black feathers like you'd expect of a crow. Instead of human feet, they are not unlike a bird's, with sharp talons. Dressed in a toga of fine black cloth, a gold belt clasps at her waist. A gnarled wood staff is in hand, with numerous gold charms hanging from it. Some even jingle softly as she walks.

Just seeing this woman puts a fear into me the likes of which I've never felt. All I can do is kneel there, knees quaking as she strides towards the beheaded body of Kane.

Stopping at his corpse, she shakes her head and sighs, still scowling. Raising a withered hand that sports claws instead of nails, she intones something in Sumerian, though I can't make all of it out.

At her words, Kane rises out of his body, his spirit red in color and holding his head with his hands, as if he is in pain. It's easy to tell that he's confused, yet when he lays eyes on the woman, he cowers fearfully.

"It wasn't my fault," he complains bitterly. "I swear. It was that bitch. I almost had him!"

To say that she doesn't believe him is an understatement. She is completely unimpressed by his excuses. In fact, she even rolls her eyes before responding.

"Silly mortal," she chuckles darkly. "Do you really think I care if you succeeded or failed in derailing my sister's plans? You were simply a plaything for my amusement. Come now. I have a number of delights for your eternity."

"No," Kane screams angrily. "Give me another chance! I can succeed. I can!"

Stopping, she levels a baleful gaze at him. "Oh no. This was your chance, and you failed. Now come, child. I have a busy schedule."

"But I can be useful to you," he stammers. "Surely, I can help you with your plans on Earth?"

A glare is leveled at him, but I shiver nonetheless. "Why would I, a Goddess, ever trust a man who believes raping women is acceptable? While I may choose to use you, you are naught but a tool, little boy. Now, come with me. Your punishment awaits."

All I can do is watch as Kane tries to run. With a wave of her hand, he is pulled to her grasp. Raising him up, she throws him to the ground. When he strikes the earth, his spiritual body disappears with a puff of red vapor.

The woman cackles evilly. The sound sends a chill down my spine and creeps into my very soul. The dread grows until I feel almost ready to lose consciousness.

With a gasp, I wake in our bed and sit straight up, looking wildly about the room. With only the night light on we are cloaked in shadow. Next to me, Chloe murmurs softly and reaches for me.

Taking a deep cleansing breath, I try to calm my erratic heart rate. Suddenly, she jerks awake, breathing hard as she sits up abruptly. This sends my heart rate racing again as I seek to calm us both down. Instinctively, I know she's had the same dream.

"It's okay, Angel. It was a dream."

"You, too?"

"Yes. It was the battlefield again…"

"Who was that woman? The one that took Kane's soul? It was horrifying! Not that he doesn't deserve it, but…"

I shake my head. "I guess she's the one who brought him back. Perhaps Ereshkigal."

Chloe shudders and lies back on her pillow. I slip in behind my lady. As soon as I wrap my arms around her, she breathes deeply and calms herself. I do the same. I think for a while on the dream and believe she

315

does too, but soon enough, her breathing evens out, and I sink back into sleep with her.

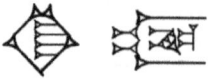

As I slowly wake, I find Beast holding me tightly to him, and I revel in it. The recent awful events are behind us now. Beast and I are still healing, both physically from the wounds of battle and emotionally, for me, at least. I am cautious enough with his health to insist that I do most of the driving in bed. So far, he hasn't argued.

I fervently hope we are going to see some peace. While I'm certain my husband would be a pessimist in this regard, I can only hope he's wrong. Yes, I'm sure I'll never shake the thirst of the Angel of Death, but I do long for a world where our children can grow up in peace.

The sound of Jimmy and Leah giggling filters in through the door. A grin slowly forms as I snuggle against my man. With a mumbled groan, he stirs and I gaze up, soaking in his features. I get maybe a minute before I'm locked with blue eyes and a bright smile.

"Morning, beautiful."

My heart melts. "Morning, handsome."

As usual, I see he doesn't believe me. That's ok. I'm not giving up so easily. He's going to learn that I think he's handsome if it kills both of us. Fortunately, we have many years ahead of us for me to wear him down.

"The kids are up, and Nena brought them home," I whisper.

Beast chuckles. "I can hear that. I guess we should get up. I'm sure Jimmy is looking forward to playing Super Mario Cart with me. Ever since he found the video games, he's been excited to play."

I can't help but laugh. Beast being home convalescing has put our boy in a great mood. He's gotten to play with daddy every day before and after school. Leah joins in, helping daddy lose, of course. Their antics give me much amusement.

Beast and I roll out of bed after sharing a quick kiss. Then we dress and head into the closest thing we have to a living room.

Nena is already on her way out of the bunker. "Good morning, Angel, your children have something to show you." Beast and I exchange a glance, and go into the room with the children.

"Thank you, Nena." I call after her. "I owe you!"

In talking with Nena after the whole ugly affair was over, I found out the dream I had of Liz and Kane in the bunker was no ordinary dream.

Nena was actually there. According to her, it was evil magic, and they were trying to break me, make me doubt reality. While she sought to protect me from Liz, she had not expected Kane to be there. Still, she saved me from their... what—evil spell?

All I know is that Nena is truly a godsend. Smiling at our nanny, I turn my attention to my kids. My husband is simply standing there, unmoving.

"What?" I ask as I edge in beside him. Jimmy has placed Leah on one side of the room, holding on to a chair. He is backing away from her saying, "Wait, Leah, wait a minute. Stay..." I think I know what's going to happen, but I wait to let it unfold.

Once Jimmy is across the room, he says, "Okay, Leah! You can do it! Come to me!" He is making silly faces at her, amusing her to no end, as it always does. With a giggle, hands outstretched, she toddles across the entire room toward Jimmy. She has taken short steps before, and teetered around, but this is real walking, straight to Jimmy. My heart swells with joy.

Once she reaches him, she giggles and smacks his face with her typical open mouth, slobbery kiss, and he hugs her quickly. Then he turns her to face Beast and I. I know what he wants as he looks at us encouragingly.

I move to stand beside Beast, and say, "Leah! Sweet, brilliant girl! Come to mama and dada!"

She looks to Jimmy first, and sees that is what he expects, so she takes a first unsteady step toward us. Then she is half-running, half-walking to us, landing safely in my husband's arms. We hug and praise her. I look over to Jimmy who is beaming in pride, yet, is also holding himself a little separate. That won't do. I see Beast has noticed this, as well.

"Call her again, Jimmy, this is wonderful!" He grins and calls out, "Leah, come to me, Leah!"

She giggles when she hears his voice and squirms around in my husband's arms. He puts her down and goes to steady her, but she pushes his hands away in a show of independence.

"Immy!" our daughter cries, and walks happily to Jimmy, followed by Beast and I. We hold our family closely to us, and, I must admit, I am so proud, that happy tears flow.

My husband is talking to Jimmy now, "How did you get her to do it? She's walking early."

Jimmy is all too happy to explain how they practiced while they were in the vault in hiding, and how Nena and Leah had long conversations about walking. And, how they wanted to surprise us as a special treat. The tense look has gone from his eyes, and I squeeze him tightly and tell him he is our sweet boy.

317

Chapter Thirty-Nine

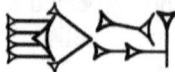

Captain Schaffer walks into the Intelligence Operations room. The IO Department is responsible for gathering information, intercepting radio transmissions and observing areas through what satellites were still functional. Before the Collapse, it was a data hub, working with NSA and CIA to track hostile targets about the globe. Now, it was simply their eyes on the world.

As the XO for the base, they called her first if and when they found something worth reporting. Given the state of the world, she got called in a lot these days.

Not that they had much to worry about. The Collapse had wiped out great swathes of population around the globe. There wasn't a major functioning government anywhere, at least as far as they'd seen.

The population centers of China were dead zones. The only people living in that once great country were in remote farming areas and a couple military bases, but certainly nothing major. In fact, it looked like the bases were acting like mini-dynasties with warlords carving out fiefdoms.

Russia was in a similar state, but with no apparent government activity at all. There were plenty of armed people, but they had left the cities. Large agrarian towns were the only civilized areas. They were walled off and well-defended, beating back the packs of armed gangs that roamed the land.

India, Burma, Vietnam and the other countries in that section of the globe were no different. A lot of people were killed in a combination earthquake and tidal wave. Those few who survived moved into areas that more readily supported life.

Then there was the Middle East, much of which was now an irradiated wasteland. When the global economy collapsed, the various Islamic countries saw this as an opportunity to remove Israel once and for all. The Jewish country was overwhelmed and without allied aid, responded with nuclear weapons.

Schaffer was in the control room when those hostilities started. All they could do was watch in horror as nuclear detonations went up all over the place. Not long after, a convoy bearing an ISIS flag fought its way into Jerusalem and the city was enveloped in nuclear fire, as well. The holy land that was wanted by everyone was now desecrated by radiation and desired by no one.

The United States didn't fare much better. All the major cities were smothered in anarchy and violence. Many burned in orgies of destruction that made Ferguson look like a campfire. Most military bases went into lockdown, but that didn't help. Someone noted that it was like people were just spontaneously going insane. Most places were ghost towns now, but if she's learned anything, it's that life still finds a way.

"What's up, Harris?" Schaffer asks upon entering the room.

"The Gunnison area has had some interesting action." Quickly, he's tapping on keys.

As Schaffer approaches his console, images are already populating the screen. They are satellite views that start painting a picture of a defended Colorado town.

This area has been on their radar for a while now. Apparently, they were led by an individual they had labeled the Gardener. This man was easy to spot. So far, he was the only person wearing a white mask. Some of the intel personnel jokingly called him the Lone Ranger. The reason they called him the Gardener was because most every morning he was spotted working the gardens in the little enclave.

It appeared the Gardener had helped lead the few Air Force personnel in Nellis and evacuated them to Crested Butte, Colorado. Since then, they have built up defenses across that town and in Gunnison. Within just a couple years, they controlled the entire valley that ran from Gunnison and into Crested Butte.

This didn't just include walls and moats. It was easy to tell that mortar pits, machinegun nests and the like had been set up. A small enclave was present between the two towns at a natural choke point. It was here a large number of their defenses seemed to be. That made sense, as Gunnison was more open, making it far more difficult to defend. Schaffer could only see that changing over time.

The next series of frames come up, and she gasps. "What is this?"

"An army," Harris notes the obvious. "It marched all the way from Las Vegas. I think it's what was left over from the Nellis incident."

Incident. Such an interesting way to put it. A massive number of people had been laying siege to the base. In the end, two C-130s left the air field and then Nellis went up in one huge explosion. It's gone now. Nothing but charred craters and burned-out hulks.

"What has been going on?"

319

Harris grins wildly. "At first, it didn't seem worth mentioning. The Gardener took a dozen people and started a guerilla war, a very successful one, I might add."

"Yeah?"

"It appears they lost two of their team, but they probably killed several hundred for each person they lost."

Schaffer's jaw dropped. "Are you kidding?"

"Nope," he shook his head. "They were that effective. Of course, these raiders were also tactically stupid. That tends to help."

"Not unusual. So why did you call me here?"

The images shifted. "Because the major part of the army was a front for a smaller group that infiltrated the area and tried to take over. But the Gardener's people proceeded to wipe the invaders out. They also employed a Hellfire off one of their drones."

"Shit!"

This is something they had been worried about. General Vogel had surmised it was quite possible they had evacuated personnel with technical skills. That made them a possible threat. The fact that they wiped out an army of thousands, even if they were raiders, was cause for alarm.

"All right. Print all this out, and I'll deliver a report to the General."

"Yes ma'am."

As Harris starts printing out the images and data, Schaffer is thinking. Based on their last conversation, she knows the General will want to take steps. She's just not sure his "steps" will be a good idea. Maybe, if they can talk to this Gardener, they can learn if these people are friends—or foes.

Epilogue

ᚠᚱᛗᛟᚠ

"Viv, I had no idea you felt this way."

Mike has finally woken up, and now there will be hell to pay. I've just declared myself, and now? Well, maybe once this is over, I can go live on top of the mountain. By myself. Forever.

Mike is looking at me like something that just crawled out of a UFO. I feel my heart cracking because clearly my affections are unwanted.

"I'm sorry. I thought you were dead. I wasn't going to say anything, ever. You were getting back together with your wife." He has no idea. Of course, he doesn't. I've been careful. So fucking careful. Tears flow slowly but constantly from my traitorous eyes. Every feeling I ever hoped to avoid is flooding me, swamping my good intentions. I give up my plan to be a hermit. Instead, I want to sink into a hole and die.

He looks puzzled. Then he speaks, "We... no, Viv we're not getting back together, but we agreed to be civil because of the kids. They don't need to see us fighting with everything else that's going on in the world. We're still divorced, or whatever. We don't need paper anymore to tell us what to do."

It's easy to tell that his eyes are filled with concern. Slowly, he reaches toward my face, my tears. I sniffle and try to comprehend what he's just told me.

"You're not... together anymore?" I am not sure about that. But then, when I think about it, I realize they haven't really been more than courteous to each other. My jealous eyes could only see them together. I hate myself a little bit more, but the ache of believing he loves someone else is fading.

"No. She's actually been seeing someone up Crested Butte way, Mayor Johnson's brother, Joseph."

I am oddly relieved. And still embarrassed. "But that doesn't matter. It's not like I'm..." I can't make the words come out right. "Look, it's not like I'm trying to force my attentions on you. I feel how I feel, but that's not your fault. But, I promised myself if you lived..." I sniffle again, dig in my pocket for a handkerchief and blow my nose.

321

I feel stupid for being here, mooning after him. I am not a person who enjoys having my soul on display. It's definitely time to go. "I am really glad you're going to be okay, but, yeah. I'd better go." I know my voice is stiff, but it's the best I can do right now.

"Viv! Wait!" he says, before I can get more than two steps away. "Just… hang on there."

My heart practically stops. I can't hope. I know I need to resign myself to feeling like a fool in front of him forever. I sigh. Then, I square my shoulders to turn around. My daddy didn't raise me to be a coward.

"Why?"

"Viv, I can't say I love you."

Fuck. I half want to break down in tears and half want to punch him, and I am leaning desperately toward punching him. I really need to get out of here. And, he's talking again. Damn it.

"But I want to find out if I can. You are…" he gives a short laugh, "you're uniquely you. I never imagined you cared for me, so it's going to take a minute to process. But don't go. Please?"

"Why?" I feel my traitorous heart quivering, hopeful. This is not what I expected. Now what do I do?

"Because I *want* to get to know you. I want to find out. I could love a woman like you for the rest of my life." His face is earnest. Hell, he looks like I feel. "I didn't think you even liked me, so..."

A laugh escapes me; a stupidly girlish laugh I immediately wish I could call back.

"I couldn't have that, Mike. Makes me look weak." I feel like my voice is quivering, too. I still want to sink through the floor, but part of me is afire with hope. I try to hold it all together. It's hard.

"And you're not weak. Never that." His face is bemused, hopeful. Worried. "But what if I'm not the man you think I am? I mean… you don't really know me."

"Don't know you? You're kidding, right? I've *seen* you the entire time I've been here. Only you. Nobody else even comes close. I've seen you with your kids. How well you treat others. Some say you were half in love with Chloe before Beast performed his Jesus routine." He looks startled at that, but he lets me continue.

"I've seen you leading people, never taking a wrong or dishonorable step. My…" I can't help but choke up a little. "My dad would have loved you. And my mom. She would have trapped you like an animal and brought you home as a present for me." Goddess, I miss them so much. I haven't spoken about them to anyone, and here I am spilling everything I am for this man.

The silence is long and awkward, and I am tempted to leave again, but my heart insists I stay and find out what he wants from me. Finally, he speaks again. "Let's start slow then. God knows you don't need to set a trap for me, I am a willing captive." He grins a sideways grin that is his alone. That almost breaks me again. I want to touch him so bad, but I manage to keep my hands to myself a while longer.

He pats the bed beside him. "Come over here, and tell me more about you, Viv."

"We'll have to make it quick," I reply softly. "As soon as news gets out that you're awake, Mr. Beast is going to enforce my punishment of three weeks guard duty at the top of the mountain for disobeying orders."

Mike laughs, rich and deep and my heart stutters. "At least you still have triplets out of the deal and no one died from your actions. Come here."

I move slowly so I don't fling myself on him the way I want to. When I sit on the edge of the bed where he patted, I feel weak and strangely like crying again. I am so, so fucking lost.

He reaches out for me, taking my battle-roughened hands in his. Before he touches me, I regret every callous, every scar. For the first time in my life I wish I was petite, dainty. Girly, like Chloe can be. *Fuck.*

But as soon as he ever-so-gently takes my hardened hand in his massive paw, I feel an almost physical shock. *What was that?* I look up at him sharply and see that he felt it, too. We stare at each other for a moment, grin, and then laugh together. My hopes soar. I've wanted this moment for so long, and now it's here. Oh Freyja, don't let me screw it up.

www.ingramcontent.com/pod-product-compliance
Lightning Source LLC
Chambersburg PA
CBHW071240170626
46809CB00001B/23